THE BOOMER

THE
BOOMER

A STORY OF THE RAILS

Harry Bedwell

INTRODUCTION BY
James D. Porterfield

University of Minnesota Press
MINNEAPOLIS   LONDON

PUBLISHED BY THE UNIVERSITY OF MINNESOTA PRESS
111 Third Avenue South, Suite 290
Minneapolis, Minnesota 55401-2520
http://www.upress.umn.edu

LIBRARY OF CONGRESS CATALOGING-IN-PUBLICATION DATA
Bedwell, Harry, 1888–1955.
The boomer : a story of the rails / Harry Bedwell ; introduction by
James D. Porterfield. — 1st University of Minnesota Press ed.
p.   cm.
Includes bibliographical references.
ISBN-13: 978-0-8166-4906-8 (*pbk.: acid-free paper*)
ISBN-10: 0-8166-4906-5   (*pbk.: acid-free paper*)
1. Railroad stories. 2. Telegraphers—Fiction. I. Title.
PS3503.E223B66 2006
813'.54—dc22
2006015931

Printed in the United States of America on acid-free paper

The University of Minnesota is an equal-opportunity educator
and employer.

15 14 13 12 11 10 09 08 07 06   10 9 8 7 6 5 4 3 2 1

CONTENTS

INTRODUCTION

JAMES D. PORTERFIELD

". . . the glamour and the glory of railroading"

ALMOST FROM their inception in 1830, America's railroads provided both settings and situations that attracted the nation's fiction writers. From Nathaniel Hawthorne's *The Celestial Railroad* in 1846 to David Baldacci's *The Christmas Train* in 2002, trains and the environment surrounding them have intrigued and entertained readers. Especially in the period from the late 1800s through the mid-1950s, railroad fiction as a genre within Americana literature was found regularly in mass-market periodicals such as the *Saturday Evening Post,* in special interest publications such as *Railroad Magazine,* and in trade publications such as *Railway Mechanical Engineer.* A bibliography of the genre (a work in progress) identifies nearly fifteen hundred short stories, two dozen anthologies, and a dozen novels as the body of this work. This does not include the more than fifty mysteries that involve trains or the hundreds of titles written for children. In 1946 the *Christian Science Monitor,* in a review of one of the anthologies, described it as "packed with action, adventure, and heroism . . . good reading for any evening." On another occasion, the *St. Louis Globe-Democrat* concluded railroad stories make "entertaining yarns."

Collectively, this "thin slice of literature" was named

the "Railroad School" by the late Frank P. Donovan Jr., America's leading authority on the subject, in his book *The Railroad in Literature.*[1] In his view, the most compelling of these works were created by men who worked for the railroad before or during their writing career. Three writers in particular stand out for the quality and realism of their writing as well as for the breadth and depth of their portrayal of railroading:

- Frank Spearman was a banker at a railroad division point, McCook, Nebraska. While not a trainman, he was known to be a sympathetic listener. He authored two anthologies of railroad stories and four railroad novels, including the western crime novel *Whispering Smith,* which was made into a movie three times.

- Frank Packard, more widely known for his Jimmy Dale mysteries, produced the famous Medicine Bow Trilogy, three collections of short stories set in and around the fictional Medicine Bow division. He also wrote one railroad novel, the mystery *Wire Devils,* about a band of renegade telegraph operators who staged train robberies.

- Harry Bedwell was the only one among the three who was a lifelong railroad man. His sixty short stories and one novel make him the most prolific of the members of the Railroad School. The "boomer" Eddie Sand, his most frequent central character, was drawn from Bedwell's own experiences. Experts and laymen alike regard Bedwell's novel, *The Boomer: A Story of the Rails,* as the best American railroad novel ever published.

Few readers would disagree with Donovan's assessment of the skill of these writers and their authenticity as recorders. Even today the stories make good reading indeed, packed with interesting characters, lots of action, exciting plots, timeless themes, and often unusual denouements. Reading them gives an understanding of the industry that played a critical role in building America and insight into the men—and they were overwhelmingly men in that period—who built and maintained the railroads and operated the trains. In fact, almost exclusively through these stories comes an appreciation of what it was like to work for the railroad, a heavy and dangerous, yet alluring, industry that was found in every part of the country because it was the predominant way to move goods and people for any distance. In capturing this work, Bedwell and the others inadvertently preserved a rare firsthand piece of industrial sociology.

"Boomers" were an elite, if not always welcomed, fraternity among railroad men. Skilled at one or more aspects of railroading, they were also driven by a defining element of the American character, a desire to wander. As a result, boomers, unlike their counterparts in the "home guard" (railroad men who continued to work for a single railroad and who sometimes resented the boomers), traveled the length and breadth of the land and worked for a living wherever they found themselves. Their presence in and contribution to the railroad scene is well known to railroad and social historians and to railroad fans. An American archetype, boomers are one of the unique characters railroading gave to American culture, which includes locomotive engineers, Pullman porters, and telegraph operators.

The term *boomer* had its origin in the 1820s and 1830s when it referred to men who followed boomtown camps. "Their common practice," wrote *Railroad Magazine* editor Freeman Hubbard, "was to follow the 'rushes'—that is, to apply for seasonal jobs when and where they were most needed" by the railroads.[2] It was not entirely in jest that a fine distinction was made by these men between themselves as "boomers," who traveled and worked, and "hoboes," who traveled but did not work, and "bums," who neither traveled nor worked.

Harry Chester Bedwell was a boomer. He was born on a farm near the remote village of Kellerton in southern Iowa on January 8, 1888. Kellerton was a stop on the Chariton–St. Joseph Branch of the Chicago, Burlington & Quincy Railroad. As a boy growing up on the prairie, he was drawn as so many were to the activity surrounding the arrival and departure of trains at the station. He was also enraptured by the fact that the railroad station telegraph operator (op) could communicate with anyone anywhere in the world and thus learned the news from near and far before anyone else in town. Thus smitten, he could hardly believe his good fortune when, at the age of fourteen, the Kellerton op offered to share the mystery of the telegraph keys with him if he would but sweep out the station, carry coal in for the stove and keep its fire burning, take the U.S. mail that arrived on the trains to the post office, and keep the station's books. Bedwell considered this cheap tuition because what he learned enabled him to travel and work—to boom—throughout the West.[3] At the age of seventeen, he was given his own station to manage in Andover, Missouri, and from there he went on to forty-one different stations on five railroads: the Chicago, Burlington & Quincy, the Denver & Rio Grande Western, the Atchison, Topeka & Santa Fe, the Union Pacific, and the Southern Pacific. His career took him from Iowa and Missouri to Utah, Oregon, and California.[4]

The experiences Bedwell had in these diverse settings— some common to railroading everywhere, others unique to specific settings—fired his imagination as a writer. He began writing for publication in 1908, when the *Los Angeles Times Illustrated Weekly Magazine* published his "Lure of the Desert," and he continued to write until just before his death on October 4, 1955. Bedwell translated his experiences into stories like "The Screaming Wheels," in which the crew of a train closely following another train hauling explosives suddenly finds they are being chased down the mountain by four runaway cars loaded with sheep, and "Smart Boomer," in which a momentary—if understandable—lapse in a passenger engineer's attention to the rules and orders that control every movement of his train places him on a single track already occupied by an oncoming passenger train. His last story, "Avalanche Warning," was published posthumously in the *Saturday Evening Post* on May 11, 1957. A vast majority of his work was published in *Railroad Magazine,* where thirty-four Bedwell stories, features, and "True Tales" appeared between 1909 and 1955.

"Railroad operation," wrote Robert Selph Henry in the anthology *Headlights and Markers,* "is a matter of many men doing hundreds of different sorts of work, and of many companies serving all sections of the continent in all seasons of the year. It calls for working together all along the line—teamwork of the highest order. That's the normal railroad operation, but it is difficult, if not impossible, to make a story of the day-by-day meshing into a smooth-working whole of all these parts."[5] The best stories, as Henry went on to point out and as Bedwell knew, grow out of something going wrong. And in the world of railroading that Eddie Sand encountered in the golden age of American railroading, early in the twentieth century, so much could go wrong.

A railroad, a dictionary typically reports, consists of two steel rails held a fixed distance apart on a roadbed; vehicles, riding on flanged steel wheels, are guided and supported by the rails and are connected together into trains propelled by motive power as a means of transportation. Such a definition conceals the scope, size, and importance of the industry in America. This river of steel rail made up a circulatory system that propelled all the nation's other industries. The definition also misses the fact that the movement of "trains propelled by motive power," especially in the days before computers and sophisticated communications equipment, was at times a breathlessly exciting, hair-raising adventure not to be undertaken by the timid.

Even those familiar with railroading today may be unaware that at its peak the industry was ubiquitous, central to America's culture and commerce, indeed, central to its towns and cities as well. National in scope, it was the only industry to have major operations in every state of the Union and in tens of thousands of its communities. In 1920 it employed 2,076,000 individuals (Wal-Mart, by comparison, in late 2005 reported employing 1,260,000 people in 3,779 stores of all kinds in the United States).[6] With only minor variations, the approximately one thousand railroads then operating over 430,000 miles of track followed a universal set of practices. The complexity of those practices, rules for safe operations that evolved over the one hundred years the industry had been in existence, required specialized knowledge on the part of its workers.

To keep the trains moving, the company established a timetable for operating employees showing, in its broadest sense, when trains should depart their stations or terminals, the routes they would follow—with arrival and departure times for intermediate locations—and when they should arrive. Into this mix, made up of both high-priority freight trains and passenger trains, were added "extra" trains, including unscheduled freight trains, special trains such as those hauling fans to a sporting event or Boy Scouts to camp, and trains out on the line doing maintenance work. In addition, there might be multiple sections of a single train (for example, four individual trains of fourteen cars each might make up one evening's run of what appears on the timetable as a single passenger train). To stir this pot further, delays, such as those caused by inclement weather, mechanical failures, and accidents, all with possible myriad variations, almost guaranteed that a day's schedule would not go as planned. In *The Boomer*, for example, ride along on a run of train 47 and experience all that could go wrong on a single movement of one train—among perhaps ninety or more trains moving each day—over just one division.

In an attempt to cover every possible situation likely to be encountered when executing the timetable, unscheduled train movements and movements at variance with the timetable were initiated and controlled by train orders issued by the railroad to the affected train's engineer and conductor. Further, train movements within a division—a geographic territory that was the principal operating unit of a railroad—were overseen by that division's chief dispatcher and his staff of subordinate dispatchers, in cooperation with the chief dispatchers from adjoining divisions and with executives at corporate headquarters. Along the routes of the trains, station agents and tower operators oversaw the passing of the various trains, both those on the timetable and the extras, and reported their passing to the chief dispatcher's office by telegraph or, as the twentieth century progressed, company telephone. If a variation in the timetable occurred—whether initiated by the dispatcher or in response to a notice received from out on the line or to facilitate the conduct of operations under changed circumstances—the dispatcher would wire new orders to the agents and operators whose routes were affected by the changes. The agents and operators would, in turn, signal the affected trains that new orders awaited their arrival at the station or tower and pass the new train order to the crew. To operate and survive in this environment, Eddie Sand notes, you had to be "geared to the speed of railroading."

From this environment Harry Bedwell, the editors of *Trains* magazine claimed in noting his passing, "could take the basic elements of drama on the high iron—say, heavy traffic running into a blizzard with an indecisive soul in the D's [dispatcher's] chair—and smoothly tighten it up into a nightmarish epic."[7] Ward Allan Howe, writing in the *New York Times* after Bedwell's death, said that "his name is synonymous with authentic railroad literature."[8] Frank P. Donovan Jr. summarized his opinion of Bedwell's storytelling ability in the title he gave his brief biography, *Harry Bedwell: Last of the Great Railroad Storytellers*.

A boomer's capacity to roam and to find work made him the perfect character to carry a work of railroad fiction. Bedwell, in an essay published in 1937, wrote that boomers "were a restless breed with tingling feet, and their lives were high adventure. Arrogant and belligerently proud of their craft, generous and cheerful under stress and strain, dubious and pugnacious when all things seemed serene, they were nonchalant of hardships, virtues, and veracity. They were the glamour and the glory of railroading."[9]

Eddie Sand is the vehicle Bedwell chose to portray these qualities. In *The Boomer,* Sand participates in a series of exciting episodes across America that require him to interact with brakemen, conductors, engineers, train dispatchers, superintendents, and others in the railroad community, as well as with townspeople, including women. The book, based on seven Eddie Sand stories published between 1936 and 1941, reveals all of the tricks trainmen used, as one reviewer noted, "[to] see to it that the trains do not bump into one another, suffer derailment as a result of a storm, or encounter any one of a dozen accidents that

trains are heir to."[10] In that it is as current as today's head-
lines. See, for example, the episode that opens chapter X,
wherein a dispatcher's sudden order to shift the routes of
two trains passing at a terminal fails to take into account
a locomotive switching cars on one of the tracks involved
in accordance with the known timetable. And it was something for which Sand was well suited, for "the flow of swift
rail traffic was in his blood." He'd learned "you were a
sucker if you got sore and lost your head when things broke
all at once. Keep your mind on each swift move and take it
fast and careful."

Here, too, find the boomer's struggles with restless-
ness and speculation on its origins and effects. Sand, for
example, observes, "There's a lot of places I've not yet seen
which I'd like to explore." A short time later he reminds
Mr. Barabe, a division superintendent he's encountered
before, that Barabe's whole world has been his desk, and
adds, "Some day you'll die here, mister. . . . And where'll
you have been, and what'll you have seen of all the good
Lord has put in this pretty fair world for you to observe?
Mister, you're only going this way once, so you'd better
look around." Elsewhere, he thinks, while advising another
op, "whenever you lingered in one place, you always got
yourself entangled in other people's problems. . . . Drifting
simplified life."

One continuing dramatic situation centers on whether
or not he is about to settle down, to undertake, as he says,
"the upkeep of a blonde." Or of a redhead: "[H]er suggestion [that he settle down] touched the alert sense [he'd] developed in the endless struggle to keep the howling trains
on the wing. Women, redheads specially, like to stab the
schedule. The iron trail and the careless road were their
enemies." Of an even more threatening combination, management and a woman, Sand observes, "They'd give you

a place of authority behind a desk, and that kept you tied. The circle of your leash held you to a pin point that would quickly grow monotonous. You had to live with a steady job, and a homestead, all the days of your life. The more you acquired, the more worries you had. Position and property—and babies. They all added up fast and kept your restless feet from the careless road."

The Boomer was published on July 16, 1942. It earned acclaim in the press, where the *New York Times* praised it as "a pleasant, readable story, dealing knowledgeably with a world one knows little about, and not without thrill and adventure."[11] *Library Journal* noted it was a "welcomed" book "written with understanding."[12] And the *New York Herald Tribune* referred to it as "an exciting yarn in sinewy prose . . . Eddie Sand is a genuine and winning character. . . . It has almost everything except sound effects."[13] *The Boomer* was chosen as one of the 1,322 books to be printed as inexpensive paperbacks, known as the Armed Services Editions, for the U.S. armed forces during World War II. A total of 106,000 copies were distributed to the military.[14]

This reprint contains the entire text of the original novel, including a postscript, "About the War," inserted just as the book went to press. In addition to this introduction there is a new glossary to explain appropriate railroad terminology and slang and a bibliography listing the complete works of Harry Bedwell, articles published about him, and reviews of his works. In his 1937 essay, Bedwell noted of boomers that "we'll never see their like again." This reprint of *The Boomer* provides an opportunity to revisit "their like" in a significant, well-written book that captures an important national industry at its peak, portrays the interesting and adventurous circumstances to which railroaders were accustomed, and illustrates a way of life that was common in its day but has disappeared today.

NOTES

1. Frank P. Donovan Jr., *The Railroad in Literature* (Boston: Railway & Locomotive Historical Society, 1940), 6.

2. Freeman H. Hubbard, *Railroad Avenue: Great Stories and Legends of American Railroading* (New York: McGraw-Hill, 1945), 334.

3. Anonymous, "Round Trip," *Saturday Evening Post* 220 (March 27, 1948): 10.

4. Frank P. Donovan Jr., *Harry Bedwell: Last of the Great Railroad Storytellers* (Minneapolis: Ross & Haines, 1959), 17.

5. Frank P. Donovan and Robert Selph Henry, eds., *Headlights and Markers: An Anthology of Railroad Stories* (New York: Creative Age Press, 1946), xi.

6. H. Roger Grant, *Brownie the Boomer: The Life of Charles P. Brown, an American Railroader* (DeKalb, Ill.: Northern Illinois University Press, 1991), xii. The Wal-Mart data were obtained during a telephone call to a representative of the media relations department for Wal-Mart in Bentonville, Arkansas, on March 26, 2006.

7. Anonymous, "Second Section," *Trains* 16, no. 4 (February 1956): 57.

8. Ward Allan Howe, "Direct Rail Coach to the South," *New York Times,* September 20, 1959, XX17.

9. Harry Bedwell, "When I Was a Boomer Op," *Railroad Stories* 21 (April 1937): 115.

10. John Cournos, "A Saga of the Rails," *New York Times,* July 19, 1942, BR4.

11. Ibid.

12. Helen Ripley Burdett, "Bedwell, Harry," *Library Journal* 67 (July 1942): 629.

13. George Conrad, "The Boomer," *New York Herald Tribune,* July 26, 1942, VII10.

14. Donovan, *Harry Bedwell,* 76.

THE
BOOMER

A STORY OF THE RAILS

I

THE MAN seated by the door to the chief dispatcher's office said, "That sun finally gets you." He had mild, bewildered eyes. He was jack-knifed over in his chair and his elbows were braced on his thighs. His hands hung down between his knees.

Eddie Sand turned a page of his book. "It sure does," he admitted without looking up.

Wooden awnings slanted low over the narrow windows, but the desert sun thrust hard, white light into the battered hallway. Outside, the heat danced in a thin, fog-gray radiance over marble-gray flats.

The man cracked his knuckles and worked his knees fanwise, as if they generated his thought processes. "The sun gets you," he nodded confidentially. His long hair hung like looped curtains on either side of his puckered brow. "The sun and the silence," he added.

"And the heat," said Eddie Sand from behind his book.

"Yeah, the heat," the man considered. "But that don't seem to bother so much. It's the sun just hanging there all day, glaring. Like it's sore at you. And it's so still you can hear yourself think, like little wheels clicking in your head. Except when a train is busting by." He studied Eddie's calm concentration with puzzled interest. He asked, "Is that a good book?"

3

Eddie sneezed and blew his nose and said, "Uhum."

"Mebby I ought to read a book."

"Might be a good idea," Eddie ventured. "But take it easy."

"You going to ask the chief for a telegraph job?" The man seemed bothered about that.

"Yeah," said Eddie. "I thought I'd see if he needed a good brass pounder."

"He'll send you out on one of them jobs where there's just a telegraph station set on the desert all alone, with an order board and a passing track. And after while the sun'll get you—the sun and the silence."

"It sure will," Eddie agreed, "if you stay long enough." Conversation didn't interrupt his reading. You were trained to do a lot of things at the same time when you worked the wires. You developed compartments in your mind that functioned separately, without confusion.

"Well, I stuck out there for five years, mostly alone," the man offered. He fanned his knees back and forth and his locked hands pumped up and down on the fulcrum of his elbows. "The chief sent me to Gravel, first thing, and I been there ever since. He just now called me in. I bulled a train order, and he says I need a change." His knees slowed down and his hands drooped between them suspended despondently. His daunted eyes searched Eddie's tranquil face anxiously again, and then they explored the floor.

"But now I'm here, I kind of want to go back." He cracked his knuckles. "Nights are pretty good," he brooded. "There's things of nights—kind of like friendly spirits. The stars come down close and whisper to you. And there's no sun." He raised his head and smiled amiably. "It's kind of companionable then."

A switch engine stamped by in the yard below, shoving

a string of loads down the ladder track, and the station shuddered to the blasts. A passenger train yelled disdain as she flung out of the desolate yard, and the echoes bounced on the naked flats. Telegraph sounders muttered beyond the partition, weaving a metallic blanket of sound. A flick of desert breeze, like sandpaper, ran across the hall. Eddie sneezed in his kerchief and read.

A decisive step resounded somewhere beyond the well of the stairs. There was a suggestion of war drums in that obstinate stride. When Superintendent Barabe crossed any space, it seemed like conquered territory thereafter. He swung around the stairhead and seized the knob of the door to the dispatcher's office as if he expected it to fight back.

The man by the door stood up and smiled, vaguely polite. Eddie didn't raise his eyes from the printed page. The door opened with a smothered explosion, and then Barabe paused. He had caught sight of the head studiously inclined over the book, the white sunlight striking a glint of red in the hair, the imperturbable, sharp-edged profile. He let the knob slip back in his relaxed grip.

"Eddie Sand!" he exclaimed.

Eddie closed his book carefully on a marker. He unfolded his considerable slim height and gave the superintendent a brief, wary look.

"How are you, Mr. Barabe?" he inquired.

The superintendent came back with big hand extended. "Three years, and a little over," he reckoned. "I was wondering just the other day."

"I got another cold in my head working up north on the Great Northern," he explained, "and it wouldn't go away. So I came back to see what the sun was like down here."

"Come into my office," Barabe invited heartily, "and let's hear where you've been."

But Eddie held back. "No, sir," he objected. "Any time I've gone into your office, I've come out with a load of trouble. I've made up my mind to live to be a very chipper old man, but I'll never make it if I let you arrange the time between now and then." His grin was slyly stubborn. "All I want is a nice, quiet telegraph job that won't interfere too much with my reading, out where the sun shines warm all day—up until I get this cold out of my head. I was just waiting here to see the chief about it. After I get over this attack of distemper, I'll be moving on again. Right now, I think I'll go look at the Gulf of Mexico when I leave here."

Barabe chuckled like the rasp of a buzz-saw through hard wood. "And all I want," he stated, "is to hear some of your tall talk of what you have been doing since you left us."

"You sure you haven't got a tough job for me, like the one I got all busted up on by that bandit?"

"Conversation is all I want of you," Barabe declared, and he urged him down the hall.

"You watch out the sun don't get you," the man called after them.

In the big private office where shutters held back the lashing sun, they recalled past times when death and disaster moved boldly about the Desert Division, and Eddie had become accidently involved with a Mexican patriot from across the line who was called *Relampago*. Then Barabe got a brief picture of Eddie's jaunty drift since then: night operator at Arkansas Junction high up on the Colorado Midland, third trick dispatcher on a little line in Missouri, a day job in a yard office in Indianapolis and then the inevitable return to the West again.

Barabe studied the boomer. Once he had given Eddie a watch on which was engraved the Southwestern Pacific's appreciation of his cunning and courage at a time of great hazard. Neither Barabe nor the S-W. P. were liberal with reward or praise.

"A lot of fun," Barabe agreed at last. "But a waste of time," he added bluntly. "And where does it get you? Why don't you stick with us and land some place in the higher brackets? You've got the sense."

He liked smart help, and Eddie was smart. On the job he did his work with cool, watchful precision, and he could spot a crisis before it developed into a disaster. He'd like to harness the boomer's ability to his division. But he sensed, behind those deliberate gray eyes, an insurgent element that would be hard to chain.

Eddie shook his head. "There's a lot of places I've not yet seen which I'd like to explore," he said.

"I thought," Barabe took up his crafty designs, "that time you were here before, you might settle down. Seemed as if you might. You'd made a reputation with us, and you were bound to go up." He gave the boomer a bland look. "Now you're back, you'd better consider this a good place to stay. Reputations get dusty when they're stowed away. You don't grow younger, and some day you'll find yourself stuck in some hole, doing a dime's worth of telegraphing because you can't get anything else. Or maybe out on your ear and no place to light."

You felt him shy from the restraint Barabe was trying to put upon him. He was a veteran of the high iron, but he wasn't much more than a kid. He couldn't be concerned with the distant future. His eyes smoldered as he brooded on some obscure concern.

"That man waiting to see the chief," he murmured. "He seemed like he'd lost some of his marbles."

Barabe frowned. "Griggs?" he snapped. "Something went wrong with him. He's mentally unsound. It doesn't look like we'll be able to use him any more."

A spark glinted in the eyes smoky with thought. "How long have you been on this job, Mr. Barabe?" he inquired softly.

"Fourteen years," Barabe answered with the pride of a strong man in a hard job well done. "And they've been mostly fighting years. This has been a tough division to tame."

"Had a lot of fun doing the work?" the boomer probed.

"It's been a heavy responsibility at times," Barabe admitted, and the lines of his face slackened. He was all at once a little tired. "You don't expect that to be fun. Life is serious business, Eddie, and it gets more complicated as it goes on. You've got to take it that way if you ever amount to anything."

"You've sat there for fourteen years," the boomer mused. "And during all the while you've never encountered much beyond this desk. All that interests you comes and goes across that thirty-six square feet of flat surface." His eyes drifted beyond the hot, flickering flats. "You've never heard the Feather River go raving mad down there a thousand feet below the high iron. You've never listened to the big jacks snarl coming up to Arkansas Junction, where the line slips off to climb to Leadville. You don't know the smell of magnolias on a wet night down South, or the tang of the north woods when they drip with the night fog."

Light flickered in his careless topknot like friction sparks. You couldn't foretell this kid's flash-point. He blew up over the blamedest, most frivolous things. The hard lines in Barabe's face tightened.

"But that doesn't get you a seat at thirty-six square feet of space like this," he growled. "You don't even own a place to sleep."

Eddie tapped the big desk with a probing finger. "Some day you'll die here, mister," he assured the brass hat kindly. "You'll crumple up on this desk, and die. Or else they'll retire you, and you'll die in bed immediately thereafter, because all the strain has been removed from that tough heart of yours. Then somebody else will sit behind that work bench and do about the same as you've done, till it's his time to go out." His lips slid out in a tight, bright smile. "And where'll you have been, and what'll you have seen of all the good Lord has put in this pretty fair world for you to observe? Mister, you're only going this way once, so you'd better look around."

Barabe thrust out his chin and set himself for one of his famous blasts. But it didn't get beyond the clipped mustache. The bright eyes met his firmly, with careless gravity, and the brass hat felt a sudden, weary impotence. He took a quick glance back at the drab years of struggle. They didn't reveal any brilliant patches, and he turned from them at once.

"Go on," he snapped. "Let's have some more of your bright sayings."

"That man Griggs, waiting to see the chief," Eddie nodded. "He got so, out there alone on the desert, he was holding conversations with things he couldn't see. His thoughts got to ticking in his head. All very friendly, and I know just exactly how he felt, because I've been there. Now that he's away he wants to go back, and you won't let him."

"Well, what's your answer to that?" Barabe demanded.

"Just like I've said. Both of you've stayed too long in

one place. Sun and silence, or just the grief that is shoved at you across a desk. You ought to circulate."

"Some day," the brass hat declared, "somebody will break your damn neck for being so bright."

"It's been tried," he nodded tranquilly, and sneezed and blew his nose.

Barabe banged forward in his chair and his shrewd eyes became predatory. "All right," he said. "Go on down that careless road and see where you come out. Meanwhile, we've got a job for you some place. Let's see where it is."

He pushed a button and told the redheaded kid who slid in to ask the chief to step over.

Chief dispatcher McKeon, bald and turbulent, erupted through the doorway, then paused and stared resentfully at Eddie.

"A little late, ain't you?" he snarled. "Three years ago it was when you thought mebby you'd be right back."

"How time does fly," Eddie murmured.

"You're still pretty lanky, but I guess that don't mean you've missed many meals. What's the matter with your nose?"

"Mac," Barabe interrupted, "Eddie has a bad cold and wants a job where the sun shines bright and there isn't much to do. You need a man at the Cinder Patch. That ought to be a good place for him to dry out."

"Yeah," agreed the chief, "but I could better use him—"

Something stopped McKeon, a recollection plucked from the dry air, or a sign from Barabe. Eddie caught the check and came to attention. These two gray, conniving brass hats were full of guile and deceit.

"Yeah," Mac decided. "I guess that would be the best place for him and his sniffles."

He studied them sharply. "The Cinder Patch hasn't

some special kind of trouble you want shoved onto me, like you did at Pigeon Pass when that Lightning man kicked me in the stomach, has it?" he inquired.

Barabe scoffed. "All you'll have to do at the Patch is a nickle's worth of telegraphing."

But Eddie wasn't sure. Handling fast rail traffic, you developed an instinct that warned you of the impending, and it seemed now trying to tell him there was something else at the Cinder Patch beside a few train orders to copy. Barabe was wily and hard. He wouldn't hesitate slyly to hand you a package. Almost Eddie spoke and said he would not go. But his pride in his ability to handle any job they pushed you into, and a lurking curiosity to look behind the furtive signs and signals that passed between these two crafty officials, held up the words of refusal. Besides, Barabe was becoming more willful with the years, and some one ought to take something out of his arrogant eye and obstinate chin before he developed into a rawhider.

"The reason I say the Cinder Patch," Barabe added smoothly, "is that you'll have the day trick. The other operator is an old head, but he prefers to work nights. That's a break I'm giving you."

Buck Barabe never gave you a break he didn't profit by. Eddie was assured that the brass hat was sending him to the Cinder Patch to perform some task that hadn't much to do with his daily trick. He smiled a bright, hard grin that made Barabe suddenly reflect.

II

THE SUN was making its final effort to carbonize the world as he came out onto the station platform. The yard grunted and chuffed with switching. The heat crawled into your pores like acid. You could feel it bite into inflamed lungs. The smell of coal smoke sharpened the thin, lifeless air. A switch engine hurtled past, and a pinman yelled from the footboard, "Hey, Eddie! When didju git back?"

Hi Wheeler, a lanky brakeman in a thousand-miler, ambled up from the yard office. He sighted Eddie and paused. His long face twitched in a fiendish spasm of delight, and he came on at a giraffelike gallop, his big feet thundering on the planking of the platform.

"Eddie!" he exulted.

In his exuberance Hi forgot that the boomer had been trained in wrestling, and that it was hard to fathom the quick hitches he could paralyze you with. He slapped Eddie's back like the kick of a mule. He roughed him with lusty hilarity, and knocked off his hat and mussed his hair.

Eddie let his book slip from the clasp of his elbow. A half-Nelson is hard to get on a man as tall as Hi, and it doesn't, anyhow, punish enough. In a quick reach he caught the brakeman's wrist and twisted it into a hammer lock and tightened it till Hi yelled from a contorted mouth. He bore down with his knees pressing on the back of Hi's legs, and the brakeman knelt helpless on the platform.

Eddie kicked him benevolently in the pants and let him go.

"Seems like yesterday," he remarked, and picked up his book and his hat. "You do stick around in one place," he chided.

"Imagine it!" Hi exclaimed, cautiously straightening the kinks out of his long wheel-base. "You ain't changed a bit. And still readin' that book. You goin' back to work for this outfit?" he pleaded.

"At the Cinder Patch, beginning day after tomorrow morning."

"Haw! Hi scoffed. "You don't work at the Patch. You just try to live. If you don't shine till then you can room with me tonight and ride out with me on Eighty-two in the morning. I got the parlor job on that rattler."

The low sun thrust a flinty glare under the wooden awnings over the stark street. Figures drifted in that stagnant light like fish in a glass tank. Saddle horses under wide-skirted saddles, and horses hitched to spring wagons, drooped three-legged at the hitching rail which extended the length of the block. The thin sound of voices flitted in the air like ghostly echoes.

Hi turned in at Mark's bar.

"Don't Barbabe ever hit you with the old Rule G?" Eddie asked. That was the decree prohibiting railroad employees the use of intoxicants or frequenting places where they were sold.

"Just once is all he ever strikes you with it. That's when he catches you. After that you're through for good. He's gettin' fierce," Hi added morosely.

Events multiplied vaguely. Hi sneaked hot sauce into Eddie's drink. The boomer spat it from his scorched mouth and pleaded for something cold to quench the conflagration. Then Eddie came back from regions beyond with hammer and tacks, and while Hi related ancient conquests

among the blondes to the preoccupied barman, he nailed
the bottoms of his trouser legs to the floor. On his next
abrupt move, the brakeman fell down and half undressed
himself. Then they moved on in search of beefsteaks.

"Eddie," Hi gloomed, "where have you been since
you left?"

"Here and there."

"I'm gonna skin out of here," Hi brooded. "This is
gettin' to be a dog's life."

"You'd better not go for any boomer notions, and start
drifting about," Eddie warned. "A blonde is going to hang
wedding bells on you some of these times, and the upkeep
of blondes is terrible."

"Don't I know it," said Hi bitterly. "But I'm about
through with Barabe. He's beginning to rawhide you
now."

Eighty-two was a mixed freight, forty-seven cars.
She lumbered out of the yard and took to the gray desert.
Conductor Doran got himself, his orders and his waybills
assembled at his little let-down desk in the caboose. Eddie
climbed into the cupola where Hi Wheeler was folded
moodily in a swinging chair.

Hi's features recorded a hard night and he tasted his
tongue with disfavor.

"A man's a damn fool," he remarked.

Eddie opened his book and read placidly.

Hi regarded him with sick and hopeless eyes. "Don't
that make a revolt in your stummick, readin' in this rollin'
caboose?" He put his hand to his mouth and violently restrained a burp.

"Next time, don't drink that barbed-wire-and-chew-
ing-tobacco that Mark tries to slip you after the third
drink," Eddie advised.

The desert ambled by, torrid and savage. Waldo and Morena, lone telegraph stations like sentry boxes set on the grim landscape, tipped their semaphore arms politely in turn and let them by. Half-naked operators signaled ribald insults to the passing crews. Eighty-two paused to set out a load and pick up two empties at Keen, where there was a store, a feed corral and a wagon road. Hi grumbled morosely at having to get down and help the head brakeman do the switching.

At Salon, another yellow daub on the desert, they were given the board, but a scarecrow of a man stood before the station and waved them down with a suitcase.

"What the heck!" Hi snarled, and slid to the floor.

Eighty-two slowed and snailed. The scarecrow swung aboard the rear end of the caboose. He batted his straw suitcase against the railing and his shell hat came off. Hi speared the hat out of the air and pulled the ragged man onto the platform and tossed the head end a highball.

"Where you goin', Macgonegal?" he demanded.

"To the big city," the man shouted, his voice out of control with excitement.

He wore button shoes with all the buttons gone, cotton pants and a collarless shirt. The shell hat was an oddity in the desert at that time.

"Meet Eddie Sand," Hi introduced. "He's another no-good brass pounder like you."

Eddie peered down from the cupola and said hello.

"I've heard of you," Macgonegal piped. "You was here three years ago, and you got busted by that *Relampago* guy. He was a wingdinger, wasn't he? I've been operator at Salon five years, and this is my first leave of absence."

"Have all you lightning slingers got to stay here five years before you take time out?" Eddie inquired politely.

Macgonegal deposited his shell hat and his suitcase and began to explain. Eddie resumed his reading. Macgonegal's high-pitched, turbulent voice flowed on above the rumble of Eighty-two's progress. Hi made rotary motions with his forefinger around his ear and winked a blood-shot eye at Eddie.

A green dot of irrigated alfalfa swam out of the restless gray landscape. The train checked and stopped at Marco with the engine at the water tank west of the station. The little settlement showed the length of the train ahead of the caboose.

Macgonegal was to transfer here to Twenty-eight, a following passenger train that wouldn't stop for him at Salon. He gathered up his shell hat and his straw suitcase.

"You'd better stay aboard and ride up to the station," the conductor told him. "We take the hole here for Twenty-eight to pass us. No use walking all that way in this heat."

The conductor went down the steps and forward along his train. Hi glanced back at the rails, distorted in the distant mirage.

"Twenty-eight ain't due for eighteen minutes yet," he grumbled, "and I ain't goin' to stand out there in that sun and flag. I'm goin' up and see can I get me a cold drink at the station. I feel like I got clinkers where my stummick ought to be." He followed his conductor down the steps and forward.

Macgonegal's plaintive monologue wove into the hot silence. Eddie marked his book and came down from the cupola and went out onto the rear platform. Macgonegal followed.

"Did you ever have them come right up to the door of nights, when the moon's big, and hear them whisper— you know, kind of excited, as if they was telling each other how you looked? It makes you feel funny at first, but you get used to them, and you try to fetch them in for a talk." Macgonegal reflected and smiled wistfully.

The rumble of drawbars began at the head end and ran down the length of the train. The caboose started with a jerk. Eighty-two rolled, then picked up speed rapidly. She wasn't heading into the passing track. Hi came trotting back over the top of the train in the white sunlight. He slid down the ladder at the front end of the caboose and stamped out onto the rear platform.

"The dispatcher done give us enough time on Twenty-eight to get to Acid," he snapped wolfishly at Macgonegal, "and we're highballing right out of town, instead of waiting for her. You'd better unload quick, fella."

The hogger was picking her up fast to make Acid on the time allowed him by the dispatcher. Eighty-two's speed was growing with every turn of the drivers.

Macgonegal's high-pitched voice checked, and then wandered on. He took up his suitcase and went carefully down the steps. The cinder path leading to the station flowed under him like a swift, dark stream.

"The funny thing, you just don't seem able to actually see them." He puckered his brows up at them in a dubious frown. "But you know they're there, and they listen very obliging when you talk to them. Sometimes it seems like they answer—you know, not words exactly. You just kind of get it out of the air."

The quick bark of the locomotive's stack streamed back at them and was flung across the desert and washed up on the distant slopes.

"Oh, for the love of Mike, unload!" Hi yelled desperately.

Macgonegal smiled politely. Calmly he tucked his suitcase under one arm and set his shell hat firmly on his head. He nodded to them a genial farewell, and then he stepped blithely from the bottom step. Instead of a one-handed backward swing from the grab iron, with which all trainmen drop from a fast-moving train, Macgonegal merely walked off into the atmosphere.

Startled, Eddie and Hi watched a phenomenon of momentum.

Macgonegal's feet spurned the cinders at first touch, and for a space he floated. He came down in a quick slide that ended in a split-second pause. He flipped over in a contortion that was almost too fast for the eye to follow. He went into another slide that took him to the shade of the water tank. And all the while he held his suitcase grimly clamped under one arm. It banged and scraped and came apart. Its contents dribbled out on the platform. Stray garments, caught in the draft of Eighty-two's passing speed, raced vainly after the caboose as it drew away.

Macgonegal sat up. His shell hat was broken and jammed about his face. His few clothes had been mostly torn from him, and his person was slightly pin-cushioned with cinders. He pulled the ruined hat from his head, and waved it in gallant farewell to the two on the rear platform sliding into the desert.

Hi looked round-eyed at Eddie. "Old Macgonegal bounces good," he said with admiration.

They climbed back into the cupola. The whine and rumble of the rambling freight train, the blanketlike heat, grew to a monotony of sound and torture. Mountains came in close, then edged away to the horizon. Hi opened a cupola window and then closed it quickly.

"That air feels like a pretty fair grade of emery paper," he complained.

Eddie blew his nose and read his book.

"Your conversation," Hi remarked after more scorched miles, "is sure irritatin'. Almost as bad as Macgonegal's. But we're comin' to the Patch, thank God, and I won't have to endure it much longer."

Eddie closed his book. "If," he menaced, "you arranged with the hogger not to slow down too much to let me off, I'll pull the air on him, and I'll twist your damn neck besides."

"In my painful state," Hi mourned, "I forgot to arrange that with the eagle-eye. But I'll bet," he grinned, "you wouldn't bounce as good as old Macgonegal."

The dun-colored station with a pencil-like semaphore came out of the shimmer. The train checked and the caboose crawled by the little structure. Eddie stepped off, and Hi handed down his suitcase.

"I hope a sidewinder bites you in the ear," the brakeman made his cheerful farewell as Eighty-two plodded on into the baking solitude.

The semaphore squawled as the arm was thrown out above him. Its joints hadn't been oiled, perhaps ever. Russ Kruger, the night operator, came to the door of the station. He was a big man, growing fat. He was languid like a complacent cat, and he had a cat's distant, mistrustful air. His sleepy eyes seemed always adrift in his round, dull face. He wore ancient khaki pants and the remnants of a shirt. Nothing else.

"You look mighty pretty, all dressed up," Russ Kruger brooded over Eddie with his aimless eyes. "I ain't had any new clothes since I came out here, five years ago. Guess mebby some of these days I ought to go in and buy me some."

Eddie gave him a quick scrutiny. "Yeah, you ought to do that at once. And not come back."

A long ridge sloped down to the back of the station and

circled westward and climbed into smoky mountains. Before it a glowing flat, palpitating like hot clinkers in a vast firebox, swept away and edged into a dim range. Nothing moved under that platinum arch of sky except the flicker of a restless mirage.

Time got lost here, except as an item that dealt with train schedules. Otherwise, it stood still and listless in a hot vacuum. The world seemed to check and stall on its orbit and turn heedlessly on its axis like a ball suspended on a string. All day the sun lashed the red flat they called the Cinder Patch.

There was no work to do except copy an occasional order and report the trains by, cook meals and make your bed. The trains slammed by, and then the silence came back and the sun blazed; or the stars grew thick in the sky and came down close for a startled stare at the blasted earth. Nothing else—except if you stayed long enough there did seem to be something that came in out of the silence and stood close beside you, very companionable. But then you got so you wanted to touch it, and after that they took you away and you didn't come back.

The desert heat burnt the dull northern fog from your mind and left it as clear as sunlight. He could now make a shrewd guess at why Buck Barabe had insisted on sending him to the Cinder Patch when the bald and turbulent chief had wanted to put him to work at another station.

III

THE LEVEL sun thrust a clear column of light through the station's bow window. It reached the length of the narrow telegraph table that fitted into the bulge. Eddie lounged there and read, with an ear attentive to the instruments and the approach of Seventy-nine.

Russ Kruger tinkered with one of his inventions, a two-knob telegraph key. He worked at a table littered with small tools and scraps of material. His breathing was moist and erratic. His talk wandered in short excursions in all directions.

"You see how it'll eliminate the wrist movement," he rambled. "Don't put any strain on it. Operators with broken-down wrists, it'll make them as good as new."

He didn't expect a reply. He held arguments with himself, and he talked as he thought, at random. Eddie stopped reading and considered him.

Smoke boiled suddenly from the skyline to the east as Seventy-nine topped the rise.

"He'll be throwing off that beefsteak we wired him to get for us," he reminded Russ. "You watch when he tosses it, so it don't get lost in the brush. I'm hungry for cow tonight."

Russ moved out into the sunlight with a slow, listless flow of big muscles, his bare feet treading as silently as padded paws. His sleepy eyes didn't blink in the hard, level light.

Seventy-nine called sharply for the signal—four long shrieks of the whistle. Eddie pulled the left lever and the westbound board bowed to her from its high pole.

"Thank you!" the freight train shouted.

The engine rocked by, her stack sputtering in a powerful rhythm. The freight cars scrambled after, the clattering wheels absorbed in a frantic effort to keep pace in the line. The little station shuddered. Eddie leaned on the table and watched the bucking cars flicker by.

A brakeman, blurred in the dust that smoked up from the wheels, stood on the lower step of the caboose. He leaned out a little as he slid near, and then he straightened with the toss of a long arm. A brown paper package shot out of the blur. It turned over slowly as it took a high arc. At the top of its climb it planed off and descended swiftly. It just missed Russ as he ducked gravely, bowing like a big turkey gobbler picking up grain.

Eddie stepped aside as the missile dived in at the end of the bow window. It swept across the long telegraph table in a quick slide. It uprooted a sputtering relay and broke the resonator from its iron stand. It flung pens and pencils about the office and hurled ink wells against the wall. Then it plunged through the west window and bounded away over the cinder platform.

Eddie followed the flight incredulously as the beefsteak created its swift havoc under his nose and leaped from sight.

"It just did miss me," he grinned. He glanced out at the rear of the fading Seventy-nine. "That would be Hi Wheeler," he decided.

Russ came in examining the pulpy package of fresh meat. The wrapping was torn and mangled into the steak.

"It ought to be pretty well tendered up," he figured.

"Now I wonder if I can get the cinders out of it?" he frowned.

"Look, Russ," Eddie urged. "You are the inventor of this organization. First thing, you'd better see if you can tinker up those busted telegraph instruments, while I scrub the ink off walls and ceiling."

Russ's sleepy eyes turned to the telegraph table. They dilated and glinted with resentment.

"Hi Wheeler did that!" There was dull, animal ferocity in his tone. "He's always making small of me. Some time I'll fix him." A yellow fire flickered under his narrow lids as he turned to stare at the smudge of thin dust and smoke far down the line. "He's jealous because I can invent things. He's always playing tricks."

Eddie said sharply, "Forget it! He didn't do that on purpose. Hi is a good guy."

Russ muttered as he began repairing the instruments.

There was a bench under the lean-to shed on the west side of the station where the operators filled and cleaned the kerosene lamps. Of afternoons a breeze came up from the Gulf of California with some freshness of the sea remaining after its torrid journey by land. Toward evening, when he had slept the day in the oven heat of his bed room, Russ contrived here at some of the more unwieldy of his many inventions.

A passenger train stormed by, and presently Eddie came into the shade, two train order hoops in his hand. They had just been tossed back to him by the crews of the train after he'd delivered an order to them on the fly. He watched Russ at his tinkering, and then he grinned. He wandered about the station, gathering scraps of material. He returned presently and began redesigning one of the order hoops.

He lapped a foot of old air hose around the top of the loop and bound it there. He sawed two six-inch lengths from a redwood scantling, soft and light, and sand-papered all sharp corners and rough surfaces. He notched them in the middle and tied each to the hoop at the end of eighteen inches of cord. He made a careful job of it.

Russ stopped his tinkering and watched him. He was puzzled and suspicious, his slow thoughts trying to trace the boomer's designs in this quaint project. He caught Eddie's eye, and lowered his lids in pensive evasion. His bare, brown foot explored the ground, fumbling. His toes tested a small stone and picked it up and tossed it with a turn of the ankle at a blinking lizard.

"What you doing there, Eddie?" he muttered. "You tryin' to be an inventor too?"

"Not me," he denied cheerfully. "I haven't got the sense. I'm just rigging a little package for Hi Wheeler."

Russ brooded, his eyes smoky. His prehensile toes fumbled and coiled about loose pebbles and flung them away.

A nerve tightened in the back of Eddie's neck. The rummaging toes were like tentacles, and then they closed in the hard grip of a trap. Things like that developed in sun and silence. There were some, the rawhide men, who throve on them. They broke the rest in time.

He sniffed and blew his nose experimentally. His cold was gone, and it was time for him to drift again before they got inside your head and started you talking to yourself. Down to New Orleans where the stern-wheelers kicked up the muddy Mississippi, and the air was humid. See if the L. & N. didn't need another good brass pounder.

He inspected his contrivance and took it into the office. He wrote a note and attached it to the clip of the remade train order hoop.

The sun was burning itself out over the peaks when Seventy-nine roared over the horizon and blasted for the board. He gave it to her, and when the engine had rocked past he stepped out in front of the station and signaled the rear end that he had a message for him.

It was Hi Wheeler's day on this run, but you couldn't be sure that he wasn't off on some escapade. He stood back a little from the rolling cars till he made sure it was the ramshackle brakeman who stood on the bottom step of the caboose, one hand gripping the railing behind him, the other ready to snare the hoop.

He stepped in close then and extended the hoop and let it go as Hi thrust an arm through the loop and swooped away with it, calling insults as he shot by. Eddie watched closely the resultant actions and reactions.

The air hose had added just enough weight so the hoop didn't stop in the crook of his elbow, but shot up Hi's arm. It bumped him along the jaw. The two pieces of light redwood swung wide at the ends of their length of string, and looped over his head. One reached across the top of his hat and rapped him between the eyes. The other came around from the left, wound the cord once about his neck and slapped him on the ear.

Hi bounded up the steps to the platform and tore the thing from him with frantic grabs of his big hands. He got it untangled and he studied it cautiously, holding it at arm's length, prepared to duck any further attacks from the contrivance. Warily he detached the note and read it.

Dear Mr. Wheeler:

Hereafter, when you unload a cow at this station, please set her out on the siding and not in the office. Animals, other than trainmen, are not permitted in the depot.

E. S.

On the rear platform of the fading caboose, Hi wildly made the sign of the double cross and his derisive yell came back faintly with the dying racket of the train.

Russ had been watching from the doorway.

"You didn't make that right, Eddie," he complained. "I'll build one that will make Hi Wheeler look small. I'll tie spikes to it."

"Listen, Russ," Eddie pleaded, "that brakeman is just acting the darned fool for fun. Don't you pay him any mind. You keep working on that key of yours. You've got something there."

Whenever you lingered in one place, you always got yourself entangled in other peoples' problems. The world was full of the kind who were forever in trouble, and they insisted on unloading their difficulties on you as soon as you knew them even slightly. One way or another, they tried to get you to pull their chestnuts out of the fire. You had to keep moving to avoid entanglements. Drifting simplified life.

The hot quiet intensified as the sunlight faded swiftly. Russ roasted himself in the kitchen over the coal range, cooking supper. He was a good cook, meticulous.

The restless impulse to flit had been building up its pressure inside him again, and he couldn't subdue it much longer. His mind played indolently over a mental map. New Orleans, he decided again. And then his thoughts slid on to Walley Sterling. It was a year and over since they had met in Detroit, and he'd only heard of Walley by rumor since then. A quick desire to hear the "send" of that remarkable hulk of humanity stole into his languid thoughts, and he reached for the message wire key.

Walley might be in North Carolina, South Dakota, or any place else. He got cut through to relay offices in El Paso and Denver and Salt Lake City, and to an operator in

Tucumcari. He made inquiries and asked for help; and he sent a deadhead telegram to a home guard operator he knew in a dispatcher's office in Kansas City, all in quest of Walley Sterling. None of the operators he contacted had heard of him recently, but they would try to locate him in their territories by wire. Walley was well enough known to the craft to be finally located.

He took up a book, and put it down. Recollections of Walley made pictures flicker in the dying twilight. Walley was a genius at life. He was neat and disorderly, tireless and lazy. He had a round placid face and a deceptive bland eye. Life in no way perturbed or baffled him. Most men liked him immensely, when he wanted them to, and Eddie grinned as he recalled the girls Walley had taken away from him, just for the heck of it.

He looked fat, but he wasn't. He'd once trained to be a wrestler, and that had amplified his burly physique. Then he'd suddenly decided that it was too strenuous an occupation, too much effort to put into earning a living. He'd learned something of other crafts meanwhile; printing and engraving, machinist, blue printing and telegraphy. He had a vast curiosity about all human activities, and a mind like a steel trap. He'd decided, after a review of the opportunities, that the telegraph operator earned his wages in the easiest and most pleasant way. Jobs were plentiful all over the country, and a railroad man could get a pass to where he wanted to go, or else find an agreeable local passenger train conductor willing to carry him free on the cushions. That covered your hankerings to travel.

Eddie had come out of the prairies, learned the trade "hamming" about a country station, and was being moved from station to station as relief man on the line along the Missouri River, a green boy of sixteen who had arbitrarily added two years to his age to get a job, a rebel kid who would fight for his rights with impatient, willful alacrity, wide-eyed at all the world; a good operator, lacking only seasoning, when they shoved him into the St. Joe yard office, a hot telegraph job. The pressure here was intense, you worked with the fastest in the craft, and a kid might have fallen down for lack of confidence.

Walley, a young veteran by then, had paused at that yard office on his way to some other place. Boomers would split their last dime with you, or give you a poke in the eye, whichever they considered you needed most. Walley nursed Eddie through those initial uncertainties and taught him life and how to live it.

But there was a price. Walley kept himself fit by wrestling with any opponent he could find, and Eddie was his elected victim while they were together. Besides having the skill, Walley was twenty-five pounds heavier. Eddie had at first fought that overpowering combination hot-tempered. Walley promptly disciplined him the hard way, mauled him and made him like it. It took time, but he tempered his revolt. Eddie was long and slim, light-boned, and he took some hard punishment before he learned to control his fury and caught the knack of tricks and holds and the use of his greater speed.

Walley was rugged. He devoured life, clowned it, clamored for more. Eddie had a lean and studious look. You only got a hint of his stubborn violence from the shine of red in hair. It was the attraction of opposites, and that association had extended intermittently through ten years as their wayward trails converged, sometimes by accident, often on appointment made when one searched out the other over wires across wide spaces of the continent. Then they met, to work a while together, or merely to revel and then move apart again on their separate, endless drifts.

The stars hopped through the blue-black sky like popping corn. The telegraph wires moaned outside, but there wasn't any wind. Must be the heat.

They both had inward depths they liked to retire to in solitude; dim, quiet recesses that prolonged companionship intruded upon. They both shrank from too close an intimacy over long periods. It was a feeling of aloofness you developed as you wandered alone. But their minds always clicked and sparked on their brief contacts.

Russ brought a lighted lamp and set it on the telegraph table. The flickering silhouettes receded beyond the yellow light.

"Supper in eight minutes," Russ reckoned with precision.

The sounder in its resonator spat his call. He answered with quick fingers on the key. The brass tongue flowed into the metallic speech of an operator in the dispatchers' office.

"I got that guy Sterling for you. Hang on and I'll cut him through."

There was a pause, and then the sounder chattered crisply.

"Hyia, Red Indian? I've been trying to reach you over in Montana. I'd traced you that far. What's the matter, get the croup again?" The brass tongue snipped the letters faintly, dragging in the signals over the bulge of the world. The swift, incisive send was a familiar, friendly hail from the careless road. Eddie was leaning across the table, his face close to the resonator.

"Just the sniffles," the words slid out on the thin wire to—"Where are you at, Walley?"

"Up here on the coast of Oregon," the sounder said faintly. "I just pulled the pin and was looking for you."

"I'm about ready to bunch it, too. Thought I'd head down to New Orleans. Want to go along?"

"Listen." Walley could make the instrument sound confidential. "Remember that green-eyed gal I took away from you down in Louisville, because she nearly had you hooked?" There was a faint, ironic chuckle in his send. "She wrote me a letter, and it made me hanker for the Blue Grass again. I promised her. After that I thought I'd rattle around the East. You mosey on down south, and when you get tired of the moon on the levees, and the Creole gals, come on up the east coast. Keep in touch with Walker in the HU office in Cincinnati. I'll do the same, and we'll get together back there some place."

He shot it rapidly, in adroit abbreviations. It tied up traffic on a number of wires when you were patched through, and the wire chiefs would be on the necks of the boys who cut you through if you talked too long.

"Sure!" Eddie sent. "Give Kate my love and affection, and you be good to her, 'cause she's a nice girl."

"O. K., Red. And if any blonde gets serious with you, you'd better let me know at once," Walley added, blandly paternal, and the flickering brass tongue was rigid and silent again.

The ocean was gray with fog up there on the coast of Oregon, and the rivers flowed into the sea from sand-banked estuaries where the salmon ran in September.

"Come and get it," Russ said from the kitchen doorway at his back.

IV

YOU HAD a dragging feeling, a perpetual desire to sit down; and then you wanted to get up again and go somewhere—but there wasn't any place you cared to go. A haze edged into the sunlight. The phantoms the heat made on the clinker flat slipped away.

The top of his head felt stuffed with coarse wool. He thought vaguely it might be a return of his cold, but his nose gave up no evidence of it. Russ abandoned his many inventions and moped and muttered. Eddie heard him in his sleep during the night, prowling in and out of the station.

The vacuum tension tightened sharply as that day began. Then at noon clouds boiled up from the south and shut out the sun. An hour later a blade of lightning ripped the rolling mass, and the vast stress broke with the crash of thunder.

Russ, asleep in the back bedroom, awoke bellowing like a hurt animal. He charged through the station. His bare feet slapped the floor in scattered explosions. His ancient nightshirt tugged at his knees and nearly threw him.

Half-gallon drops of rain slammed on the roof and a tongue of lightning stabbed a telegraph pole. A ribbon of fire flitted down the wire to the station and unrolled a ball of flame on the office floor. Fuses went out in tight puffs of smoke.

Russ leaped and yelled and bolted for the door. The lightning ran over all the seething sky, and now the rain came in driven sheets. They lashed the hillside into gleaming cascades and swept smoking across the flat. The storm seemed trying to make quick compensation for its long absence.

Russ stopped by the semaphore and stood with his big, sullen face lifted and let the driving rain flow over him. In his night shirt he looked like a heathen priest making incantations.

Water shouted in the barrancos. Eddie replaced the burnt fuses and the wire circuits closed. Russ splashed back and stood in the doorway, dripping and muttering in a kind of chant. Lightning licked down and stamped the earth while the thunder blasted. The sound of running water deepened to a roar. The telegraph instruments awoke to recount the storm's devastations.

Gullies that hadn't felt water for months brimmed and gouged out new channels. Sections of the main line began to weaken. Slow orders went out to all trains on the Desert Division. Section crews pumped their hand cars up and down trying to prevent washouts, and a work train with an extra gang was put together and moved out into the storm area.

A freight train went by at fifteen miles an hour. A passenger train, three hours late, followed. Darkness shut down early and the lightning retired to the horizon.

A break developed in a low pass near Sunbridge, a blind siding west of Cinder Patch. The water had dug a channel along the rails and undermined the ties, then washed them out. The work train pushed doggedly to it and threw a shoo-fly around the break. The telegraph operator, sent out with the work extra, cut in his portable set of instruments and kept the harassed dispatcher informed of conditions there.

Russ went on duty, and Eddie cooked supper. He made a two-gallon kettle of coffee. It was chilly now, and he lit a fire in the heating stove in the office, and put the coffee on top of it to keep hot. The rain drummed in a steady, stubborn rhythm.

At seven o'clock a section gang pumped wearily in from the east and ran their hand car onto the passing track and tramped into the office. The Mexican section hands pulled their ponchoes over their heads and dried themselves by the stove. Their wet, dark faces gleamed like dull copper in the yellow lamplight. Their soft, alert eyes followed Eddie and they murmured politely and smiled as he poured them hot coffee. The section foreman hung over Russ at the telegraph table, dictating a report to the roadmaster.

"That roadbed just ain't got no bottom," he told Eddie as he blew on his coffee.

The roadmaster ordered the section gang to continue west to Sunbridge, checking conditions and making repairs where they could. The hand car moved west, the men bending mechanically to the dipping handles and the two dim lanterns swung on the car winked out in the vast, wet dark.

Seventy-nine came snailing in an hour later, and grunted to a stop. Hi Wheeler stormed into the station, gasping profanity, water streaming from his slicker. He blew a stream of it from the end of his nose and took off his rubber hat and flipped it so that water sprayed over Russ and the train orders piled on the table.

An operator would rather you assault his person than disturb his train orders. He is charged with their proper handling and delivery, and that responsibility involves lives and equipment. Russ stood up, muttering. He took an angry step toward the brakeman, soft-footed and ominous. Hi yelled derisively and fell into grotesque fighting postures, clowning. Russ's eyes turned a smoky yellow.

Eddie intervened. Obsequiously he helped Hi out of his slicker and then threw it over the brakeman's head and held him struggling. Hi twisted himself free but prudently refused to attack in return. He was more rowdy than usual. He had been bumped off the rear end by an older man and had in turn bumped the head brakeman. So he was riding the engine cab that night. That had made him irritable, and the storm had inflamed his high-strung spirits.

Russ sat down, scowling. Conductor Doran splashed in and talked through him with the dispatcher, who ordered Seventy-nine to wait at Cinder Patch until the section gang which had proceeded him reported from Sunbridge.

The engineer and fireman ducked into the office to get the news. They were all suddenly relaxed from the strain of the run through the storm, and they blundered about in the little office and scuffled, cheerfully abusing one another and the two operators. They bumped into Russ, who was copying a "hold" order, and he opened the key and bellowed at them to be quiet. You are always under stress when you work with the dispatcher. Tonight the juice was weak in the wire and Russ had to strain his senses to catch the faint clatter of the sounder. The uproar made it still harder for him to catch the order. He fumed and pulled the resonator close to his ear.

Eddie poured coffee. He listened with ominous courtesy while they gleefully libeled the beverage and himself. Russ finished copying the order. He glowered at the crews and moved restlessly in his chair, fingering the key morosely.

It was past eleven o'clock.

"I'm going to bed," Eddie declared, "and if anybody

tries to interrupt my slumbers, I'd be glad to break him in two. Or would you guys rather I wrung a neck or two before I retire?"

They applauded his decision, but declined to offer a neck. He took a lamp from the kitchen. His bedroom was next. He could hear the horseplay begin again in the office as he undressed, and he listened suspiciously for signs that they meant to gang up on him. He paused as he was about to blow out the light. He turned it low instead. That way it would smell up the room, but the wary sense that could spot impending trouble had been bothering him all evening, and now in the quiet of his room it began to prod. He knew a crisis walked out there in the storm, the same as you knew what the sounder was saying, what it portended, even when you had your mind concentrated on some other task.

He listened again to the explosion of voices in the office, and the shuffle of feet and the faint rattle of the instruments. But there wasn't anything ominous in these noises. He got into bed. The rain hissed at the windows. Then all sounds drifted into the distance and died.

After that first dive into oblivion had relaxed him, vague shapes began to move on the other side of slumber. A train rolled through the storm that should have been held somewhere. Then it was gone from hearing. A goblin shape swooped down through the rain, trying to destroy it. That warning sense became restless again, then it moved sharply.

He turned over. The thing jabbed him and he opened his eyes and reached for his watch. It was one thirty-five. He tucked his arm under the covers. Rain scratched at the windows. There were no voices in the office now, and no tramp of feet. The telegraph instruments were quiet. He stared at the low flame in the lamp till he was sure of another sound that flowed through the noises of the storm. It seemed like a saturated purr of mirth, but it wasn't funny. It eased to a fat, breathless chuckle, then it began all over and came up to a rumble of crafty laughter.

He slipped quietly from his bed. That laugh wasn't at any nice, harmless joke. He knew now, as he put his feet into cold slippers, that he'd been waiting here at the Cinder Patch for this to happen.

He turned up the light and went through the dark kitchen and opened the door to the office. Seventy-nine had gone. Russ sat at the telegraph table. His lips were twisted in a sly grin, his haphazard eyes peeping behind the folds of the contorted smile. His big body shook with turbid mirth. He caught sight of Eddie and the laugh broke into a roar.

"Ho, ho, ho!" The old chair quaked under his convulsions. "They won't make small of me again. They point their fingers so sly like this, like I'm crazy." His finger made circles around his ear. "But they won't think so any more. They won't play tricks on old Russ again."

The cold, wet air at the back of his neck didn't come from the storm. "What did you do to them, Russ?" He couldn't get the stiffness out of his lips to grin. "I'll bet it was good."

Russ's eyes showed yellow flickers. He was eager to explain.

"You know just beyond Red Dome." He snatched a pencil and diagramed. "The track goes around the bluff in a short curve, sharp like this, and then follows along right under the mountain. There's a deep gully here, you remember, with a short trestle across it." His pencil scratched and darted. "The section gang that went west, they reported at Sunbridge that they had just got across that little trestle beyond Red Dome when a wall of water came down and took it out. The foreman said they heard it coming and they had to pump like hell or they would have been caught in it. I bet that gang was scared."

His wet chuckle began again.

"So what did you do, Russ?" The words tasted as if they had come out of cold salt brine.

"I heard Sunbridge report that, and then the dispatcher told me to tell Seventy-nine that she'd be tied up here till morning."

The rumbling laugh swelled in his big body and spilled into the quiet room. Then he looked at Eddie slyly.

"You see what I did, Eddie? Those crews scuffling about my office and making jokes of me till I can't hear the dispatcher. All so smart, with a finger pointing like this. I didn't tell them what the section foreman reported."

The confused eyes focused triumphantly. Eddie reached for a breath of air and held it down along with his furious impatience.

"What did you tell them, Russ?"

"I just made up an order myself that let them go on to Sunbridge, and I told them the foreman reported the track in good shape. Hardly any slow track even. So I got rid of them and their noisy jokes, and I played one little joke myself. That engineer and fireman so smart, and Hi Wheeler with his tricks, all of them in the cab together. I bet the water is twenty feet deep in that gully, and they won't know till they are in it with the engine. Ho, ho, ho!"

Handling swift rail traffic trained you to get the picture clear and quick. Don't get yourself in an uproar. Take it fast and careful.

"That's a good one on them, Russ."

He didn't know how long Seventy-nine had been gone, whether there were seconds or minutes to go on, or if it was already past doing anything about. It was one of those times when you did everything there was to do, with speed and caution, till you knew the answer.

"That's a good one, Russ. But the S-W.P. is short of motive power as you know, and that locomotive on Seventy-nine couldn't ever be fixed up after she dived into the gully and pulled a bunch of cars in on top of her. You'd better let me tell them at Sunbridge to send out and stop them before they get into that washout."

"Not on your life, Eddie. This is my little trick. I worked it all out fine. They have joked me and made little of my inventions and it is my time now." He stood up suddenly with his back to the table. He frowned. "Maybe Hi Wheeler is a friend of yours," he said suspiciously. "Maybe you like him better than me. But he played tricks and he pointed with his finger like this. He won't do that any more to old Russ. You stay away from the key, Eddie. I am in charge now, and you can't touch the key."

With the rain gumming Seventy-nine's carbon headlight, the three in the cab couldn't see the washout till they were in it. There wasn't any more time to argue Russ out of his joke. He moved in on him with the skill that Walley had taught him.

Russ was watching him with resentful cunning. He gauged the boomer's intent and he stooped and snatched the lighted lantern from the floor beside the table.

"You keep away, Eddie. You played a joke on Hi, and I got a right to do the same. You're just mad because mine's better." He swung the lantern back in a short crook of the arm for quick striking.

Eddie locked a grip on that big arm. He twisted it across his shoulder and heaved. That should have thrown Russ over his back in a flying mare, but he was an inert mass with no spring or give. Eddie's feet slid half out of his slippers and he lost most of the power of the lever he had made to toss him into a stunning fall. Russ slid over his shoulder and dropped to the floor like a bag of grain. The lantern rolled away under the table and sent up a ribbon of black smoke. He kept his grip and kicked off his slippers and added a murderous crotch hold. But Russ was apparently insensible to the hurt of that grip and wrench. Eddie quit punishing him and rolled the dead weight against the wall and held it there.

He could feel sudden life surge through the big body. Russ doubled his knees and wedged his bare feet under Eddie's rigid arms at the shoulders. The prehensile toes came up fumbling, working in toward his throat. They wiggled and clawed and crawled in, and ripped his pajamas. You could imagine it was something scaly aiming for a choking grip, if you let your mind drift that way. He tightened his hold in a quick twist, and at last pain worked into Russ's consciousness. He grunted and his legs straightened. Eddie bounced and slithered from that catapult and banged against the opposite wall.

Red moons wheeled about the yellow flame of the lamp. He got his breath under his aching ribs as the drilled instinct lifted him to his feet in a rebound off the wall. Walley had hurt him as bad as that any number of times. Walley instructed thoroughly.

Russ lumbered at him like a crafty bear. He avoided him till his breath stopped hurting, then tried to get behind him for a hold. But the room was too small to maneuver in. He got a big arm into a hammer lock and came in close with his head over Russ's shoulder; and they struggled and stumbled. They knocked over the stove and it broke and live coals spread upon the floor. They got under his bare feet. Gas and smoke choked the little office. Russ wrenched free and his two big hands slid up and came together about his neck, and clamped.

He hadn't been as merciless as Walley had taught him. He'd hampered himself by trying not to hurt Russ too much. The red moons turned to a scarlet glow as the fingers worked into his neck. He thrust his hands upward through the loop of the heavy arms and prized with the wedge of his forearms. He locked his hands at the back of Russ's neck and jerked the head downward and brought his knee up to meet the chin. The contact numbed his leg. Russ sagged then, his knees unhinged and he lay down quietly on an elbow, then flattened on his face.

He dragged him clear of the smoking coals and stepped over him to the telegraph table, and his hand slipped to the key. It wasn't well-controlled as he pounded out the call for Sunbridge.

"SB, SB, SB," the sounder hammered urgently.

Sunbridge wasn't far from Red Dome, and they might get an engine to the break before Seventy-nine rolled into the gully. They could set off fuses and maybe light a fire with oil waste and show the headlight as close on the other side of the flooded gulch as they could get. If they made enough light, it ought to stop the freight before she got into the water.

"SB, SB, SB," his call went on doggedly, reaching through the storm.

The coals on the floor glowed and crawled into little flames. The rain clawed ceaselessly at the windows. The flames multiplied about the baseboard and smoke banked on the ceiling. It stung his nose and scratched his throat. The operator at Sunbridge was likely dozing and he wasn't familiar enough with that call for it to arouse him at once. His hand steadied and he flung the call desperately across the desert in crisp signals.

The fire snapped and spread along the wall. It licked at

the tatters of Russ's shirt. Russ shuddered and choked. Eddie's eyes were scorched and he ducked his head into the crook of his arm and breathed carefully.

"SB, SB,—"

The circuit broke and the key went dead under his fingers.

"I, I, SB," the sounder came back stolidly.

"Get this quick!"

The smoke licked in under his arm and scorched his lungs. The flames chuckled as they climbed the wall. He had to reach for air, try to find whiffs of it in the choked room. He didn't have to think out the clipped sentences he shot at the Sunbridge operator. The situation was printed in his mind and it flowed through his fingers in brief statement and command.

Sunbridge paused an instant with open key when he had finished. Then he flashed back a quick "O. K.," and the solitude swarmed back to the Cinder Patch with the rain pounding the roof and the flames licking merrily up the wall of the little office. The obligation had passed to the nimble fingers of the operator crouched over his portable set in a chill boxcar under a dim lantern out there where the extra crew worked to maintain a shoo-fly.

The fire sang as it reached for the ceiling. Russ rolled and coughed. Eddie pattered into the kitchen, hopping on his blistered bare feet, and snatched a bucket of drinking water. He flung it in a sweep at the jumping flames and tipped the bucket to retain a quart and poured that in Russ's face. He sprinted to the water barrels beside the main line and sank the bucket into the nearest one.

That fire was stubborn. On his second trip with the bucket he slid out of his pajama coat, soused it into the barrel and came back to throw water and beat the fire with

his streaming jacket. Nearly naked, drenched and battered
and scorched, he fought the flames till they smoldered and
died. Then he dragged Russ to the back bed room and
heaved him into bed.

V

THE MORNING sun sparkled cheerfully on the desert, and authentic steam came from the clinker flat. A freight train pushed up from the west and rattled over the passing track switch points and grunted to a stop before the station. It was Eighty-two of the day before, carrying the white flags of an extra because she'd been out too long to claim her schedule rights. The crews of Seventy-nine and Eighty-two had evidently turned around at Sunbridge, because Hi Wheeler swung down from the locomotive.

Eddie eyed him ominously from the doorway, but the brakeman shook his head meekly, then rolled it in a backward gesture to indicate Barabe who had followed him from the cab to the ground. Hi came close.

"The Old Man was out there at Sunbridge all night and he's spittin' spikes," he mumbled. "If there's anything you want me to say, tell me now and I'll repeat it word for word."

"After I've said my piece, there won't be much to add."

"Go as far as it seems fit," Hi nodded. "I'll vote for it. We didn't miss headin' into that gully by much. I'm glad you loved me enough to save me from death by drowning," he grinned.

Russ Kruger lifted a frightened voice from his bedroom. "You ain't going to let them hurt me, are you, Eddie?" he called.

"They don't come that size, Russ. You just take it easy."

Barabe's eyes were fringed with tight, jaded wrinkles. His mustache sprouted in tufts and gray stubble crowded in on it from his cheeks. It bristled from the set of his jaw as he eyed Eddie.

"If I have the straight of what happened here last night," he said, "we'll have to put Kruger in jail, and prosecute him."

"Yeah?" said Eddie. "What for?"

Barabe blinked tired eyes. "Why, didn't he try to head Seventy-nine into that washout at Red Dome?"

"I'd not blame that on him," Eddie snapped.

"All right, then." Barabe's voice was thin with slipping patience. "Who was it?"

"It was mostly you, mister." His blistered feet tormented him and he had to breathe lightly inside his battered ribs. His temper was jagged. "You wondered what it was making some of your operators out here in these desert stations go blewy. You're not able to understand that the sun and the silence gets inside your skull after just so long; and you wouldn't come down off your high seat to find out. It was just an epidemic of some kind. Just lucky, you thought, when I showed up. Sure, send Eddie Sand out there, and he'll find out what it is. Well, mister, I did."

The bristles on the jutting jaw rippled like grain in a wind. "Look here, Eddie, you can't talk to me like that!"

"You want a report, don't you? Well, set yourself, because here it comes." It felt like his tongue was dripping acid. "It's hard to get men to stay out here for any length of time. When you do get one that will, you just keep him on till his sap dries up and he goes wing-ding." Barabe's assured conceit always started him orating, telling 'em off, trying to take some of the starch from that jaw. "Then when he shows up at headquarters, like that fellow Griggs when I hired out this time, you cut him off and let him go. You can't use him any more. But, mister, you can't slough your responsibilities. Whatever happened here last night is your fault. And I'd be tickled to go on the stand at anybody's hearing and say so under oath."

Barabe took a furious step. Eddie came down from the door sill and waited hopefully. He drew a long, gentle breath and held it against his sore ribs. He'd put a hammer lock on him and gratefully break him in two. Barabe stopped. Eddie shrugged into a flinch and went on with his lecture.

"If you don't look after your men better, they're going to hit you with something that'll knock you loose from your job. And if you don't send Russ to the hospital and keep him there till he gets straightened out in his mind, I'm going to raise cain all up and down the line till you do."

He stared belligerently and waited. But Barabe's eyes were on the smoking flats, brooding, as if he were bitterly considering point by point the swift denunciation.

"O. K., then," Eddie said. "I'll now point out four examples of what it is to keep on working for the S-W.P., as you asked me to do. There are Griggs, Macgonegal and Russ Kruger. And there is you. All of you stayed in one place doing the same things too long. You've all lost too many marbles."

He turned back through the doorway.

"You'll have to send a couple of operators to the Cinder Patch, because Russ is going to the hospital and I'm about half way to New Orleans right now." He limped into the bedroom and grinned at Russ.

Barabe peered in at the doorway. He studied the

wrecked and burned office. His wrinkles relaxed in a shrewd smile and the bristle went out of his stubbly jaw.

"Having Eddie around," he decided, "is like associating with a stick of dynamite."

Hi Wheeler grinned and drew his sleeve across his nose.

"Yes, sir," he agreed politely. "Dynamite is right. And when he blows up, things do come apart. But at that," he considered slyly, "he's a mighty handy hunk of explosives to have around when needed."

"Yes," Barabe considered. "Yes," he decided definitely, "I've found him so."

VI

HE CAME out of those unmarked days like struggling
back to consciousness from the ether of a major operation.
His first dim, rational thought was that he was again pay-
ing high penalty for trying to keep pace with Walley
Sterling when Walley was in one of his vivid moods; and
then he shut his mind to the blunt ache of body and spirit
and turned it to the immediate circumstances. A perfunc-
tory check of his pockets verified the depressed hunch that
the session had been expensive.

Hi Wheeler snored in the red plush seat of the coach
beside him. A very disagreeable sound. The tranquil local
passenger train clanked and stumbled over high joints and
low. He reckoned gloomily that the budget of the Spring-
field, Omaha & Denver for that fiscal year hadn't been
adequate for proper maintenance-of-way, and that there'd
be other drastic economies on the Sod Line. His luck had
ebbed with those trailing miles from the East.

You could wear yourself out disputing the inevitable,
but it got you nowhere in all directions. He reckoned the
imminent future glumly, but without prejudice. He'd not
make the cooler regions of the Rocky Mountains, as he'd
intended, till he'd recuperated his fortunes and his vigor.
They'd both been badly battered in that reunion with
Walley. He'd have to get a job, and shortly.

Cinders rattled flippantly on the coach roof. Humid

sunlight flickered on green corn sliding by, and the endless
right-of-way fence made a running blur that throbbed at
the back of his wrenched eye balls. Telegraph poles stalked
solemnly past the window, each one flicking his raw brain.
There was some slight panic in his stomach. The situation wasn't suitable in any of its parts.

Hi Wheeler strangled as if he had swallowed his
tongue. He opened vague eyes. They became limpid with
distress as they focused on Eddie's face.

"Mister," he croaked, "you sure remain rapidly with
that guy Walley Sterling. Is there any drinking water in
this coach?"

He arranged himself carefully on his feet and shook
out his double-jointed length and moved drearily toward
the water cooler.

He hadn't been able to connect with Walley in the
East. That green-eyed girl in Louisville had nearly nailed
him down, the way she had Eddie, and Walley had been on
the flit to avoid any entangling recoil. Eddie trailed him no
less than ten days behind, after he'd come up from the
South, and then had lost him entirely. He'd spent nearly a
year back there. There'd been a night telegraph job on the
B. & O. in Maryland, where he'd caught up with his reading, then a relief dispatcher's chores on a short line in
Jersey and last a tower trick on the Pennsy where the
gorge pinches the four tracks down to three as they swing
into Johnstown. Then a late spring had erupted all at
once and brought to a fierce ferment the latent urge to
migrate westward. That had developed into a longing for
the thin air of the altitudes and the sound of the big Mikados' heavy tramp on the grades. The East didn't suit
him. He'd come out at the break of summer, bent upon
reaching the cooler heights of the Rocky Mountains in one
trek.

Hi Wheeler, on an excuse to visit his sister in Illinois, had come up from the Southwest and met him in Chicago. Walley was reported somewhere north. From a yard office, Eddie got plugged in on telegraph lines radiating for five hundred miles as he searched for him. He'd located Walley in a Pere Marquette dispatchers' office out Grand Rapids way, and Walley had taken time out and come in for a convivial reunion. They'd foregathered with other "rails," boomers of the iron highway like themselves, and home guards who were wishful to stray upon the careless road, but lacked the courage to cut adrift. That, as well as he could remember, had developed into a lurid affair, promoted by Walley, all very beguiling at the time. He now found that he didn't specially like to revel. But he took it stoically.

At the end he dimly remembered floundering through a web of railroad yards searching for a westbound local passenger skippered by a conductor who would carry them free on the cushions; and there had been bibacious farewells with what seemed a multitude. Somebody made a speech. The time that intervened since then was fitful and lurid with lights and somber shadows. He didn't even recall when the train had begun its run.

Free transportation was your legitimate perquisite on the rail lines you helped operate, whether the brass hats in the swivel chairs approved or not. But everything else you paid for. The minimum equipment for a boomer on the drift was a good blue suit, in definite repair and press, ample eating money and a proper shave and hair cut at all times. Otherwise, you were likely to be shunned as a tramp. It was a proud craft. There were only a few thin dimes remaining in his pocket. He'd have to go to work for the S. O. & D.—the Sod Line—for a season. And the Sod Line appeared to be retrenching. He got a book out of his suitcase in the rack above, and began to read in lieu of breakfast.

Hi came carefully back along the aisle. "My God! You still readin' that book?" He'd been talking to the brakeman. "We ain't headed exactly in my direction," he complained. "I'm kinda on the wrong train."

"Yeah," Eddie nodded. "I know. Walley and those savages figured you were going south and I was heading in a westerly direction. So they split the difference and routed us in between."

"That bunch could figure out the most things," Hi gloomed. "The brakeman says there's a line branches off at the junction—at division headquarters down here a ways that'll take me south to Kansas City. I better head that way."

"You going back to work for Buck Barabe?" Eddie murmured.

"Yeah," Hi decided. "I guess I will. And then there's Gladys. Did I tell you about her?" His eyes lost some of their dead fish look.

"You told me," Eddie said. "Often. Ever since you've been along."

"I guess I talked considerable. Mister, what a time we musta had!" Hi brightened. "I bought me a quarter section of land down there that'd nearly starved a guy to death. Gladys don't particularly like railroadin'." He brooded blissfully. "This is a tough life you lead," he patronized.

"That's so," said Eddie. "But don't ever say I advised you to become a wedded farmer."

In the station restaurant at the junction, Hi's prospects began to glow when he found that his ham and eggs were going to stay put.

"I could fix that ranch up nice," he beamed, "and when

you got to be an old man, you could settle down with us to a peaceful old age."

Eddie gave him a bleak look. "You won't live that long," he stated.

Hi stacked cup and saucer and knife and fork on his plate and slid off the stool.

"Well," he grinned, "I've had a nice time at your party, and I'm now going back and quit havin' such. My train leaves for the south right now. I'll give your love to Gladys."

"Let me know how it comes out." Eddie was skeptical.

Hi swung aboard the dingy branch local as it moved out of town.

The dull, limitless prairie swung in on the little city from the circle of the horizon. The dry, strawy smell of a meat packing house stifled the air. The chief dispatcher on that division didn't need an operator. Eddie found one more agreeable westbound passenger conductor, and the flat, drab country drifted by again.

He'd come out of the plains more than ten years ago, a kid telegraph operator with a wild urge to see all there was out beyond those hot reaches that had seemed then like an endless blank wall shutting away all the glamor of the world. It would be like doing penance for the vagrant years to be isolated here again. And he wasn't penitent. But you wore yourself down uselessly trying to frustrate your ordained fate.

At the third division point, on the second day, he found a chief dispatcher who could use him at a country town station, nights, and he drifted reluctantly into Auburn as quietly as a straw on the hot breeze. Night operator for the Sod Line at Auburn, a big country town in the exact center of a bowl in the earth that the sky fitted over in a similar featureless bowl. Lumber yard, coal yard, a Stand-

ard Oil tank enclosed in a high fence, grain elevator and
stock pens, all clustered about the railroad yard. The gods
of the high iron were jealous of the drifters and they became punitive at the most unhandy times.

He settled alertly to his duties. And one of the first
items noted in the big red station on that first night was
that there were three telegraph keys on the long table: One
for the dispatchers' wire, one for the message wire, and a
third, with a separate sounder but no relay, he didn't know
about and couldn't quite understand.

In the first lull, when the second trick dispatcher quit
spitting train orders at him, he opened that third key and
thereby contacted destiny. He made some tentative I's to
attract attention, and then he sent into the null:

"Who'n hell's on this wire?"

The void remained mute for a space. But presently the
circuit came apart and the sounder began a desperate struggle to commit itself. The Morse was terrible, ragged and
stumbling. The sounder broke and repeated on every other
word. The contest continued for violent seconds, and at
last the meaning and intent of it came out of the obscure
clatter and registered on his acute ear as he pieced the
grotesque eruptions in his mind.

"This — is — a — private — wire — to — Madden's —
home. If — you — are — the — new — night — operator
— don't — get — fresh — and — use — swear — words."

Eddie grinned. Madden was the agent, his immediate
boss, but it wouldn't be that old-timer who was mangling
the Morse code.

"Who are you?" he spelled out slowly.

A question mark sprawled back at him, and he repeated.

"I am JQ," the sounder retched.

Those two letters are a handful for the personal sign of

an operator, hard to shape with an untrained wrist. An expert would hesitate to choose them as an identification tag. For a "ham" to pick them was ostentatious.

He sent: "Much obliged to meet you, JQ."

JQ pondered that for some time. Then the sounder stumbled an O. K. and was silent.

Telephones were then big wall contrivances, installed mostly by the farmers who had formed their own little mutual companies. This telegraph wire had likely been long ago strung between the agent's home and his station. Now, some kid in the family was learning telegraphy, Eddie decided, with his talent as yet almost entirely undeveloped. He went back to the rounds of the night bob with no inkling that he had touched fate with the tips of his long fingers.

He'd been right in his guess that the Sod Line was curtailing expenditures. That was a two-man job he worked alone, a feverish trick with the double track hot with traffic most of the night. Solid trains of livestock thundered by to market, so many and so close together at times that three or four were run in sections of a passenger train and kept on passenger train schedules. Red ball merchandise extras clanked up and down, and way freights snorted in and out of sidings to let the fast ones by, and to service the wayside stations. Local passenger trains threaded through the stream of traffic, and trans-continental limiteds flung themselves screaming at the far, low horizon. You didn't lay out the hotshots without a peremptory letter from the superintendent for the first offense. On the second, you were stood upon the carpet of his office and dealt with harshly. The brass hats had despotic powers and were very, very arbitrary.

You had to break yourself in to the work, because there was no one else on duty at night to give you instruction.

You just caught on by being alert and smart. But he'd been doing that ever since he went adrift down the careless road. He'd been all the way along the line from night jobs in lone block towers to the heavy strain of the roaring terminals. You had to be capable of learning a new job fast.

Mostly you worked with the dispatcher, copying orders, reporting trains, answering his questions. You always had one ear on his wire and were prepared to drop everything to answer his peremptory call. And no matter what else you were doing, everything that went forward on that wire trickled through an ear and lodged in some dim section of the mind where you could dig it up at once if you needed it.

This second trick dispatcher here wasn't too effective, he decided as the first evening wore through. The man had little, overdone artifices on the key when he wanted to be nasty. He was always insolent. He made a tremendous clatter of speed that had too much hurry. He seemed rash and headlong, and he was certainly harsh and arbitrary and inclined to go up in the air. He snapped at the operators. He terrified the young, unseasoned telegraphers, which wasn't safe practice in handling heavy traffic from a distant point.

Furthermore, he juggled the minutes. He tried to make them do more than their sixty seconds of duty. Unexpectedly he would give a storming stock train as little as three minutes on a following passenger train's time, and insist that the stock train's hogger clear the next block ahead of the first-class train on that slim margin. When there was barely time to make the maneuver without scrambling the threading traffic, he would switch a train over to the left-hand track against the normal flow, to run around a slower one in the block.

It unraveled the kinks in your hair, the way he cut the

corners close. Some of his smart manipulations of the storming trains fitted too snugly. A cool, adroit dispatcher can accomplish this smoothly, if his operators are alert and working with him in confidence. But this man was in a constant state of high pressure, fighting his help. Eddie decided that he was young and cocky and hadn't got himself into enough serious trouble to calm him down. But he was headed for it.

Late in the evening he suddenly sprang one of his trick maneuvers. Sixty-two, a red ball, had gone east at ten fifteen. Her engine had developed leaking flues and she was making poor time. The dispatcher instructed the operator at Oswego, next station east of Auburn, to let him know the instant her headlight showed, and then kept asking him if she were yet in sight. She wasn't at eleven five. The dispatcher called Eddie and snapped at him:

"Let me know the second that stock extra east shows. I'll cut him over to the westbound track there, if the red ball hasn't cleared ahead of him at Oswego by then."

"How do you cut him over?" Eddie asked.

The dispatcher blazed an impatient explanation. "I'll give you the order for the red ball, then you chase down to the switch and throw it and signal him to take the crossover. You'll have to move fast. Slow operators don't last long on that job," he snarled a warning.

Eddie followed through carefully. He watched the darkness to west till the yellow disk of the stock train's headlight showed. He flipped the key and sent, "Extra east is coming."

They split the seconds then in the swift operation. The dispatcher flashed at Oswego, "Is Sixty-two in sight?"

"Not yet," Oswego clattered.

"Thirty-one, copy three," the dispatcher shot back, and to Eddie, "Nineteen, copy three," in swift, abbreviated signals. The brief order flowed from the sounder.

Oswego repeated it then Eddie drummed it out in a quick patter. The dispatcher completed the "19" to Eddie, and added, "Now hop to it."

He guessed that he had first glimpsed the headlight less than three miles away. During the time consumed in copying and repeating the order, the train had been rolling down upon the station at speed, slowing a little as it neared the red light of his semaphore. She was headed into the yard by the time he'd scribbled a clearance card, torn two copies of the order from the manifold, snatched a lantern and dashed for the crossover switch stand.

The dim flare of the headlight reached to him as he rounded out of the station. He tucked in his chin, let the power into his long legs, and spurted. The exhaust died as the engineer shut off. The hogger would guess what he faced when he spotted Eddie's lantern streaking toward him.

The yard lights bobbed in his vision as his feet tore at the cinders. He sucked in a lungful of warm air and held it and drove for the crossover switch light that jumped and goggled at him ahead in the hot darkness. He skidded to a stop beside the stand and thrust his key into the lock. He swung the lever over and clamped it down and slipped the padlock in place. He straightened then and tossed a quick highball to the engineer.

The whistle yelled twice. Softly the exhaust began again, and there was a mumble of slack being taken out of the long train. That dispatcher raised heck if you didn't take advantage of every second he gave you. The engineer wouldn't lag. He'd hit the crossover at the maximum speed that would take him across safely.

Sod Line economies hadn't allowed them to furnish hoops to deliver train orders on the fly. He fluffed a copy of the order from his finger tips and raised it aloft as the locomotive plunged at him. He held the lantern up beside it with his other hand. You had to stand far enough away to be missed by the engine and close enough for the fireman to reach and snatch the proffered order as the train charged by.

The headlight, and the two white marker lights below, made a quick triangle above his head. He caught the flicker of the firebox, and the heat of steam blew across his face. Smells of hot oil and cinder dust boiled up from the clanking drivers. The fireman leaned out from the cab steps, scooped the order from his hand and yelled an offensive remark. The engine slammed at the crossover, and cattle cars grunted as they swerved over to the westbound track. A taillight swam through the darkness as the rear end rocked toward him. The tempo of the wheels slamming at the switch points increased. The engineer was impatiently building up his speed before his train was across. The cars, wrenched from their line of flight, rocked wildly. Cattle complained with frightened, foolish cries.

A light bobbed from the steps of the caboose. He eased closer again and held out the order, and it was snatched from his hand by an unseen trainman. The caboose careened and bucked as it flicked across like the snapper of a long whip. Profanity, faint and bitter, came back from the stock attendants drowsing in the caboose as they were thrown about in their seats by the corkscrew twist of the crossover. Red taillights flared in his eyes and moved swiftly away. Silence of the country night crept back slowly as the clatter of the train died under the dim stars. The scent of curing hay and hot dust came back to drench the air.

"Slick—when it works," he decided, and turned the switch and went back to the station to report Extra 626 East by at 11:16.

VII

AUBURN sprawled sun-scorched in the center of hot fields. Breakfast time was afternoons on the night trick, and your sleep was restless these humid days. He urged himself along the wooden sidewalk without enthusiasm.

The red depot palpitated like an oven doing Saturday baking. Ninety-one, a way freight, clanked slowly up the house track. A brakeman stood on a boxcar near the middle of the train, his long figure cut into the steel gray of the summer sky like a semaphore, his arms extended, signaling. He eased the engineer down and spotted the car he was standing on at the high freight platform at the rear of the depot.

The conductor came forward from the caboose with a handful of waybills. The agent met him on the platform with waybills of his own, wet from the copying press. They made an exchange.

A thousand times you watched the quick distribution of merchandise and still you couldn't keep your eyes from the maneuvers. The head brakeman cut off part of the train and set the cars at unloading places throughout the yard. Then he backed the engine down to the stock pens on top of two cars of hogs, ready loaded.

The hog buyer was wetting down his pigs. He had employed two boys, one for each end of the long wooden pump handle which swung from the middle. The boys

58

alternately put their weight on the handle and pulled down and sweated in streams. Their fee, you could guess, would be five cents each. The buyer squirted water from the three-inch hose onto his panting animals packed in the stock cars. The head brakeman tied the engine on and dragged the squealing hogs forth and tied them into the train.

At the station, the student operator had broken the seal of the merchandise car and recorded it. He and the rear brakeman shoved the running board from the platform to car door. Train crew and station force began rolling and carrying merchandise from the car to the platform. They called each piece in a practiced chant as they took it out, and the agent checked it on the waybill.

"J. J. B., a keg of nails. Make it two."

"W. J. R., a box of drygoods."

"O. K. B., a parlor work bench." (A sofa.)

The voices mingled and collided in the still air. The brakeman took up a box as if it were heavily weighted, struggled with it, lugged it to the car door. He handed it to the big student. It was, in fact, a box of soda crackers, very light, and when the student seized it and lifted it with all his strength, the box flew over his head and knocked off his hat. There was a pause for ribald enjoyment.

They loaded eggs in cases and tubs of butter, and a dozen coops of chickens were added to the contents of a stock car.

"That's all."

The rear brakeman swung his arms. The engineer whistled off, carefully took the slack out of his train and moved out of town. The head brakeman climbed onto the side of a car and walked forward over the top. One at a time and far apart, the conductor and then the rear brakeman swung onto the caboose. The engineer had his train moving fast by the time the rear end reached the station. Each of the trainmen ran a little way with the train and then snatched the curving grab iron with both hands and was tossed onto the rear steps.

Eddie went into the station through the waiting room and unlocked the office door. He stopped abruptly just inside. He felt the slight, cool tingle at the back of his neck set off by that acute sense which warned of a proximate hazard. He grinned now after that first pinch of nerves. This didn't look perilous.

A girl sat on the telegraph table, leaning on her hands, swinging her legs. She had dark red hair and distant gray-green eyes, a small freckled nose. She was dressed cool and she wasn't hard to look at.

"Hello," she greeted. It wasn't a warm salute, and there was some slight condescension in the brief remark. She seemed involved in a remote consideration of a more amiable existence. She was maybe just under twenty, and she was likely afflicted with the long, long thoughts of youth.

"Good evening," Eddie said cautiously.

Her eyes withdrew from some dim futurity and stared at him with slow disenchantment.

"You are the new night operator," she decided without interest.

He admitted that with a nod as her faculties retraced their flight into the far places that girls' thoughts stray. He waited for her play.

"I am Janet Madden," she explained, as if that settled something. "Your name is Sandy," she added dogmatically.

"Sand," he corrected her. "Eddie Sand."

"Oh!" She studied him sharply. "You used profanity on our private wire last night," she charged, and stopped swinging her legs.

Eddie stared. "You aren't," he begged, "the JQ who answered me on the agent's private wire?"

She nodded. "I am his daughter." She was entirely returned from those outer mysterious regions, and now there was a trace of ordinary feminine curiosity.

"O. K.," he agreed. "If you say so. But I didn't really cuss. That was just a little impious inquiry."

"It indicated the way in which your mind runs," she assailed him. "You should discipline it, or you are liable to expose your real character."

"That wouldn't bother me," he assured her. "Anybody that's interested can look into it at any time he likes. I'm not modest. And when I get around to exposing my mind, it shows up pretty livid sometimes."

"I thought so." She was now trying to be judicial. "You are what they call a boomer, aren't you? A drifter. Which is in some sort of degree a tramp."

Redheads began by being willful while young, and grew domineering as they went along—if you were submissive. A recollection singed his temper. As a craftsman, her Morse made his soul screech. A grownup oughn't even attempt to read the wire or remark on it if he was as clumsy at it as she had been. A ten-year-old should do better.

"By the way you handled the key last night," he said grimly, "I wouldn't know how you understood a word I sent—profane or otherwise. You're old enough to have learned it better by just being around where they use telegraph instruments."

Her legs began a slow, irritated swing. "It isn't hard to learn," she said, and eyed him balefully. "I haven't tried yet. I haven't been interested. To any one with sense it is quite simple. Curtiss Halman learned it right here in this station within six months, and within a year he was one of the best on this division. Right now he is the best," she boasted.

"Up to and including the minute I went to telegraphing on this division," he nodded. "That now puts him in second place. And now you can tell me who this Curtiss Halman is."

"He is the second trick dispatcher," she stated triumphantly.

"You mean the one I was working with last night?" he demanded.

Janet nodded. "It wasn't three months after he came into this office as a student operator before he was as good as most of them out on the line. Six months after they put him out as relief man, he was an operator in the dispatchers' office. And within the next year he was dispatching trains. Curtiss is going up to something big."

"He is," Eddie agreed. "And how he knows it. But he'd better be a little more careful or he'll go on to something so big he won't like it."

"You would be jealous. Every operator on this division is. But they still try to imitate him." The dust of freckles faded under a hot flush. "Look at Peck Frim," she said scornfully. "He has been student operator in this station for six months, and what has he learned? Dad says it was only spoiling a good plowboy to bring him in off the farm and try to make a railroader out of him. And Curtiss says Peck will never amount to anything. Curt talks sometimes of taking up something else, where his ability will get him more."

"He will certainly be taking up something else," he nodded, "if he doesn't stop cutting corners."

She smiled suddenly, and the freckles wiggled on her nose. She withdrew again to some recess that would be hard to find. And that way she made a bright picture. The dark hair glowed like a sunset cloud. Her lips curved to some remote and pleasing image. Redheads could be fascinating when they turned on the charm. But Eddie wasn't impressed. You started by falling for their romantic moods, and ended by buying furniture on the installment plan. He'd seen it happen.

The day force trooped in from the wareroom.

Madden, the agent, was an old-timer, a little gray and slightly stooped. He had shrewd, twinkling eyes. He reported the local to the dispatcher. Then he took up his round of duties, answering the wall telephone, selling tickets for the impending local passenger. He worked at the easy, methodical pace of a veteran.

Roy Dent, the clerk, was a little grasshopper of a man, cheerful and quick and accurate. He checked rates and extensions on the waybills and shoved them on to the student to expense. Roy had begun as a student intent upon becoming an operator, but he had never been able to fathom the instruments. Something had been left out of his construction, like a person tone deaf to music, and he couldn't master the knack of reading the chattering sounder or make anything on the key that much resembled the Morse code. It was all just noise to him. So he became a clerk, keen at accounting. He'd go up to the auditor's office some day.

Peck Frim, the student, the "ham," began filling in the freight bills in a large, awkward hand. He was big and ramshackle, shy and slow-moving. He had deliberate tenacity, a stubborn way of proving things for himself in spite of ridicule. There were several reasons which Janet Madden hadn't mentioned why Peck had deserted the farm to become a railroad man. Most of them were Janet herself. His dogged adoration of her had begun and grown through their school days. But with no apparent return on her part at all. She considered him dull, too predictable. Peck was aware of this, but he set himself to overcome it. He had an obstinate endurance that kept him going long after the less hardy had dropped along the way. He hadn't made much progress so far in learning the complicated transportation game, it was mostly just a confusion of details, but, like the man who lost five hundred dollars in the poker game, they hadn't yet bluffed him.

You could read most of that in the look on Perk's face as he watched Janet go dreamily out of the office. It was whimsically pessimistic, stubbornly hopeful. He had some dim realization that he wasn't geared to the speed of railroading, but he was desperately trying to increase his own ratio, fumbling for a place in the machine he could fit into so that he might win that girl's approval.

But that wasn't the way you succeeded in life. Eddie doubted that women inspired you to great endeavors. That took you away from them and their domination; and they hadn't the stamina to keep on building toward a far distant end, battling cheerfully through the inevitable failures to real achievement. They were concerned mostly with immediate events. Tomorrow was to them a dim time away.

Then he faintly realized he was being supercilious about it. Inclined to tell 'em how. He grinned. He'd come along through a like background and had gone on the long drift; had mastered his craft, and maybe was a little cocky. You felt old and wise at twenty-seven, but you hadn't learned it all.

The crowd in the waiting room and on the platform increased as the time for the arrival of the local drew on. Roy Dent was now at the counter, checking baggage, receipting for outbound express shipments. Peck Frim was outside on the freight platform, assembling all the effects to be loaded out.

His mind edged into speculation upon all the ambitious and venturesome youth that the railroads had engrossed in their expanding departments. The long surge of westward migration that had absorbed the lives and energies of so many for long generations, had spread thin and become almost static. These later generations, with the inherited restless instincts of their forebears, had been aroused to the challenging cry of the iron horse. It had taken the place of the covered wagon for the nomadic ones.

The steel highways had offered the wistful, wide-eyed country kids the only opportunity to evade the drudgery and narrow existence of isolated farm life. They took you across a world that glowed in bright pictures against the dull background of this colorless landscape—to roaring cities, to the exhilarating mountain heights and the far blue seas. The romantic places that kids dreamed of here in the rolling prairies. Even the songs they sang of these drab planes were laments, sad and lonesome.

There was little training for other crafts here in the reaches of small communities. To become a telegrapher and station man, you did the heavy work, the drudgery, about the depot, and picked up your knowledge as best you could. For train service, they put you through a quick, preliminary training as student brakeman and then you had a job. They liked to bring the kids in off the farm so green that they had to tie them up alongside the main line till they got used to the trains and wouldn't scare and run away. That kind were easily disciplined.

But they weren't all competent. Those who didn't at once become adept were dropped, and they went sullenly back to the farms, or tramped the country as itinerant laborers. Peck, hulking, slow, deliberate of mind, would find it hard to speed up to the increasing tempo of the high iron. Transportation was becoming more complicated, requiring a brisk and accurate handling of traffic as the trains multiplied and increased their running time. If you hadn't the ability to perform to that rising velocity, you were shoved aside.

A hum of voices floated through the open windows. Town and country folk in search of diversion in the idle hours after five o'clock supper, attended the passing of the evening local. Girls gathered in groups. In the bare space between sidings, men and boys played catch and pitched horse shoes. The editor of the Auburn Globe bumbled about.

The hack came from the hotel and the drayman brought a load of drummer's sample trunks. The pitch of excitement on the platform grew as engine smoke smudged the sunset. The train clanged in, tainting the lifeless air with its dark breath.

Passengers and express, baggage and U. S. mail were hurried off and hustled aboard. The brakeman and the station force, with the help of the undertaker who had come to receive it, carried a corpse in its big wooden box from the baggage car. The noise of the throng was hushed to a murmur. Hats came off.

" 'Board !"

The engine's bell rolled and Twenty-one clanked and chuffed into the twilight.

The crowd broke into sections. The elders trailed toward the post office to await the distribution of the mail. Boys and girls mingled and strolled off in couples under the dark trees along the wooden sidewalks.

Madden came back into the office. He counted out some change for the ticket drawer, checked the closing numbers of the tickets with Eddie, and said good night.

Peck and Roy came in after stowing express and baggage in the wareroom. Roy could still crack chipper jokes after the long hot day's work. He hooked his coat on his arm and went home.

Peck lingered, hunched on the long telegraph table. He said diffidently at last, "Mr. Sand, would you mind if I came back later after supper and practiced my receiving? I've got a dummy set in my room I practice my sending on, but I don't get much time in the day to take it from the wire."

He had a bothered way about him, as if he were always conscious of his awkward bulk and the continued mild derision he incited. No one had ever helped or encouraged him in his efforts to become a railroader. He looked straight at Eddie with serious eyes, his long homely face slightly set.

"Sure," Eddie agreed. "Come along."

Peck began a slow glow. "That's mighty kind. I don't seem to catch on very fast." He opened up under Eddie's amiable eye. "Mebby you can tell me if I'll ever be able to pick it out."

"Don't worry, old-timer. Relax. I'll show you how it's done."

Peck stumbled over his feet going out. He was back within an hour, tense and worried. He sat at the telegraph table and tried to copy what the dispatcher sent as the trick man snapped his orders up and down the line. He puzzled and frowned and laboriously wrote an occasional word he caught from the brass tongue. But he couldn't read much of the splattering send of Curt Halman. It made him tighten up inside and the dots and dashes wouldn't register in his mind.

Eddie studied him and nodded and began his cheerful instructions.

VIII

YOU DIDN'T have to feel omniscient when you picked out the private weft in the familiar, milling scene. He knew the pattern from his younger years. He grinned as he watched Twenty-one drag her length alongside the station platform and stop. Young Curt Halman, that second trick dispatcher, was there, taking the admiration of his people. Janet hung on his arm, and Peck Frim watched him wistfully, and failed to duck out of the way of five sacks of mail the train clerk dumped on top of him.

Curt had come down to Auburn on his day off. First, he'd displayed himself about Main street. He was well-considered in his native town. He was the bright boy who had made good in the city. But even his friends' considerable estimate of him wasn't as high as he appraised himself. He was glossy. His hard hat and his clothes were bright and new, his conversation assured. He had a round face with hard dark eyes stuck into it like raisins, a round body and plump hands.

After he'd exhausted the tribute of the town, he'd hired a rubber-tired livery rig and taken Janet and a basket lunch to the woods by the river. Eddie reckoned that Peck had watched them drive away, and was grim for the remainder of the day as he suffered despair at ever attaining to that position in life.

Curt was to take Twenty-one back to the city, and

when he and Janet walked onto the station platform, they'd been at once surrounded and set upon by the young of their kind. Curt and his success were popular here.

Peck would have to make two trips to the post office. He took one more wishful glance at Curt in his clean new clothes, with Janet beside him, surrounded by esteem. You couldn't handle freight and express and mail and baggage all day in the heat of summer and keep even overalls neat. Peck heaved two sacks to his shoulder and trudged doggedly up the street.

Janet caught sight of Eddie as he walked toward the station door, and called to him. The chattering circle of young people opened, and he was facing Curt Halman.

"Mr. Sand," Janet said primly, "I should like you to meet Mr. Halman. Curtiss, this is the new night operator."

"Oh, yes," Curt acknowledged with a cool, quick look. His little dark eyes were hard and bright. His mind was active in a good many directions at the same time. "I guess you have worked with me the last few nights. I remember now when you came on. Look here, Sand, you weren't too quick answering me a couple of times last night. You can't be slow on this job."

They liked to strut before the homefolks, and that was natural and very human. He'd likely have done the same if he'd ever gone back. But Curt's quick rise had thrown him too far off balance. He'd get hit with a disaster one day that would jar him to his heels. You got along better with these arbitrary ones if you punched right back.

"Mister," he said, "you don't have to fret about the delays I'll hand you, unless you go to rawhiding. Now, I'll tell one. I can't be outside delivering an order and answering you at the same time. Don't overlook that, like you do some things."

A flutter of quick breathing came from the girls.

They'd enjoy this. Curt winced, and then his lively eyes snapped.

"A smart boomer," he sneered. "A tramp operator who knows too much about how to avoid work and responsibility. I hear you've already worked for ten railroads. I can see why that is. You won't last long here, either."

"Right!" he agreed. "It isn't a spot I'd like to linger in. But I've never been kicked out yet. You'll learn that if you try to do it yourself."

He grinned a brief glint of teeth, and turned and walked into the station. That might have developed into something if he'd remained. He'd have to overcome that obstinate impulse to dispute. Specially with the men at headquarters. It relieved your feelings, but it got you nowhere.

Janet came into the office as Twenty-one pulled out.

"You were awfully mean," she fussed, "and deliberately insulting. Curtiss won't stand for that. He told us so."

You couldn't tell for sure if she were really hostile, or was merely fitting him into some fantasy she'd contrived in her mind. He had a spooky feeling he'd better not try to find out.

"I'd say," he suggested, "that Curt and I'd better battle it out between us. You know how a third person sometimes gets stepped on in a fight."

She caught the chill gray of his eye then, and her little golden freckles were half-submerged in a slow flush.

Peck had another attack of diffidence when he returned to practice that evening.

"Sure you don't mind my hanging around?" he begged.

"Old-timer, you come when you like. We've got to make a telegraph operator out of you."

Peck mused. "I thought you were like that. But Janet

told me she doubted it. She gets ideas that I can't understand."

"You'll likely find out more about that as you go along," he grinned. "Now, let me hear you send some on the agent's wire."

The kid had a heavy, trampling send. His big hand worked the key as if he were intent upon annihilating it.

"Look," Eddie instructed. "Take it easy. You're making too much work of it. Now, I'll send to you slow enough for you to take every word. Unhook yourself and write it down."

He began sending from a newspaper. He had a sure, smooth send, as tranquil as flowing water. He had a feeling for the capacity of the receiving operator, and he fed it to Peck gently. The kid relaxed slowly and began to write.

Janet, at home, broke in.

"You are on the wrong wire," the sounder convulsed.

Eddie sent back slowly, "I'm sending for Peck to practice his receiving. You'd better try to copy some yourself, if you think it is so easy to learn."

She got that after he'd repeated. "I will!" You could tell she was suddenly excited about it. The sounder choked up and strangled as she sent, "I'll show you how easy it is for smart people."

Peck flushed. Eddie retarded his pace still more, and sent slow, clear stuff. Peck began to catch more words and write them down in his big, awkward scrawl. He exulted when his pencil caught full sentences. When the lesson was over, he went to his room a good deal more confident than he had ever been.

But Eddie doubted if he'd ever make a good operator. That fine, quick sense that could instantly catch full meaning from swift, minute sounds, had been left out of his structure. The best he could expect was some degree of skill that would keep him in the lesser jobs.

Thereafter, almost every evening, when he wasn't busy with the dispatcher, Eddie sent to them both. Janet was suddenly interested in rapidly mastering telegraphy, and sometimes after Peck had gone to his room, Eddie sent to her alone. They chatted back and forth, and their conversation became more amiable. She caught on quicker than Peck, and she gloated over that. Redheads liked to excel, he observed, and she was eager to exult over the kid. This was going to be tough on Peck's progress in love making, and Eddie tried to puzzle out some way to counteract her growing arrogance.

He began to realize that she responded with quick alacrity to his hand on the key, to absorb his thought as if that thin wire tied their inner beings together in a kind of astral contact you couldn't put a name to.

There were ticky things in telegraphy. Through it you sometimes tuned in on elements you couldn't otherwise touch. For one thing, the constant reading of the swift chatter of the instruments trained your hearing to an acuteness that picked up sounds which the normal ear didn't catch. You got meanings from slight tones by some sense that had been dormant since prehistoric man came down out of the trees. You could learn things about a person, by working with him on the wire, that you'd never acquire by intimate association. Your fingers on the key tapped an inscrutable force that came through faintly at times to your blurred consciousness. He'd experienced it, and he'd heard crack, high-strung operators mention it with a dubious grin.

He wondered if they hadn't opened that subtle channel of relationship. But it was dangerous, he decided, to get entangled in these obscure intangibles.

"Better practice your sending more," he warned her abruptly one night. "It still sounds like an inebriated woodpecker."

But she wouldn't be discouraged. Ten days later she came to the station and she challenged, "I can receive faster than Peck right now. You send at the rate of about twenty words a minute, and see which one has to break you first."

Eddie swung into an even, slow send. But Peck was flustered by the challenge and broke first. Janet exulted.

"You're doing all right with a high-class operator sending to you," Eddie grinned. "But let's see how you copy from Curt. He's just starting to send an order. See can you get that."

He pulled the resonator close to her ear and she took up her pencil. A train order is brief, follows a limited number of forms and is easily read. But Janet couldn't get started on this one. Her pencil circled helplessly above the paper. It wavered and stood still without recording an item from the instrument. A slight paralysis came over her. She stared dumbly at the sounder.

"That doesn't seem so plain," she flushed. "And of course Curt sends much faster than you have been."

"Curt gets more people than me rattled," Peck nodded. "I got some of that order, but Janet fell down on all of it. He can't send clear, like you. It's kind of twitchy, like he's straining himself."

Eddie revived the theory that one quick way to teach a timorous person how to swim is to throw him into deep water and let him figure it out. He considered it several days before he decided to thrust sudden responsibility upon Peck and see if the emergency wouldn't cure him of his irresolution. He framed it cunningly.

The dispatcher called while Peck was at the telegraph

table, and Eddie told the kid to answer. Peck thumped out a reply.

Curt signaled him to copy an order.

"You take it," Eddie told him casually. "You can get it. I've got to catch that extra down at the other end of the passing track waiting to follow Nine out. I forgot I had a message for him."

He went out the door and into the darkness and tramped rapidly down the platform. Then he turned quietly and slipped back to just outside the doorway.

Curt had begun to send the order. You could see that Peck had long felt the vague and dreadful responsibility that an operator assumes in handling trains. He'd brooded on it in the back of his mind ever since he'd started in the Auburn station, and now he was suddenly confronted with the thing. The traffic must roll without hazard or delay. A train order contained a lot of dynamite. He was alone, faced by the waspish sounder and the fateful order that the brass tongue babbled.

He pawed a manifold from the rack. He fumbled for a stylus and the thing slipped from him and rolled in scared hops across the table. He snatched it as it leaped for the floor. He gripped it so it wouldn't escape again. He smoothed the tissues and stared dumbly at the sounder in the hooded box.

He got the order number and half the address. Then his faculties cut out. The rest was just noise, without form or significance. He made impotent loops in the air above the manifold. His eyes glazed into a stony focus. Blood drummed in his ears and subdued the sound of the instrument. He choked and reached for the key and broke frantically in terror-stricken haste.

Curt repeated as far as he had gone in a blast of fury.

He burned numerals and flashing letters into the kid's quivering soul, and then tore on with the order.

But Peck couldn't write down a word of it. The sounder mocked him with metallic gibberings, shattering his senses. It was all sound and fury, without meaning and without end. He felt that he held all those rolling cars and the lives and fortunes of passengers and crews in the aimless, looping hand that clutched the stylus. And that hand wouldn't function. His senses were frozen in a vast void and then they collapsed on a cold blast. The sounder menaced him like chattering death.

Eddie had seen high-strung kids go through telegraphers' terror on their initial attempt to work with the dispatcher alone, but you'd not expect a fellow as deliberate as Peck to come apart under the strain. This had been a bad guess.

People walked by on the wooden sidewalk before the station in the dim light of street lamps. A whispering group of girls had paused behind him, and he turned at last as one moved in closer to him. It was Janet.

"What is Peck doing?" she murmured. "Trying to really copy an order from Curt?"

He nodded grimly. You started a little trouble and it immediately developed into a drench of complications. He wished bitterly that she had kept her little freckled nose out of this.

Peck arose slowly from the chair as the order streamed at him. Some magnetic power dragged him reluctantly to his feet. The sounder spat and snarled. Peck lifted one foot and put it down in the seat of the chair. He hauled the other up after it, and crouched there on his heels, his chin on his knees, his arms wrapped around his legs. His unblinking eyes were fixed on the fluttering brass tongue in a marble stare. But no comprehension of what it jabbered could penetrate his benumbed consciousness. All the knowledge of telegraphy he had ever learned fled from him in terror.

Janet laughed softly in Eddie's ear, a mocking titter that he didn't like. She was really amused at Peck's antics.

"Wait till you try it some time," he warned, and tramped into the station, whistling cheerfully. He had caught the order from the doorway and set it in his mind.

Curt had finished sending, and had waited for the order to be repeated, and now he was snapping furiously, "Go ahead, Auburn!"

Eddie opened the key. "You didn't get it all?" he asked Peck. "O. K., I know what it is. See if this isn't the way it went."

He repeated it briskly on the wire from memory. Curt completed it, then demanded, "What's wrong with you tonight? Drunk again?"

Eddie flashed back, "If you want to find out for sure, come on down and see for yourself."

"I might do just that," Curt sputtered. "I'll bust that order to Nine if the extra gets to Tucker before Nine gets to you. Stand by for some quick work this time, or I'll turn you in."

"Help yourself," Eddie said agreeably.

He wrote out the order, checked it carefully and tore off the tissues.

"That guy is plenty smart," he hooted, "but some day something's going to catch up with him that'll bite out the seat of his pants."

Peck got down out of the chair. He fumbled out a kerchief and swabbed his forehead. Then he saw Janet standing in the office doorway and the slow red burned into his blanched cheeks.

Janet laughed. It was a merciless trill. The burn went

out of Peck's face and his ramshackle frame gathered in and braced stubbornly. His eyes smoldered.

"You think it's funny?" His voice came from a dim cavern inside him.

She turned quickly and went out.

"Eddie," said Peck desperately, "I can't read that man. He just scares every bit of sense out of me. I guess I'm through being a railroad man."

"Not yet," Eddie snapped. "Lots of operators have done the same as you did, and come out good men. And they didn't have a goop like Curt to work with, either. If that fathead slapped you in the face, what'd you do?"

"I'd bust him one, I reckon," Peck decided.

"Well, that's what he does all the time on the wire. Slaps operators he wouldn't stand up to face to face. He's got some cowed, but not many. Are you going to let him run you off the line?"

"Well, now," Peck brooded, "maybe not."

Presently Janet came in on the private wire from home.

"Anybody going to practice with me tonight?" she inquired.

Eddie looked at the sounder. These redheaded gals sometimes looked at a thing around a lot of angles. You couldn't be sure what they saw.

"Right now," he sent back, and then he directed Peck, "Get your pencil and go to work on this."

IX

CURT HALMAN didn't come down to Auburn that week, and Janet was pensive. Peck surprised Eddie by taking advantage of Curt's absence and the girl's mood to invite Janet to Sunday dinner with his folks out on the farm. Then he immediately blundered by asking Eddie to go along.

"Look," Eddie pointed out impatiently. "When you take a girl buggy riding, you don't want another guy along. Get yourself organized."

"That's not the idea," Peck flushed. "We're just going out home for dinner. She ain't my girl. She don't like a guy who crumbles taking a train order. It's just, you know, friendship."

Eddie blazed at him with unaccountable temper. "If she was Curt's girl, and I wanted her for mine, I'd sure give him a run for his money. He'd not miss coming down a single week without being sorry, if I was trying to beat his time."

"Gee, Eddie! I didn't know you could be so fierce."

"Listen, fella. Anyone's got to prove he's a better man than I am before I'll believe it." There was a glint in his eyes like sunlight on ice. "Now you get in your work while you've got the chance."

"But ma and pa want to meet you," Peck persisted. "And Janet said specially she'd like for you to come along.

You can sleep till noon, and we'll pick you up when we come from church."

"All right," Eddie warned. "But I'm telling you that I'll likely cut your throat and Curt's too. If I fall for Janet, the both of you can go jump in the river, and I'd try to see that you did it."

Peck was flustered. "With you and Curt as rivals," he muttered, "what chance have I got?"

"Not a one," Eddie stated, "unless you buck up and go to fighting."

That Sunday afternoon caught up with Eddie folded in a big rocker on the wide back porch of the Frim farmhouse in the shade of a maple tree as big as a circus tent. He had been stuffed with a quantity of chicken and gravy, mashed potatoes and pie. He was gorged and comfortable and with no desire ever to move again.

Janet and Peck were washing dishes in the kitchen, and Pa Frim ground on an ice cream freezer and sputtered and breathed hard. Ma Frim stood by and supervised.

"I declare," Pa Frim panted. "Seems like she turns stiff enough now to be done, Tillie."

Ma computed the power he was putting into the crank and shook her head.

"A mite more," she urged.

"She's froze as tight as ever I'll make her," Pa declared.

Ma opened the freezer and scooped heaps onto plates. Eddie took his and groaned and dug in.

Pa glanced at him and lowered his voice.

"Seems like, Mr. Sand," he said, "that boy of ours ain't ever goin' to amount to much as a railroader. Tillie and me worry a good sight about him. He could do better right here on the farm with us. But he's got the railroad bug. Wants to be like Curt Halman." The old man shook his head. "And Curt tells me Peck won't ever be any good rail-

roadin'. Says it ain't in him, and I guess Curt ought to
know. He's done right well with it." He peered at Eddie
urgently. "I wonder, could you kind of talk to Peck, and
mebby show him he's wastin' his time tryin' to learn to
telegraph? He likes you, and he thinks you're smarter than
Curt. He'd consider it from you, and I'd take it kindly if
you would."

He was gaunt and toughened by toil, and he'd likely
been worried by mortgages most of his life. There was a
sod house dug half way into the rise just off the back
porch. They used it now as a cellar to store canned fruits
and the root crop and milk and butter. But the Frims had
begun their married life in that little room—a bride in sun-
bonnet and a slashing young buck. They'd toiled here ever
since, through lean, hard years, shut away from the outside world, digging out a small competence. They weren't
as smart as some, but they were determined and inde-
pendent.

Now they were uneasy about their son, suspicious of
the world he was venturing into. It looked treacherous, and
it didn't seem prosperous. The Sod Line didn't pay the stu-
dents anything. The old folks had to finance Peck's educa-
tion in railroading. That was likely a strain. But mostly
they worried about the boy's future.

"Peck may not be as smart as some." The old man
leaned closer, his troubled eyes on Eddie's face, awaiting
a verdict. "But he's got something that'll take him a lot
farther. He's sturdy and reliable and he's got the will to
fight a thing out." Eddie pondered and nodded encourage-
ment. "One thing," he said, "he's had very little encourage-
ment from anybody—including you. A pat on the back
right now might be worth a lot to him. I'm not a parent,
but that's my idea of being one." He grinned. "Me, I root
for the home team most when the going is toughest. Peck's

a good kid, and it might surprise you how smart he'll turn out to be."

Pa Frim stared and clicked his store teeth. "I declare," he muttered. "Nobody ever told me that about Peck before. Did you hear it, Tillie?"

"I heard it. He's our child, ain't he? Somebody's got to be proud of him."

"Well, well," Pa reflected. "Mebby we have been a little skimpy with Peck. If that kid did come out on top— say, it'd make some folks around here look small."

Peck and his mother went upstairs to pack his clean clothes for the week, and Pa went off to water some stock.

Janet toled Eddie, groggy and protesting, across a pasture to the trees by the creek bank. She was cheerful and more than half contented. The dark red glowed in her hair in the spotted sunlight under the trees. Her eyes flickered with some deep, quiet amusement. She was flatteringly attentive, and her smile turned often his way.

"Isn't this peace and quiet better than the roaring road?"

Indian summer had come to the prairies, and a tranquil hush was on that vast land. Creek smells came through the gossiping cottonwood leaves. The air was like fragile silk, and her words strung out across the serene, pungent sunlight like falling bright leaves.

He had a feeling like drifting in narcotic fumes; and then her suggestion touched the alert sense you developed in the endless struggle to keep the howling trains on the wing. Women, redheads specially, liked to stab the schedules. The iron trail and the careless road were their enemies. He realized that he'd got himself detoured from his resolve to pause here only long enough to recuperate in all departments from that fling with Walley Sterling. And now it was Indian summer, and he wondered uneasily why that old urge hadn't sent him on his way.

"Sure," he answered her lazily. "I like it—for Sunday dinner like the one we just had. But I guess not otherwise. I'd get lonesome for the sound of fast wheels clicking at the rail joints when they're going some place else." He glanced at her shrewdly. "And the way the sounder snaps when a good dispatcher is lining them up," he added slyly. "I often get curious about some other territory than where I am at, and I've got to go take a look. You couldn't do that with stock to feed and water."

"You want to go on like that forever?" she puzzled. "Just drift, never settled to a—a home and constant friends."

The fireside made a nice, comfortable picture. Security from rough weather, an explicit alliance, profound associations. They said life was constructive, and all these things made it so. You didn't foregather with casual, disorderly drifters and acquire a headache and go broke. You became a home guard and got bitter heart-burning from your snug bed at three in the morning when you heard the lone wail of a hotshot fleeing in the night.

"Those things don't come by fasting and prayer," he complained. "They strike, like lightning."

"And you have never been stricken?" she asked.

She was artful enough. She'd pitched the tone of her query so you might consider it an overture. But whether genuine or provocative and just for the hell of it, he wouldn't know.

"I've been exposed," he admitted, and grinned.

The bright head bowed to consider that. She lived in a couple of worlds. She could dream up romance and fantasies of daring hazards. The girls were still reading *When Knighthood was in Flower*. She'd likely thrilled to intrigues and the clash of swords in the dark and a handkerchief dropped from a casement. But she'd turn away from adventure if she met it, and she'd never let her feet stray down the careless road.

Her ability to judge life and those who lived it around her was growing. She was rounding into the more thoughtful years when existence began to bear down. Maybe she was considering Curt more temperately. If she ever did get a focus on that glossy young man, he'd never dominate her brisk imagination again.

"I can't understand being restless," she brooded. "But I suppose it's because I like people better than places."

That quick mind had picked out the answer at once. The thrill of her swift judgment slightly dazzled him. His thoughts deflected into seductive vapors. She was lovely and vital, and there was stern stuff besides. She could be yielding, but she'd fight like the devil for what was hers. He considered if she might be the woman who would compensate for the loss of freedom to move on when that keen impulse to migrate with the birds overwhelmed you. It was a powerful pull, that desire to drift. It dragged at your thoughts and showed you alluring pictures away over the rim of the horizon, and you were miserable till your restless feet were on that jaunty way again.

But it could be a lonely road, with no familiar faces and no hand raised in greeting. The right woman might be able to destroy that urge and tie you to a fireside. He wasn't discontented with anything at this moment. And that, he realized suddenly, was a bad sign.

He fought his way out of the cloying fumes. He wondered uneasily again why he'd remained here so long after he'd recovered in all ways from that session with Walley. You'd better be wary of these romantic thoughts. They'd trap you. Redheads were pretty realistic in the final analysis. Some were quite capable of deciding your destiny for you.

But the fireside reflections kept recurring as they drove to town toward sunset, and the close, warm presence of her reminded him that there were more amiable ways of life than the long drift.

They let him out at the station, and the thunder of the limited as she swept by screaming seemed to challenge those long, indecisive thoughts. The taillights flared angrily and faded through the prairie dusk, and her lonely cry trailed back as she sounded a crossing warning. He stood there till the deep velvet silence came back, but he still felt the faint tug of the undertow her passing had set in motion.

X

THREE LONG freight trains got tangled in Auburn's stuffed yard at the same time. The double track was roaring, and Curt Halman wasn't handling the traffic skilfully. Jams like this were showing up all across the division, and the dispatcher was harassing everybody without helping them much. Eddie lost his temper once and spat back at Curt.

One of the freights cut itself in two and ducked out of the way and waited for room to do some switching. The other two finally sawed their way out of the yard and moved on again. Curt raved, and that didn't help the situation in any of its parts.

Then when things were beginning to cool off, a westbound passenger paused an instant to let off an old lady. A son was to have met her, but he wasn't there. Old ladies instinctively shifted their troubles to Eddie, and this distracted mother was on his neck while he answered Curt's snarled queries and between times tried to reach her offspring on an impotent country telephone line.

He got some one on the telephone, evidently the progeny, but the man was either hard of hearing, or else the connection was bad. He kept yelling, "Hey?" and "What's that?" and at last Eddie raised his own voice and yelled back. The old lady complained in a high-pitched voice.

It was just one of those nights.

Then Curt interrupted again, ablaze with a close-fitting bit of strategy, and he shot it at Eddie in his galloping Morse. Extra 672 East and Extra 689 West should pass each other at or near Auburn. Because the eastbound block wasn't yet clear of one of the freights that had sawed out of the Auburn yard, Curt planned to cut Extra 672 over to the westbound track there.

"I think Extra West will clear you before Extra East gets in," Curt fluttered, "so you won't have to delay the 672 more than just enough to slow him for the crossover. It will be close, but if you watch sharp and move fast, there won't be a minute's delay." He sent slower, as if being confidential. "I'll give you the order and leave it up to you to see that Extra East don't take the crossover till the westbound is by you. Here it is."

Events began to crowd in again. The old lady complained and expostulated. The telephone, with the receiver down, sounded as if it were being violently ill. Extra West blasted the "approaching station" whistle, and the headlight of Extra 672 East streaked out of the prairies like a fleeing moon. Curt poured out the train order with all the jumpy speed he could manage.

It was a swell situation to distract and divide the mind.

He copied the order and repeated it. Curt shot a complete and added, "Now hop, and don't bull it up."

But he didn't hop at once. This operation was being jammed through, and he had a feeling that there was a loose item rattling around that hadn't been included. Curt shouldn't have completed the order till Extra West was by, because it put the responsibility and control of the following maneuver up to the operator. The dispatcher was delegating his guarding hand. And there was something else wrong here that he couldn't quite locate in the confusion.

He sensed another fault that he couldn't put a finger to in those first turbulent moments, and he opened the key again and sent, "That doesn't look right—"

Curt cut him short. "Get out there and shove the eastbound over when it's clear for her. I'm dispatching these trains."

"I guess you are," Eddie admitted, still dubious.

You were a sucker if you got sore and lost your head when things broke all at once. Keep your mind on each swift move and take it fast and careful.

He could hear the roll of the westbound's exhaust and the clank and roar of her long train. He tore off two copies of the order. The old lady's protests followed him out into the starlight.

The cool air on his face was a quick bracer. The westbound slammed by, passing him as he ran toward the crossover switch. Dust from the racketing wheels washed over him. The eastbound's headlight sprayed the station with thin light. The engineer would have her shut off by now, coasting under control, watching for signals, ready to run again or choke her down to a stop if the red board held.

The westbound would be well clear before the other reached the crossover. He swung into a sprint. The taillights whipped past him. By Curt's direction he was now free to signal the eastbound over to the other side and deliver the order as she went by. But he still had a kind of conscience-stricken feeling that he'd overlooked a stray element. He checked at the stand.

He threw over the lever against more than the drag of the switch points. He swung a highball, notice to the approaching hogger that he had an order which would clear the red light at semaphore and switch. But he couldn't put much zip into the high toss of the lantern. There was a drag on it.

The freight's engineer began working steam again as he acknowledged the signal with two quick snorts of the whistle. He picked up his speed to take the crossover and be on his way again.

Eddie felt that something was crowding in and about to happen. The taillights of the westbound faded under the dark line that broke the arch of stars. The thin glow of Extra 672's headlight slid along the ground and climbed into his eyes. Suddenly he knew, the way you feel there's something alive in a dark room with you, that there was a moving part somewhere in this traffic that didn't fit. He turned in a quick search of the yard. A misty disk caught in the corner of an eye and he wheeled toward it.

A headlight showed down there in the ruck of cars at the east end of the yard, coming out of a siding onto the westbound main line. He could hear the slow chuff of the engine's exhaust above the racket of Extra 672. It was the freight train that had been dodging about the yard for the past fifty minutes, trying to do her switching. Now, in some impatient shuffle of cars, the engine had pulled out onto the westbound high iron to move over into some other section of the yard. She was out there with the assurance that there'd be nothing close behind the 689. They were protected that way by the block. And they wouldn't know that Curt had unexpectedly ordered the eastbound to cut over, and they'd move out right in her face.

The headlight of the 672 was almost on top of him as he flipped the handle of the switch stand and threw it over so as to keep her headed down her own main line. He swung a brisk washout, the lantern signal to set your brakes. The engineer flung an angry screech of the whistle at him as he roared by, and sparks lit along the line of wheels as he kicked ten pounds of air under his train.

That was tight.

He hadn't been trigger-quick to catch all the swirling pieces in that setup. He should have caught Curt's error the second he took that order. But he'd forgotten for a few seconds that there was an engine working in his yard, and he'd nearly dumped a storming train into her. Curt had sure got under his skin.

Back at the station, he pacified the old lady. He got the telephone operator on the line and asked her to have the son come and get his mother. Extra 672 stopped with her caboose beyond the station. The conductor came in, belly-aching. Eddie called Curt.

"There's a freight train been switching in this yard for about an hour," he sent. "He has nothing that I know about to tell him an eastbound train would use the west-bound side through this station." With a man like Curt you told as little as you could get by with. "He's liable to break out and use the main line himself any minute," he admonished. "For all I know, he is using it. So I didn't turn the 672 over. I stopped him," he sent truculently. "Now, let's start all over again. Bust this order, because I'm not going to deliver it. Then go on from there."

Curt paused for a dumfounded moment. Then he blasted.

"I'll get your head for this. That freight switching there has no right out on the main line without a flag. You've laid out a stock train, and we can't overlook that. You're through."

"Listen," Eddie snapped. "That switcher may have a flag out against westbound trains for all I know. But he might not be looking for anything running against the flow of traffic. I'm the guy that don't take that kind of chances. She's set here just like I've told you."

But Curt had to bicker about that before he accepted it as a fact and picked up from there.

"I'll bust that order, but it will mean your job."

"O. K.," Eddie agreed. "And I'll give you a break. I'll make no report of this unless I'm asked. If I am, I'm going to have to say some things you won't like. It's up to you."

In the quiet, just before midnight, Curt called him back.

"I've been thinking about that mixup," he sent cautiously. "It looks to me just like one of those things. We'll forget it."

"It's up to you," he repeated.

Five days later, Eddie was relieved at Auburn and called in to headquarters. You never knew, when they peremptorily stood you on the carpet, whether you'd get a kick in the pants or a pat on the back. Swivel-chair brass hats were unpredictable. Curt might have caved and decided to make his own report first, before word got around. He faced the old gray chief across the big table and withstood his cold scrutiny blandly.

"Apparently," the chief said, "you are able to think fast and decisively in the clutches, and I know a good operator when I hear him work. I've a pretty fair idea what happened at Auburn the other night," he said and paused and waited.

Eddie looked blank.

"Nobody reported it," the chief picked up his level tone, "and I'll not revive it now. I'm setting you up to a telegraph job in this office of mine." He turned off the chilled scrutiny. "It might make you stop and think, the next time you feel like rambling, when I say you've got a good chance to go on up from here."

"Thanks," said Eddie.

XI

A HALF-DOZEN lights glowed in the dispatchers' office, funneling down yellow cones onto the telegraph tables from round green shades. The table tops were cut into segments by glass partitions, and sounders chattered briskly and relays muttered in the little compartments.

Eddie squirmed into a new position in his chair before the typewriter. He pulled the resonator on its iron arm closer to his ear and his accurate fingers rippled over the keys in short bursts as he copied messages from the Omaha office. He was only semi-engaged with that task. He sat inert while he caught a sentence from the brass tongue. Then he transcribed it in a quick patter of type. The telegrams dripped slowly from the machine.

Copying occupied only a dim recess in his thoughts. You developed a faculty of dividing your mind into a number of compartments that worked independently of one another. The messages flowed into his ear and out through his fingers in typed lines as mechanically as any other part of the equipment, without leaving a memory of them as they sifted through. He speculated on his personal problems. He was aware of the night chief brooding in an orange wedge of light at the big table facing the length of the room. The chief computed outbound tonnage in the yard and checked his motive power. He spoke to the yard office on the telephone, and then to the roundhouse.

Curt Halman worked at the trick dispatchers' table. His plump hand was busy at the key, or making quick entries with his pen in the train order book or on the long train sheet. Two operators farther along the line of tables sent from stacks of messages and reports, scribbling the time on each with his left hand as he finished sending it. Another copied consists.

Curt seemed to be simmering more fiercely than usual. There was sly talk about the office that the chief had slipped it to Curt that he knew about what happened at Auburn that night, and wasn't pleased. Curt wasn't considered the fair-haired boy he had been. Some of the starch had been taken out of him.

The clatter of sounders ebbed as the evening wore on and wire traffic slackened. Two operators turned out their lights, conferred with the night chief, and went home.

Janet edged back into his thoughts. He eased farther down in the chair and lost all cognizance of the messages that pattered from his fingers. Her glowing hair got tangled in the funnel of light falling from the shade just above his eyes. He caught the quick smile that made the freckles dance on her nose. She'd kissed him goodby and said she was sorry he was going.

Well, he'd been kissed before. He grinned. But maybe not in just that way. It'd seemed different, anyhow, and he wasn't easy in his mind about it. Maybe the gods of the high iron had decided he'd gone far enough along the careless road, and had checked his pilgrimage here and were about to bind him to this pointless speck of creation.

The moon can soften a man up, and that had been a humdinger of an Indian summer moon. Walking home with her in the dappled shadows under the trees that last night in Auburn, he'd felt a kind of smoky serenity. He hadn't been wary. Like this, on the drift, with most girls you made your play after you'd told them you'd be gone from there in a very short while. And then you kept reminding them you were just passing through. He considered that last sharp moment with her when he'd almost said he wouldn't go—without her. The quick, warm kiss had brought the words almost past his lips. But his restless past had stirred in slight cautious rebellion and he hadn't quite said them.

"Goodby, old drifter. Maybe we will meet again. You do go back sometimes, don't you?"

Her misty hair glowing in the moonlight blurred the long dispatchers' room. The gossip of the sounders moved into a dim section of his mind and faded out. He slid away quietly to some becalmed state that wasn't bad at first. A bright spot, and serene. But the shine wore off, and he was back in the dusky room with the undertone of metallic sound flowing through it. He couldn't lose himself for long.

He felt funny, in a kind of quiver, but it didn't seem as if he wanted to go any place. He couldn't quite gage if it were a remembrance and a nostalgia for the girl in the moonlight, or the willful craving to be on the move again. He couldn't remember ever being undecided about such a question before. The thing began to fret him, which wasn't a condition he would allow.

Curt was fighting his division, tearing into the job of keeping the trains rolling, in a hot, rash impatience. Curt couldn't hold on to his temper or his deliberate judgment. He raved at the operators and sent angry notes to the train and engine crews. He stormed at everything that went wrong, and there didn't seem to be anything exactly right that night.

Something was biting him sure enough. Maybe he was trying to redeem himself with the chief by some extraor-

dinary maneuver. Kid stuff. Eddie caught the vicious snap
of Curt's sounder as he snarled at some night operator
who couldn't keep up with his erratic send. Better take it
easy. You laid yourself wide open to error if you got yourself and your helpers in an uproar.

The night chief swiveled out of his chair. It was time
for his evening snack in the station restaurant. He looked
once at Curt, and then went out.

A switch engine, shoving a Pullman up beside the
station, clanged to a stop below and panted as she rested.
A freight train hooted a derisive farewell as it pulled out
of the east end of the yard. The soft patter in the room slid
into the background of his thoughts. His fingers moved
over the typewriter keys in a heedless, mechanical rhythm.

He could remember saying fond and final farewells to
girls at gates in picket fences all back along the careless
road, and none of them had been like the one with Janet.
That Indian summer moon had put the brakes on him. He
was scheduled out of here a long while ago, but his feet
wouldn't begin. They'd never missed an excuse to travel
before. Maybe that glow of coppery hair and the soft curve
of smiling lips had snarled him. The web of iron highways, stretching out over the rim of the world, receded
beyond the horizon of his thoughts and left him suspended
here where he'd thought he'd never want to stay.

There was a pause in the easy, streaming babble of the
sounder at his ear. The Omaha operator clucked thoughtfully. Then he eased into a query.

"You got a brass pounder working in your office name
of Sand?"

"Yeah," said Eddie. "I'm him."

"Guy in Denver wants cut through to you. Says he's a
friend of yours. Want 'im?"

Denver? He wondered what stray comrade of the iron

highway was stranded there and wanted a telegraphic loan of cash.

"O. K.," he said, and suddenly Walley Sterling's crisp send leaped at him from the resonator, the incisive letters exploding with cool, casual arrogance. Walley was in Denver! He'd beaten Eddie to the altitudes. You couldn't check or detour that massive man when he got under way.

"Guess I ran around you somewhere down there on the flats," Walley sent, and you got the sensation that his words came down from some lofty pagan retreat. "I'd never thought you'd stop in the shoals. I ran into Hi Wheeler down Pueblo way, and he told me. What'n hell didja tie up there for?"

"My health," Eddie lamented. "I felt like a poisoned pup after that session in Chicago."

"Mebby the fifty bucks I borrowed from you stopped you in the wrong place," Walley suggested.

"Didn't know you took fifty off me," he clattered plaintively. "Which shows how bad wrecked I was."

"Hi, hi," Walley made the sound of derisive laughter. "You ought to practice more. You can't get toughened up to the butterfly life while you cower in the country. You were babbling about the mighty and magnificent mountains when you left me, and it kinda got me wishing for them myself. I came out, thinkin' mebby I'd run into you. Instead, you snuck off into the hazel brush," he reproved benignly. "Well," he made the sounder drawl, "it's getting crimpy here, and I thought I'd drift toward New Mexico and warm weather. If you get cold, come winter, why don't you slide on down where there's sunshine?"

"I would if I thought I could get an Indian to scalp you," he chanted.

"O. K., Sorreltop. Any time you want that fifty bucks, come and see if I've got it. I'll send word to the HU office here when I've made up my mind where I'll be. Keep your shirt tucked in, and don't let a blonde take you. Adios."

"Keep your nose clean and your vest buttoned up," Eddie advised. "And I hope you strangle."

The little brass tongue froze in an empty silence and left a lonesome void under his ribs. You were a mile high in Denver. The air had a zing, and the mountains were cut into the sky that arched so high you stretched on tiptoe when you looked up at it. The big Mikes bellowed and stamped coming up to Soldier's Summit, and compressed air snarled savagely when the hogger kicked the brakes under his train on the snaky grades.

He slid down in his chair as the messages began to flow through his gliding fingers again. Pictures shimmered under his eye lids: High, lonely passes that throbbed to the pound of the Mikados' stacks, like you had your head in a barrel; where blizzards fought among the crags and the rotary plows drilled deep channels through a wilderness of snow. The smells of cold, dark pine and the faint, bitter taste of engine smoke in the thin, keen air.

And then he wondered sharply why Hi Wheeler was down Pueblo way. That didn't fit.

An interruption in the chatter of the sounders pulled his mind back, and he glanced at Curt. The dispatcher's small, dark eyes protruded in a shocked stare at his train sheet, and his round face was blank and opened at the line of his mouth. His plump hand clung to the key as if the knob was the only hold he had on a situation that was coming apart. He wet his lips and began to pump at the key with stiff fingers.

Curt was in trouble again.

The night chief hadn't come back. Eddie checked the operator who was sending to him and made the sign that he was called away. He crossed the room and stood by the dispatchers' table.

Curt was calling Auburn, tearing out the signal letters and flinging them into the dark over the roaring division.

"19, AU, AU, AU—19, DS." His fingers clawed out the call in a tight, breathless suspense that tried to drag a reply in out of all that dim space.

Eddie glanced at the train order book. The last entry was timed twelve minutes before. He made a quick study of the rows of inked-in figures on the train sheet. Curt had tried that maneuver of shoving a train over to the opposite track, and it had apparently somehow trapped him again.

That last order had cut an eastbound stock train, Extra 682, over to the westbound track from Tucker, through Auburn, to Oswego, to run her around an overloaded coal train. And this time he'd overlooked a lone helper engine westbound that had left Oswego eighteen minutes before he had issued the crossover order.

There were two OS's on the train sheet that had just now been recorded. The ink was wet and unblotted. They showed that Extra 682 East had just now gone by Tucker, where she'd been cut over. But Light Engine 929 West had passed Oswego thirty-one minutes ago. They were heading toward each other at a considerable rate of speed, both on the westbound track.

The delayed OS from Oswego was puzzling at first. And then he made a shrewd guess why it had taken the operator half an hour to make that report. Curt had been keeping his wire hot all evening, and the operator at Oswego hadn't dared break in on him to give the OS at the time the engine had passed his station. Curt would have scorched him if he had. The operator had gone on to other duties, and when Curt had called him to take the order which should have protected Extra 682 to Oswego, the dispatcher's furious impatience had caused the night man to overlook reporting the light engine then. And the delayed OS had likely caused Curt to miss the presence of the lone engine on his train sheet. The dispatcher hadn't checked carefully to make sure he had Extra 682 fixed on every opposing train before he cut her over. Then the operator at Oswego had just now come to life and reported the helper engine, which had brought its presence to Curt's mind.

But you couldn't see that this was fatal. The Auburn telegraph office was still between the two trains, and that operator wouldn't be far from his instruments. The coal train was likely passing him just now, and maybe he was out there delivering something to her on the fly. But he'd be back in the office before either the lone engine or the stock train reached him, and he could amend Curt's blunder. There didn't seem much chance of a head-on.

But Curt, crouched before the dispatcher's table, his elbows braced on the long train sheet, ruled and lettered and inked with the record of all the train movements out there in the dark, seemed to think there was. He jerked out the Auburn call with stiff convulsions of the wrist, and he sweated and his eyes peered in a stark stare from the intent pucker of his cheeks.

"AU, AU, AU—" The harsh call went on in a kind of droning thunder that spread out over the crowded double tracks. "AU, AU—"

That night operator was too long away from his key. Eddie got a hint then of something come unjointed at Auburn station. There was a breakdown that was developing into a dangerous situation.

The seconds stole away while Curt tossed his call, and a tight nerve coiled in the back of Eddie's head as he reckoned time from the train sheet. The lone engine was due at Auburn within seventeen minutes. You didn't realize how brief that amount of time could be until so much depended upon it.

Then the circuit came apart at last, and the sounder went dead. Curt clamped his key shut and held it down desperately. The straining quiet chased the dull thunder of the call into the far darkness, and Eddie felt the breath go thin and hot in his throat as he stared at the motionless brass tongue, waiting for it to move again.

"I—I—AU," it came alive at last, limping. Then there was a pause that ate up lean seconds while the operator continued to hold his key open.

That answer hadn't burst from the sounder with the abrupt snap of a trained telegrapher. It fluttered, dubious and frightened. Eddie caught in those few uncertain snicks a familiar quality of send that took him back to the long evenings of practice with Janet and Peck. And suddenly he recognized that light, hesitant touch. It was Janet who had answered Curt's call. He couldn't guess why. But he was certain that those murmured signals had been made by the girl, and that she was confused and scared.

"I, I, AU," the sounder struggled again, and then the circuit closed timidly.

XII

"THIRTY-ONE, copy six," Curt rattled. "Order No.—"

But Janet couldn't take it like that. It was too fast and bewildering for a ham. She broke at once, and there was another long pause that got lost in a distant field of silence. Then the sounder rattled faintly once, in an infirm question mark. She hadn't understood a single letter or numeral of Curt's violent signals.

Curt strangled. He muttered and tried again, slowing his sending pace. But his hand had no cunning, his nerves were screaming. The letters hopped and exploded under his fingers. He broke himself and repeated.

"Thirty-one, copy six. Order No. 92, C. & E. Ex. 682 E. & Lt. Eng. 929 W." And then the portentous period and pause before he sent the body of the order.

Janet broke again and held her key open while she tried to reconstruct in her mind the sense of those clattering symbols. But there was nothing familiar to her ears in the harsh clucks, and presently she made another question mark, dragging it out with trembling fingers.

You could feel her panic growing as she huddled under the shaded oil lamp, alone in the gloomy station. The cold snip of the instrument had shaken all the confidence out of her and left her collapsed over the telegraph table, quietly freezing with dread. The little brass tongue was a tormenting fiend. Her mind was in a tight tumult, and Curt couldn't get his signals through that frightened confusion. She had caught the note of alarm transmitted by his plunging send, and she wouldn't now be able to read a word he offered.

Curt paused and stared up at Eddie. He seemed about to howl. A drop of perspiration slid across his chin and dropped onto the train sheet with a soft hiss. His lips moved.

"She can't get me—she's scared." He goggled at the boomer. "She did all right early in the evening. Then she had trouble copying an order I put out there, and I didn't give her any more. She just OS'd the trains as they went by." He moved his tongue across his lips. "I can't think why she's scared to work with me," he complained peevishly.

"Why is Janet on duty there?" Eddie asked.

"Madden is sick, and the night operator has worked two days and nights. The chief let him off this evening for rest till midnight. We're short of men and can't relieve Madden or send another operator."

The Sod Line had shaved the budget for that year, and there wasn't a relief man to fill in for the sick. Railroaders always managed to keep the traffic rolling somehow.

"Why wasn't Peck put on instead of Janet?" he asked softly.

The seconds slid away with the slow swing of the big clock's pendulum. The gap between the two trains was closing with every deliberate tick.

"That dumb kid? I wouldn't work with him. I made them put Janet on. She's a pretty good operator. I just don't know what's got into her. She worked all right with me at first."

Curt had thought that by putting Janet on the job, instead of Peck, she'd sit there and listen to him run the division. Eddie twisted a grin. He'd thought Curt had been trying to do something to impress the chief, and all the time he'd been making his play at the girl.

"It don't add up," he said.

Telegrapher's terror had hit her when she was faced with the intricate operations of moving all those trains, and she wouldn't now come out of her panic while Curt tortured the wire. Her nerves had been strung tight by her first responsibility for the safety of the trains, and he'd shredded them to strings. He wouldn't be able to reinstate her confidence within the slipping seconds allowed.

O. K. If you were the right kind of operator, you could exert more influence on some people over the telegraph wires, if they were tuned in right. There were elements you could blindly manage that you couldn't otherwise contact at all. She had responded with alacrity to his hand on the key, absorbed his intent and purpose in a kind of astral contact. They'd come pretty close together in a quick understanding that had nearly reached its climax that last night.

"Get up, Curt!" he said.

The lean, implacable minutes dripped from the clock. Curt's jaw unhooked as he stared up at the boomer.

"What?" he said. "What did you say?"

"Get up," he ordered. "I'll take over." He was set for a quick hold. "I can make Janet understand me. She's done it before."

Curt read some swift violence in the level eyes. He half arose, and then hesitated.

"Move!" he snapped.

Curt unfolded his knees and pushed back the chair and

stood aside. Eddie dropped into the chair and hitched it up to the table and reached for the key.

The dim dispatchers' room, spotted with yellow light, slid out of his consciousness. He relaxed his fingers and made some brisk I's and sent amiably, "Who'n hell's on this wire?" and closed the key.

The silence widened in quiet ripples out beyond the circle of light on the train sheet. He could hear the switch engine's pump throbbing just below the window. You couldn't help the tightening around your stomach, even if you were entirely confident. She'd decipher that first jocose remark he'd ever made to her on the wire. He'd repeated it to her often enough since then. It had become a comradely call. She'd remember that, and all their associations, and she'd come out of it.

Her reply came sliding in from the miles of darkness with a flutter of the brass tongue. It said *clump, clump*— and made another question mark.

He flinched. The room was suddenly hot and airless. A vacuum began to absorb his convictions. And all the time he was conscious of the time. You could count the fleeing seconds without a glance at the clock. That half-strangled interrogation warned him that the minutes remaining were moving away with the steady stride of the pendulum.

"This is Eddie, Janet." He tried to insinuate a personal and private note in his send, as if he whispered some sugary secret. "How are you doing?" he inquired blithely.

The passenger train yelled at the lower end of the yard and glided to a stop by the station platform below. The switch engine coughed as it came out of the siding and pasted the Pullman onto the rear end.

Janet would be pulling herself together before the telegraph table, staring at the instrument, recognition of his hand on the key rising within her. She'd feel that astral touch through all those miles of wire, and she'd respond. His nerves began to tighten like strung threads as he waited for her to reply.

Clump, clump, the brass tongue coughed.

There wasn't much more personality in those frightened sounds than the squeal of an ungreased axle. She was just a scared girl, likely beginning to cry, and he'd not be able to get a spark of recognition from her.

That light engine was in sight of Auburn by now, and the hogger of the stock train would be winding her up, blasting to get around the coal train and back on his rightful side of the double track. You'd never guess how precious seconds could be until they were scarce.

"Janet," he tried again, "this is Eddie. Can't you read me?"

Maybe there was some one in this world who could lure her back to confidence within the next three minutes, but he knew by all those inscrutable instincts he'd privately taken pride in that he'd never be able to arouse her. You were born with a conceit that you had a certain power over women. It was rooted like an ancient tree, and it took dynamite to demolish it. He'd just now been blasted, and the hollow left felt like an aching cavern inside him. Curt looked badly mangled, and between them they were going to be implicated in a head-ender that would be destructive, and likely tragic.

He glared at the mute sounder crouched in its hooded box, as if he would wrench some reasonable response from it. And abruptly it did retort. The brass tongue jumped and banged out letters as if the key were being stamped upon.

"Hey!" it exploded. "Janet's fainted. What's the matter?"

Eddie jumped. That ponderous, trampling send was a

familiar shout slamming in out of the weird darkness. There was only one big hand that could make it sound as if it originated in a machine shop. He'd tried often enough to teach it cunning on the key, but now he knew he'd never heard another send as agreeable. Peck Frim was on the wire.

Eddie stretched a sickly grin. Sure, that awkward ox would be about the station as long as Janet was there.

Curt sucked in his breath and reached for the key. The boomer brushed his hand aside. Curt would scare the daylights out of the kid too, and you couldn't waste a single second now. The gods of the high iron had relented just so much. He paid them a hearty reverence.

You mustn't let hustle and panic get into your tone on the wire. Take it easy. You might use up the last second by being cautious, but you had to make it unconcerned. If one touch of terror got to the kid, he'd be useless too.

"Hi, Peck. This is Eddie." He cut it enough to make it casual, used their personal signs, and he sent with steady assurance, clear and quiet. "Have you got both boards out?"

Promptly Peck answered, "No."

"Put both of them out. Say when."

The sounder clicked open and was silent.

He pictured the kid as he got out of his chair and walked with the stamp of big feet to the end of the long table. He'd pull one lever at a time and the semaphore arms outside on their high pole would be flung out horizontally and the dots of light up there would turn red. You could stop any train, from the charging limited to the crawling freights, with that speck of red in the dark.

But he realized with a flick of cold needles down his back that none of his images that night had turned out real. Maybe Peck was sitting dumbly at the table figuring out the brief command in his mind. He'd take a lot of time to sift the signals through his slow thought procedures. There wasn't, he knew now, any astral processes to get at that kid. That lone locomotive would be right at the station. Peck might at the last second hesitate to take the responsibility of checking the engine, and he might let him by before he set his board against westbound traffic.

He felt as if the kinks in his hair were unraveling. He could hear Curt keep wetting his lips. If Peck came back with that stuttered question mark, Eddie felt he'd just go up in a puff of smoke.

The sounder slammed explosive Morse at him.

"Both boards out. I just did stop a light engine west. Made'im slide'em. Is that right?"

His breath stopped choking him and he steadied his hand. "That's right. Hold him. Now, copy an order. Do you get me?"

"Sure," Peck tramped out. "Easy. Go ahead."

Let the kid take it through. He'd picked up the responsibility. Ease him into the water this time, and let him build up his own confidence. He'd copied a hundred train orders from him in practice. Keep to the regular send of the drill.

"Order No. 92."

He let it flow quietly from his fingers. Peck broke once, but without a show of panic. Then, when Eddie had finished it, Peck carefully pounded out what he had written, repeated the order to the last period.

Eddie sent, "That's O. K., Peck. Get the trainmen's signatures, and repeat them to the dispatcher as soon as they've signed."

"O. K., Eddie."

He went on, "You've done a good job, Peck, stepping in when Janet couldn't take it. You'll likely get a letter from the Old Man saying so. And a telegraph job besides. You're good enough now, kid. Stick out your chin."

"Sure will," Peck exulted. He paused, and then blurted, "Janet's come to, and she's trying to cry on my shoulder. What do I do now?"

"You big oaf, let her do it. As long as she wants to."

"What's a oaf?" Peck fumbled suspiciously.

"A nut!" Eddie raved. "Get busy and comfort the girl."

There was a longer pause, and then the sounder sputtered, "Hey, Eddie. I kissed her, and she kissed back!"

"Very, very elegant," said Eddie. "Let the traffic wait till you get that situation entirely cleared up."

The night chief, chewing a tooth pick sauntered in. He veered and came to stand beside Eddie. He glanced at the train sheet and then he took up the order book. He spat out the tooth pick and his eyes puckered as he looked at Curt.

"What's been going on here, Eddie?" he demanded.

The boomer stood up.

"There she is." He spread his hands in benediction over the train sheet. "There she is, with all the wheels on the iron—and rolling."

He went back to his table. He called the Omaha operator and started the stream of messages through the typewriter again. Quietly his mind took up its separate concerns. The messages dripped unheeded from the machine in slow, yellow drops. He was aware of the sharp tone of the night chief and the mumble of Curt's replies.

He grinned as he considered the restless element that had been bothering him, but that vague grin wasn't quite authentic. Encounters like this lifted you out of the dull routine and made you live high moments. They were good to remember at the times you didn't do quite so well.

Pictures drifted in the back of his mind. The flicker of yard lights in great terminals, and banks of signals on high interlocking plants that bridged the four tracks. A stark semaphore thrust up out of the blank desert like a slim finger pointing at the exact center of the blazing sky. The sting of wind off the ruffled blue of the Great Lakes, and the long ridges the Gulf of Mexico built and flung upon the white beach. The tramp of the big jacks on the hill.

There couldn't be firm alliances or lasting associations when you couldn't resist that impulse to drift. When that restless feeling came over you, it tortured you till you took to the careless road again.

Swift chatter of the telegraph instruments and the surge and thunder of traffic down the high iron. Denver was a mile high above this flat land, and maybe forty-eight hours away. The mountains leaned back against a sky that arched so high you stood on tiptoe when you looked up at it.

XIII

THE TAG end of Fall had been wet and sunless. It rained when it wasn't sleeting. The prairie mud was without bottom; a godless land deserted by the sun. The weather had never made him melancholy before. It must be the weather, though.

The chief dispatcher gave him a pass to Omaha, and said he ought to take a leave of absence till he got over whatever it was that ailed him. Instead of just quitting. But Eddie thought he might have to travel a long way before he found the sun again. He'd likely not be back.

Omaha looked like something the Missouri River had become irritated with and shoved aside. It still rained when it wasn't sleeting. He veered south. He rode the cushions "on his face" to St. Joe. That city had the strawy odor of meat packing plants, and no sun. He wheeled westward.

Local passenger train conductors were obliging through three consecutive division points without a break, while more murky flat country, spiked with dead corn stocks, wandered by coach windows dulled by rain. At last mountains smudged the sky and drew near enough for you to be sure they weren't just more rain clouds. The sun promised beyond the range, but at that next division point he had to transfer to the Anaconda Short Line, and he ran out of benevolent conductors. The reason they were no longer accommodating, it developed, was a trainmaster who was out to make a reputation for himself. He was named Bull Keeley. An operator in the ticket office explained it to Eddie.

"You can't get squared out of here with any of these skippers," he stated in disgust. "This Keeley-cured trainmaster has just recently come to his high post, but already he's got the scalps of a number of trainmen curing by his fire. Your head's cut off if you get caught carrying rails on the drift. He hates 'em."

"You sure he's that bad?" Eddie asked incredulously.

"Listen," begged the operator. "He'd soak a conductor twenty brownies if he caught him carrying his grandmother's picture without a ticket. Keeley's kin to somebody high in the general offices. We got a new bunch running the A. S. L., and no telling what'll happen."

Eddie said that there must be a special corner in hell reserved for such officials. Then he sought more deadhead transportation in the freight yard. It was a mile down there from the passenger station. He heaved his suitcase to his shoulder and splashed through the drizzle.

You could smell the high country. A grim peak tore belligerently through the curtain of clouds and leered down at him. The wet air bubbled. Lines of freight cars huddled dumbly in the damp. Switch engines coughed as if they had the croup. The battered yard office came out of the mist and he veered that way.

A long man in rubber hat and slicker that covered him like a tent, ducked out of the low doorway and ambled forth into the rain. He tucked train-book and waybills and tissue orders into his pocket. Eddie paused and lowered his suitcase. A nose protruding beyond the dripping brim of the rubber hat was the only visible feature, and the slicker would conceal the identity of your twin brother. But that rambling, double-jointed pace that seemed as if it was four-legged, couldn't be duplicated. It was Hi Wheeler.

"Mister," Eddie piped politely, "could you spare a poor guy two bits?"

Hi Wheeler skidded to a stop and pivoted. His long face divided in half. "Eddie!" he yelled, and embraced him in the folds of the slicker and trampled his toes with his huge rubber boots and pounded him on the back.

Eddie wedged an elbow into his ribs, and Hi grunted and let go.

"You ain't gentled much," he complained, and rubbed his side. "You look like you been eatin' regular, but there's a look in your eye. Where'd you just come from?"

"Back there about where you left me," he admitted.

"In them mud flats? What happened to you?" Hi scrutinized him carefully. "It must'a been a woman," he decided.

"Well," Eddie pondered, "yes and no. I've not made up my mind for certain just exactly what it was."

"Then it was a woman," Hi stated. "You look like you been hit by somethin' and was still scared. Wimmen'll do that to you."

"O. K.," said Eddie. "We'll let it ride. Now suppose you bring me up to date on your own personal history. How come you left the S-W. P.? Did Buck Barabe finally catch up with you, or did a gal get you to write her a letter that you didn't want to hear read to the jury?"

"Doggone, Eddie!" Hi grinned. "It was amazin' how I got myself all crossed up. This gal Gladys—did I ever tell you about her?" He looked pensively at his boots and chuckled.

"I remember you saying a lot of things about her, back there in Chicago, but none of 'em registered in my mind."

"Well, sir," Hi chortled, "Gladys is a clerk in Sko-

winski's, and I knowed the minute I'd bought my first pair
of gloves off'n her that I wouldn't ever be happy without
her."

Eddie stared. "You mean you wanted to marry her first
thing?" he demanded.

Hi gave a bright nod. "And that still stands," he said.

Eddie upended his suitcase and sat upon it and stared
dumbly. This didn't sound reasonable. Hi often became
exuberant over buxom blondes. Frequently one had him
groggy for a time. But never for long. His considerable
technique had up to now saved him from a drastic alliance.
He'd lightly lose his heart, but not his head.

"It was just like that!" Hi said, and snapped his fingers. "By the time she'd given me my change, I was ga-ga.
And by the time I'd bought another pair of gloves off'n
her on every trip, in and out, for thirty days, she said it
looked like I ought to be diverted." Hi nodded compla-
cently. "Either buy pants and shirts, or save my dough.
Then she decided I'd save it. She's a great gal, but a little
rigid about my conduct."

Eddie sighed. "Look, Hi," he said, "I'd better know
the worst at once. Tell it to me just as you remember it."

"Some of it wasn't so good." Hi darkened. "I couldn't
seem to keep my feet on the ground. And when we'd decided to get married, I just fluttered like I was about to
fly."

"Who decided that?" Eddie asked sharply.

"Why, it was kinda in a session between us," Hi ventured vaguely. "It was pay day, and I'd have enough left
over to buy me a new blue suit, which is how come I had
the nerve to approach her on the subject. And then on the
way home afterwards, I stopped in at Mark's to get my
check cashed."

He brooded over that night. "You're kinda obliged to

buy a drink when Mark cashes your check," he muttered. "I did, and it went right to my stummick. The darndest thing." He gave Eddie a puzzled, pleading look. "So I bought another one, just to see. There was something wrong some place, 'cause that'n also had a delayed fuse to it." He pushed back his rubber hat and wrinkled his brow. "But when it finally let go, it nearly took the top of my head off." He spat emphatically. "I remember some time after decidin' to have my old suit cleaned and pressed, instead of buyin' a new one. And then the call boy found me. I was wanted for an extra west."

Hi shook his head sadly. "Down in the yard, after I'd run into most everything else, includin' telegraph poles and flat cars and a yard goat that snuck up on me, I ran into old Buck Barabe. Hard." He laughed far down in his diaphragm. "Mister, that was an encounter. My luck had quit me that night the minute I left Gladys. Shows how necessary she is in my life. Old Buck hit me so hard with the old Rule G that I woke up next morning without a job."

"Right!" Eddie said impatiently. "But what about Gladys? Didn't she tie a can on you too?"

"No," Hi sighed. "No, she didn't. But I had to talk and make promises, or she would have."

Eddie took his head in his hands and muttered darkly to himself.

"But, lookit," Hi became pungent again. "I get a job here, and they're short of men, account of a new trainmaster that's been movin' out some of the boys. So right away I'm made an extra conductor."

"And now," Eddie brightened, "you can leave the past behind you, and forget it all, and start all over again."

"You'd think that was comin' to me," Hi beamed, "but such is not the case."

"What !" he snapped at him.

"I got enough money for first payment on the furniture, and Gladys is on her way up, and we're gonna be married. I've got to meet her at the other end of this division in the mornin'. And you've got to stick around and see me through this. It works out just right. I'm takin' Forty-seven out right now, and you're ridin' with me in the crummy."

Eddie shook a dejected head. "No," he declined. "Much obliged. But I'd better not be a party to this."

"You've got to, Eddie. Just stick around and steer me right, in case my feet won't stay on the ground. You're my old friend and fellow confederate. It's just like you was sent down here on purpose to see I do it right."

"I don't know who sent me," he grumbled, "but whoever it was didn't have my best interests at heart."

He was wary of blithe blondes on principle. Any one of them which Hi favored so ardently would only aggravate his amiable talent for getting into trouble. How'd that wayward guy manage with one of them to supervise his existence? Not well at all, Eddie informed himself; not in any department.

"You goin' to run out on me?" Hi lamented.

At that, there was something inscrutable here, he decided with a chill. Their branch lines had run down to a junction, and at the exact instant Hi was headed into a crisis. If he'd arrived at that yard office twenty seconds later than he had, they'd have missed each other. Fate. If you believed in destiny you'd have to go along with this.

"All right," he agreed. "But I'll not hang around after you're tied. I just couldn't take that."

"Doggone!" Hi exulted. "We're gonna make somethin' out of this. Come on. I'll stow you in the caboose."

They tramped across the sidings to where a freight train was set to take to the high iron.

"But lookit," Hi cautioned. "If that trainmaster shows up, I'll have to hide you while he's around. I've already had some trouble with him about overtime, and besides he'd fire anybody for carryin' love and affection free on any of his trains."

"As low as that? Wouldn't even carry an honest rail even in the caboose? Somebody ought to do something to him."

"They will," Hi promised. "He just ain't met the right man in the dark yet. We'd a fine old superintendent named Welby. A swell brass hat. I only got ten brownies off him so far."

"He must be ailing to let you off that easy," he judged.

"He was sick and had to go to the hospital," Hi admitted. "The talk is he won't have a job when he comes out. This Anaconda Short Line had just recently been taken over by a new outfit, and they been cleaning house. This Keeley is one of the new bunch, and he's hard after the Old Man's job."

"And he's liable to get yours, too, if he catches you carrying me. You sure I hadn't better take my foot in my hand and walk?"

"You get aboard that crummy!"

The hind brakeman had a fire going in the iron heater, and the caboose felt comfortable. He stowed his suitcase under a bunk and hung up his rain coat.

"What'd you ever do with that farm you bought for my old age?" he inquired.

"When it come right down to it," Hi said, "Gladys didn't fall for the idea. They been drillin' around that section for oil, and there's a chance we can sell it for more'n I paid. Gladys would have been up here before now, but she's been on a dicker."

"Did she sell it?"

"She ain't said." Hi pulled down his rubber hat and opened the back door.

Eddie looked at him sharply. "Ain't said? Isn't the place yours? Wouldn't you have to sign the deed?"

"Naw," said Hi. "I deeded it over to her before I left down there." He shut the door and clumped down the steps.

Eddie reflected. You couldn't figure if the happy ones were always dumb, or if they just seemed that way because they were joyful. He whistled softly as he got a book out of his raincoat pocket. He stretched out on a cushioned seat and began to read.

XIV

FORTY-SEVEN, a mixed freight doing local work, whistled off and rattled over switch points as she snaked out onto the main line. Hi and his rear brakeman swung aboard and they headed into red streaks of sunset that broke through the clouds. The brakeman put out the rear marker lights and lit the lamps. Hi worked at the little desk.

The busy speed and the stubborn, muffled rumble of the moving train made you feel tucked-in. You felt at home in a caboose, the way you do in a farmhouse kitchen. The ghosts of a thousand sturdy meals, ingeniously cooked by trainmen on the small round top of the drum-bellied heating stove, were faintly there among the shadows. There were the smells of a dozen brands of tobacco, some of them with a range of forty yards, but all mellowed by time and the milder mixtures of old leather upholstery and signal oil. It was a snug, tight feeling, with the wash of the rain at the little windows and the brisk rhythm of wheels clicking at the rail-joints. Dim lamps in brackets and lanterns, red and white, by the back door. Above, in the cupola, the faint outline of the rear brakeman, lounging there on lookout. The high wail of the engine's whistle trickled back, a thin challenge.

Eddie dropped his book and dozed.

Station and yard lights showed ahead, and then the

lights of a town drew in around them. Forty-seven eased
to a stop.

"We got some merchandise to unload and empties to
set," Hi said. The two trainmen went out.

The wind came through in weary sighs. The engine cut
off and nosed about the yard. Hurrying feet slapped on the
packed wet cinders outside and the caboose shuddered as
someone sprang up the steps. Hi stormed in, tossing his
lantern angrily, livid language on his tongue.

"That blamed trainmaster is here," he snarled, "and
he's gonna ride through to the terminal with me."

Eddie closed his book. "Oh, well," he said with some
relief, "it's just fate working in the dark, first one way and
then that. She's now relented and is sparing me the sight
of you being tied in wedlock. Is this a town you can rent
a bed in which to sleep?"

"You ain't stoppin' off here, mister," Hi stated flatly.
"Why doggone, didn't you drop in straight from above
to see me through my nuptials? Just one nosey brass hat
ain't goin' to part us now."

"Maybe not, but I'm not going to ride the rods."

"You don't have to," Hi said cheerfully. "There's an
emigrant car in this train, with a kid in charge of the livestock. I stopped as I came back and took a look and talked
to the boy. It's O. K. with him, and he's got it all fixed
comfortable. Come on."

"Has he got a light I can read by?"

"Aw, sure," Hi assured him grimly. "And hot and cold
runnin' water, I guess. And they most usually have maid
service in them zulu cars. There was a lot of other critters
in it besides the kid, and none of them raised any objections to you ridin' with 'em."

Situations always got more complicated as you went

along. He put on his rain coat and followed Hi down the steps.

"Old Bull Keeley," Hi muttered darkly, "says we're too slow gettin' over the road, addin' up overtime and usin' too much slack, which they call coal on this pike. He's with us to demonstrate how to make schedule." He paused and slid back a boxcar door. Pale light wedged out into the rain. "Here he is, son."

Eddie climbed and squeezed inside.

"You see he rides nice and comfortable."

"Betcha." He was a chunky kid with a brush of yellow hair. He straddled a bench under a lantern hung by a long wire from the roof, and he cleaned a set of harness. "My name's Chad," he said.

Half the car was stacked high with household goods and farm implements. Two big draft horses and a cow stood in straw up to their knees. The sleek animals stared at Eddie with mild curiosity.

"The mare's name is Carrie," Chad introduced, and made a swift, shadowy gesture.

Carrie nodded briskly and put out her nose at him.

"The horse is Boxer."

He didn't catch the signal, but Boxer shook his head wisely and snorted at him.

"This is Miss Murphy," Chad indicated the red cow.

Miss Murphy lowed, and then at an impatient sign from the boy, she bawled loudly.

"They've got nice manners," Eddie said. "How do you teach them?"

"You just got to know a little more than they do," Chad said.

Eddie grinned. "A lot of people ought to realize that before they try to instruct their betters," he allowed.

He slid the door to and took down a rocker from the pile and sat down.

"Want to read that book?" Chad found a candle and dripped wax on a packing case and set it there. "Pull up to that," he invited.

The light from the flame widened and brought out a head with horns and whiskers that peered down at him from a pile of packing cases. Eddie found himself clutching his book. The thing clattered down nimbly and jumped to the floor.

"Ba-a-a!" it challenged him. It took a tentative nibble at the book. It was a huge billy goat.

"That's Barbecue," Chad announced. "You leave him alone," he ordered the goat.

Barbecue gave Eddie a resentful eye and went to lie in the straw at Carrie's feet.

A hair trunk in the shadow at the end of the couch moved and stood up. Its mouth opened in a scarlet yawn.

"That's Pomp," Chad enumerated. The dog waved a bushy tail and held out a polite paw. The yellow light ran in glinting streaks over his long coat. "Dad's driving the sheep through, and Pomp and Barbecue started with him. But they ran away and came back to me when they found I wasn't going along."

"Both of them trained on sheep?" Eddie asked.

"And cattle, too, Pomp is," Chad nodded. "Dad's got the other two dogs with him."

Pomp curled up on Eddie's feet. Chad sponged a tug over a pan of lather, his hands moving swiftly. It was an orderly outfit, properly disciplined. A keen kid.

Sounds of switching subsided in the yard. Sheep bleated and called in distress, and men's voices drifted in angrily on the wet wind. Boots splashed outside and the door squealed open a foot. Hi's head and his lantern hung on the sill.

"Nice time we're havin' loadin' them ba-bas," he snorted. "What I mean, a nice time not shovin' them aboard. I had to get out for a minute before Keeley and me got to namin' each other. I'm gonna speak my mind to that man one of these times."

"How come you've got to load the sheep?" Eddie asked.

"We had an empty which should have been set for loadin' by the local this mornin', and then we was to pick up the load this evenin'. But somebody slipped," Hi grumbled. "Keeley says we've got to load them and take 'em along, but the sheep don't know that. They won't come aboard. And Keeley and the herders can't make 'em. If you like good, clean fun and want to learn some sheepmen's way of sayin' things, slip over to the pens."

"Not interested," Eddie yawned.

"I hope," Hi fretted, "them critters don't hold us up so I'll be late meetin' Gladys in the mornin'. She might not understand that."

"In case you personally want those woolies loaded," Eddie offered, "and nobody else is able, Chad here would be glad to see it's done."

"Betcha," said Chad.

"Yeah?" said Hi. "You're pretty artful, but how you gonna make sheep do what they don't want?"

"Just say you want it done," Eddie grinned.

Hi rubbed his wet nose. "Doggone," he muttered, "just when we got a chance to slow down this buzzard who's tryin' to hurry us up, and I could get in some nice overtime, which is badly needed on account of matrimony, then I got to be in a hurry to meet my gal. But Gladys won't like it if

I'm not there when she arrives, so we'd better get goin', if you can do it."

Chad wiped his hands and slid into his slicker.

"Come on, Barbecue," he ordered.

The goat got up suddenly from the straw and shook himself and confronted Hi in the doorway. He lowered his head and sniffed at the trainman's face. Hi strangled and stepped back. His rubber boots tangled in his slicker. He tripped and fell in the mud. His lantern bounced and rolled away.

Barbecue sprang to the ground beside him and muttered in Hi's ear. Eddie and Chad got down and untangled him and helped him up.

"I ain't had a drink since the one Barabe fired me for," Hi explained, "but I wasn't sure that wasn't what I thought it was."

Barbecue followed at Chad's heels as they crossed the yard. The long chute at the stock pens twinkled with lanterns. They climbed the fence where a car was spotted. The dim light showed the runway packed with sheep. They had halted on an invisible line just short of the open doorway of the car, and they milled and refused with dismal protests to go inside.

Chad pointed to a worn depression in the chute floor at end of the running board. It was filled with water.

"They don't like to cross that," he said, and dropped to the ground and walked away in the dark toward the back of the pens. Barbecue trotted amiably beside him.

Bull Keeley and two sheep men were in the muddy space between the flock and the car. You could spot the trainmaster at once. He had heavy, hunched shoulders and a head set forward between them without much neck. He'd hung his lantern on the side of the chute, and sizing him up under that fitful light you'd guess he was one of those pushing kind that had come up by tieing in with any influence he could manage.

But he didn't know about sheep, and he was obstructing the men who did. He panted from his exertions and he muttered as he crowded in and tried to start the head of the column into the car. He seized a sheep and thrust it toward the doorway. The animal whirled and crowded back into the flock.

Hi regarded this with glee. "You got to be kind to 'em," he chanted. "Pet 'em and call 'em pretty names."

Keeley paused and peered up into the darkness in the direction of the voice. "I've been wondering where you'd gone," he growled. "Get down here and go to work."

"That ain't in my working agreement," Hi jeered. "I just herd freight cars. But I got a better critter than you and me both that'll get them bleaters aboard for you. He knows about sheep."

"You heard me!" Keeley yelled. "Get in here and help."

Hi began another jocular refusal, but Eddie kicked him and closed his mouth. Chad came back and climbed the side of the chute.

The flock became agitated in the dark at the farther end of the chute. The stir moved forward. Barbecue's horns and whiskers showed in the light of lanterns as they tossed above the backs of the sheep. He came out at the head of the pack and paused.

"A goat!" bawled Keeley. "Wheeler, are you trying to be funny with me?"

"You better treat him kindly," Hi warned. "He don't like some folks."

Barbecue paused and eyed the trainmaster. He rocked gently back and forth on his legs like a hobbyhorse. He muttered darkly. Then he walked into the car and paused, inviting the sheep to follow. They stared at him dubiously.

"Haw!" said Keeley. "What's he trying to do?"

Barbecue came out of the car, and circled through the flock. He nudged the sheep amiably.

"Haw-haw!" the trainmaster scoffed. "Call off your goat, Wheeler, and get in here and help shove them in. We can't stay here all night."

"He's doin' as well as you, up to now," Hi pointed out.

Barbecue made reassuring sounds in his throat. He came out and shook his head at Keeley. He muttered.

"He's tryin' to tell you to get the heck out of there," Hi called, "and let him work this."

Keeley yelled and tried to kick the goat.

Barbecue stepped nimbly aside. He looked at Keeley and came to an abrupt decision. A quick ripple ran through him and he rocked back on his hind legs. He tucked in his chin and walled up his eyes and exploded from the tension of his hind quarters. Keeley slipped as he tried to avoid him, and Barbecue's horns got tangled in the trainmaster's slicker. Keeley floundered to his knees and the goat butted him into a sprawl. He backed off and shook his head and clattered up the running board.

The sheep suddenly broke from the jam and hurried after him into the car. They swarmed over the trainmaster. Their pattering hoofs dented his back and packed him into the mud. A herder stretched a hand into the hurrying flock and dragged Keeley to the fence.

"Haw!" Hi chided. "Haw-haw!"

Barbecue eased out of the car when the last of the sheep crowded in. The sheepmen pulled the door shut and swung back the chute gates. Chad took the goat away, and Eddie helped boost him into the zulu car.

Chad went back to cleaning harness. The animals watched him with mild, affectionate eyes. The engine tied the car of sheep into the train. Brake shoes clanked as the air was connected up. Boots hurried outside and the door was pushed back. Hi set a bundle inside. The bundle stood up and murmured and blinked round eyes at car and contents.

"This is Carlotta," Hi hissed, "and she's the section foreman's kid."

"Which adds up to what?" Eddie inquired.

"What I mean," Hi said impatiently, "we've got to take her home. She's got to ride in here."

"Now, if she was a big blonde girl," Eddie suggested, "she'd ride in the caboose with you. You'd break your neck to see she did."

"Why, Mr. Sand," Hi reproached him, "talkin' like that to a man that's practically married to the sweetest woman." He rubbed his nose. "Lookit, I'll diagram. Carlotta rides up and down the line all the time alone, on visits to her grandma here, and other relatives up and down the line. Section foremen always has a lot of kin."

Two quick blasts came from the head end, and Hi turned sidewise from the doorway and swung his lantern.

"Whenever she wants to go, she just gets aboard the first train headed her way," he went on hurridly. "The trainmen always take care of her. Which is all right when Mr. Welby was runnin' the division. He'd take her in his private car, if he was all hitched up and goin' her way."

The engineer caught up the slack and the train began to move. Hi peered up at them, his chin just over the sill, as he walked alongside.

"But this Keeley," he complained. "Aw heck, Eddie! You can see how that adds up. I just asked him if we could take her home, and you know what his answer was. The very words. He just boiled over."

"Then why don't you give her back to her grandma?" Eddie demanded.

"The old lady lives in the country," Hi was plaintive. He stumbled in the dark and clung to the door jam. "She left Carlotta with the agent and went back home. Now, don't get sore. 'cause it ain't no fault of mine. She's a swell kid. Everybody likes her. Carlotta, this is your Uncle Eddie." He pulled the door shut and was gone.

Ed-*dee*," Charlotta said agreeably.

Pomp moved over and put his muzzle under her chin. She took him by the ear and held on. She wasn't more than an inch taller than the dog's back, bundled in a shawl, with a brown face and a benevolent stare. She guided Pomp over to Miss Murphy and patted the cow on her moist nose. She chattered confidently in Spanish. Miss Murphy benignly licked her face and toppled her in the straw. Carlotta scolded and Pomp barked brief protest.

"Chad," said Eddie, "how are we going to manage this?"

"She won't be any trouble," Chad said. "She's hungry. I know, 'cause I got kid sisters."

He got out a bucket and began milking the cow. Eddie set Carlotta on the couch and unwrapped her from the shawl. Chad gave them foaming cups of warm milk. Carlotta's eyelids fluttered and closed, and she leaned against Eddie and went to sleep. They wrapped her in a blanket and put her on the couch.

The smooth, slick chuckle of wheels made a drowsy sound. He put his feet on a packing case and relaxed. Chad finished the harness and hung them on the wall to dry.

Forty-seven checked. Her whistle blared angrily. She stopped and the engineer blew out a flagman. Then the whistle took up its indignant blasts again. Two men stamped forward over the top of the train. The whistle ceased and the wind sighed.

"Something's blocking the way," he judged, "and it isn't a washout either."

Presently the door slid open a foot. Rain bounced on the iron sill and a draft blew out the candle. Hi peered up at them.

"How's the family?" he inquired.

"Every time you open that door," Eddie charged, "it makes for trouble."

"That's right," Hi agreed. "This time its cows, and a bull. And the bull ain't named Keeley, either." He grinned and rubbed his nose. "He's got a nice head of horns, and he's chased our trainmaster over the pilot and up onto the boiler. And there they are. Bull Keeley and Bull Cow, out there in the rain tellin' each other what they think."

"Why don't your locomotive chase off the one with the horns?" he asked drowsily.

"Account of the cows. There's a long, narrow cut filled with 'em. Come there for shelter. And they won't be shooed out. We can't whistle 'em away, and the bull won't let us get near to drive 'em."

Eddie yawned. "Well," he said, "thanks for the information, and I'll bid you a kind good night—unless you have something else to say."

Hi pondered. "This is addin' into considerable delay, and I sure got to meet Gladys in the mornin'. Otherwise, I'd be glad to let them two bulls argue it out the rest of the night. You did right well loadin' them woolies, and I thought you might rig a way to move the cows out of that cut."

"Love is sure grand," he recited bitterly. He reached for his rain coat. "Chad, let's help him meet his destiny."

"Betcha," said Chad. "Come on, Pomp."

The head brakeman and the trainmaster stood on the running board along the boiler at the front of the locomo-

tive. Below them, in the flare of the headlight, a massive
bull menaced them from the middle of the track. His humor was sour. He rumbled and dug into the earth and
threw mud in exploding splatters with an angry hoof. Beyond him a mass of cattle was packed into a high, narrow
cut, humped up in the rain.

Eddie hung back out of sight in the dark.

"Hold everything," Hi called from beside the locomotive. "Here comes Mrs. Wheeler's little boy Hiram to fix
you right up."

Keeley cursed bitterly. He peered down and tried to
locate Hi in the flicker of the firebox.

Chad hissed, and Pomp launched himself into the light.
He circled the bull. He yipped and darted in and nipped
his heels and ducked the savage kicks. The bull tried to
keep his head to the circling fury, but the footing was uncertain. He slipped and stumbled. He charged, and Pomp
slid behind him, his yips raised in an excited treamor. He
made lightning slashes at the lumbering heels. He kept
him going till the bull crowded into the herd to escape the
flashing teeth.

Chad piped a thin whistle, and Pomp's outcry went up
to a clamorous yell. He raced back and forth and darted in
among the close-packed cattle till they began to mill. He
started a stream of them past the engine and out into the
open. He kept that moving and increased the flow as he
urged them with high cries and snapping teeth. The last of
them went by in a bawling stampede.

Chad whistled Pomp back to him.

"Hey!" Keeley bellowed, searching the dark for Hi.
"What you got, Wheeler, a circus? Where are you getting
all those animals?"

"I just pick them up as I go along," Hi explained
blandly.

"You're cute, all right," Keeley snarled. "But don't be too smart. It gets you disliked."

Forty-seven plowed on into the storm. Chad set up a kerosene stove and cooked ham and eggs.

"That fellow you call the trainmaster is kind of bossy," Chad considered.

"Yeah," said Eddie. "He's not so good."

"Seems to find fault, even when he's being helped," Chad puzzled.

"That kind's hard to satisfy."

"I didn't put Pomp and Barbecue on the shipping contract," Chad said. "They ran away from Pa and came back to me just before the train left. I didn't have time to tell the agent. Do you suppose this trainmaster'd make trouble if he found that out?" His eyes were bright and direct. Any sort of deception bothered him.

"Don't worry about it. For every mean railroader you find, there's usually several dozen that are trying to get along."

Carlotta slept in a bright trance with Pomp curled up on the other half of the leather couch. Barbecue rested at the horses' front feet. Miss Murphy worried her legs from under her and lay on her side and drowsed. The animals watched Chad benignly from half-closed eyes as he spread blankets on a packing case and rolled up in them. Eddie dozed in the rocker. They stopped at a station, and the rain seemed to condense the silence inside the caboose. He drifted into sound sleep.

The door squawled and fretted cold nerves all down his back. Hi's disembodied head stared up at him from the lower corner of the doorway, wet and harassed.

"All right," Eddie grumbled. "What is it now?"

"Tied up again," Hi complained. "Mister, it just looks like that fate you talk about ain't goin' to let me meet my gal when she comes in the mornin'. This rain done washed an old shanty halfway down a bank and tipped it so it won't clear the main line." He hung from his arm on the iron sill. He rubbed the tip of his nose on the rubber sleeve as he thought hard. "Seems as if it's all set to turn over on the track, and then we'd have to get the big hook to clear it."

"Thank you kindly, Mr. Wheeler, for waking me up," Eddie muttered disagreeably, "but what the hell am I supposed to do about it?"

"Well," Hi offered, "you been doin' right well in all other emergencies so far tonight, and I just wondered. Seems like you was sent to me by my special little guardian angel." He grinned slyly. "You can't figure it otherwise, the way you showed up. And knowin', like you do, that there's goin' to be considerable grief if I ain't there on the spot when Gladys arrives, I just thought you might think of somethin'."

"You thought," Eddie scorned him. "What with? Anyhow, a girl that's going to marry a trainman'll have to get used to his arriving when the train he's working allows."

"Yeah, I know." Hi rested his chin on his arm and stared up pensively. "But I told her—you know—that I'd be there regardless. You know how fellas talk to girls like that sometimes. And how they believe him—sometimes."

"Seems like," Eddie warned, "you're going to have to be more restrained in your statements. Chad," he called, "are you still interested in getting this guy to his nuptials?"

The kid unrolled quietly from his blankets. "Betcha."

They had run out of the wind, and the rain had thinned to a mist. You could feel the mountains hanging over you. The emegrant car had been stopped close to the station.

It wasn't a night office. They had called the agent from his quarters above to inform the dispatcher of the situation, and through the window as they passed they saw him at the key. His semaphore was lit and showed red.

The engine's whistle blasted a call for the section gang. The headlight showed them a narrow shack tipped down a crumbling bank which overhung the main line. It was an old abandoned bunkhouse of construction days. Keeley was scrambling about it in the mud, appraising the prospect by the light of his lantern.

"Chad," said Eddie, "I saw block and tackle in your car, and a lot of rope. Think your team could pull that shack down and then snake it off the track, if the section foreman and his crew helped you tie onto it?"

"Betcha. Carrie and Boxer could pull that from here to Pueblo."

"And would walk a narrow gang plank from the car to the station platform?"

"They'll go any place on sound footing I tell them," the kid said.

"Better tell the hogger to watch for your signals," he told Hi. "We'll have to set the zulu car at the station platform, and unload the horses."

"Didn't I know you was sent direct to me from above," Hi exulted.

It was like kid pranks on halloween, with their guilty schemes to cross up Keeley. The agent came out of his station as the two horses, their harness clinking, followed Chad across the gang plank to the freight platform and came down the incline to the ground level. The agent helped them carry the tackle forward along the long train.

Keeley began an uproar when he sighted the horses. "What have you got now, Wheeler? Some more of your circus?"

"Hiram of the helpin' hand," Hi chanted. "You got to keep yourself equipped for all kinds of emergencies to get your train over this division."

Keeley studied him grimly.

The section foreman and some of his crew had arrived. Figures moved through the misty glow of the headlight. Chad gave the orders, and they hooked onto a tree across the track and took a hitch on the building. The horses set themselves, but they couldn't get any traction in the mud.

"I've got some crushed rock I can haul in on the push car," the section foreman offered.

"Better do that," Chad said.

"Hey," Keeley protested. "That'll take time. See if they won't pull it that way," he ordered.

Chad looked at him. "If I told them to, they'd pull, figuering I'd fixed everything safe for them. If they slipped and fell, they'd know I fooled them. We don't work together like that."

The section gang went off to haul in the crushed rock.

The kid had pulled stumps and moved farm buildings, and he knew the tricks of ties and angles. When they had made footing for the horses, he waved all hands back.

"Sometimes these old buildings break apart and throw things," he warned. "Get 'way back in the clear."

It was a slow, dim picture in the wedge of the headlight, with the huge backdrop of night and overhanging mountains and the little dots of light the lanterns made. You could feel that quick, dramatic tightening of nerves as Chad spoke to his team. The wise old horses snuggled into their collars. They took a test pull for the feel of the load, and then dug their iron toes into the crushed rock, and pulled.

The Manila lines mumbled. The old bunkhouse

grunted. Slowly it heeled over and slid down and exploded as it landed across the main line. Somebody coughed and a figure collapsed. It was the agent. He hadn't stood clear, and a snapped brace, flying through the dark, had caught him across the chest. He was out. Three of the section men carried him to his quarters in the station and one went for a doctor.

Chad examined the new position of the structure and rearranged his lines. He snaked first one end and then the other across the tracks till it was in the clear.

"No trouble at all," Hi exulted, "When you're properly equipped. It's Skipper Wheeler who gets his train over the road in all kinds of weather."

Eddie told himself that Hi talked too much to the wrong people, and slipped along the train to the zulu car. Chad came back with his team and lead them aboard and rubbed the horses down with gunny sacks. He said he didn't think Keeley had seen where he took his team.

The engine did some switching. Chad went to sleep and Eddie blew out the lights in the car and stood at a crack in the door. A star jigged over a blunt mountain that hung directly overhead. The engine coughed at the lower end of the yard and her headlight painted a running picture of sidings and rolling stock. A lantern rounded out of the station and showed Hi's big boots striding down the platform. He peered up at Eddie.

"That agent ain't come to yet," he muttered. "The doc says there don't seem any broken bones, but he can't tell much else." He slanted his head sidewise and screwed up his face. "The dispatcher done put out an order here against us when he thought we'd be tied up here from now on, and we gotta get some more orders before we can move."

"I know what you mean," Eddie nodded. "You hate to

miss the chance to do the trainmaster deserving dirt, and make a lot of overtime while delaying him, but you can't disappoint the little woman. Is Keeley in the station?"

"Yeah, but I can say I found you wanderin' about."

"Love is blind, sure enough, or you'd see Keeley's going to find you out. I'll get you going, but you sing soft to that man."

"Doggone, Eddie!" Hi crowed. "Ain't Gladys goin' to be tickled with you."

Keeley paced the office in the gloom of one shaded lamp.

"Picked him right out of the air," Hi exulted, "and he's got enough telegraphin' in his system to get us goin'."

"You're pretty good," Keeley growled. "Seems to me you're too good to be true."

Eddie slid into the chair before the telegraph table. He checked the order and called the dispatcher and reported the changed situation. He copied two more orders and made out a clearance card and handed them to Hi. He got up and made for the door.

Keeley stopped him. "How come you're floating around this station so late at night?" The man couldn't be amiable, even when you were doing a favor.

"It isn't late for a guy to be out holding his girl's hand, is it?" he inquired.

"Been here long?" Keeley suggested.

"Just long enough," he nodded casually, and went out.

Forty-seven moved out of town. The bark of the stack sharpened and the wheels mumbled with absorbed effort. They were climbing. He dropped into the chair and it gently rocked him to sleep.

It was just after a clearing dawn, with the mountains thrust up all around and the sun edging through hurrying clouds, that they stopped at the last station before the terminal. The door of the zulu car was wrenched open. But it wasn't Hi's concerned features that were thrust in at the lower corner of the doorway. The hard countenance of the trainmaster hung there ominously as his eyes ran over the human and animal content of the car.

"Quite a family movement," he said, and nodded. "I considered this must be where Wheeler reached in for all his trick help. But I noticed the waybill calls for only two horses, a cow and an attendant. The rest of you will have to unload."

Eddie stared down at Bull Keeley drowsily. "After all the help you've used up out of this car to get your train over the road?" he asked.

Chad peered at the trainmaster from the top of a pile of packing cases and threw off his blankets. Barbecue got up and stretched. He tucked in his chin and rolled his eyes. Pomp sat up and looked at Chad. Carlotta slept.

"Makes no difference. You've got no business on this train." Keeley liked his authority. "Wheeler isn't going to pull this free ride stuff on me, after I told him not to bring that kid along. Now, you take her and the dog and the goat and get to hell out of here, or else I'll throw you out."

"I'd be glad to break you in two if you tried it," Eddie nodded.

Chad looked at Eddie and got a grin. He made a noise in his throat. Barbecue rocked gently like a hobbyhorse. He bleated raucously and bucked and flung himself at the head in the doorway. Keeley bumped his chin on the sill as he made a quick duck. Barbecue went over him and landed and skidded in the mud outside. Pomp set up an eager outcry.

Keeley began to run. He was heavy-footed in his rubber boots, and he slipped and floundered. Pomp bolted from the doorway and chased him, clamoring. Barbecue got some traction in the mud and followed. Keeley tried to turn in between two cars, but he got his legs tangled with the dog and went into a flat fall. Pomp yipped and circled. Barbecue stood over him and dared him to rise.

"Call them off!" Keeley yelled.

"What do you say?" Chad asked.

Eddie sighed and nodded.

Chad said, "Hey!" Pomp came obediently, but Barbecue backed away from the trainmaster reluctantly.

Keeley crawled up out of the mud. "All right for this time," he snarled, and stamped into the station.

Just before they left town, Hi came to the zulu car.

"Seems like that Keeley-cure man is gonna tack the hides of all of us on his own personal barn door." He considered the future darkly. "I'm fired, and the rest of you are in jail as soon as we get into the terminal. He wired the company police to meet us. Ain't Gladys goin' to have something to say when she hears about this?"

The big blondes that Hi preferred wouldn't toss you for as little as that when they had you hooked. "She'll be all full of sympathy," he consoled.

Hi went pensive. "If I was you, Eddie," he advised, "I'd unload right here. You can come in on a passenger, and I'll hold your suitcase for you. I'll take care of Carlotta, and I'll swear Chad didn't have any part in whatever they accuse him of."

"I don't run out that easy," Eddie glinted. "Besides, I'd better be there when you finally meet Gladys. You may need me then, sure enough."

Hi moved on about his duties. Carlotta awoke and chattered cheerfully. Chad milked, and filled their cups. Carlotta insisted on sharing hers with Pomp. Chad lit the oil stove and cooked breakfast.

"What do you think's going to happen?" he asked Eddie.

"We'll see what the setup is when we get there," he brooded. "You just come along and take what they hand you. Then we'll see if this Anaconda Short Line wouldn't like to stand a shipper's suit. You haven't got anything to worry about."

An hour later they pulled into the terminal yard. Keeley brought Hi, and two railroad special officers converged on the emegrant car.

"All right, you two fellows," Keeley ordered. "Unload. Bring the girl and the goat and the dog. These men will shoot either one of the animals that makes a pass at me. Now, let's get going."

"Just to keep you straightened out," Eddie said, "Chad here is a shipper, with certain inalienable rights. You'd better go easy with what you try on him. And you can't prosecute this little girl."

"Maybe you don't think so," Keeley said, "but I'm running this division now."

"Oh," scolded Carlotta, round-eyed. "Bad! Bad!"

"You're headed for a jam," Eddie warned.

"Fella," said the trainmaster, "you heard me the first time. Nobody's going to set dogs and goats on me and not be sorry for a long time. Unload."

Carlotta kissed Miss Murphy on the wet nose. She shunned Keeley and threw herself into Chad's arms when he got down and held them up to her.

White sunlight washed over the crags and flooded into the valley. It had a crisp warmth and a clean, sharp smell. It made your blood bubble. The heights swept back, dark blue against the silver of the sky. They threw down echoes of the mountain traffic in dull thunder, like the roll of big drums.

Keeley led the cavalcade across the sidings toward the station. Carlotta held onto Pomp and Eddie with Barbecue close behind. Chad and Hi were followed by the two railroad cops. Switch engines paused and hooted and crews stared at the procession as it crossed the yard. The men set up faint, derisive cheers, and then ducked out of sight of the trainmaster. Passengers at the station came out to stare at the parade as it marched onto the platform.

Keeley instructed one of the cops to keep Barbecue below until he had an opinion from the legal department on his status. Then he led the rest upstairs to the division offices.

Barbecue watched Chad go up out of sight, and muttered to himself. He twisted his horns out of the cop's grasp, and eyed the man ominously. Then he clattered up the stairs.

They trailed through the superintendent's outer office. The chief clerk, used to weird spectacles, eyed them cynically. He started to say a warning, then checked and grinned.

Keeley had been acting as superintendent in Welby's absence, and he opened the door to the inner office and strode in. Then he stopped. Barbecue nudged him impatiently. The rest trouped in.

"Will you look who's here," Hi murmured in Eddie's ear.

A big man with an untamed shock of gray hair and a palid face was at the desk. Beside it sat a thin man whose big glasses glinted eyes that seemed to instantly catch all the details of the intruding horde.

Keeley was flustered. For the moment his voice evaded him.

"He wasn't expecting this," Hi whispered.

Carlotta began a high piping. She ran to the big man

at the desk. "Papa Dan!" she chortled. Her smudged face beamed.

The big man swung her up and held her with big hands that had once done heavy toil. "Carlotta," he chuckled, and his tired face folded in a grin. "You little tramp. Have you missed your Papa Dan?"

"Poor, poor Papa Dan." She caressed his face with two soiled brown hands. "Does your head hurt any more?"

"That's Welby," Hi said in the back of his throat. "And, mister, that splinter of a man with him is none other than old Salt-and-molasses Nickerson. This is going to be something."

"Who's Nickerson?"

"Him? Why, he's the tycoon that's just taken over the A. S. L. and is trying to make a railroad out of it again. He's the new president. Fella, we're going to get this right out of the horse's mouth." Hi clicked his tongue and shook his head.

"Well, Keeley," said Mr. Nickerson, "are you at the head of this array of men and beasts?" His voice had a fine, thin edge, and you didn't want to fool yourself that those little eyes behind the big glasses couldn't uncover things.

"Yes, sir," said Keeley. He took another look at Welby. "That kid and this man here were stealing a ride in a zulu car which this boy was attendant of. And the dog and the goat were in the car too, but not declared." He gave Mr. Nickerson a quick glance. "Conductor Wheeler knew they were all four aboard—in fact. I ordered him not to let the girl ride—so I've discharged him. The rest I'm going to turn over to the chief special agent to prosecute."

President Nickerson uncrossed his legs. His glasses

sparkled like sunlight on granite, but a slight mist seemed to drift across his face. Welby's palid face hardened.

Eddie began to remember the talk about S. A. M. Nickerson. The Anaconda Short Line had been a stepchild, a sickly brat kicked around the money marts until recently when Nickerson had taken it over. He had a reputation for reorganizing incompetent lines, but they were saying he'd now got himself a railroad he couldn't revive. Where was he going to get the money to put it into operating shape, and then where was the traffic with which to pay it back to be found? Well, you got the notion that maybe those brisk eyes could search out a lot of both.

Barbecue rummaged in the waste paper basket and Pomp beamed up at Carlotta.

Hi said brightly, "I'm right glad to see you up and at 'em again, Mr. Welby. I'd like to introduce you to a friend of mine who's an operator I worked with down on the S-W. P. This is Eddie Sand."

Welby nodded. "Thanks, Wheeler. I'm glad to meet you, Mr. Sand." His voice had power and warmth. He was rugged, and you knew he'd come up through construction times. "You must be the operator my friend Barabe gave a gold watch for exceptional bravery." He smiled quisically.

"I guess so," Eddie answered cautiously. You couldn't know just how Barabe told that story. He might even have made it funny.

Mr. Nickerson crossed his thin legs. "Let's have details, Keeley," he suggested, and Keeley, set and primed, began to relate.

Hi murmured in Eddie's ear again. "Guess the president's here to turn the division over to Keeley. The trainmaster thinks so, anyhow. Listen to him pour it on. Not so good. You in jail and me in the dog house. I thought we had more sense, between us."

Keeley was making a good case for himself. Very well thought out and delivered. Eddie broke in when the trainmaster had finished.

"Mr. Keeley's most rightly in his facts, but he left out some," he insisted. "He overlooked naming the assistance rendered by the contents of that emegrant car."

Mr. Nickerson's glasses bore on him sharply. "Assistance?" he said.

"Yeah," said Eddie, and met the glare of the spectacles. "The goat did get rough with him, but I don't think Barbecue is a killer. Most of the animals in that car did your railroad some considerable service last night. Like this." And he took up the tale with sly humor and somber running comments.

You got some notion of the way brass hats looked at things when you'd faced as many across their own desks as he had. The misty look returned to Mr. Nickerson's face and increased as Eddie ran on. Hi listened with his mouth slightly ajar. He nodded and chuckled. Nickerson uncrossed his legs and reflected when he'd finished.

"It seems, then," the president said at last, "that all the creatures in that car rendered service, except the cow. Couldn't you have found something for her to do?"

"Why, yes," Eddie grinned. "She furnished rations, specially for Carlotta."

"Rather an efficient outfit," Mr. Nickerson remarked, "the way you tell it."

Welby's eyes came alight with grim humor. "His statements sound reasonable to me, because it's about what would happen on my division. I've run it for a long while, and I ought to know." He looked at Keeley. "Carlotta is Mexican on her mother's side, and she has inherited the most engaging qualities of two races." He chuckled. "She is an incorrigible tramp with a heart of gold. She has the run of the division, and a trainman who refused her a ride and proper care on the way, would find himself violently disliked by his mates."

Welby got out a handkerchief and blew his nose. "And I expect conductors occasionally carry other railroaders temporarily out of service. I don't know. I never checked to find out, because I supposed they did. A good many of our men came to us that way." He untangled Carlotta from his neck and set her upon his desk. "By which I mean to say, Mr. Nickerson, that I and most of the men have worked together so long that we pretty well know what one another of us would do under most circumstances. Yes," he nodded, "the whole episode seems plausible to me, because that's the way I'd have expected it to be done. So you see, Mr. Nickerson," he said, "whatever fault you find in this is really mine."

"I can see that," Mr. Nickerson nodded promptly. The edge of his voice was intended to cut. He got up and went to the window. When he came back his step was brisk and decisive.

"Hold onto your hair, mister," Hi breathed. "Here comes the cyclone."

"Keeley," said the president, "suppose you report to me in my private car down in the yard at two o'clock this afternoon. I'll take care of the rest of this."

"That sounds—" Keeley began hoarsely, and stopped.

Nickerson said, with that thin edge to his voice, "I'll talk to you then."

Barbecue was the only one who watched Keeley to the door.

"Wheeler," said the president, "Mr. Welby will decide

your case on its merits." His glasses glinted. "He is back on the job again."

"Yes, sir," said Hi and cocked his head as a whistle sounded at the upper end of the yard, an arrogant challenge to the stubby switch engines to clear the way. "Is that Twelve?" he beamed, and Welby nodded. "Excuse me, please," Hi begged. "I got a gal to meet." He slammed through the doorway and thundered down the stairs.

Mr. Nickerson smiled at Chad. "The A. S. L. apparently hasn't been very appreciative of services rendered," he said, "but I'll make that up to you. If you will please take your goat out of here before he destroys Mr. Welby's office, I will see that you have more pleasant experiences of us from now on."

"Aw, I've had a swell trip," Chad declared. "I didn't pay any mind to that man. We had a nice party last night." He smiled at Eddie with his steady eyes.

"You were mighty hospitable, Chad." They shook hands with friendly gravity. "And you were smart to take Keeley for just what he is."

"Animals and people," Chad said gravely, "are about alike. The bad ones just haven't been trained right." He went down the stairs, Pomp soft-footed beside him, while Barbecue clattered insolently behind.

Good guys like that you wanted to take along. They showed up, strayed a little while on your casual way, and then they were gone into a bright patch of memory. But they left you something enduring that you wove into your own pattern of existence. The people you liked were scattered all along the road you'd come. Most of them you saw only once, except like Walley and Hi, who came and went. But all those others were more potent to you than the rest of the pack of humanity. You'd not remember Keeley long, but you'd never forget that solemn, cheerful kid.

Mr. Nickerson spoke softly after a thoughtful pause. "It is easy to make a mistake when we are trying to do so much all at once," he mused. "I'm glad it happened the way it did, Dan. It made a situation clear that I might have overlooked."

The clamor of Twelve's bell bit into the high, thin air and filled the sunlit room. Carlotta put a strangle hold about Welby's neck and teased Eddie with her big, dark eyes. The unfailing pull of high iron traffic turned them all to the window overlooking the platform. The Mikado checked the line of coaches to a quiet stand beside the station. The big Mike disengaged herself from her train and moved away to the roundhouse. Another slid in from a siding and coupled into her place.

Men in overalls inspected the intimate particulars of the inert line of cars. Passengers swarmed from them to stretch their legs and sniff the sweet, sharp air. Hi Wheeler bumped and blundered among them, hurrying up and down, twisting his head on his long neck as he tried to watch all exits from the train. Passengers ceased coming down the steps, and Hi plunged aboard to search the coaches.

"Sometimes," Eddie conjectured, "you'd think Hi is dumb and acts smart; and then again you're certain he's smart and acting dumb."

Welby chuckled. "Wheeler is smart enough to keep me guessing at times," he admitted. "A little high-spirited and vigorous. But that's the way I like them."

Faintly down the hallway through the open door, you could hear the swarming murmur of the telegraph instruments in the dispatchers' office as they guarded the traffic over the heights. The keen smell of engine smoke tinged the air. Twelve's new conductor barked, and the coaches sucked in the milling crowd as her bell took up its clamor

again. The stack errupted as she moved out of the yard
at a swift glide.

Hi Wheeler stood on the deserted platform and glumly
watched her go. He was a gaunt and lonely figure in work
clothes, dark in the silver of the sunlight, and the mountains brooding over him in grim benevolence.

"That girl of Wheeler's he has talked so much about,"
Welby said in his rich voice. "She must have missed her
train. Very disappointing to Hi."

"She didn't even miss that." The boomer's eyes were
sharp as he watched that long, disconsolate figure on the
platform. "She'd have had plenty hours to telegraph him
if she'd just failed to catch her train." He shook his head.
"He shouldn't have deeded her a farm that's in the oil
boom territory." His lips curled into a tight smile. "Or
maybe he should have, at that. You can't always tell at
first glance when you're lucky."

Mr. Nickerson's glasses glinted at him shrewdly.
"Those things usually work out of themselves." He used
a crisp, confident tone. "But perhaps it might be well for
you to remain here a while in case your friend needs some
personal aid and comfort. I'm sure Mr. Welby has a place
for you somewhere on his division."

That splinter of a man could dig into a situation pretty
fast. You could always get along with the brass hats who
really knew their business. He looked up at the clear blue
sky and the bright sun on the mountains.

"I was just about to ask if you had a job of telegraphing for a brass pounder that'd at last found the sun."

XV

THE STORM exploded from the lean barrel of the pass and slapped the Imperial Limited with a charge of birdshot sleet as that arrogant train yelled twice for the board and then checked and stopped reluctantly under the unyielding arm of the semaphore. Station and section houses at Saber Summit, hunched up on the rim of the world, faded out in the blast.

Conductor Gary stamped into the office, and the wind wrenched the door from his hand and slammed it after him with an abrupt explosion. He choked and brushed sleet from his blue-and-gold uniform.

"Hey, Eddie," he strangled irritably, "what you got on the board?"

"Paint," said Eddie patiently. He took his eyes from the book he was reading and his feet from the telegraph table.

"Haw!" Gary scoffed. "Mebby you think that's a new one." He was a mettlesome trainman, forever fighting his schedule. "Come on," he snapped. "What's the delay?"

It was curiously quiet in the dusky station without the chatter of the telegraph instruments. Eddie smiled placidly to reassure the conductor. He wished some trainman less arbitrary about making time had the Limited of that date. You couldn't reason with Gary if you delayed him. And Eddie wasn't sure but what he ought to hold him here from now on. That treacherous storm had made him responsible for this crack train and its passengers, whether Gary thought so or not. But you didn't delay the Anaconda Short Line's scenic limited without exceptional reasons.

"This weather's kind of slowed things up," he said amiably.

This late storm had suddenly turned back at the break of spring to lash the mountains with a surprise raid, and catch the A. S. L. with winter equipment stowed or in the shop. All day it had trampled snow into Imperial Pass and the grade below. The cuts down there were choked. The mountain might set an iron grip on all movement on that twisting swoop. But you couldn't know for sure. The telegraph wires had gone out at noon. That blinded the division in a tempest like this, shut each train operation into a blank sphere of silence, to fumble through without protection.

Cold needles pecked at the windows. Gary shrilled his impatience.

"Let's have the orders, Eddie. We've got to get down the grade in a hurry. We took a fireman off the extra board, and he messed his fire coming up. The engineer had to shut off steam heat in the coaches to have enough power to make that last ten miles. Those passengers of mine got ugly when the Pullmans began to get cold. Specially that party in the private car."

Eddie knew he'd been waiting for that. The party in the private car had been mixed up in all the other problems he'd been considering since noon. Perched on this high skyline, he learned from telegrams overheard going through, from the gossip of the wires, that the men of that party were a committee of bankers in which this railroad was extraordinarily interested. Mr. Nickerson had to do some more financing for the A. S. L., and these men had come out from New York to inspect the property and the improvements already made and report if more funds should be made available. Mr. Nickerson wouldn't want them delayed or endangered. They would likely let the A. S. L. go back to being just another rusty streak if they were. And now the telegraph wires were down. Somebody here on the job had to pick up the responsibility.

The twilight went out as the storm dropped a sudden curtain. The wind yelled from the pass and swooped over the station. Eddie lit the oil lamps.

"Hey!" Gary's voice splintered. "Are you going to get us out of here? Know you're holding up the Imperial Limited? Give me my orders and let me go."

"There aren't any orders," he said quietly. "The wires are down; that's why I stopped you. I don't know what has happened on the grade, but it's been storming down there all day, and I'd say you'd better tie up here till the wires start working so we can find out."

Gary blew up like a package of fire crackers. "You holding me without orders? You know what the chief does to smart operators who delay Nine. Trouble with you fellows is that thinking goes to your mind." He spat at the stove and strangled. "You give me a clearance card now, or I'll have your scalp when I get in."

You had to be good to outguess a blizzard. They never performed twice the same. He was in charge at this bald spot on the rim of the world. He'd have to decide right now. Nine might fight her way through the drifts below and win clear to the high desert without much delay. Yet if she got hung up in that white hell, and her coal gave out before they got the snow fighting equipment back in operation and dug her out, a trainload of passengers and those critical bankers were going to experience real hardships, which would include hunger. Yet if you held up those bankers here, they would consider it a breakdown in operations and penalize the management in their report.

"Look," he said. "I didn't order this storm. But now it's here it comes under the head of my business. Let's figure this out."

Gary took hold of the counter and leaned forward. "I was running trains in these mountains before you'd learned to ride your perambulator." He sizzled like an ignited fuse. "There's a train load of passengers and U. S. mail and Wells Fargo express out there that I'm responsible for. You clear me right now, or you'll go on the stand in the Old Man's office and say why you didn't."

Gary was asking for it, and he couldn't blame Eddie if he got his clearance—and then ran into trouble. But an alibi didn't vindicate a disaster.

The wind eased to a chuckle under the eaves. Sleet pecked mechanically at the windows.

The telegraph sounder grunted abruptly in the lull. It paused and fluttered and slapped aimlessly. A gust boomed in the upper air and fled on across the summit as that slight, metallic sound slipped through into the room from the outer world. The instrument clacked again as the wires struggled against the weight of wind and the clawing fingers of the sleet to drag that whisper through the boisterous dark.

Eddie spun and bent over the resonator. The brass tongue gasped as if the storm was choking it. Then it stumbled into the dispatcher's call.

"DS," it mumbled. "DS."

The dispatcher snapped back a faint reply.

The sounder limped, "This is the lineman up a pole west of Granite." You could barely catch the weak, wooden signals. The man was sending with numb fingers. "Been tieing breaks in the line all afternoon and I'm out of wire.

Got this one hooked together, but it won't hold after I let it go. Wind and snow. Am going back to Marble Gate, if I can make it."

Eddie snapped the picture of the lineman strapped and clinging on his spurs to the telegraph pole in the dark and the savage gale, cutting in his portable set and working the key with stiff fingers.

The dispatcher's answer slipped back. "Hold it! Keep that line open." He snatched swift seconds from the blizzard and rapped the call for Saber Summit. Eddie's hand dropped to the key and clipped his reply.

"Where's Nine?" shot the dispatcher.

"Here!" said Eddie.

"Get this quick!" The abbreviated words fled under his cunning hand. "We don't know conditions in the Pass and down the grade. Mr. Nickerson says you are to handle Nine as you think best, for the safety of passengers. He is anxious about the party in the private car. Don't disturb their confidence in us. Don't let them become alarmed. Imperative they meet with no hardships. Contact Elder. It's up to you!"

"Okay," said Eddie. And then he sent with slow emphasis, "Lineman, what are conditions down there on the grade?"

"Wind and——"

The sounder choked and died. The storm rifled a blast out of Imperial Pass. It yelled and stamped with wild glee.

He nodded at the impotent brass tongue. He had his orders. Old Salt-and-Molasses Nickerson, thin and stooped, leaning over the dispatcher's table, his shrewd eyes glinting behind big glasses, had slipped the old railroad emergency call through a rift in the storm.

It's up to you!

He turned on Gary. Already in his mind he was checking all his possible resources of food and fuel.

"You'll be tied up here till we hear different," he told the conductor gently. "Better get your train on the siding and cut off your engine first thing and take a tank of water."

"I won't!" Gary exploded. "We haven't got coal to keep steam heat in the coaches till morning. I'm not going to stay here and freeze my passengers. They'd murder me. I'm going to run for it."

Eddie said patiently, "That semaphore up there is still on you, old-timer. You won't move while it is. And don't start getting your passengers excited. The Old Man said that."

A freckled face edged through the doorway leading to the stationmen's living quarters. The visage came apart in a bottomless yawn, which slowly subsided.

"Nice day," said Sam Dunn, the night operator, just arisen. "I'll fix my breakfast and your supper if you'll bring in the coal," he bargained.

"Coal," said Eddie, "is a material you are going to think most about and have the least of for the next several chilly hours."

Gary stamped out and the muffled chug of the locomotive came through the wind as he stowed his train on the siding.

Hi Wheeler whipped open the door and bounced inside. His passenger brakeman's uniform was pressed into sharp edges and his brass insignia gleamed in the lamplight.

"Eddie," he yelled, and crowded the stove, "I figured you'd tie us up here as soon as you knew I was handlin' the flag. Mister, we can have a nice family visit while it storms it's head off. Ain't you glad to see me?" he pleaded.

Eddie regarded him bleakly. "Blizzards always blow in the damdest things," he complained.

Hi was still a little baffled and stricken. He clowned life, but he was artless and warm-hearted, without a stint in his system. He hadn't decided yet exactly what had hit him. Maybe he never would.

"Sure," Hi agreed. "It's a bad wind that don't blow you some overtime."

Eddie put on his overcoat and went out. In his eternal drift along the high iron he had arranged excursions and special service for circuses, conventions and church conferences. But he'd never done much business with bankers in any capacity. They were supposed to be an arbitrary and disillusioned breed. He'd have to take it easy. He headed into the stinging sleet and climbed onto the observation platform of the private car and knocked on the door. A colored boy in white apron to his shoes opened it.

"I'd like to speak to Mr. Elder," he said.

"Come in," an abrupt voice summoned from beyond the door. "I'm Elder."

He was a raw-boned man without much hair, as big as a horse. Beyond him two other men sat in big leather chairs. The colored boy was arranging the dinner table in this observation section. Heavy linen and fat silver glowed in the chastened light. There was the soft warmth of steam heat. The three men were having a prudent drink.

"I'm afraid," Eddie explained, "we are going to have to hold the Limited here for a while, till we can get a snow plow up the Pass. Mr. Nickerson wired to express his regrets and concern at the delay, and he instructed me to do anything I could for you while you are held up. I am the A. S. L.'s agent here."

Elder got up with a hospitable gesture. It was a good

deal like shaking hands with a steam shovel. On his feet, he towered like a steel derrick.

"You can't do a thing like that to us." His humor was grim. "This is Mr. Osgood," he introduced a man with a marble-white face like the façade of a financial institution. There were balconies under his eyes. He made his manners with a quarter-inch nod.

"And this is Mr. Rayburn." Elder indicated a thin man with wistful eyes surrounded by wrinkles. He was collapsed in his chair, but he got up spryly to shake hands.

"I'm glad to know you," he said with precise cheerfulness. "Won't you sit down? And perhaps a little drink?"

Eddie felt suddenly like a mouse accepting the hospitality of three benign cats. The liquor had a velvety warmth with just a trace of power.

"As a fact," Mr. Rayburn said, "I started my career on the railroad. As station agent and operator on the old New Haven. A very happy experience," he added and beamed. "I was really a good railroader."

Elder bit into the conversation. "Before we again go into the fact that you and Thomas A. Edison, and some other of our great men, started life as telegraph operators, let's find out where we stand on this mountain, and for how long. What do you think, young man?"

"This storm is of course unpredictable," he said frankly. "But if it gives us a chance, we'll have the plow through within a few hours."

Osgood regarded him distastefully. "It seems to me," he deliberated, "that Mr. Nickerson should have foreseen such an emergency and have protected us from it. Apparently his organization is not good."

"And don't claim an 'act of God' on us," Elder warned Eddie. "Osgood won't have one. They're not his kind of collateral. You tell your president that the quicker he gets us out of here the better we'll like him."

"You spoke of Mr. Nickerson having telegraphed you," Osgood reminded Eddie. "Then your wires are still working," he stated. "I will have some telegrams to send after dinner."

He'd overlooked that one. It was a well-known fact that bankers were always impatiently telegraphing about something. He had handled scores of their messages, and they were usually pretty peremptory. They liked to think they were keeping ahead of events. If these three thought they were cut off from immediate communication with all their complicated affairs, they'd likely get panicky. The world might smash if they didn't keep an alert eye on it. And the Old Man had instructed him not to disturb or alarm them. Wherefore, he couldn't tell them the wires had been in operation for only a few desperate seconds since noon.

"Certainly," he said. "Shall I send for them about eight?"

"You needn't do that," Rayburn interjected. "Fact is, I should like to see if I still remember my telegraphy. I will bring the telegrams, if Osgood doesn't mind. I might even send them myself."

This was tightening up with every move. He took a wary glance at the thin man. "I wish you would," he said profoundly.

"No danger of running short of food and fuel?" Elder demanded.

"We'll take care of that," Eddie assured him blandly, and cautiously rechecked his estimates of supplies in his mind.

But he wasn't sure, as he skidded back to the station, that he had completely covered up the situation from Elder.

That grimly droll eye had penetrating power. Like all good bankers, he likely deprecated any statement made to him.

Sam Dunn was cooking on the heating stove in the office because Eddie wouldn't let him use up coal in the kitchen range.

"As soon as you get that grub down your rum sucker," Eddie instructed him, "set up a key in the kitchen and connect it with a sounder and key on the telegraph table, and attach a battery. A dummy set just between those two points." He diagramed and explained. "When this banker comes to send those telegrams, you'll be in the kitchen hooked up to his set. We'll leave the door open a little so you can hear the sounder in here, and you send back to him like you were receiving his messages in Denver."

"Yeah," protested Sam, "but supposin' they're important telegrams?"

"They won't be," Eddie assured him. "I never handled a banker's wires yet that contained anything more than instructions to be careful."

He went out and boarded the diner. The dining-car conductor said he had enough of most things to feed his passengers for two or three days.

"Except fresh meat," he added. "I don't know whether I'll have enough of that to carry me through tomorrow's luncheon."

"I hope you'll be gone by then. But I doubt it." Eddie went out and climbed under the storm curtains of the engine cab.

The engineer, folded in his seat and dozing, said he had enough coal to keep the coaches warm till morning. Mebby eight o'clock.

Eddie coaxed him out into the storm to estimate the supply of fuel on hand at the station and the section houses. There wasn't much after the drain of the winter. Mebby keep the Pullmans warm till some time tomorrow afternoon. But what the hell was going to happen after that? Stay up here and freeze to death? Mebby starve. What a railroad! Ought to've run for it down the grade. The hogger put his head into the sleet and went back to his warm cab.

Eddie roused the section foreman. Rip Biggers was a lank man and not an optimist.

"Six o'clock in the morning," Eddie told him, "get your gang out and start hauling my coal and yours over to Nine's engine."

"What about keepin' us and our families warm?" Rip objected.

"We'll save a little for ourselves. But everybody'll have to cut down and maybe bunch up at one stove. As thin as you are, it would be easy to thaw you out if you froze stiff."

Sam, at the station, had connected up the dummy set, but he was worried.

"Eddie," he complained, "it's cold in that kitchen. Can't I make a fire in the range to keep me warm while I'm foolin' that bankerman."

"We're on a stringent coal ration," Eddie told him flatly. "Anyhow, he won't keep you long."

Hi Wheeler banged in and backed up to the stove. He studied Eddie covertly. At last he broke down.

"Listen," he said wistfully, "there's a poker game going in the smoking compartment of that last Pullman." He grinned and waggled. "I feel a streak of luck comin' on. I'm just right to crack her on the nose. But I'm busted, Eddie," he complained. "You couldn't let an old friend and fellow confederate have twenty bucks till payday, could you?"

"Anything in the old sock is yours," Eddie told him

cheerfully, and tossed him his wallet. "Just save out a little eating money for both of us."

Hi fingered the worn wallet. "Okay, kid," he said softly. "I guess you and me won't miss many meals." He took out some bills and rubbed them on his cap badge. "I'm all set," he said, and went out.

"That stinger," said Sam, "sure has faith in the guys that play poker in Pullmans."

"He usually knows where to find the aces, when needed," Eddie said.

XVI

MR. RAYBURN came at eight thirty, all snuggled in a fur-lined overcoat, excited and twittery about his little enterprise. He inspected the office and sniffed with pleasure. He beamed.

"A good hot stove," he enumerated, "and the smell of copying rags. I guess every little railroad station is just about alike. This does take me back to my young days on the old New Haven."

Sam was stationed in the cold kitchen. He had rigged the dummy set and was prepared to delude the banker into a belief that the telegraph lines were in operation.

"May I practice a little on one of these sets?" Mr. Rayburn asked. "Then, if you think I still retain enough of my former skill, I would like to send these telegrams myself."

His Morse was uncertain at first, but the long-buried knack came back a little as his wrist limbered and his confidence grew.

"You never forget a thing that has been drilled into you when young," he smiled happily as he warmed up. "I believe I am doing quite well. Shall I try to get these messages off?"

"Of course," Eddie encouraged him. "You're doing all right. Just call Denver and let him have them."

Mr. Rayburn called and Denver answered promptly—from the kitchen.

The banker was shaken when he believed he was sending to another operator, and he made a messy start. But he battled stubbornly through the half-dozen messages, and he was jubilant when he had finished and got an okay from the spurious Denver operator.

"How that does take me back," he exulted. "I was a good operator in my time."

"Right now," Eddie said, "you're good enough to go back earning your living at it."

"I wish somebody would start sending," he said wistfully. "I'd like to know if I can still receive."

Eddie had to prompt Sam in the kitchen. "There isn't much wire traffic on a night like this." He raised his voice. "But about this time they usually send press reports out of Denver for the country papers."

Sam got that, and he began sending from a month-old newspaper. Rayburn couldn't get much of it until Sam's fingers congealed and slowed him down. The banker became eagerly engrossed then as his pencil caught more and more of the words clicking from the sounder. Then the cold got into Sam's marrow and he signed off.

"As a fact," Mr. Rayburn signed, "I have enjoyed this evening more than I suspected I would. A very happy time, young man. Now, let me give you the secret of my success." He lowered his voice. "It is really very simple, and I know you will appreciate it. Always," he said impressively, "be alert and resourceful in your work. Handle every situation deftly. Be ingenious. When I was with the old New Haven I made it a point to accomplish every unusual task, no matter how abruptly presented, in a prompt and competent manner." He beamed. "You see where it leads?"

"I do indeed," Eddie admitted profoundly. "I will certainly remember that."

As the wind slammed the door behind the banker, Sam crept stiffly into the office and huddled by the fire.

"Eddie," he moaned, "how do you get to be ingenious and resourceful?"

"It means the same," he said, "as keeping your nose clean."

The wind went down during the night, and the clouds collected over the ridges and dumped more snow on the grade. Rip and his section gang were out with push cars in the black of morning transferring coal to the engine. Later, a pale sun shown upon Saber Summit, and passengers emerged from the Pullmans to stretch and exercise.

Eddie reported to the bankers. The storm still blocked operations below, he said. But that couldn't last much longer.

Elder was impatient about it and more than a little incredulous. Osgood was bitterly offensive, Rayburn genially patient.

He checked the coal supply after Rip and his gang had completed the transfer to Nine's locomotive. The hogger didn't think that it would keep the coaches warm longer than three o'clock.

The wind snarled out of the Pass again and drove the passengers back to the coaches. The clouds still hung to the ridges. Eddie sought the foreman again.

"Rip," he said, "don't you think you and your gang can bring down a car of coal from the Kittybird? I thought we might get this train out of here before we needed it. But I guess not."

The Kittybird was a mine in operation at the end of a spur that climbed five miles over the ridges. It used coal for power, and once a week the A. S. L. switched two cars of the fuel up to the mine.

Rip peeked at the spur from the ambush of his sheepskin collar. Wind tore sheets of granulated snow from the shoulder where the track bent from sight.

"Sure," he agreed darkly. "All you got to do is go up there and turn a car loose. She'd fall down. But she'd splatter all over this end of the mountain and'd be considerable trouble to assemble for use. Them rails is so slick with sleet and ice you couldn't hold her back on that two-percent grade."

"On the way up," Eddie instructed, "throw gravel on the rails wherever you think you ought to. Beginning right here on the siding we'll drop the car into. Maybe you'd better find a heavy piece of timber up at the mine to tie on to the hind end as a drag to hold her back."

"We'll have to shovel our way through going up," Rip pointed out dismally. "Then when we get there the cars will be unloaded. If they ain't, they'll be in behind a flock of ore cars and we'll have to switch 'em out without an engine."

"If they're unloaded, get the crew at the mine to help load up half a car for us. They've got enough men there to push cars any place you want them. I'll give you a letter to the superintendent. And I want to send a note to Dad Carter who's trapping up on the lake. Take the Perez boy along and drop him off with the note where you can see Dad's cabin. I'll ask Gary if he won't give you his brakeman to help bring the car down."

"Do I get paid engineer's time for this switching job?" Rip asked bitterly.

Conductor Gary wasn't interested in rendering assistance. "I told you we ought to make a run for it last night," he bawled. "We're in a hell of a fix now!"

"I didn't think you'd want any," Eddie admitted. "Where's your brakeman?"

"How do I know?" Gary snarled.

He found Hi Wheeler still engaged in his poker game. He was sitting in with a mining engineer, a traveling man and two tourists from Iowa. Hi and the traveling man had most of the chips.

Eddie drew the brakeman aside with his request for help with the car of coal. Hi looked at the pat jack full he had just been dealt, and then at the salesman who had dealt them and was now moving a stack of chips into the pot. He nodded.

"Sure, I'll go," he grinned. "That guy just came into the game this morning, and he's been topping all my good hands. Anyhow, I guess I'm enough ahead to buy me that new blue suit."

Hi and the section crew went up the spur on the hand car.

At one o'clock the dining car conductor came to the station. "That's the hungerist batch of passengers I ever had on my car," he complained. "It must be the altitude. My fresh meat's all gone, and dinner will be mighty skimpy without it. There isn't a cow around here some place we could butcher, is there?"

There wasn't.

Eddie glanced out at the spur track anxiously. The wind was down again and the sun struggling out. A number of passengers had come down from the Pullmans. He caught sight of a man in a coonskin cap and felt boots leaning against the baggage truck, watching the antics of the crowd. Eddie shoved the dining car conductor aside in his rush to the door.

The man in the coonskin cap smelled of pelts and

faintly of skunk and he smoked a pipe that barely cleared the end of his nose.

"Look here, Dad," he snapped at him. "My note said for you to hurry down here."

"I know, Eddie," Dad complained, "but I had trouble findin' my other pants."

"How many deer carcasses have you got cached up there in the woods?"

"Why, none at all, Eddie," Dad denied. "You know it's ag'in the law."

"You old scoundrel, you don't pay any attention to the law, except when it comes looking for you. How much venison have you got stowed in the snow?"

Dad considered. "About how many could you use?" he inquired cautiously.

Eddie glanced at the passengers swarming over the snow, enlarging their appetites, and made a quick estimate. "Two," he guessed. "How much?"

"Well," Dad figured, "as long as they're for the railroad, they'd only be worth about fifty dollars apiece, if you don't think the warden'd catch us at it."

"Robber! How long will it take you to get them here?"

"About two hours, if I can use your right-of-way to sled'em down."

"Don't make it any longer, or I'll tell the warden myself. Deliver them to the dining car."

Sam was burning old records in the office stove by then. The three bankers came out into the growing sunlight and tramped up and down. Then they came to the station. Eddie ordered Sam into the kitchen to make noises on the dummy telegraph set to assure them that wire traffic was still uninterrupted.

"Aw, Eddie," Sam pleaded, "I ain't strong, and I'm likely to get pneumonia in that icebox."

"We're stuck with a lie now," Eddie snapped. "Get in there and get busy."

As the three came into the office, the sounder began to clatter furiously and profanely at a rate that Rayburn couldn't read. The bankers were grim. They wanted something definite.

"All this indicates extremely poor management," Osgood said with harsh precision. "I told you when this came up," he pointed out to the other two, "that I have always been dubious of these Western roads. They are never adroitly handled."

The sounder brayed as Sam sent from the kitchen, "That's the way a banker talks. 'No, no, no,' and 'I told you so.'"

"We had to be resourceful on the old New Haven," Rayburn beamed. "Alert to every emergency, and ingenious to handle it. There were great railroad men in those days."

The sounder clattered, "Eddie, you better get alert and ingenious or them guys will take you."

"Look here," said Elder shortly, "I don't like the look of this at all. We are wasting a great deal of time up here, and I doubt if we are being given all the facts. Our position seems to be getting hazardous. If you have been concealing anything from us, young man, you had better come clean."

Eddie said quietly, "I can appreciate how impatient you feel at this delay. But let me asure you that this situation is being handled by a competent railroad organization." He looked at Elder amiably. "We encounter savage operating conditions here that don't exist back in your country. Right now you are at an elevation of something over nine thousand feet. But your safety and comfort are being well protected."

"Give 'em hell, Eddie!" the sounder shouted.

Rayburn was leaning over the instrument, frowning at it, trying to read the babbling brass tongue. "That operator sends a little too fast for me," he said regretfully. "Perhaps, if we are still snowbound here this evening, I will come back and practice a little more."

"You do and you'll get shot," the sounder raved at him.

Osgood delivered a careful disgust. He suggested that they abandon the inspection trip and return to New York as soon as they were liberated from this trap.

The three went out in an ominous silence.

The sun continued to glitter through the afternoon. Dad Carter surreptitiously delivered his load of venison carefully concealed in burlap.

Then Conductor Gary and his engineer came to the station.

"Jim's got his last scoop of coal in the firebox," Gary said. "Steam's going down, and pretty quick the passengers are going to start complaining, mebby taking things apart. I'll tell them it's up to you, and they're likely to get rough. I told you we ought to run for it. Trouble with operators is thinking goes to their heads."

"Hi and the section gang ought to be down any time now with that car of coal," Eddie reassured him.

"Yeah!" Gary scoffed. "Hi is likely at the bottom of the canyon some place with the car on top of him. He couldn't keep it on the rails down that grade." He muttered darkly and went out.

At 3:45 Eddie went out on the platform for a look down the Pass. The sun was sliding toward the rim of peaks and shadows had gathered deep under the high walls. The air was motionless in the tight grip of the cold.

The spur up to the shoulder was empty. Even if they

had to reload the coal, Hi and the section men should have been back by now. For all his clowning, Hi was a top-hand railroader, smart at handling rolling stock; and you couldn't deflect him from a job he was set to. That car might have got out of control on the mine spur and worked up a speed that had tossed it down the mountain. It would be like Hi to ride it to its final crash.

The solid train of Pullmans lay like a log washed up under the dark walls. The passengers were knotting up together, their breaths making quick plumes in the pale sunlight as they talked and gestured. They stared at him. They were disquieted and they were talking themselves into a mild panic. The coaches were becoming chilly. The cold was showing its teeth on this high rim.

The three bankers came down from their private car. They moved clumsily in their heavy overcoats. They were far away from the softer elements they lived in. The snap of the savage mountain cold with its insidious menace had them worried. They were arbitrary in all their dealings, and they were prepared now to assert themselves, to foreclose.

Elder said abruptly, "Everyone knows that there is no more fuel, and very little food. You are responsible for our being in this hazardous position, and now you are powerless to do anything to relieve it. We are going to take charge now. I only hope it isn't too late."

Passengers edged closer to the little group on the station platform. Your head gets light in unaccustomed altitudes, and your nerves string up over little things. It wouldn't take much of a disturbance to stampede them. The white plumes of warm breath multiplied and fluttered like gun smoke.

Eddie said softly, "I don't suppose you have ever had to deal with crowds of people, ever had to handle an ex-

cited mob that fights its way aboard a train that has more
then enough room for all of them. Folks do senseless things
like that when they go traveling in throngs. They're sometimes pretty hard to manage." He nodded toward the
group slowly moving in on them. "You'd better not alarm
them more than they are, because you can't guess what
they'll do—except that it will be blind and destructive."

Elder drilled him with a bleak look. Osgood's gloved
hand fumbled at the buttons on his great coat. He'd lost
the knack of arranged sentences. He babbled.

"But this is dangerous, criminal; you put us in jeopardy
like cattle in a stock car. I'll prosecute—I'll sue."

"This would not have happened in my day on the old
New Haven," Mr. Rayburn nodded with satisfaction.

The sun slid down to the jagged skyline and the
shadows reached across the Summit with stealthy fingers.
The silence was like a frigid vacuum. The passengers were
all in one group now, and they inched forward uncertainly.

Sam came out of the station, his right hand tucked into
the front of his overcoat. He muttered in Eddie's ear,
"I've got the gun, if anybody starts anything."

He looked at Elder. "Do you want to take the responsibility of stampeding that crowd?" he asked.

"But, my God!" Osgood piped. "We're trapped here
to die. Can't someone do something?"

The crowd caught that. It began to buzz.

Elder snapped, "Shut up, Osgood!"

"Something must be done," Mr. Rayburn pondered.
"Something resourceful."

The rim of the mountains was scarlet with the sunset
and the red of it was on the snow. Osgood stared at the
faint crimson about his feet and shuddered in his great
coat. "A walled trap," he said.

The low buzzing sound from the crowd moved up to a

higher pitch. A half-dozen came forward in advance, and the rest followed. They shuffled slowly in the snow.

"Want to take Osgood away and let me handle these people?" Eddie suggested.

Elder hesitated. It was hard for him to stand aside in any situation in which he was involved.

"Aw, hell!" said Sam. "Want me to chase these bankers back to their roost?"

He shook his head. He turned and moved quietly toward the crowd of passengers.

They stopped. The mumble of voices ebbed into the snapping silence. He looked at them and smiled the practiced grin he used on indignant patrons.

"It gets colder than this up here in the winter storms," he said cheerfully. "And we have to take it for weeks at a time."

"Yes, but there is no heat in the coaches," a man protested sharply. "They say there is no more fuel, and there are women and children in those sleepers."

Eddie said, "And men enough among us all to see they don't suffer."

The quick jets of congealing breath plumed out and voices grumbled. They eyed him suspiciously.

Osgood muttered, "A walled trap."

The cold, biting silence slid over Saber Summit as the crowd considered that. The quick mountain dark edged in and dimmed the twilight. The unearthly quiet deepened in the half light, and then it was splintered as a high whine sawed into the crackling stillness, a sustained squawling protest that made your nerves wince and crawl. The sound ran up to a raucous wail and a tortured yell. It jarred set teeth and made them chatter.

That racket couldn't be made by anything but flanged wheels turning at speed, rounding a curve on brittle steel.

A coal car nosed abruptly around the shoulder above. It scooted down the grade at the preoccupied speed of a thing being desperately pursued, and it moved with a certitude that would be hard to check. The head and shoulders of Hi Wheeler showed above the rear end-board where he hung to the brake wheel. The car slammed and pitched over the switch-points and lurched onto the siding.

Brakeshoes smoked. Hi had tightened them to the limit of his rangy strength. The wheels took hold on the graveled rails. They exploded bits of rock that sang in the sharp air. They grumbled and grunted as the car stormed down the siding. A length of rope with a frayed end like a cow's tail trailed wildly from the rear drawhead. As the car passed the station, Hi swung over to the iron steps at the side, doubled and dipped down and unloaded. He spraddled into a deep drift and disappeared in a cloud of snow.

The car rammed the safety bumper at the end of the siding, and uprooted it. The front trucks were stripped away, and the car nosed into the snow and skidded and struck the passing track fill and flipped over on its side. Coal spewed and black dust flowed over the white ridges. The dark cloud faded out and exposed a heap of coal flung up against the fill just below Nine's locomotive.

Hi Wheeler's head came up out of the drift. He shook snow from his hair. He grinned at Eddie and pointed at the length of rope fluttering from the upraised rear of the coal car.

"My drag tore off," he yelled. "If it hadn't, I'd have dumped the coal right in the tender for you."

Rip Biggers and his crew came in sight around the shoulder on their hand car.

Sam Dunn considered the situation with satisfaction.

"Eddie," he bargained, "I'll get my breakfast and your supper if you'll carry in the coal."

Stars slipped into the deepening night. The crowd set up a scattering cheer and laughed and shouted.

Eddie turned to Elder. "How," he asked, "would you like to have venison for dinner, some that's been frozen in a snow bank for the last two months?"

"You're not fooling?" Elder demanded. "Look here," he pounced, "if you really have it, and you'll let me cut the chops and show the dining car chef how I want them, I'll—I'll buy your damn railroad."

"It's not for sale," Eddie grinned. "But you get the chops as requested."

The cold sun had come over the peaks next morning when he heard the snow plow's thunder rising in Imperial Pass. She came out, tossing a stream from her hood. The stream eased to thin jets as the snow level dropped below the big fan. The stubby train clanked to a stand beside the station and Mr. Nickerson came down from the caboose and stepped briskly across the platform to the private car on the rear of Nine.

Eddie, at the telegraph table, pulled a scratch pad toward him and indited a note.

"Mr. Nickerson," he wrote in his swift telegrapher's fist, "I slightly misinformed Mr. Elder and party on certain items, and withheld a few facts which may surprise you when they mention them." He scratched his ear with the pen. "We brought a car of coal down from the Kittybird, wrecking the car in that operation. But the coal was delivered in time to keep passengers and guests from freezing." He grinned and wrote, "I purchased two nice venison for the commissary which was illegal and cost $100." He considered. "I couldn't help Mr. Elder and party in the private car becoming somewhat disturbed. They will doubtless inform you as to how much they were alarmed." He signed it, "E. Sand, Agent."

Mr. Rayburn came out of the private car and Eddie went to meet him.

"I want to say good-by," the banker said, "and to impress upon you my little secret of success. As a fact, I believe you did get something of my meaning at once. It seemed to me you were somewhat ingenious at times and quite resourceful."

Eddie reflected solemnly. "Now that you mention it," he said, "I really think I was."

Nickerson and Elder came out onto the observation platform, and the president signed Conductor Gary to be on the way.

Eddie handed his note up to Nickerson.

Gary's "All aboard" rumbled down the Pass. He shook his fist at Eddie and yelled, "I told you—"

The Imperial Limited sounded off. She stamped as she shook loose the bearings in the frozen journals.

Salt-and-Molasses Nickerson looked up from the note. He turned his back on the bankers, and he winked once at Eddie behind his frosty glasses.

Elder stared coldly down at him. "If you ever decide to try banking," he said, "look me up. I could use a young man who readily pulls assets out of the air when needed."

He waved a grim farewell as the Limited moved down the passing track.

XVII

SUNLIGHT moved softly back and forth through the windows of the coach as the clattering local passenger train turned on the curves. Spring air washed in the scent of snow water and pine and growing grass. The mountains had dropped behind and faded to a dim cloud on the horizon. A lonely ranch house far off against the bluff by the river among cottonwoods and old hay ricks, sent up a straight column of lazy smoke.

He picked up his book and then put it down again. The fertile air wouldn't let you concentrate. Hi Wheeler dozed with his cheek in his big brown hand, his elbow propped on the window sill. He rocked gently to the sway of the coach. His long, homely face was relaxed and had the wistful look of a baffled child. He was still dazed from the low blow that gal Gladys had dealt him. He couldn't comprehend it. He'd have given her any thing he possessed and been happy if he got nothing in return but the old up-and-up friendship. Hi hadn't thought that he had merited her love and affection. She had just moved in on him, had him in dazzled, and then cut his throat.

Hi clowned and made exaggerated statements, but that was mostly in derision at himself. "I never knew folks wore anything on their feet but cowhide boots," he would explain whimsically, "till I was eighteen and come in out of the brush to see my first train." Since then he had never been out of hearing of the snort of the iron horse. He never wanted to be. But he would always be a sucker for the predatory female.

Hi strangled slightly and jerked his head and stared about. His eye found Eddie and his face brightened in a grin.

"Springtime sure relaxes you," he said. He studied the great plains slowly revolving around the clanking local. "Seems like a lot of country they've got up here," he decided.

Up ahead, a herd of cattle grazing close to the right-of-way stared comically from their white masks. They backed away as the noisy engine approached. The engineer blew his whistle and they turned and galloped off, their tails flung high.

"We had a hogger," Hi said, "down on the old Jaw Bone, a big Swede, who once run his engine over a bull. The trouble was, it was a thoroughbred which the farmer had imported at a cost of eight hundred dollars." Hi shook his head doubtfully. "Anyhow, that's what the farmer claimed. It was important money in that community, and you'd 'a thought he'd arranged to keep his bull off the railroad track." He watched the herd of white-faced cattle slow and stop and turn to stare foolishly at the train. "Anyhow, there was a lawsuit, and they put Ooley on the stand. 'When,' asks the attorney for the railroad, 'did you first see the bull?' Ooley says, 'I first saw him coming through the alfalfa.' The lawyer says, 'And when did you next see him?' Ooley stood up on the stand. 'When I next seen him,' he says, 'the alfalfa was coming through the bull.' And even after all that time he began brushing himself off. Considerable of that bull had come into the cab when Ooley's engine cut him down."

Hi yawned and rolled a cigarette. "That A. S. L. wasn't a bad outfit to work for," he said thoughtfully.

They paused at lean little towns to let off stray passengers and to unload their baggage, and express and U. S. mail; to take on traveling men and their big sample trunks. Men in boots and wide hats leaned against the stations and eyed the train solemnly.

The A. S. L. was a good outfit. In a way he had hated to leave it. When you worked with that kind of people you put down roots that hurt when you tore them up. Hi had come along like a lost kid. Well, he needed the change to make him forget Gladys, or else put that gal in the proper perspective.

The brass hats had been mightly obliging when the two of them had quit. Without quibble they had given them passes to Denver. Which showed they appreciated good men and would welcome them back. He tried to do his work so that he could always go back. He seldom did return, but it was nice feeling to know you could if you wanted to. Good boomers kept their records clean. They had a fierce loyalty for their craft.

He'd had a notion of going in and saying good-by to Mr. Nickerson. He liked that slightly bent sliver of a man with goggling glasses that never missed a thing. Then he had decided against it. They would likely never see each other again, and farewells could be embarrassing. Polite words didn't say exactly what you meant.

He glowed a little. There were a lot of good guys in this world. Did you good to work with them. Kept you on your toes when the traffic jammed. Maybe a lot of grand women, too. But he wouldn't be sure about that. They could mangle your sensibilities if you let yourself go for one, and sour your outlook. He didn't think there was one yet born who could subdue that acute, restless push that set you drifting again. Nice to think about a woman pal, but you'd better be wary.

They hadn't lingered in Denver. The hard tramp of the big Malleys on the grade didn't step up his pulse. The chant of wheels going some place else made his thoughts follow them to far distant places. Just to have a point to shoot at they had decided they would push up toward the Northwest.

Foothills closed in and you could tell by the slam of the engine's exhaust that they were climbing. A stream flowed by going the other way. The sweep of plains behind blurred in a soft, smoky haze.

Long shadows came down from the hills and the sunlight softened. Hi dozed and Eddie read till they grunted to a stop at a sprawling town where the stream widened. The inscription on the big wooden station said it was Ledge River. Beyond, he saw the familiar layout of yard and roundhouse and a barn-like structure across the way that was likely division headquarters. Switch engines snorted among the ruck of rolling stock.

"It appears," he said, "that we've come to a terminal. Looks like we'll have to unload and find us another conductor with charity enough to carry us further on our faces."

Hi blinked at the slanting sunshine and sniffed the soft air. "Me," he said, "I'm gettin' some saddle-galls ridin' behind this particular iron hoss. This railroad's got a nice sound to it's name—Puget Railway & Navigation Line. I ain't never navigated in its true and proper sense. What say we hit'em, for a job apiece?"

Eddie reached into the rack for his suitcase. "Might as well," he agreed.

The operator on duty in the ticket office said he thought the P. R. & N. L. needed experienced men, and they left their baggage with him. The operator thought he'd seen the trainmaster heading down toward the yard office, and Hi went that way in search of him. Eddie crossed to the dispatchers' office to interview the chief.

XVIII

THEY GAVE him second trick there in the Ledge River ticket office right under the guns of headquarters, which wasn't what he wanted at all. Close association with the brass hats either brought comfortable acquaintance with them, or else made you a stepchild of all the division. He was promptly made a stepchild.

He vaguely sensed that he was in the clutch of circumstance when in the late evening the yardmaster slid cautiously into the office where Eddie read placidly under a cone of light. The night yardmaster was in trouble, seeking a refuge. The superintendent was on the prod, and the dinger was desperately trying to find a place of concealment until the punitive wrath of the Old Man had subsided. He appealed to Eddie for help.

Eddie wasn't yet familiar with the human elements of the Ledge River Division. Some organizations fitted together like the fine works of a watch. Others were held insecurely in the fumbling grasp of one man's hand. He had guessed tentatively that the latter was in effect here. But on any railroad you were obliged to assist an associate who was in wrong with an official. He suggested to the dinger that he stand alongside the high ticket case, out of line of the windows. It wasn't a qualified hiding place, but the only cover available in the bare office.

It didn't avail. O'Conner, the superintendent, by some

keen Celtic instinct for quarry, had trailed the yardmaster
through the stuffed yard, and he came upon him plastered
against the ticket office wall, trying to shrink his two-
hundred-and-some-pound bulk into the slender width of
the case. The Old Man pounced.

Pressed for time and space, the yardmaster had in-
stigated a hazardous switching operation that had put a
car of baled hay on the ground upside down. That had
blocked the ladder track and uprooted a switch stand.
O'Conner blasted. He menaced the dinger with fists as big
as drawheads and rode him right down the line. The yardmaster remained flattened against the wall and took the
stormy rebuke stoically.

Eddie's eyeshade was pulled down over his nose. Undisturbed, he read on through the uproar.

Abruptly O'Conner subsided. His craggy face discarded the storm cloud that had tortured the bald headland. The lightning died to a distant glimmer.

"Now that we have settled that," he said with entire
satisfaction, and dusted his hands. His probing eye fell
upon Eddie, still reading placidly, and he stared. Anyone
who could remain inanimate through the storm that had
just torn through the office was a peculiar specimen to
him. When he roared everyone ducked. The distant glimmer flared up again. "You are the new man here," he said
with marked restraint. "I hope we make it pleasant for
you," he added.

Eddie put down his book. He said cautiously that it'd
been interesting so far.

"A boomer brass pounder," O'Conner chided, "from
every place but here, and you will soon be gone from this
place."

Eddie admitted that he'd been around.

O'Conner was frustrated for the moment. The huge

Hibernian was like dynamite with the fuse ignited. The sizzle wasn't especially alarming, but it always ended in an explosion that took things apart.

Eddie calmly set off another blast. His critical eye for defects in methods had lit on one that his experienced railroad sense told him was dangerous. He couldn't let it slide.

"It looks to me," he pointed out, "like it's perilous, the way we put out train orders through this station. We've got no telegraph instruments in this office, but every other office on the line has. So the trick dispatcher has to telephone the orders to us over the city phone after he's issued them by telegraph to the other stations involved. That makes them two-legged."

"Yes?" said O'Conner incredulously.

"What I mean," Eddie pursued blandly, "the trick man gets in a tangle of traffic, with everything crowding him, and it's easy for him to forget to telephone the second leg. That sometimes adds up to a cornfield meet. I'm just remarking," he remarked, "because I've seen two-legged orders smear things up bad."

"Yes?" said O'Conner ominously.

"I asked the lineman about it," Eddie went on, "and he said it'd require only a couple poles and a few hundred feet of wire to bring the telegraph line over here from the dispatcher's office. He has that on hand. All he needs is an order from you. I thought it my duty to bring it up," he added tranquilly.

The yardmaster flinched and choked on his breath.

O'Conner's pale eyes hardened to a cloudy granite as they raked the boomer. "He consulted the lineman, he says," the Old Man rumbled like an earthquake, "and he considers it his duty to bring it up. A glum boomer who reads a book and makes suggestions." The rumble deepened "The young man comes to us all bright and shinin' with idees about how to run a railroad—very efficacious." The storm cloud whipped across the bleak crag. "But here, my brilliant young drifter, I'll tell you what your duty is, and there will be no need remindin' me."

He went out and slammed the door.

The yardmaster controlled his breath. "A glum guy who reads a book and makes bright suggestions," he quoted bitterly. "Swell advice you give me on a hide-out. Now look, boomer," he invited, "if you want to get by with the Old Man, you keep your notions all buttoned up and a deep secret from him. Else he'll bounce'em right off'n your head."

"So he's like that," Eddie considered, and took up his book.

Next morning, the chief dispatcher had a call out for him.

"I thought," the chief reproved him, "that a brass pounder who's been around'd know better than to tie into the Old Man. He don't like other people's schemes."

"I just advised him against two-legged orders," Eddie explained.

The chief shuddered. "Anyhow," he admitted, "he didn't maim you. But I wouldn't trust him not to a second time. He's ordered you to Mammoth Pit." He paused to make it impressive. You had to play fair with the boomers or they wouldn't come your way when you were short of operators. "It's a workhouse," he added.

"Okay," said Eddie.

"But nobody lasts on that job," the chief insisted. "Fact is, another man walked out on it last night. The Old Man's just handing you a package."

"I'll handle it," Eddie stated.

The chief was puzzled. Boomers passed up the dull drudgery of big station jobs. The expert telegraphers usually refused the weary pencil work of making the endless station reports. He examined the boomer's slim length carefully. His blue suit was pressed, and he didn't look as if he had missed any meals lately. The drifter wasn't on the rocks. The chief wondered why he would stick around and take punishment when he'd eventually move on anyhow. Then he noted the shine of red on the upper end of that long exclamation point. Maybe he was obstinate. They came that way some times.

XIX

MAMMOTH PIT was a cheerless spot in the highlands, entirely begrimed with coal dust; a one-man job, agent and operator, where there should have been three. Trainloads of coal to waybill, herds of empties to order, flocks of messages and train orders to handle. A workhouse.

The station was set between the passing track and the high iron. Sidings and coal spurs and ladder track fanned out in a crazy web. Two switch engines blared and snorted all over the place.

Eddie hunted up the yardmaster.

"Yeah," said the dinger, "you're the glum guy who reads and recommends. Well," he decided, "you won't have time to peruse that book here." He squinted. "We'd get along better if you'd turn around and go right back where you come from. You fiddle-footed birds see too much that ought to be rectified."

"I'll stick around," Eddie decided.

The yardmaster fished for a bunch of keys. "They'll unlock everything at the station," he allowed. "There's likely several days work to be caught up. I hope you like it here as long as you're able."

The chief hadn't overstated. It wasn't a task the drifters undertake. Boomers like the brief telegraph tricks to keep the roaring traffic on the wing. The Mammoth Pit job was a snarl of monotonous details. It took long

182

hours, into the night, to keep the work cleaned up. He ran it with stubborn, imperturable industry.

At the end of the first week, O'Conner had the chief call him on the wire to verify the fact that he was still on the job. No sign of the usual grief and disorder had come from Mammoth Pit since he had gone there, and these two grizzled brass hats were dubious about that, a little uneasy at the silence where there had been turmoil. It was the anxious relief after a long pain in the neck.

Eddie told them he was still holding her down. And he added another recommendation.

"You'd better have some more sidings laid in this yard," he sent on the wire. "They get so jammed sometimes that the switchmen have to use the passing track and the house track and the ladder to make up trains. You're going to be tied up tight here some of these times so you can't move a thing, or else something'll bust and spread traffic all over the district."

O'Conner wasn't a telegrapher. He dictated his reply to the chief, who relayed it to Eddie as well as the Morse code could manage it. Which was hot enough to blister.

Eddie sent back that he had merely thought it his duty to report conditions.

By then he had become the entire division's main aversion. The men didn't care for a slick boomer from the outside who horned in on their family disputes. They were accustomed to O'Conner's blasts. The Old Man wasn't as bad as he sounded. A smart boomer who strayed in and tried to reform the system of operations would have to be slapped down. They followed hostilities with raffish glee through furtive bulletins the operators sent about on the wires. The Old Man would pin his ears back good. They were delighted when finally Eddie stepped into a situation that subjected him to ridicule and harsh discipline.

He had worked late, as usual, and was closing up, when a way freight paused in the starlight at Mammoth Pit to make a pickup. The caboose pulled up before the station. Hi Wheeler was the parlor man, and operations stalled while Hi told the conductor stories of the escapades he and Eddie had collaborated in along the iron highway. The conductor interrupted that to say he was tired and wanted to get in.

There was an empty boxcar on a spur off the team track to be picked up. To get it into the train legitimately, the engineer would have to head in and pull the car out of that dead-end stub, and then maneuver all over the yard to get it behind the locomotive. The most expeditious way to place it properly was to make a Dutch drop, a flying switch. That was a hazardous operation, forbidden in one of O'Conner's bulletins, but the crew had gone through a hard trip of many delays, the men were all tired and eager to be into terminal and in bed, and the conductor gave the nod to the illegal Dutch drop when Hi argued for it. The two moved forward toward the head end.

The engineer brought his engine back through the team track and headed into the spur and tied onto the empty car. He backed up at a brisk speed, checked briefly to give slack for the brakeman to uncouple. Then, freed of the boxcar, the engineer raced out onto the team track, followed more slowly by the car. He reversed his engine quickly and headed up the siding past the switch, which the head brakeman closed behind him, and on past the rolling boxcar as it coasted onto the team track behind the engine, where it could be picked up and coupled into the train.

It was a swift, smooth bit of railroading, minutely timed. It took good men to bring it off without disaster.

Eddie watched the engine come out of the spur and roar ahead in time to avoid the boxcar, the two moving pieces of equipment missing each other by scant inches.

He saw Hi's lantern swing up the side of the car and stop beside the brake wheel on top. He was outlined among the stars an instant and then disappeared against a background of trees as the car slid down the siding.

That car had developed considerable momentum by the time it clattered over the switch points onto the team track. He heard the strangled rasp of the ratchet as Hi spun the wheel to set the brake. The sound was choked off abruptly in a metallic gasp. The car didn't hesitate. It continued down the team track at an increasing speed. There'd been a slip in that trick bit of switching. All the elements hadn't clicked in tune.

The car moved on unchecked, and there was no further sound of the ratchet. Evidently the hand brake had fouled. The car slammed through the spring switch onto the main line and slid away into the darkness. The lantern still burned calmly at the brake wheel on top as it dropped down the grade.

The empty was loose on the hill, with Hi Wheeler evidently on top struggling with the defective braking equipment. It had a long descent on which to ramble, but Eddie was relieved to remember that there weren't any trains in its path near enough to collide with it before the opposing grade brought it under control. No traffic hazard, but somebody would get mauled when O'Conner heard about that Dutch drop.

Eddie had jumped to the conclusion that because the lantern still winked on top of the runaway, that Hi was there too, gamely doing his duty. He hadn't unloaded before the car slipped into high speed because he probably didn't know whether anything was coming up the grade

behind his way freight, and now he'd likely break his fool
neck if he tried it on the jagged hillside. He would be
plastered all over the slope if he did. He was stuck with the
insurgent boxcar until it was controlled.

Then he realized that the empty might develop enough
speed on those swooping curves to take flight into the timber. At high speed that top-heavy boxcar was likely to turn
over on one of those abrupt bends. After that, they'd pick
Hi out of the treetops in small pieces.

Under the pressure of these crowding events, a number of other items crowded into his mind. The air had been
cut out of the caboose when the way freight first arrived.
That was also prohibited by the Old Man, but the night
crews often disregarded that order and cut out the air here
so the crummy could be dropped off without delay as they
entered the terminal yard.

These cabooses had four-wheel passenger-coach trucks,
heavy and frictionless. You could push them about by hand
on level track. If there was slack to uncouple it, the crummy
could overtake the fleeing boxcar, tie on and check it; and
the caboose would stay on the rails long after the empty
had taken to the timber.

It was only one jump to the coupling lever. Eddie made
it while these undigested reflections careened through his
mind. He was heaving on it with savage jerks before any
sober second thoughts could occur. The mechanism clanked
and grunted. The coupling lever came up.

The caboose inched backward before he gave it a shove.
He swung onto the step and ran through the aisle to the
rear platform.

That crummy was free-rolling. It immediately picked
up an oily speed, and then stepped up to a breathless rush.
The heavy trucks appeared to feel that they were back in

passenger service. They flashed down the grade, chanting joyously at the rail joints.

The lantern beamed benignly on the rambling car ahead. He had no doubt but that Hi was there beside it, valiantly trying to rectify the defective brake and check the car's flight. A brakeman and his lantern, at night, were as inseparable as a man and his pants. You were certain they would always be paired. It would be indecent otherwise. Yet it had happened that Hi was parted from his light. Eddie was still in the clutch of circumstance. The improbable had happened, and Hi had been wrenched from his glim. But the darkness had hidden that accident.

When the boxcar had cleared the spur switch, Hi had given the brake wheel a preliminary spin, then swung on it; and he put his exuberant weight into the swing. Then something in the mechanism caught. Instead of winding up the last slack in the chain, the wheel froze suddenly in his hands. The momentum of his hard body tore loose his hold.

Hi spread-eagled in thin air, turned over in flight, lit on his heels on a crumbling fill and slid into a pool of stagnant water. The breath was knocked out of him. He nearly drowned in six inches of water. It was a minute and fifty seconds before, half-strangled, he crawled out of the pool. By then the boxcar was flashing down the hill, and Eddie had the caboose in furious pursuit of the abandoned speck of light on top.

The night operator at the Brier Patch, asleep, with his head in his arms, on the telegraph table, was awakened to a stunned consciousness by their passing, and he wildly reported that two heavy blasts had gone off right under the floor beneath his feet. But he could find no damage done.

The agent at Crescent, properly asleep in his bed in the upper story of his station, fell down the dark stairs and jabbered at the dispatcher that a pair of rockets had gone by and nearly blasted the windows out of his depot.

The dispatcher began to rave. What the hell was going on out there? Those operators on the east end must have been poisoned by something they ate—or was it what they'd drunk? What were they trying to say? Explosions and things tearing by in the night. What'd they think the Old Man would say when he heard about this?

It took the caboose three miles to gain the last two hundred yards on the boxcar. Eddie overhauled it at last, and juggled to a coupling. He was vexed because the brakeman didn't appear at once to assert his gratitude and assist at the hand brakes of the crummy. It was a tough job for one man to bring the two cars under control and stop them at the passing-track switch at Ripton, and then let them into the clear. He searched the car, but no part of Hi was there except his lantern.

"Joined the birds," Eddie decided dejectedly, and crossed to the Ripton telegraph office to report.

XX

WHEN THE insane details of that wild affair finally trickled through to Eddie in the Ripton telegraph office that night, and the size of his error was born to him by the clacking sounder, he was badly scorched. He passed the word to Hi Wheeler that a beautiful friendship was forever blasted. Next time he'd let the brakeman break his long neck, and be damned to him.

Hi hooted. He had crawled out of the foul pool and spent the time of the chase safely at Mammoth Pit, being censured by his conductor and derided by the rest of the crew. They nicknamed him Mud Turtle and that epithet stuck to him as long as he was with the P. R. & N. L., and beyond. He was glad to divert the division's ridicule, and he piled it on. He said it seemed Eddie was getting a little strung up over his feud with the Old Man, a little too quick on the trigger.

But even in the heat of exasperation, Eddie didn't forget the immediate future. He conspired with the train and engine crews of the way freight on their report of their conduct in the misadventure.

Nothing quite so intricately funny had ever occured on the Ledge River Division. That delirious escapade brought forth prolonged spasms of gusty merriment, restrained a little while O'Conner made a tumultuous investigation.

Eddie was ribbed without restraint or mercy. He took it with a grin and admitted he'd been impetuous.

There wasn't much the Old Man could do to the crews involved. In connivance with Eddie, they neglected to admit the Dutch drop and the lack of air in the caboose, and the mechanical department verified the bad-order braking equipment on the boxcar. That left no broken regulations of record.

But O'Conner knew in his bones that he hadn't been given the whole story in reports and hearings. He pounced upon Eddie.

"You are the kind of railroader," he told the boomer, "that is always looking for somebody else to make the errors. Like the section hand watching to see is everybody's tools off the track when the train approaches, and 'tis his shovel gets run over."

Eddie grinned and said he'd only done his duty as he'd seen it.

"There is little cause for levity," O'Conner erupted. "Now, that report you made me. It told me nothing at all. Tell me what happened up there at Mammoth Pit before you went off down the hill in the crummy."

"Didn't the crews report it?" Eddie asked blandly.

"Report!" yelled O'Conner. "They tell but the half of it. I will have the rest from you."

"I don't write the other fellow's reports," Eddie said.

O'Conner was set to blast. He restrained himself just under the detonation point. "I have not enjoyed such a fine brawl," he muttered, "since I fired Tim McGurk five years gone. I will decide presently what is best for you."

"Before you do that," Eddie advised, "you'd better put some more sidings in the Mammoth Pit yard. You haven't got enough room in it right now to whip a cat."

The Old Man scorched him with a look. "I would have

thought your last attempt to rectify conditions would have cured you of making recommendations," he said with restraint. "I remember once you complained of two-legged orders as well. Maybe it would be better if I retired and turned the division over to you to manage."

"I'd be willing to handle it," Eddie admitted modestly, "till I got a better job."

O'Conner's ways were set in concrete. He was an explosive fragment erupted from the old construction days, a vivid relic of those brawling times. He dominated his division with the rowdy discipline learned in those distant, disorderly years. He didn't know any other method of conduct. He had a warm, Irish heart deep inside of him, but it was protected by boiler plate.

Eddie cheerfully admitted to himself that the Old Man had all the best of their embranglement so far, and went back to work the Mammoth Pit job.

As he was preparing to close the station, so that he could clean up the pencil work uninterrupted, a switch engine shoved a string of loaded coal cars down the passing track by the office. The yard crews were plagued with the congestion and they weren't cautious. The head car in the string suddenly dumped its load. Coal exploded in a black cloud and sprawled over the siding. The rear trucks of the car became entangled and jumped the rails.

The yardmaster's voice resounded to the outer reaches of his domain and fetched the section crew. The foreman inspected the derailment and sent his gang of Indians down into the supply yard. They came back shoving a push car loaded with new ties. But the foreman stopped them before they moved the load over to the passing track, and he anchored the push car just off the main line.

Eddie listened to the altercation between the yardmaster and the foreman that followed. But apparently they weren't speaking English as it is commonly used, and he remained unenlightened. The dispute ended abruptly when the foreman and crew straggled away down the supply spur.

"That gandy dancer," the yardmaster reported, "is half Injun and half enjineer. There's a festival cooking tonight among the red men, and he has to officiate. He's through for the day. He ain't in any way going to assist in cleaning up the passing track till morning."

Eddie's critical eye noted a hazard. "That supply track has considerable pitch to it," he pointed out, "and the foreman's left the push car of ties with only a chunk under one wheel to hold it. Sure would take a ride down that swale if that block got removed."

In the flare of sunset, without interest, the yardmaster viewed the length of the spur far down through the yard to where it curved parallel with the curve of the main line beyond the bunkers and ended in a bumper. "I said you'd see too much that ought to be rectified," he considered darkly. "But that comes under the head of the section foreman's neglected business. Mine's keeping empties spotted and the loads lined up for the road engines."

"Yeah," said Eddie, "it does seem so."

"You better tell the dispatcher," the dinger decided, "that the passing track is blocked and won't be in service till morning. I'll clear Spur Three for trains taking siding to meet here, and they'll have to head in and back out, instead of heading through. He'll have to figure that delay."

The trick dispatcher was snowed under. He took the news of the blocked passing track, remarked his bitter opinion of yardmasters, and went back to ranging the division, exploding train orders, prodding reluctant freights and untangling traffic snarls.

Eddie locked the door on the inside and worked late on

accounts. He was off duty and the dispatcher didn't bother him further. But the thread of the tale the telegraph instruments wove ran through the back of his mind while he wrote up reports.

Nine was late, and the Hawk was later. The dispatcher, threading the crowding trains two ways on a single strand, couldn't keep them on time. These two had a timetable meet at Mammoth Pit, and the dispatcher gave Nine forty minutes on the Hawk, so she could make that appointment. Nine was the inferior train and had to take siding. The dispatcher told her to use Spur Three to clear at Mammoth Pit.

It seemed to him, as he cast up the station accounts, that the dispatcher was restricting the Hawk's engineer, holding him back to forty minutes late, if he were trying to make up lost time. The high iron was hot, the pressure was on the lone dispatcher under a cone of light in his aloof office, making quick reckonings from the inked-in figures on his long train sheet. It was easy to miscalculate when traffic jammed the single track. But maybe there was a slow order out somewhere, or the Hawk would be stabbed by another meet. It was habit, following train movements in the back of his mind while he wrote up reports. He didn't have all the items the trickman had to consider. He wondered what condition he hadn't caught from the wire that had caused him to restrict the Hawk. The order to her was put out at Ledge River.

The racket of the switch engines died in the yard. The quiet of late evening brooded over Mammoth Pit. Eddie yawned as he struck a balance. He put his reports in the tissue book and squeezed them in the copying press. He leaned on the wheel of the press and waited for the reports to cook.

Nine hooted for the station, and the dim radiance of

her headlight flickered on the bow window facing the main line. Her bell tolled and the throb of her exhaust eased. She was slowing for the Mammoth Pit yard.

He glanced at the clock. She had fifteen minutes to clear before the Hawk was due on her time order. He whistled thoughtfully as he checked back on the situation which the babbling sounder had sketched, and he wondered again what had stuck the Hawk forty minutes. But that, he decided, was the dispatcher's headache. He yawned again as he waited for his reports to cook. The glimmer of Nine's headlight grew brighter as she came down the main line.

He couldn't say for certain why he remained here to be persecuted by this workhouse. Maybe to discipline his vagrant spirit. But that wasn't likely. The old timers would scoff if you talked about the gods of the high iron. The title was a little too lurid. But they believed in secret in a vague deity special to the iron highway only, that arranged good fortune and bad for the men who ran the trains and guarded their movements. Some weren't above carrying charms and making incantations. The blamed old frauds. He grinned and whistled a drowsy tune. He was trying to believe he was staying on because a phantom of the rails had conjured him to remain for some hidden occasion.

A swift shudder slipped through the quiet darkness. It came up from the flooring and fluttered gently at the windows, a brief shock like the echo of a distant explosion. It was so faint that you would scarcely have noticed it if it hadn't been an accustomed sound, but there was power in it like a far earthquake. The tune dried up on his lips and left them in a pensive pucker.

Those dim reverberations cuffed his mind back to the immediate moment. It was the sound of the Hawk hitting the diamond of the crossing two miles to the west. It had the brisk impast of high speed. The Hawk was close at hand and the hogger had her latched out. His eyes slid back to the clock as he made a quick estimate. She was twelve minutes ahead of her time order.

The soft chuff of Nine working steam came nearer down the main line from the east, moving slowly. The crew likely didn't know the exact location of Spur Three and was searching for the switch stand in the web of sidings under the glare of her headlight. With his eyes still on the clock, he reckoned closely that she wouldn't clear in time to let the Hawk by, if the Hawk didn't slow and stop to her limit of forty minutes late at Mammoth Pit.

It looked to him as if all these crowding items were going to end in a telescoped tangle. Some one had slipped. But that futile chase down the hill in the crummy had made him wary of snap decisions. He went back over the details he had gathered from the wire with quick care. Nine was here loitering into the clear. On the time order she needn't hurry. But by the sound she made when she hit the diamond, the Hawk was certainly ahead of her schedule as laid down in that same order.

The picture assembled in the dim quiet of the office as he leaned against the copying press and considered intently. He couldn't add it up to any answer, except that the Hawk had missed its leg of the two-legged order. The dispatcher, crowded with the surging traffic, had overlooked telephoning it to the Ledge River station after he'd put it out by telegraph to Nine. And without that restraint the Hawk's hogger had nipped twelve minutes off his lost time. He had hit the diamond at a speed that indicated the engineer had no intention of slowing for the station. By his rights, if he hadn't been restricted, the main line should be clear through the Mammoth Pit yard.

The slow exhaust of Nine died, and then picked up again. She was heading into the spur.

This might not be so critical as it looked. Maybe another illusion caused by a detail he didn't know about. Like Hi falling off the boxcar. But you couldn't tinker with events that were moving at high speed. You'd have only one snap shot at this one. He'd give the division another good laugh if that was the way it turned out.

XXI

ALL THE probabilities moved clearly through his mind. There were a myriad of them swarming in. You had to snatch the essential items and keep strictly to them when time had dwindled to a handful of seconds. There wasn't a lighted lantern in the station. He plucked a dead one from the shelf with the instinct that on duty at night you always carried a lantern. You couldn't check the Hawk in time if you went down the main line to flag her. The main came in on an inside curve, and her hogger couldn't see your signal until he blasted into the yard.

The wooden platform boomed under his long stride. The night air slapped him in the face. The push car was nearer than he'd reckoned, and he scraped his shins on the protruding load of ties. The car began to roll on the grade the instant he kicked the block from under the wheel. His shove increased its speed so quickly that he nearly lost it in the dark. The dead lantern in the crook of his arm swung wildly and slapped him behind the ear as he scrambled aboard.

It was a good thing that foreman hadn't anchored the car better, or he couldn't have got off to a quick start. He changed holds cautiously and crawled forward over the splintery ties. His knees were pinched between the timbers as the push car rocked and took the grade of the supply track in a glossy swoop.

197

The Hawk's headlight cut a wedge through the thin velvet of the darkness, swinging toward him on the arc of the curve. The superheated exhaust cracked and stuttered above the absorbed mumble of the push car's wheels. Her whistle stamped out the long wail of "approaching station."

This was going to be tight. You could do a lot of things in sixty seconds, but it left no period to rectify errors committed along the way. All the indispensable items now had to fit, and all at once. The Hawk and the push car were rapidly reaching a juncture. When that came he'd have about three short seconds to do whatever showed up that he could do. He didn't know the yard very well. He'd have to make a wild guess as to when and where to unload. He felt for the foot brake as the headlight sprayed him with speckled light. The roar of the Hawk leaned against him like a high wind. Then the light was blinding, and the ecstatic exhaust and the pound of brasses crashed over him. He shoved down on the foot brake with both hands.

That Injun-and-injineer foreman kept his equipment in good shape. The brake grabbed and screeched and held. The check of the car was so abrupt it nearly projected him out ahead of it. He pivoted on a stiff arm and abandoned the vehicle in a sidewise convulsion. He kept his feet by the practiced digging in of heels and swung over to the main line.

The light eased as the locomotive loomed above him. The purr of the stack beat against his chest and crammed air back into his lungs. The Hawk wasn't slowing for the Mammoth Pit yard.

He swung the dead lantern and tossed it at the flaring disk of the headlight. The glare streaked out of his eyes and steam scorched his throat. He caught the vague ricochet of the lantern along the boiler. The cage frame exploded signal oil and broken globe as it was flung back at the cab. It ducked into the front window. The engine boomed past, and dust and hot smells swirled through the dark. The coaches slid by, chuckling amiably at the rail joints.

A ragged clatter broke out down at the end of the supply spur as the push car loaded with ties was stopped abruptly by the bumper. A dull explosion kicked the darkness and compressed air screeched as the Hawk's hogger gave her an emergency application. She lost her decisive gait as brake shoes clamped and jets of fire licked at the wheels.

He cut across the yard inside the curve of the main line. The Hawk's rear end squalled by before he reached the station platform. In the wedge of her headlight, Nine moved on Spur Three, her taillight winking solemnly in the glare. You couldn't tell, till the Hawk's engine had howled past that bleary marker, whether she would clear. It was that tight.

Train and enginemen of the two schedules were brawling at one another by the spur switch when Eddie drew near. They were trying to place the blame for that close one.

A rugged figure came off the rear end of Nine, and O'Conner erupted into the altercation and doubled its clamor. The dispute flared as the Old Man dug for cause and effect. Watches were compared and events reviewed. The Hawk's engineer reported the lantern that had hopped in through the glass of his cab's front window and hung up on the Johnson bar. He told it defiantly as if he doubted it would be believed.

The reason Nine had used Spur Three was kicked about. The two-legged order was hauled out and disputed. The Hawk hadn't received it at Ledge River. The dis-

patcher had failed to telephone it to the station. The
Hawk's hogger had no instructions to run forty minutes
late. An ominous silence fell.

Red and green switch lights blinked and goggled in
the dismayed quiet. The safety on the Hawk's engine lifted
and tossed a plume of steam as she popped. The men were
still, vague shapes in the dim light of lanterns and the
flicker of enginemen's torches. They braced themselves
against the menacing hush, waiting for the Old Man to
blast. The two trains crouched in the restless shadows.

O'Conner walked slowly toward Eddie. He studied the
boomer as if his Celtic soul were disturbed by elfin fancies.
"Warnin's and prophecies come from you like an oracle,"
the Old Man brooded. "I wonder can you now foretell
what is about to happen to you?"

You could mark the rising pressure as if you watched
it on a steam gage. Trainmen's brass insignia winked in the
trailing glow. Eyes glinted from the smudged faces of
enginemen.

Old-timers would jeer at talk of the gods of the high
iron. But some potent, omnipresent energy sure arranged
your wayside stops to suit its purposes. When that design
had been achieved, it released its restraint and let you drift
again. O'Conner felt it now and was troubled.

The tension ebbed away as Eddie considered how this
willful affair had worked out. Then his mind moved ahead
on the careless road with clear precision. He caught the
racket of the loggers' furious little saddle-tank locomotives
huffing importantly as they twisted through the spotted
sunshine, with their lines of log-loaded flat cars snaking
out behind on insecure tracks laid on top of the ground.
The smell of sawdust and the high whine of great saws
and the placid blue of the sound far below.

"Figure it this way," he offered: "The score adds up

to about even, counting that I objected to the way the section foreman anchored his push car. If he'd done it better, I'd never've made it in time to check the Hawk."

O'Conner pondered. "I have not enjoyed my job so much since I was a foreman in the old construction days," he said plaintively. " 'Twas in my mind to give you a quiet telegraph job, one that would little interfere with your readin' of that book. But now I know the two of us cannot work on the same division. 'Twould disorganize it badly, and there would be little traffic moved. Which leaves me no choice but to fire you, much as it grieves the heart of me."

"I will agree to that," Eddie agreed cheerfully. "But I did shade you a little in the final total. I ran this job that you thought I would fall down on. And for that you owe me something."

"Name it," said O'Conner promptly, "and 'twill be yours."

"A pass to Seattle," said Eddie, "and your blessing."

" 'Tis a shame," the Old Man brooded sadly, "that I cannot do more."

XXII

THE SMOOTH, muffled sound of heavy Pullman trucks gliding swiftly under him, and the clean smell of fine linen sheets, edged into his dawning consciousness. The light woolen blanket nestled softly to his cheek. There was the unaccustomed air of subdued luxury and rich, quiet orderliness and the sense of calculated speed.

Drowsy thoughts began to float through his mind as he lay in the snug berth. There were compensations for winning to the higher places in big railroad management. You slept warm and soft, and you ate regularly of good foods. When you toured you merely ordered your private car tied onto the rear end of a hotshot passenger train, and traveled with all the comforts of home. Servants to make life easy, clerks to attend to the details of your job. The way he felt now, he could lie here and dream out the whole career.

The rich smell of coffee drifted through the car and pulled his mind awake. He grinned and opened his eyes. Anything was likely to happen to you when you associated with Walley Sterling. This couldn't occur any place else in the world. A boomer brass pounder riding in a vice-president's private car, sleeping soft and eating rich.

His thoughts darkened. His luck was, as usual, spotted. He had been happy and contented for a long period up there in the Northwest, where Walley had joined him;

Walley working alongside part of the time, and within visiting distance the remainder.

For once the big, amiable cyclone had been serene. The universe was for the moment entirely in tune with him. He was in a philosophical mood, subdued and lazy. The cheerful pagan hadn't even seriously tried to break Eddie in two in their wrestling bouts. It was one of those times when he retired into benign lethargy, storing up energy for his next furious venture into some physical and mental extravagance. He worked his easy trick, and then lounged in the sun and considered mining propositions brought him by slick promotors and shaggy prospectors. The sublime way he handled these interviews gave you the startled feeling that Walley might even pull a fortune out of some forlorn mining enterprise. There wasn't any limit to what he could do when he put his mind and energies to it.

The letter had taken thirty days to catch up with Eddie. The envelope was scarred with reforwardings. There was no return upon it, and the thing had originally been addressed on a typewriter, yet he knew before he opened it that it was from Peck Frim. Peck managed a typewriter much the same as he did a telegraph key—emphatically. He batted it with heavy blows of his strong fingers, and the resultant imprint was like blurred engraving, where the letters didn't cut through the paper altogether.

The warm surge of thoughts which the feel of it had brought was a little mixed. That big, lumbering oaf was the honest salt of the earth, a boy to take along. Still, his mind moved on to Janet at once. It was a hell of a long while to remember one kiss, and the glow of moonlight that got tangled in her hair. But he was aware that the incident had haunted him quietly all along the way he'd come since then. It was one of those incidents you picked

up on the careless road and couldn't leave behind. The
moon could sure soften you up.

He didn't want to open the letter. Yet his fingers slid
quickly under the flap. Likely the type on the machine
hadn't been cleaned since the ancient typewriter had been
sold to the railroad. The paper was raised in blisters around
the indentations that Peck's pounding had produced.

"Eddie, there's been a lot of changes on the old Sod
Line since you've been gone," Peck had slammed out.
"But in some ways it seems just yesterday you were here.
We've got a lot of big new motive power, they've length-
ened the division because the engines can go farther and
faster, and there's been a good many changes in the per-
sonnel besides. Some improvements, and some that aren't.
You'd hardly know the place."

Peck was trying to be offhand and was sweating over
it. The furrows in the paper dug deeper.

"I seem to get along about the same. Sometimes I do,
and then again I don't. Janet worries when I get in a little
jam, and that panics me some. But you'll remember I went
off the old chump pretty easy back yonder."

His probing thoughts slowed and focused. It felt like
a thin jet of cold air had whistled through his brain.

"You know," Peck plowed on, "letter-writing don't
come easy to me, so consider this as a long epistle. You can
guess what the rest of it would be. We would like to hear
from you, or maybe you could stop over when you are
going through. Janet has been dinging at me to write, but
I keep telling her you would sure look us up if you came
this way."

He'd held the letter tight in his fingers and stared out
of the upper story window of the yard office. The saw-
mill's stack smoked stolidly in the center of acres of neat,
high piles of lumber. A little saddle-tanker snorted out of

sight among the symmetrical heaps. The main line curved around the mill property like a steel belt. The low sun made a gun-metal sheen on the river.

There were actually hard strata of ferocity deep inside him. He'd felt a cold fury that tasted like brine on the back of his tongue. Good guys, honest and simple, couldn't get by without somebody knifing them, just because it was easy. And that wasn't the half of it. This time, it reached beyond Peck to Janet. They were in trouble, and Peck was asking for help, whether he realized it or not.

He'd have to take the road back again. Maybe he would always be bound in some way to that dull, limitless land of his birth. Likely the gods of the high iron, who were jealous gods, must chastise your wayward spirit just so often.

Even in a state of suspension, Walley could exert a bland and decisive influence upon events. He probably gaged Eddie's plight without its being expressed. And by divination he'd learned, or sensed, that the private car of one of the railroad's vice-presidents was held up there in the yard for repairs. It was dead-heading to St. Paul from Seattle, and in charge of the V. P.'s secretary and a chef and a porter. Next, Walley found that he had known the secretary in some previous existence, and he had genially talked him into letting Eddie ride east with him, when the car was again in repair, as far as Fargo, North Dakota. That hadn't been difficult for Walley.

Corless, the vice-president's secretary, was at the breakfast table in the observation section when Eddie came from the dressing room. City newspapers had been put aboard during the night, and a stack of telegrams, handed up at the last station, lay on the white cloth.

Corless was stalky and agreeably assured. He had the endurance to work long hours, and an amused eye that gave the impression he was smiling pleasantly all the while. He knew how to make himself indispensable to the mighty, and with luck he would go on up to a title and perhaps a private car of his own. He wasn't obliging just from good nature. He had an eye always to the main chance. Walley certainly must have had something on this smart boy to induce him to take Eddie along. But he was cheerful about it. He would always make the best of any situation. A valuable trait.

Corless chatted briskly of the news and the stock market. He dug into the telegrams and his observations became pungent with criticism of high officials and low.

He wasn't awfully well grounded in traffic and train operation. You could tell that from his lively remarks. Eddie considered dispassionately that he himself was better trained, sounder, than this young fellow who was going up in the railroad game. Mostly what Corless had to carry him along was a hard geniality and a sustained hustle. He put on a good show of efficiency.

Eddie thought of that soberly in the atmosphere of that luxurious private car. The careless road was just a pleasant phantom trail you followed, but it took you to no particular goal. You were at liberty to shrug off the entire situation when a place and its people oppressed you. And that made you intolerant of a number of things you likely ought to learn to endure, for the good of your soul. With that restraint and a dogged determination to keep on plugging at any task, you might climb to an agreeable place of affluence and authority, with a fine apartment and a private car for your delight.

Shadowy thoughts of a steadied, resolute existence kept floating through his mind as he abandoned Corless and the private car and drifted southward in smoky coaches through wide prairie country.

The Missouri River was the same old muddy wash, but there had been a good many improvements on the Sod Line. He sensed it in Omaha, and he saw it from the cupola of a caboose headed east. The roadbed was solid and smooth under the clanking trucks, and new block towers reared up along the main line between the old stations. Towns seemed to have grown and multiplied, and the country looked fat and fertile. Maybe it was in comparison to the great blank spaces of the west. Maybe his point of view was changing.

Division headquarters had been moved to another town, and the old chief was gone. The new one was aloof in a private office of his own. That was a novelty. No chief he'd ever known would sit any place but in the room with the operators and dispatchers, where he was instantly available when trouble broke. This one had come from the East, a laconic young man, evidently with a future. He was wary of boomers, but he needed operators. He gave Eddie the choice of three jobs. Eddie learned where Peck was stationed, and chose a trick at an adjoining tower.

XXIII

FROM THE upper story of Hobart Tower, Eddie regarded the rolling countryside, green and peaceful in the dying sunlight. The tower was planted in the deep country, but the works of man crowded in all about. Farm buildings and live stock were all over the landscape. He wasn't sure, but that it seemed comfortable and companionable after the lonely desert stretches and the grim mountains that bounced the echoes from the big Malley's for a hundred miles.

Busy double tracks cut a gash through the amiable contours of the land. He had an order board, a passing track whose switches he could throw from the tower, and a crossover from one main line to the other, all manual.

His first concern was with the dispatcher. You had to try to get along with the trick man. He listened to his clattering send. There was something familiar in his little overdone mannerisms.

"He thinks," Eddie decided, "that he is a fine and efficient fellow." He cocked a dubious ear. The sounder rasped like an irritated rusty file, harsh and arbitrary. He frowned. Then the sounder spat the Hobart Tower call, and he answered slow and placid.

"Has extra west showed yet?" the dispatcher pecked at him.

He felt a cold sprinkle on his back. "That's Curt Halman," he informed himself, "or his ghost. And I thought they'd fired him for good for overlooking that light engine." He opened his key. "Not a single sign up to now," he drawled his answer with exaggerated calm.

"Listen!" Curt Halman blazed back impatiently. "You must be new here. Get this: you answer me brief and accurate. When I order you to do a thing, don't hesitate or make remarks. I won't tell you again."

He knew now why he had hurried back here to the prairie country.

"Just like it was yesterday," he sent serenely. "It's the same old delirious Curt."

The circuit snapped open, and then there was a cautious pause. It picked up words with bewildered incredulity. "Who—are—you?"

"Your old friend and fellow confederate, Eddie Sand," he chanted.

The next pause lengthened to thirty seconds. "Okay," Curt said slowly at last. "Things are different here now. The incompetents are gone, or on the way out. There won't be any more trouble like there was with the hams when you were here before. You'll have to keep lined up, or you won't last."

He thought of the brisk, laconic young chief alone in his private office. Curt would fit that young official's specifications for a trick man very well.

"Yeah," he sent. "You told me that before."

His immediate problem was to find food and lodging for the duration of his stay. There wasn't such a spot in sight, unless you considered the farmhouses squatted under the bright green trees. He studied these with considerable interest.

"I'll not be surprised if they grow chickens specially to eat," he confided to himself hopefully, "and cook them as is proper and succulent for provender. Let's see if Peck can't give us aid and comfort."

He called Malin Tower, where he'd been told Peck held the second trick, and presently the old familiar trampling send answered him. He grinned with delight at the sound of that awkward clatter, and then he sent blandly, "I've just come onto the second trick at Hobart, and I need a place to reside."

Peck made some diffident I's while he pondered. Then he pounded out, "I've got a place you could stay, but my wife thinks people ought to be clean. Some boomers ain't."

The word was out that a new drifter had come to Hobart, but apparently his name wasn't yet known to Peck. Some tramp telegraphers must have been working the division recently, and their habits and conduct hadn't been good.

"Can your wife cook?" he inquired.

"And how!" Peck exploded with enthusiasm. "She has to, and lots of it. I grew big and it takes victuals to keep me in working order."

"Tell you what," Eddie offered. "We'll look each other over, and if I stand the missus' inspection, and the grub is half what you claim, we'll make a deal. How far do I have to walk?"

" 'Bout two miles. It helps you relish the cooking. I have to walk four miles each way to work."

It wasn't unusual for station men with families to board the floating bachelors, but he hadn't counted on moving in with Janet and Peck. He'd planned to maneuver from a refuge of his own. The capricous influence that seemed to be handling the incidental arrangements was leading him irresistibly up to a certain point. Then it would likely desert him.

Rail traffic was booming. At that end of the division

a steady stream of coal trains swung onto the main line from a branch. Short hotshot freights swooped by and chased the longer, slower merchandise trains into passing tracks to let them by. All classes of passenger trains clamored for the block and blasted the freights out of their way. A busy spot, but you didn't have anything else to do except keep the trains from tangling. He decided cautiously that for a change it was more agreeable than a lonely night trick in the far west.

As he worked through that first evening and on toward midnight, he quietly inquired into the recent past of Curt Halman. He got the record from crews who paused at Hobart Tower, and from cryptic conversations with other operators on the message wire.

Curt had somehow crawled back into service when a new set of officials had taken over the division, and he was really going up this time. He'd somewhat subdued his old trick of cutting corners, but it still cropped up when the going got congested; and any one that gummed his smart handling of traffic was sure in trouble. He's taken some scalps. The new brass hats seemed to think a lot of his judgment. Specially the young chief, who in turn was supposed to be close to the Old Man. Curt seemed to think that everybody out there on the line conspired to slow down train movements, to outwit him. You still couldn't argue with him, or ask questions. He had a special dislike for boomers. He put the skids under them at the bat of an eye. Eddie grinned at that. He could understand Curt's bitter regard for the drifters.

At midnight, on instructions from Peck, he hiked east along the right-of-way to the next road crossing, and waited. Presently down the main line a gangling figure ambled forth in the moonlight and an amiable bellow shook the night as it approached.

"Hyia!" it said. "My name's Peck Frim, and I'm mighty glad to meet you. I didn't catch your name. Here, let me have that suitcase."

You'd as well have tried to resist a Mallet. He tucked Eddie's luggage under his arm as if it were a folded newspaper.

"Look," said Eddie, "I didn't contract for porter's service along with my lodgings."

Peck stopped and peered. The suitcase slid from under his arm. "Eddie," he said, and stopped. Then, "Janet said you'd come."

It was as easy as that for Peck to let go his troubles. You could feel them ooze out of him. He got his senses gathered together at once and picked up the suitcase. He chatted like a guileless calliope as they tramped down the country road in the quiet of the night. He didn't answer questions. He just blew off steam.

The countryside slumbered. One dim square of light advanced out of tree shadows. A gable of an old two-story house was wedged into the foliage. There was a picket fence, vivid white in the moonlight. Peck broke open the front door with an abrupt explosion. He said, "Hey, Janet! Look what I found," with a gusto that fluttered the shingles.

"Bring it in," came the cheerful invitation from the rear of the house, and Eddie's heart throbbed in blunt, hard beats.

"Does she stay up for you?" he marveled in a hushed voice.

"Stays up, or gets up," Peck said. "It's a big job— keeping me nourished."

An oil lamp beamed benignly on a flowered table cloth in the big old kitchen. Janet had arranged dishes of food under the shaded glow. The light got tangled in her hair,

the way he remembered. She turned as Peck clumped into
the room. He kissed her with the sound of a parted air
hose, and stood aside.

The big gray-green eyes reached for Eddie and hovered
there. A warm glow lit in some depths behind them. She
smiled quietly, and the freckles on her nose jigged. She
stood there quite still in the mellow lamplight for him to
see. She was going to have a baby.

He blinked once as if a beam of light had struck him.
Then his mind swung back to cold clarity. The gods of the
high iron had now assembled the elements of this tangled
encounter. The coincidents had all occurred, and the affair
was now in his lap. It wasn't surmise or superstitious belief. It was a fact of natural phenomenon, the same as the
sun rising at its appointed time in the morning, after a
dark night.

"I've got the second trick at Hobart Tower," he said
from the back of his mind, "and Peck allowed if I passed
his wife's inspection as to cleanliness, you might house
me for a while."

"It's just going to work out fine," she glowed. "Even
better than I thought."

His eye wandered to the table, and he stared. A stack
of quarter-inch thick slices of very likely ham showed
richly on a platter. A great loaf of bread and about two
pounds of butter adjoined. There were at least three
pounds of cheese and a pitcher of milk. A plume of steam
blossomed from the coffee pot on the stove.

"You expecting a lot of company at this time of
night?" he asked blankly.

"Oh, that," she laughed. "It's just Peck's midnight
snack. There is plenty more in the cupboard."

Nobody was abashed. It was as native as walking into
your own home—if you had a home. These two had taken

him into their lives. No matter for how long or to what distances he wandered, he would be a part of their existence.

The big kitchen glowed with paint, bright-colored, a cheerful room for brimming, happy life. There was no evidence of distress here. He wondered what it was that had pulled him across half a continent.

Peck stoked and commented obscurely with his mouth full. Little puckers of worry straightened out of his brow. He beamed on Eddie and waggled. Janet passed food and encouraged Eddie to gorge. She smiled parentally, like a mother pleased at the return of a wayward favorite son. It was a little dazzling to a drifter whose abode was usually a bleak room in the station living quarters, or a dingy chamber in a boarding house.

This could grow on a man. He ate and admired Peck's capacity for food. He was at home here in this bright room with these enduring kids. He got the definite feeling that he had come a long, wandering way to find this serenity. The careless boomer trail faded out behind in trailing mists. He let the placid life submerge him. It almost seemed there in the stillness of early morning as if he had come to the end of his wanderings.

They gave him a big, high-ceiling room upstairs. It smelled of starched linens and scented soap. The bed barely interrupted his plunge into slumber. A thought trailed him into the soft oblivion: Whatever else was troubling Peck and Janet, it wasn't malnutrition.

XXIV

THE EARLY sun and the sound of a great voice awoke him. He peered sleepily through the curtained window. Peck, carrying a pail of milk, was urging a little Jersey cow through a gate into a fenced square of clover. The placid beast moved deliberately in spite of the giant's stormy pleadings to hurry. There was a neat barn and shed and chicken runs with snowball fluffs of feathers clucking therein. A huge sow with her litter of pigs crunched and grunted in a pen. A truck garden adjoined, and beside it a patch of bright green corn. All the structures were in repair and newly painted.

Peck turned toward the barn while Eddie goggled. He came out at once, leading a fat mare, harnessed, and attached her to a cultivator. The two began moving up and down the rows in the truck garden.

Eddie sighed and relaxed. Evidently, one job wasn't enough for the vast energy of that ramshackle lad. He'd deserted the farm to become a railroader, and now he was spradling the issue by doing both. He gave it up and went back to bed. The details would work to the surface shortly and he'd understand the situation better. Meanwhile, it wasn't yet six o'clock. He went back to sleep.

When he went down stairs, Janet quickly fetched him bacon and eggs and spuds and hot cakes.

"Look," he pleaded. "You measure out my food in

ratio of exactly one-eighth of what you feed that man of
yours."

Peck's voice, lifted in raucous song, floated in through
the open windows as he followed the brown mare back
and forth across the garden. Janet turned to watch him,
and Eddie caught a sudden mist in her eyes.

"He is so happy you are here," she said. "It's the first
time he has sung for a long while."

"Call that singing?" he muttered.

She giggled. "Whatever it is, it's good to hear."

"Quite a plant you have," he suggested.

"You didn't expect to find us in this kind of a situation,
did you?" she asked.

"Lady," he rebuked her, "I just never expect anything
till it comes along and happens."

She smiled at him with that paternal understanding.
She wasn't any longer a girl, fumbling at life. She was a
woman who had come to grips with existence. She was
fighting.

"You are always the man in the tower," she said.
"What ever comes in sight, you make a note of it. The
rest isn't any of your concern—till it's brought to your
attention."

"Sure," he admitted, "and I have a tough time getting
along with my own immediate surroundings, without taking in more territory."

"But you came a long way to us," she suggested softly.

"Just passing through," he said.

"Peck has had a time of it." Sunlight, flooding
through the windows, got tangled in her hair. "His
mother was in the hospital for a long while, and then his
father. They both died there. You know, it was like one
of those endless nightmares to him. Afterward, when he

sold the farm, and had paid all the bills and notes, there was just enough left to buy an equity in this little place."

He looked at her reproachfully. "How come nobody wrote me about that?" he asked.

"I was the only one who could do anything for him then," she said. "He just had to grow out of it."

Peck would take the loss of the old folks pretty hard. She must have had a time keeping him sane.

"Then there was a shake-up on the Sod Line, and Curt Halman got back in the dispatchers' office." She looked at him steadily.

"Yeah," he nodded. "I talked to him on the wire."

"He hasn't changed for the better." She wasn't bitter about it. She was just putting up a fight. "Peck was getting along all right in the jobs he bid in, till Curt came back. Peck isn't a brilliant railroader, but he is a good worker and dependable, and people like him. Curt throws him all off, as he used to when Peck was a student. Curt harasses him on purpose. He would have had Peck fired long before this if it hadn't been for me."

Eddie stared into his coffee cup.

"Curt has been trying to take me away from Peck," she said simply.

He couldn't see the bottom of the coffee cup. A red mist slid into the bright morning air, and there was a rumbling in his ears like he'd taken too much quinine.

"That is the reason I decided to have a baby just when I did," she added, "when we really couldn't afford it." The red mist moved out beyond the open windows. "I thought perhaps it would show Curt exactly how I felt, and maybe arouse some latent manhood in him."

He'd tightened up inside till it hurt. He moved in his chair to loosen up.

"You see, Eddie," she said, "with Peck's railroad pay,

and this little place, we can build and raise a family, and amount to something. He isn't the brightest man in the world, but he is the best. This way, we can pay off what we owe and make something of life. He can do that if he isn't imposed upon." She smiled proudly. "This place was all run down and dilapidated when we got it. And look at it now."

Peck's voice swirled exuberantly through the kitchen. The red mist melted slowly in the sunlight. He considered clearly all the harsh elements that would be arrayed against these two in their struggle for security and happiness. He firmly subdued the cold fury that tried to stampede him. He'd have to keep his mind clear and alert.

"Curt went crazy when he found I was going to have the baby," she said. "He will get Peck's job the first chance he has. He told me so." She nodded earnestly. "That is why I sent for you." She smiled with complete satisfaction. "But don't tell Peck," she warned. "He would pull Curt apart like a fly, if he knew what I have told you."

He took hold of his thoughts and turned them around. She was fighting hard and clear-headed. That was the way to tackle your troubles.

"Peck would make a messy job of Curt," he admitted. "I could do it much cleaner." He tried to grin. "But nobody has to worry about that. Curt isn't smart. We showed him once that he wasn't, didn't we?"

"Yes," she said. "You did."

XXV

THE SUN slid down to the low, tree-feathered horizon and the sky glowed with soft shades. Up here in the tower you dominated all the landscape, while in the mountains there was usually higher country all about, and you felt insignificant wherever you were. The sunlight here was milder, too, and it didn't break out in violent colors like it did when it went out over the high peaks. The green of pastures and fields was maybe more alluring. Up there in the altitudes it was dark and somber, except when the aspens caught fire with the first frost.

Three coal trains scrambled by. He had to check the last one to hold it to its proper interval from the one ahead. A through passenger swooped out of the west, a dusty green streak in an aura of sharp, thin smoke.

Curt Halman, in his usual tearing hurry, was nagging Peck again. Curt had recorded Peck's O. S. of an extra west as by at 5 :47 instead of 5 :37, the time the train had actually past Malin, and he had made dispositions computed on his own error. This had disrupted his lineup and caused a delay that would show up in the 8 :00 A. M. report.

There was some slight similarity in the figures three and four in the Morse code. Peck's send was deliberate. Curt, Eddie reckoned, had impatiently jumped to a conclusion before Peck had completed his report, and had jotted

the time on his train sheet as he thought it should be, not
the way it was sent.

Curt scolded in an angry clatter. "It's just another in-
stance of your stupidity. You seem to get worse instead
of better. I'll have to turn this in."

"I've got it down on my block sheet as 5:37," Peck
insisted anxiously. "I'm certain I O. S.'d it that way."

Eddie glanced at his own block sheet and cut in: "I
took the time when Peck reported it to you," he told Curt,
"and I've got it on my sheet as 5:37."

Curt blasted. "Listen, boomer! I've told you before I
didn't want anything out of you but what I asked for.
Maybe you think Frim will be easier on your board bill if
you back up his alibies. Now you line up, or I'll line you
out."

Maybe that didn't help Peck any. But it showed Curt
that Eddie was keeping a constant eye on him. It might
make him slow up.

Up here in the secluded tower your speculations flowed
in and out of the traffic. Those two kids were making a
gallant effort to maintain that neat homestead. They were
putting into the building of a home, and a competence, all
their skill and cheerful effort. The thing they'd have to
guard against was the same that most honest and indus-
trious folk watch—the guy who thought he was a genius,
with opposing ideas in his mind.

A man wasn't competent to judge a woman's intents
and purposes. That wheeze was likely as ancient as the one
about "the good old days." Janet was going to have a baby
on the theory that it would make Curt ashamed of himself
. . . The telegraph sounder babbled its record of fleeting
time . . . It gave you the equivocal feeling that her logic
was faulty, but she might be right. But he didn't think so
. . . An amiable local passenger cleared the block and

rambled into the dying sunset . . . Curt sure liked to tamper with dynamite. When a woman decided to have a child, you interfered in no way, unless you were prepared for disagreeable consequences to yourself.

Daylight faded slowly. Extra 2727, a long coal train, lumbered into the Malin block at 7:32. Close behind it came an impatient hotshot freight, Extra 1618. It would take the coal train ten minutes to clear the Hobart Tower, while the hotshot behind it would do the same in hardly more than half the time. Curt was fussing about it. He'd planned that the Extra 2727 should make Toban, beyond Hobart, to let the hotshot by, and he was trying to make that stick. He lined Eddie and Peck up sharply as Peck reported the coal train by his tower.

"Clear the 2727 the second she's by you," he snapped at Eddie. And then to Peck: "Let me know when Extra 1618 shows."

The hogger of the 2727 had his train swinging along nicely coming down the grade approaching Hobart. Eddie leaned out of the tower window and watched her smoke boil up from the cuts. She swung into sight and called for the board.

"Coming," Eddie reported to Curt, and an instant later, "Coming," Peck reported Extra 1618.

This was going to be tight, to clear the block without checking the hotshot. Curt was tieing himself in knots.

He watched the line of loaded coal cars rolling and swaying by beneath.

"He's asking for the board a second time," Peck stamped out.

The coal train wouldn't clear in time. The hotshot would have to stop at Malin, and then start up again against the hill.

Curt held his key open indecisively.

"How near is he by you now?" he asked, and Eddie told him, "About half by."

By the rules, the hotshot was stabbed for a stop at Malin. But Curt decided against that. He flung at Peck, "Give Extra 1618 the board. Clear him at 7:43, and Hobart you clear Extra 2727 at the same time."

Curt was cutting another corner. He was sending the hotshot into a block that wasn't absolutely clear, and asking the operators to fake the time to keep the records straight.

He glanced at the clock. "A lot can happen in sixty seconds," he reflected, "but who am I that hesitates to lie for an atom of time, when I've stretched the truth all out of shape without regret? All the same, that's not operations as prescribed."

The faint scent of dust rolled up from the clucking wheels below. The train checked slightly as the engine hit the upgrade out of town. The cars mumbled attentively, the gear clanking.

"Then," Eddie advised himself, "on the one-hundredth-and-oneth time, something goes blooey, right in your face, and you're in a jam."

The abrupt explosion of compressed air rattled the tower windows. Brake shoes grabbed with a savage roar. Wrenched drawbars grunted. Spurts of fire licked out of the grinding wheels. The coal train writhed and howled to a stop. Five cars and the caboose hadn't yet cleared the east end of the passing track.

"And this is that time it didn't work," he remarked. He opened the key and flashed to the dispatcher, "Extra 2727 broke an air hose, and she's stopped dead with her hind end still in the yard."

Curt wasn't quick to get that. He hesitated for six valuable seconds. Then he called Peck.

"Is Extra 1618 by you yet?"

"Caboose right here," Peck slammed back.

Curt faltered. He couldn't quite keep up with the exploding events. Eddie estimated calmly that he delayed for just the margin of time that allowed the 1618 to get away from him. Then he woke up.

"Stop him!" he clamored at Peck. "Get out there and stop him!"

Not a chance, Eddie decided. There were dragging seconds of silence, and then Peck came back on the wire.

"I couldn't get him," he sent raggedly. "He was fading out around the first curve and didn't see my washout."

"Not at all competent," Eddie considered. He leaned out of the window and glanced along the stalled freight train.

The head brakeman had come back along the train and paused where the air hose had broken. The conductor was hurrying forward. The rear brakeman came down from the caboose with a spare hose. It was the time of day when you couldn't see with a lantern, or without one. Theirs made swaying dots in the light velvet dusk.

"Hey!" Eddie yelled at the rear brakeman. "Get you a couple of fusees and ramble back there and protect your hind end. Go away back."

The brakeman glanced up at him and plodded on toward the head end.

"We don't herd 'em around careless, like you're used to out in the wide open spaces," he called back genially. "We got a block system here that protects us. It's them levers you've been working. Hadn't you noticed them?"

That hotshot would make it from Malin to Hobart within six minutes. She would be spilling out of the cuts right on top of the stalled coal train in not very many flying seconds from now.

Curt was clamoring Eddie's call wildly, but he paid him no heed.

"Hey, wait!" he yelled at the brakeman. "The dispatcher let one of those bob-tails into the block before you cleared me. He's on his way, and coming fast. You get back there and stop him, or he'll be into your kitchen door and half way up to the engine. I mean *run*."

"What you talkin' about?" the brakeman demanded. "He ain't allowed to do that."

"Just for the hell of it," Eddie assured him, "you'd better believe he did. It looks like the flicker of his headlight just over the hill. Get out and gallop!"

A faint moan drifted gently into the evening quiet. It hit the brakeman like a club. He dropped the hose and dived into his caboose. He came out running. His lantern streaked up the main line like a scared rocket. That stinger was a good sprinter. And he'd figured a fusee would show up better than a lantern in that uncertain light.

The headlight of the hotshot made a dim glow in the last cut, and then she twisted into the straightaway. The hogger was wheeling her. The long seconds pounded deliberately as he roared at the dot of light streaking toward him. Then the flare of a fusee bloomed in a red warning. The engineer blasted a brief acknowledgment to the thin, expanding glow.

That hogger could juggle the air. He let off just so many pounds, a quick and accurate application that checked her smoothly and then took hold with a stubborn grip.

Eddie nodded approval and turned back to his key and broke in on Curt.

"Yeah," he sent calmly, "Extra 2727's got his flag out, and it looks like the 1618 is going to get himself stopped before they kiss."

Curt held his key open and made no reply for sixty seconds. Then he turned irritably to straightening out the tangle.

Eddie called him just before he went off duty at midnight. "It's all right with me the report you make, just so you don't try to blame Peck," he sent. "I might have to go higher up if you did that."

Curt sent furiously, "You'd better pipe down, boomer. I could make it tough for you ever to get another job on any railroad."

"Yeah, but take it easy," Eddie warned.

Peck was anxious when he met him at the crossing on their way home.

"Think he'll try to hang that one on me??' he asked.

"Look," Eddie invited. "There just isn't any telling what that monkey will do. But he ought to be cunning enough not to try it. However," he instructed, "if any investigation is made, don't answer any letters till I tell you what to say."

"I won't," Peck promised.

XXVI

A LITTLE uneasily he began to wonder if the careless road could compensate for the comforts of home. He seemed as firmly fixed in the Frim household as any member, present or expected. There wasn't a thought in the head of either of them that they withheld from him. Sometimes he sweated over a hoe, or managed a paint brush, or helped Janet with minor household chores. And liked it all. He even protested against Peck's violent eye in the selection of colors on his paint jobs.

"You seem," he pointed out, "to like'em mighty bright."

"I guess," Peck finally admitted, "it is a little gaudy. But that's the way I like it."

You couldn't attempt to modify Peck's tastes after that.

You forgot that domesticity was a trap, that possessions hampered your mobility, and that permanent human ties delayed your abrupt decisions to migrate by discussion and compromise.

Janet's time drew near, and Peck became helpless in his anxiety. Amused at first, Eddie began to feel the tension of the coming crisis. At the last, he was nearly as wrought up as Peck. When the night came, the chief dispatcher didn't have anyone to relieve Peck of his trick, so Eddie arranged with the third trick man at Marlin to work in Peck's place, and he rode to Malin on a freight, after his tour at Hobart, and worked the third trick.

When he arrived home in the morning, Peck was white and shattered—and grinning.

"It's a boy!" he raved, nearly wringing Eddie's hand off. "And listen," he shouted, "we're going to name him Eddie. Janet says so."

He tried to make Peck take some rest that day, but the ramshackle wreck couldn't compose himself. He offered to work in his place, but Peck wouldn't have that. They went off together in the afternoon, and Eddie warned him to cut in his head.

"You've got an infant now," he pointed out, "besides everything else you possess. Keep your feet on the ground and your mind on your work. You get in trouble easy when you're not thinking."

He wasn't unshaken himself. He had to force himself to rigid forethought as he took over his trick, checking the train orders carefully, impressing the lineup of traffic on his mind as he caught it from the sounder.

Operators came on the wire to congratulate Peck, to remark broadly. Peck was still in a high state, and the ribbing apparently exhilarated him still more. Eddie frowned.

Curt called.

"I hear there's a new baby at Peck's house," he sent. He almost made the sounder sneer. He slurred the signals, as if there was something nasty in his mind.

"Yeah," Eddie answered him cheerfully. "A fine boy."

"Does it look like Peck?" Curt jeered. You could feel the venom flowing through the circuit.

Something wound up inside of him. It would be a very inviting job to break Curt in two. But you had to be smart when events got tangled.

"You know how it is with babies," he said smoothly.

"They don't look like much of anybody at first. They've got to grow into their resemblances."

"That one will never grow into anything that looks like Peck." Curt's hand on the key was going out of control. He was trying to make the words suggestive. "I'll be out to look it over."

"If I were you," Eddie drawled, "I wouldn't. Remember I said so."

Curt made a derisive clatter and turned to prodding the traffic viciously.

Eddie eyed the sounder malevolently. And for one of the few times in his life he knew how fear could claw.

Stubble fields made brown squares among the faded green pastures. The country smells had a sharper tinge.

A mixed freight on the passing track below gave a strangled toot. He leaned out of the window. The train had been tied up there since early afternoon with an engine failure. A machinist had come down from the shops and had been tinkering with the locomotive. The conductor now stood below.

"Hey, my friend," he called up politely, "How's to slip us the block? That nut-splitter says he's got this hunk of scrap iron all cobbled up to the extent we can now shove along. Any chance to let us ramble?"

"So far as I know," Eddie told him, and turned to the wire to tell the dispatcher.

Curt was still on fire, fighting and prodding, and when Eddie tried to interrupt him, Curt snapped back, "Keep off this wire. Can't you see I'm loaded up?"

He cut in again a minute later, trying to explain that the train was ready to move, but Curt blasted him off the wire again.

He called down to the conductor, "Curt's burning'em

up and I can't bust in on him. Didn't he annul your running orders when your engine died?"

"He did not," the conductor reported. "We're still in circulation and ready to move. To hell with'um. Give us the block and we'll be on our way. If we wait for that hot potato we'll be here till the hog law gets us."

Eddie checked cautiously, but he found no reason for not giving the extra the block. Curt would likely wake up and rave at him when he finally took a report of her. However, the running orders were still in effect, in which case Eddie's only duty was to see that he was expedited.

He called Peck at Malin on the message wire, and got the block. He cleared the freight.

"Thank you kindly, sir," the conductor bowed. "It's been swell knowing you. Come and see us any time you're in town."

He watched the train snake out of the siding and wind slowly away through the cuts in the fading sunlight. Curt was still on the prod, and he sat with his hand on the key, ready to report the extra the instant the dispatcher would take it. Then a freight conductor called him on the telephone from an industry siding a mile to the east. The train-man dictated an order for empty cars, and he reported two bad orders that the car-tink would have to fix up before they could be moved.

The conductor was shouting over the inadequate old telephone to make himself heard; and then Eddie had to interrupt him to give Peck the block for a westbound coal train. It was one of those jumbled situations in which you had to be alert to several operations at the same time. With his ear to the telephone receiver, straining to catch the trainman's indistinct words, a dim section of his mind registered what was going forward on the dispatcher's wire.

When the conductor had finished, he turned back to the telegraph table; and then the order that had slipped faintly into his consciousness while he was on the phone began to form into a brief, clear sentence as he heard Curt snap, "Complete at Malin at 6:47 P. M." and then the query, "Is he coming?"

Peck answered him, "Right here. I'll have to run."

"Get down there and highball him through," Curt clattered.

The import of the order was clear now, and Eddie's hand pounced on the key.

Curt's mind sure ran in vicious circles and furious patterns. His ego was on fire tonight, and without proper caution or consideration he'd slipped into that dangerous strategy that had gotten him in trouble before. He was cutting a westbound passenger train over onto the eastbound track, Malin to Toban, to get it around a coal train. Peck now had that order, had set the crossover switch from the tower, and was heading down the stairs to deliver the order on the fly. Both of them were blind to the fact that the freight train, which had been hung up at Hobart Tower, had moved into the block to which Peck was about to divert the storming passenger.

Curt had evidently passed up the delayed freight on his sheet as fixed at Hobart. Peck, in his abnormal state of mind over the advent of his first offspring, and confused by Curt's exasperating rush, had overlooked the fact that he had already given the eastbound block to Eddie.

He made the sounder shout, "Hold it, Peck! Don't deliver that order. Are you there—"

Curt cut in then. "Sign! Sign!" he rapped.

"This is Eddie at Hobart. Peck, hold that—"

Curt blazed, "What in hell are you messing in for again? Now, stay off this wire till I call you. Malin, don't delay Seventy-seven." He began calling another tower, all wound up in his plans and dispositions.

Eddie cut in again crisply, "Hold that order, Peck," before Curt broke in again.

"I'll have a man down there on Eight to relieve you," Curt sent gleefully. "Meanwhile, you be careful how you handle things, because there will be a special agent with him, and the first thing he'll want to know is if you're sober."

Eddie opened the key and held it that way for silent seconds. Peck had either caught and heeded his warning, or he was down the stairs out of hearing, sending Seventy-seven on her way.

"Listen," he sent at last, "if you cut Seventy-seven over, you'll never sit in a dispatcher's chair again." Curt didn't break in. "Peck," he went on calmly, "don't let her by. That extra east that was tied up here is already in the block."

Curt opened his key, then closed it quickly. The quiet extended out over the countryside. The seconds seemed to drip away like retarded drops falling from a height. Twilight deepened.

The circuit broke at last, and the little brass tongue babbled breathlessly as Peck's huge hand banged the key.

"I got you, Eddie. I went down the stairs as far as I could, and still keep my head in the side window to hear you." Peck had cut in his head when operations tightened up. "Just so I'd have a chance to deliver the order if you changed your mind." The words began to stumble. "Seventy-seven's slowing for the board. And I just now saw I overlooked—"

Eddie interrupted Peck's confession of error. You were liable to babble too much about your mistakes immediately after they occurred.

"That's fine, kid," he sent. "Now, take it easy."

He grinned as he thought of Peck's disorderly length dangling down the stairs while he hung to the window ledge, listening to the exploding sounder, set to stop Seventy-seven, or let her go. In that position his big feet would reach nearly to the ground.

He sent to Curt, "I tried to tell you when Extra 2727 East left here, but you wouldn't listen."

"I thought," Curt faltered, "that I'd annulled his running orders when his engine died." He was confessing what he would later try to cover up.

Walking home together at midnight, Peck canvassed the situation gloomily. "I sure booted that one, didn't I? They'll cut my neck off right up under the ears." He reflected darkly. "This'll likely mean we'll lose the farm, 'cause we can't keep up payments without my job." The dust of the road exploded softly under his dejected stride. "Even when you work like hell for it, I guess it's expecting too much to be able to keep all I've got." He was trying to stand up to disaster.

"Look," said Eddie patiently, "this isn't over yet. Keep your pressure down."

"I can't guess what we'll do, or where we'll go," Peck brooded. "So I'd better tell you now that Janet and me— well, look, Eddie: You've done things to us—kind of shown us what a white man really is like." He frowned. "But it seems like it's more than that, too. It don't sound like much," he floundered, "when I say we feel as if you were one of our family." He shook his head impotently. "It's more than that," he said. "We'd both take it kindly if you'd always consider whatever kind of roof we've got over us is yours."

The trouble with associating with people like this was that you were lost without them. They made your heart take root, and when you tore up those roots, they hurt like hell for a long while thereafter.

"I guess," Peck broke up his gloomy thoughts at last, "I ain't smart enough to get along well. That's tough on Janet—and the boy," he added sharply.

"The world," said Eddie, "is full of mistakes. One isn't going to bust things wide open."

"Toughest thing I've got to do now is tell Janet."

"You're not going to tell her yet," Eddie stated flatly.

"But I got to," Peck cried. "It ain't honest if I don't."

"You'll lie to her," Eddie ordered, "and to anybody else, just as long and just as hard as I tell you to. Don't talk to anybody about this, and don't write letters on the subject."

"O. K., Eddie."

XXVII

IT WAS blamed easy to be destructive, plenty hard work to build. Anybody could find an excuse to criticise, to kick things apart. It took a good man to be thrifty, when one little error could wreck a long job of putting together. It wasn't much consolation to consider that the destructive ones often came to a bad end in the course of time.

Eddie examined his own record critically. Maybe it was luck, added to eternal vigilance, that had kept his record pretty clean. He'd tried hard enough, because your mistakes could be costly to a number of other people, perfect strangers. And the hard, close association with that robust breed of railroad men generated a loyalty to the iron highways, like fidelity to your country.

He'd had some brief citations from the seats of the mighty, and that gold watch somewhere in his plunder which Barabe had had engraved and presented to him. He wondered if any of those men in the swivel chairs would remember him now. If they did recall him at all, it would be vaguely and without a sense of obligation. They were busy folk; and besides, the gratitude of kings wasn't to be depended upon, especially after a lapse of time. That would also apply to brass hats.

But he knew somewhere in his system of reflexes that it wasn't exactly like that with them. The brisk encounters in grim operations left deeper than ordinary impressions.

Those men you worked with in the tight moments of minor and major crisis weren't merely ships that passed in the night. Maybe you never saw them again, but some were more potent in their absence than your closest associates of the moment.

Buck Barabe, square-jawed and abrupt and about as direct as a sledge hammer. He'd consider a request for favors quite coldly and from all angles, and then ignore it. Mr. Welby, gray and kindly, would consider it, but probably not seriously enough. Old Salt-and-Molasses Nickerson, with his glinting, prying glasses, had acknowledged in writing that he owed him something. But the president of a railroad under reconstruction had clerks to handle such items. He never saw them. And that blazing Irishman, O'Conner. You couldn't even hazard a guess what he would do—except explode.

It wasn't easy to go back and remind them of services rendered above and beyond the line of duty, and request a little something extra on that account. Asking concessions from brass hats came hard.

The mills that ground out the red tape on the Sod Line mixed the items of that evening of errors and set them forth in written statements, more or less accurate and somewhat vague, and dropped them in a ragged file on Superintendent Nathan's desk. The Old Man studied them, and then penciled a memo to his chief clerk to have all the parties involved present in his office at ten o'clock on the day after tomorrow.

"I've got to tell Janet now," Peck pleaded with Eddie. "She'll know something's wrong because we're called in to headquarters."

"I'll do the lying for you," Eddie promised. "I'll make it that we're going in for examinations."

They were nearly all assembled in the superintendent's

outer office when Eddie and Peck arrived. The rest
straggled in immediately after. Curt Halman came last. He
didn't even give the rest a glance, but stood talking in
private to the chief clerk. You knew he had his story all
neatly arranged, and he would be shrewd and relentless in
putting it over.

The train and enginemen were subdued and cautious.
They hadn't been at fault, the way they looked at it, but
you never could foretell what would come out of one of
these hearings. Peck Frim was through, and that was a
shame. Everybody liked Peck. All of them would give him
the best of it if they could, but with Curt gunning for him
there wasn't a chance. Curt was going to have a time saving his own neck. But he was cute enough. Even Eddie
Sand might be in trouble. He was in the clear by the rules,
but brass hats could twist the regulations into funny
shapes. A new bunch rode the swivel chairs now, and you
couldn't guess what they'd do.

The chief clerk glanced at the clock and got up and
wandered toward the superintendent's private office. "The
Old Man," he said cheerfully, "acts like he'd had barbed
wire and chewing tobacco for breakfast this morning. So
none of you'd better expect anything but the worst of it."

He went in and came out and stood in the doorway.
His wandering eye settled at last on Eddie in a mildly
incredulous stare.

"You're Mr. Sand?" His eyebrows went up whimsically. "Will you please step into Mr. Nathan's office? He'll
be ready for the rest of you in a minute," he added to the
room.

The men stirred uncertainly in their chairs as their
glances swung to Eddie. They were suddenly suspicious.
This boomer out of the West was maybe going to talk out

of turn. He might even be a spotter. They set dicks in like that sometimes. This could develop into something bad.

Eddie walked to the doorway, and the chief clerk stood aside and closed the door behind him.

Superintendent Nathan was gray and sharp-eyed and incisive. He was frowning at some yellow half-sheets on the desk before him. He raised his head slowly at last and probed the boomer with his needle eyes.

"So far as I know," he clipped out his words, "you are in no very serious trouble here, and yet you have asked officials for whom you formerly worked to recommend you to me, as if you were in a terrible fix. Are you into something I don't know about?"

Eddie could feel the dampness in his palms under his tight fingers. He was taking this harder than the hazards you encountered out on the line. At least one of the brass hats had heeded his petition, but you couldn't guess to what extent. Likely some clerk had handled his appeal, and there'd only be mention of the length of his service, and if it was good. That wouldn't give him the edge he needed. It would only appear presumptious to Nathan, make him resentful.

"I asked some of my previous bosses," he said, "to vouch for me so you would consider what I have to say more seriously than a statement I'd make at the hearing."

"What is it you want to say to me?" Nathan demanded. He wasn't amiable.

"It's about young Peck Frim," he dived. "He made one of the mistakes you're investigating today. I'd like to see he gets all the consideration that a good, loyal employe is entitled to." He tried to think out his words carefully. "His wife had their first baby the night before, which apparently was as much of an ordeal for him as for her. The chief couldn't have him relieved for a day or two while he was under that strain, so some of the rest of us operators arranged to take his trick for one night." He watched Nathan covertly. "I'll admit he wasn't quite all there the next night, when we nearly pulled a bad one. But there were contributing incidents that I hope the investigation will bring out." He put his hands in his pocket to keep them from wandering about. "And I'd like to point out that he was quick to catch the mistakes, and to act instantly to rectify them. He pulled us out of that hole."

He didn't seem to be making any impression on that lean, dry countenance. It was about like holding a conversation with yourself. He began to talk faster, because he expected to be interrupted at any moment. Nathan had turned his swivel chair and was staring out of the window.

"I'm just asking that you give the kid some kindly justice—the three of them—that will likely pay you big some day. He's reliable—a good man in any organization. He'll never set any rivers on fire, but he'll be there till the last dog's hung. And he'll remember this mistake he's made, and the way you treated him, a long while after you've forgotten it."

He stopped because he had to swallow three times to get the starch out of his throat.

Nathan said coldly, "You raised all this tempest to save that boy's job?"

"It's important to him," he said.

"But why did you think it necessary to bring all this pressure to bear on me?"

"I didn't know how much it would be—I didn't know if any of them would answer my telegrams at all. I just shot the works."

A shimmer came across the sharp eyes. "You must think a lot of Frim."

"He's a good guy, and happiness is hard to come by. It don't make you feel well to see it destroyed."

Nathan took up the four yellow half-sheets and slid them across the desk. "You certainly did shoot the works to preserve it," he said sharply.

Eddie's eyes developed a startled stare as he glanced through the telegrams. Then the type began to blur. He'd braced himself against sanguine hopes, and the sense of the messages was hard to get all at once.

Barabe wired Nathan: "Any consideration you feel you can give Operator Sand will be greatly appreciated by me. Thoroughly trustworthy and a good man."

Somewhere behind his iron visage, Barabe actually had a soul.

Welby's telegram said: "Competent and absolutely honest."

Old Salt-and-Molasses Nickerson arranged it all in that tone of finality you couldn't dodge. "If Telegrapher E. Sand has a request to make of you, please grant it, and advise."

That thin, dogged dynamo meant it, and he would follow through to see it was done.

O'Conner, the wild Hibernian, went into some detail. The sense was contained in the last paragraph: "I fired him once, but would consider it a favor if you would let him go and send him back to me. Any other concessions he asks I would appreciate you confer and charge to me." There was just a faint qualification in his final statement. "He won't lie to you for his own protection."

Nathan's voice came out of the distance. "Between ourselves," he said, "how do you rate all those commendations?"

"I guess," he muttered, "by doing the thing that had to be done at the moment." That didn't sound like what he meant, but he'd have to let it stand. A lot of it was in those men themselves—the quality of their leadership. They were alert on their jobs twenty-four hours a day. He put the telegrams down carefully. "Can you see your way clear to let Frim down with a stiff reprimand?" he asked.

"Oh, that," said Nathan. He stared down at the yard where the switch engines snorted and scurried, shuffling the traffic. His thoughts seemed to wander out over the hills, beyond the skyline, maybe away back there in search of his youth. A smile flitted an instant, light and quick, and then he turned back to his desk.

"I'll handle Frim's case so he won't be badly hurt," he said. "I can't do as much for that trick dispatcher," he added. "However, what concerns me most just now is why a young man like you, who has the esteem and confidence of officials like these," he put his hand on the telegrams, "hasn't remained with one of them and gone up to a high place in railroading? Where are you headed for anyhow?" he frowned.

It was the old intolerant question of a man set on the hard and narrow road to success, following it with blind determination to climb as high as he could, whether it made him happy or not. Yet Nathan's query was half startled, as if he had suddenly wondered if he hadn't missed something important along the way.

The tension eased out of the boomer. The sounds of the iron highway came up from the yard—the clang of engine bells and the stamp of exhausts and the solemn rumble of drawbars. A long, thin switchman on top of a rolling string of cars slid along the bright sky, his arms extended, waving as gracefully as a dancer. A stock train clanked into the yard and sent up the faint bleating of sheep. Far out on the prairie the limited shouted her insolent warning. The restless traffic moved with the minutes, day and night.

From the north, beyond the Great Lakes, from far up in the lonely stretches of Canada, a faint tinge of autumn drifted through the room. It was the first faltering suggestion that summer was dying.

Illogically the words of an old song got tangled in his thoughts. "Fall time in Georgia, comes but once a year." The slow melody beat in his pulse. "Catch a 'possum by the tail, or catch him by the ear."

The season when wild fowl migrated wasn't far off. Right now their primeval monitor was sounding a faint, restless call. Some day soon, at a sharp signal that couldn't be heard, the immemorial instinct would send them hurtling through leagues of space to a distant pin point on the earth they could hardly have known existed. Great flocks of them—and in pairs. He wondered if there were lone rovers of the skies.

"Where am I headed for?" he said, and stared at the horizon. "I think I'll head south with the first frost."

XXVIII

HE MOVED about the big room, dressing himself after a shave and a bath in a tub that was nearly as large as a gondola. You could feel the heights out there, bright in the thin mid-day sunlight, the peaks and bald ridges rolling somberly into a far, burnished horizon. He had a short, fierce rush of exaltation. He felt as if a drag had been unhooked from him and he was the old careless drifter again. And now he knew he didn't want to be anything else.

He'd made the long trek to the mountains on Hi Wheeler's insistent pleas, but that was just an excuse which only hurried his return a little. It was sure good to be back in the altitudes. Your problems came out in clear focus in the high country. You could think straighter, and you seemed to have a firmer hold on life.

It showed he was getting a wider view when he could consider his present condition with satisfaction. As compared to a substantial home, boarding house life had its compensations. The rules were few and simple. You paid your rent promptly, avoided disturbing others in the house and didn't destroy the furnishings. You weren't obligated to be there at any specific time, or at all. Your living quarters weren't under constant scrutiny. They weren't a sacred sanctuary, like a home where you withdrew with whatever other members of a family you had, and shut out the world and its dog, with a woman in charge who insisted on certain proprieties and rules of orderly conduct. He was very well pleased to be in the exact situation he now was.

Hi Wheeler opened the door as if he'd expected to find it fastened and was determined that shouldn't check his entrance. He threw his hat and gloves on the bed and raised his voice in vociferous greeting.

Your room here was your own private concern, Eddie considered, pleased, where your friends came and went with no formality or self-consciousness. Usually they didn't even bother to knock, and they dropped things on the floor heedlessly and without remorse. Their stay wasn't interrupted by household schedules, and if they came to borrow, they took whatever it was, if they could find it, whether you were there or not. A pleasant habit, if you believed in reciprocity, and only infrequently inconvenient. A very satisfactory male arrangement.

Hi had just come in from his run over the sullen grades, but that hadn't subdued his exuberance. He remarked, and he asked questions about Eddie's tour of the prairies and the south.

"The Deep South," Hi drawled with satisfaction. "Mister, them black-eyed girls sure've got personality. Did you tell any of them about your old pal Hiram? You sure look pretty with your hair all slicked down."

"I left word," he said, "that if you showed up to be sure to lock everything and put the sheriff on the alert."

"Yeah," Hi nodded brightly, "but I could talk them out of that. I speak the language. Tell me, how'd you do?"

"Fair," said Eddie.

It had been restful in a way. Working the extra list took him to little southern towns that drowsed all day, and then went to bed early of nights. It was a little too calm and leisurely, gave you too much time for brooding, when

what you needed at the moment was vivid action so as to
keep your mind off life's deeper human relationships. His
roots had gone down farther than he'd thought, there with
Janet and Peck.

"Even the trainmen are polite," he said darkly. "It's
hard to get used to. You stab a crew a couple of hours, and
then just hunker down in your office and shoot the breeze.
Schedules are merely printed to hand out to inquiring
strangers, but in no way to be maintained. The crews have
to keep up their family and social relations all along the
line. Handling freight and passengers is just an excuse.
Everybody's kinfolks down there."

"Ah, a lovely country," Hi murmured happily. "The
old folks at home." He sighed, and then discovered briskly
that he was hungry. "If you'll wait till I slick my hair down
like yours, I'll give Mrs. McGurk's grub a whirl with you."
He plunged down the hall to his own room, leaving his hat
and gloves.

It was noon dinner time at Mrs. McGurk's, but Eddie
had his breakfast. Hi kidded the old maid school teacher
with polite and preposterous compliments, while Mrs.
McGurk beamed on him with her blind marital smile. She
was an insidious matchmaker. Two department store
clerks, in high, starched collars, ate rapidly and in silence.

They went to Hi's room afterward, for their first long
talk since Eddie had come west.

There was still that puzzled, hurt-dog look in Hi's eyes,
away back beyond the impish twinkle that glinted there
incessantly. That affair with Gladys still bothered him. He
didn't readily forget. He was still bewildered and per-
plexed, trying to find some justification for her desertion.
He hadn't the flexible nature that recovered quickly. He
couldn't be philosophical about that unfortunate encounter.
That lanky boy from the hills was made of tough fiber.

He'd likely never be quite content till he'd made dead sure about that hearty blonde. He was hard to disillusion.

Eddie went out and took to the slanting streets that dipped toward the railroad yards. You could breathe that sharp air clear down to your toes. The sunlight seemed to strike into your pores. A lot of vitality in that old sun. It washed down over the peaks and saddles and flowed into the deep high bowl in the mountains that held the town.

Crestline, a division point on the Empire Line, was scattered all along the sides of that bowl. At the bottom was collected the roundhouse and shops and the huge granite station with division offices above. Good times had expanded into a national boom, and the railroads were busy. The yard down below was packed with freight cars, and raving switch engines sorted them out. High on a rock dome on the other side of the bowl, the Western Empire Hotel brooded in the white light, a massive structure designed in the likeness of an old world castle. Cable cars, like scrambling bugs, moved up and down the abrupt incline of the rock dome, carrying the traffic from that high hostelry to the platform beside the grim, granite station. In the era when western railroads went in for all kinds of development, the Empire Line had built it as a tourist hotel, and made it a nationally-known resort; and now that good times were here again the place was crowded with affluent sightseers.

Sounds of switching muttered along the high walls. A black cloud boiled over the rim of far peaks. Lightning glinted in the sunshine. The elements up here were savage and abrupt.

He detoured on a short-cut through the tie yard, heading for the station and his four o'clock trick. A switch engine rested where the stub sidings spread out among the tie piles. An engine foreman and two switchmen were clustered about Roger Preston, the assistant trainmaster, at the end of a string of empty flat cars. They debated with a solemnity that wasn't credible. Switchmen were notably prankish, and Roger Preston was a fraud official, son of the president of the Empire Line, sent here to serve his apprenticeship in railroading, with a title and authority, but no knowledge of operations. These stingers would delight to trick him in some phony maneuver.

The foreman was muttering over a switch list. "Old Hollihan," he complained, "keeps this tie yard like a chicken pen. Where'n heck is the old bender, anyhow?"

"He's likely hid out sommers," the pinner offered.

Roger Preston scowled at the list, and then at the piles of ties that crowded the supply yard. In front of each rick was a stenciled sign on a stake, indicating that the ties therein were either hewed, sawed or culls.

Roger grumbled, "He wants six empties set to load hewed ties, but they're scattered all over the yard. And so are the sawed ties, and he wants four cars set for loading that kind. If you set the six cars for hewd ties, then how are you going to squeeze the four cars in between them at the sawed tie piles?" He shook his head dumbly.

"That's it exactly," the foreman nodded. "And we gotta do it before that manifest shows to be broke up." He lowered his eyes and straightened his mouth with the back of his hand, hiding his derision.

Roger's father had begun his rise at Crestline when he had been made assistant superintendent. Evidently he had sent his son here to start him in the same position as an inspiration. But it wasn't working out that way.

The foreman watched Roger with grim amusement. "His old man," he mumbled, "must hold about the same theory the fella had who sold a dog and guaranteed him good on coons. When the man who'd bought the hound turned him back as no damn good as a coon-hunter, the fella who'd sold him said he thought sure he'd be good on coons because he wasn't worth a hoot for anything else. I guess Roger's pa found he wasn't good for anything else, so he was certain to make a good railroader."

Roger came back from a prowl among the piles. "I don't know, Bill," he said. "Don't seem to me as if it could be done."

"Why," suggested Eddie, "don't you spot the signs to the cars, instead of the cars to the signs?"

"How do you mean?" Roger demanded.

"Like this," Eddie showed him. "Shove the string of empty cars into the tie spur, and then pull up the signs and place them beside the cars. That'll make it like the switch list says."

"Sure!" Roger bellowed. "Set the signs to the cars— its easier. Just like that!" He threw a huge arm about Eddie's shoulders and urged him across the yard toward the station.

Roger was burly and blonde and heedless. In college he had majored in athletics, but now fat was beginning to overlay hard muscles. He had a ruthless and selfish disregard for the feelings and the property of others. The men distrusted him and disliked his dumb interfering in work he knew nothing about, yet they had some faint, indulgent fondness for him. It just didn't seem possible that the son of old Computin' Sam Preston could be so ignorant. He might be spoofing, too.

Eddie shrugged the heavy arm from his shoulders. He said quietly, "Tom Brannon is in a jam with the superintendent for bringing Sixty-seven in ahead of schedule when there were slow orders out."

Roger chuckled deep in his barrel chest. "I scared old Tom out of his pants that day," he said gleefully.

"That's what I hear," Eddie nodded. "You got aboard Tom's engine somewhere along the line, took over the throttle because you had the authority, and beat her all the way into Crestline, in spite of soft track and Tom's protests."

"'Protests' isn't the word," Roger grinned. "Tom threw fits all over the cab."

Eddie said softly, "Tom will likely lose his job, if you don't clear him."

"There're lots more jobs, aren't there?" Roger asked carelessly.

"Look, my friend," said Eddie sharply, "are you talking sense?"

"Sure," Roger nodded.

"You never had a job you had to keep in order that your family could eat, have you?"

"Of course not. I've mostly tried to keep out of work. And from what I hear, you're usually moving on from the last job you had."

"Tom Brannon has a wife and five grand kids," Eddie suggested.

"Stout fella," said Roger.

"It's sometimes tough going, keeping a family like that, stretching the old pay check to cover shoes and grub—and doctor's bills. Did you ever have anybody you cared about get dangerously sick?"

"No," said Roger easily. "Neither one. Nobody sick, and nobody I cared about."

"You've missed something," Eddie considered. "Who raised you?" he asked curiously.

"I've tried not to miss anything good," Roger said blithely, "and nobody raised me. Mother died before I can remember. The first thing I learned was that you can bluff servants into letting you do anything you want, so long as you don't tell the boss. My dad wasn't home much, so I had a good time of it. In boarding school I learned to kick and gouge for what I wanted, if they wouldn't give it to me otherways. It worked something like that in college."

He wasn't being apologetic. He was merely reciting the facts of life as they had occurred to him. He believed he'd gotten along very well with his simple system.

"Meanwhile," Roger went on placidly, "dad married again and started another family. I went home after they'd kicked me out of college. But I stayed only a couple of days. I didn't get along with the new outfit. There was a step-mother who hated me on sight, and a half-brother, so high, who mistrusted me from the start. Dad can manage a railroad, but not a family."

"Maybe then," Eddie said, "I'll have to explain what I'm talking about. The superintendent is blaming Tom for bringing his train in ahead of schedule, directly against orders, and he has pulled him out of service. Tom's afraid to tell the Old Man the truth, because you're the president's son. So is everybody else that had anything to do with it."

"Should I worry?" Roger demanded. "Those fellows ought to kick and gouge for the things they think is coming to them, like I do."

Sunlight glinted on the web of polished rails. A road engine moaned softly behind them, and they moved out of the way.

"Sickness in the family," said Eddie, "and hounding creditors, can sap a man's courage."

"Well, what do you want me to do about it?" Roger demanded impatiently.

"Go tell Mr. Monahan exactly what happened. Clear Tom. It would sound better if you told him straight out yourself, than if I had to do it for you."

Roger checked his easy stride abruptly. "So you're going to tell Monohan, if I don't?" he inquired ominously.

"That's right," said Eddie.

A dusky shade crept into Roger's pink cheeks. His eyes hardened to a pale ice-blue. He bulked beside the slim boomer, big enough apparently to crush him without much effort. He was the son of Samuel Preston, president of the Empire Line, accustomed to underlings who were meek and obliging. He glowered at Eddie, cunning as a predatory young bear.

Eddie watched him coolly. He seemed only mildly curious about what Roger was going to do about whatever he thought was wrong. The spare length of the boomer looked as if it might be fine steel, and the glint of red in his hair could indicate dynamite. Roger frowned.

"I don't see what you're getting all steamed up about," he complained angrily.

"It would do you good if you'd really try to find out," Eddie murmured.

This careless brass pounder from everywhere had Roger baffled. He couldn't seem to make him fit in at any given point. He hedged.

"All right," he agreed. "I'll tell Monahan. I don't mind. Is that all it takes?" It didn't embarrass him at all to back down.

"That's all," Eddie said cheerfully.

Down below them, at the west end of the yard, two rivers, the Music and the Mad, flowed together at the base of a bald headland—the Pinnacle. The ceaseless, sullen mutter of the wild stream mingled in an undertone that crept unbroken through the brisk sounds of switching. The main line skirted the north bank of the Mad River, crept along a bench blasted from the face of the Pinnacle, then crossed the canyon of the Music in a single span.

The clang of construction came up sharply above the snarl of swift waters. The spans of a new bridge crept out toward each other from the rock walls of the gorge, paralleling the main line on the headland. Donkey engines puffed out there on the lengthening steel frame. A big crane crouched on the main line under the abrupt wall of the Pinnacle and deftly swung heavy material across to the new structure. A new main line swung left from the station and approached the bridge on a high ramp above the rocky channel of the Mad River.

"All that construction runs into money fast," Eddie estimated.

"Shows you how my dad makes adverse circumstances work for him," Roger said. "His engineers found that the Pinnacle wasn't safe to take the traffic, that the vibrations of the trains was tearing it to pieces, and that some of these years it would let go and drop the main line into the gorge. That meant they'd have to cross the juncture of the two rivers with a bridge."

He gave a fat little chuckle of jaundiced glee. "Just about that time Kincaid Brothers decided to build their own line into the Shire Valley."

Steam plumed from the crane crouched under the Pinnacle, and its long steel arm plucked a girder from a flat car in front of it. The arm swung the heavy piece easily across to the bridge. Workmen wigwagged, and the crane operator eased the girder into place.

"Dad and his associates," Roger said, "had financed the Kincaids to open up the mines and the timber of the Shire, and the Empire Line built a branch to tap it. The Kincaids got rich—and greedy. They decided not to split their profits with dad and the Empire."

The thin air had a sting that made your blood bubble. The sounds of traffic and construction rang musically against the high walls above the sullen murmur of racing water. Roger picked up his feet quick and clean, cat-like.

"And so," he said, "they did some quiet looting of the property, and then shut down to force the others out. They tied in with the P. & W. Railroad, our competitor, got a right-of-way along the Music to connect with them, and started to build a railroad of their own. They were to cross under the Empire Line there at that bridge across the Music, and dad couldn't stop them. But when his engineers found the Pinnacle was faulty, he got a franchise to build that new bridge across both rivers. That blocks the entrance to the Shire; enough anyhow so that the Empire can fight the Kincaids in the courts for long years. Meanwhile, the Empire abandoned its branch into the Shire. The Kincaids have been out of production for a very long while, and a while ago they woke up and found themselves broke."

"Those big boys do murder one another," Eddie said.

"Fella, you don't know how right you could be," Roger declared. "The fact is, the Kincaids began their careers as outlaws. I found that out when I stayed a summer with them in the Shire. I never told dad. Maybe I should have. Now that they are broke, they may take up their old profession."

Passengers, loafers and train crews stood about the wide station platform. The little tram car was nested in its berth ready to swing guests up to the hotel on the bald rock above.

Bernice McFee, a stenographer in the superintendent's office, came out of the stairway door, a bundle of letters in her hand. She began stuffing them into the mail box beside the station. She made a drab little blot in the slanting sunlight, downcast and waif-like. She was poorly dressed and shrinking. Her thin face was apprehensive.

"Hi sweetheart," Roger hailed her gleefully. She was the kind of person he liked best to torment.

The girl flushed. She stood by the mail box and glanced about quickly as if she were trapped.

"I've certainly got to make good on my promise to step you out," Roger chanted. "All you've got to do is say when we go."

A knot of passengers laughed slyly. The girl wheeled and made for the stairs. Roger turned in beside her and slid an arm around her waist. She twisted out of his embrace, and her eyes suddenly blazed.

"Oh, ho!" Roger cried. "This way, then." He took her arm. "You look fine when you're angry," he laughed.

"Don't forget about Tom," Eddie called after him.

"Right away," Roger flung back.

XXIX

BURTON, the baggage smasher, opened the door at the rear of the ticket office. He squinted as he searched in the light and shadow of shaded electric lights, low-swung over desk and counter. He said plaintively, "They's eight hundred and thirty pounds of excess on that drummer's boxcar trunks, Eddie, and don't let him tell you different."

It was raining, and Burton's slicker dripped water in a widening pool about his rubber boots.

"If they go to makin' them trunks any bigger," he explained patiently, "they're gonna have to furnish me a house mover's outfit."

"Thanks," said Eddie without turning from the ticket window.

The ticket clerk was swamped, and Eddie, in charge of the station on second trick, was at the other wicket inscribing an itinerary for a little old lady who was of half a mind to visit her daughter in Indianola, Iowa.

With Eighteen nearly due, the pressure was on. The big waiting room was restless with tourists and bellboys and porters from the hotel.

Subsidiary instincts kept you aware of what was going on about you. That was your training. He was aware of a man and a woman and a little boy who slipped quietly into the waiting room through the crowd, and settled in a far dim corner. There must be something odd about them, for each time his glance went through the room his eyes paused an instant on the three. Some peculiarity there that his preoccupied mind couldn't quite catch.

Eighteen snorted in through the rain, and the waiting room emptied with a rush. Those three remained in the dim corner. He decided at last that the singularity was in the appearance of the woman, but he couldn't quite name it. She was tall and stiff, and she made no movement, seemed unwilling to change her stark position.

He couldn't make out much of the man under a wide hat pulled down over his eyes. The boy, likely about seven or eight, had his feet tucked under him on the seat, his arms around his legs, his chin on his knees. He had a vague expression as if his thoughts wandered through great spaces, dreaming.

Seventeen was soon due, and passengers crowded in again. Big Bud Salverson came into the office and then went out through the wareroom. Big Bud was the chief of the Empire Line's special police, something of a noted western character. You wondered what he was on the prowl for.

When Seventeen had gone, Eddie got up from the telegraph table. The waiting room appeared empty now; and then a shadow stirred in the far corner. It was the boy, and he was alone. The kid was slumped in the seat, his legs dangling. He was asleep. He was draped over the bench like an old rug.

The kid whimpered. Then he cried out and sat up, his hands clutching. Eddie opened the office door and stepped into the waiting room. The boy's startled, sleepy eyes studied him as he approached.

"My name is Jasper," the kid said. He seemed anxious to have that understood at once.

"And a very good name it is. Mine's Eddie."

The coat and knee pants, the stockings and the shoes, all needed drying out and mending and cleaning. So apparently did the boy. One side of his face was slightly swollen. The end of a red welt that came up over his shoulder showed on his neck at the edge of the collar.

"Lonesome?" Eddie asked.

"I don't know," the boy said vaguely. "Maybe." He tucked his knees under his chin and stared solemnly. "Do you run this station?" he asked.

"Right now I am."

"May I stay here for a while?" the boy asked quietly.

"Sure, old-timer. For about how long?"

"I don't know," said Jasper.

"When are your father and mother coming for you?"

The kid said, "I don't know."

"That was your father and mother with you a while ago, wasn't it?" Eddie persisted.

Jasper's solemn, sleepy eyes wandered away. "They said I wasn't to talk about that," he said.

"And they didn't say when they were coming back for you?"

The boy shook his head.

"Have you had your supper?"

Jasper said hopefully, "I have a dime."

You could let it go at that and return to work and forget it. He went back to his key and asked the dispatcher if he could be out for thirty minutes.

"If you'll take about eight good fingers of Bourbon for my cold," the dispatcher replied, "you can be gone for an hour."

The kid's eyelids were fluttering again.

"Let's get something to eat," Eddie suggested.

Jasper hesitated. "I don't know what they will do about that," he murmured.

"I'll take care of them," he promised.

Outside, the rain swirled in a thin mist.

"Just a dime's worth is all I may have," Jasper said sleepily as they climbed the slippery sidewalk.

He unlocked the front door of his boarding house and tramped down the hall to a lighted kitchen at the farther end. Mrs. McGurk sat in a rocker beside the stove and peered at a newspaper through spectacles perched on the end of her nose.

He spoke rapidly, in the vain hope that he might get his story told in one breath, without interruption.

"Mrs. McGurk," he said, "I have a friend here—"

"Who is hungry," Mrs. McGurk broke in ominously without lowering the paper.

She was entirely right so far, he admitted. "But there is the further matter of lodgings. And then he ought to be dried out."

"Then he is not sober," Mrs. McGurk stated with deadly calm.

He contradicted her hopefully.

"Prove it," she invited.

"Look," he pleaded. "It's a dark and stormy night, and a kind, Christian woman like you—"

She cast her newspaper aside impatiently and snatched the glasses from her nose. "Christian, says you, and carousin' about yourself with your disreputable friends—" She broke off and stared at the rumpled figure beside him. She said, "You are always picking up strays. Where did you get this one?"

Jasper said drowsily, "Just a dime's worth is all I may have."

Mrs. McGurk gave Eddie a black look. "You know no more than to drag the child through the wet. Scat!"

He edged backward into the hall. "He can sleep on the couch in my room," he called, and fled.

The third trick man relieved him at midnight. Rain slid over his face, cool and soft, as he climbed the abrupt street again. He felt good. Eight hours on this job was like a flick of time. Windows glowed in the upper story of the station where the trick dispatchers kept the two-way traffic from tangling. The misty lights of the town climbed the steep shoulders.

There was unaccustomed light for this time of night in Mrs. McGurk's parlor just off the hall. He thrust his head inside that plush sanctuary.

A sputtering gas stove had raised an immoderate temperature and filled the over-furnished room with lethal fumes. Mrs. McGurk rocked solemnly in a big chair and stared back at him as if rebuking him for being alive and cheerful. Bernice McFee, the drab little stenographer from the superintendent's office, rested sadly on the sacred davenport. She was woeful, and showed it.

He quickly digested the evidence of his eyes, and grinned. Pint-sized Johnnie McFee was on another spree, and his daughter, Bernice, had sought the shelter and solace of Mrs. McGurk and her hospitable roof till the minute tempest had abated. Little Johnnie, on a bender, made two times the noise for his size, but he wasn't dangerous.

"How's Jasper?" he asked.

"Asleep in the room next to mine," she said gloomily, "and you will not disturb him. He has been bad treated— beaten, by the look of him, and he is tuckered out. Where did you get him?"

Eddie explained.

" 'Tis a matter for the police," Mrs. McGurk decided. "We will take care of it in the morning."

Bernice smiled at him, a dieaway turn of the lips, but it did light up her thin face and make her look, with her hair down and loose about her shoulders, and that robe which showed off her nice figure—well, dammit! He was encouraged with himself to find that he could look at a girl that way. The light glowed and rippled in her burnished hair, and her face was small and exquisite. The altitudes sure perked up your imagination. She should be studied and her mode of getup mended—by some other good man!

"You lunch is ready in the kitchen," Mrs. McGurk croaked.

His landlady was enjoying a gloomy occasion. He restrained his mirth. Little Johnnie McFee was on a bender, and the old hens about town, in anguish, were putting the heat on his daughter, as if he was acting hellish—little Johnnie, old and dried up, who hadn't a bad intention in his shriveled system, and wouldn't be able to manage one of any size if he had. He eyed the two impishly.

"There aren't any house rules that forbid you joining me in a bit of nourishment, is there?" he inquired elaborately. "Anyhow, that gas stove will strangle you if you remain with it longer."

"There are times," said Mrs. McGurk, "when I've been bad tempted to put strychnine in your coffee."

"Likely that wouldn't harm it any," he pointed out. "It often has that taste now." He gestured politely. "I'd be delighted if you'd join me in the cup that cheers but does not inebriate," he offered, and turned down the hall to the kitchen as they stared at him resentfully. That hadn't been a suitable allusion, with Johnnie on a bust, but at the moment nothing you could say would be appropriate.

They followed him into the kitchen. He turned up the gas under the coffee.

Mrs. McGurk was an old croaker, the last person this girl should come to for sympathy, because she would get it in bucketfuls. These Irish were a little touched. They believed in fairies—and likely Santa Claus. Intoxicated, Johnnie McFee became a Celtic king. So what? It was a drab world for the fanciful. If you could occasionally make it potent for a night, there oughtn't to be any objections—unless you became unruly and tried to destroy the place.

Eddie ate heartily and tried to relieve their gloom with his bright reflections. Johnnie McFee was a section foreman, with a long and honorable record, mild and efficient and loyal. He was beloved by his superior officers and by his fellow workers. He'd probably done less wrong than most. There were, Eddie believed, no saints left in this benighted world, and people who lived in glass houses shouldn't take a bath at night with the lights on.

"Men!" said Mrs. McGurk bitterly.

XXX

THE CHIEF of police was moulded into his big chair, placid and inert.

"But what does the kid say for himself?" he repeated doggedly.

"Nothing," said Eddie.

"Ain't he got no other name than just Jasper?"

"If he has," Eddie said, "he won't give it to me yet."

"Ain't he got no folks?"

"He won't say. The couple that had him with them evidently mistreated him some, and otherwise scared him. He won't talk, because they told him not to. He won't even say where he comes from." He studied the chief skeptically. "What's got me puzzled is why they abandoned him at the station after staying there with him for a couple of hours."

"Funny," said the chief.

"While they were there, and the waiting room was crowded for Seventeen," Eddie said, "Big Bud Salverson came in. I didn't notice those two after that."

"Which means what?"

"I don't know. It just occurred to me."

"Why didn't you bring the kid down here to me?" the chief complained irritably. "I'd 'a made him talk."

"He's been through more than is good for him already," Eddie explained. "He's got to stay in bed for a day or two, the doc says."

"All right! All right! Bring him in when he's able."

Down at the station, Hi Wheeler, in clean overalls and jacket, ready to go out on a merchandise, lounged on a baggage truck and waited for him.

"A very funny thing," he told Eddie. "I just talked to Mrs. McGurk, and I saw Jasper. You know what? We brought them three in on the local freight last evening."

"Where'd you pick them up?"

"At that old freight shed at Mather," Hi said. "We had a meet with Eight there, and we pulled into the siding. It was rainin', and the three of them was camped under the shed, with a fire going on the cinder platform." Hi took a spit. "It didn't seem right to me to let the woman and the kid stay out there in that cold rain all night, so I asked them didn't they want to ride into Crestline. They didn't at first," Hi said, "and then all at once they climbed aboard the caboose." He spat again reflectively. "It was the woman that decided it. I can't tell you how I know she did, because she didn't say a word. She just made up her mind, and that's what they did."

"Didn't they talk about anything coming in?" Eddie asked.

"Not that I heard. Look, Eddie," Hi insisted, "my mother raised me to be polite to wimmen."

"And a very good job she did," Eddie approved.

"She'd be tickled to hear you say that," Hi said wistfully. "But what I'm getting at is I didn't feel like being mannerly to that woman. She kind of made the hair rise up on the back of my head."

"I had the same feeling about her, clear across the waiting room," he nodded.

He went into the station and the brisk action that swept him through the swift hours of feeding traffic to the impatient passenger trains. The quick rush of minutes washed over him and receded, and he emerged into the keen midnight air like a terrier after a plunge into a cold stream. The job was as absorbing as that. His spirits climbed to the sharp stars. Fine to be in the heights, working the mountain traffic.

The elation ebbed as he opened the front door. A bright light glowed in the kitchen, and a shadow moved against the farther wall. Only somebody's dire distress could keep Mrs. McGurk out of her bed, and it was likely she wanted to share the grief with him.

"You," he charged, peering cautiously, "carousing around at this time of night."

" 'Tis the work," she sighed, "that keeps me from my bed." She folded an iron board and stowed it away. "Bernice came to me again late this evening, and I was advisin' the poor girl."

"Is Johnnie still on his bender?" he inquired. It was said he never protracted them.

"No," she grudged. "Tonight he is at home and remorseful. 'Tis another misfortune that worries the girl," she mourned. "And then I bethought me that I had better iron Jasper's clothes which I washed this day, there being little enough of them, and him up tomorrow."

He eyed her suspiciously. The woman was full of guile. And wily. He fingered the little pile of clothing to see if any was hot from the iron. They were not. She was fraudulent with that ironing board. Then the feel of the garments attracted him.

"Hey," he said, "have you observed that these clothes are made of very good material?"

"That they are," said Mrs. McGurk.

"Well?" he said.

"I was thinkin' the same thing," she nodded.

"Jasper hasn't talked yet?"

"He hums to himself," she said, "and he looks at the pictures in the book I gave him. But he will say nothing of himself." She sighed heavily again. "Sit down, sit down," she invited. "You act as if my food does not tempt you."

He sat and bit into a sandwich. She poured two cups of coffee and eased into a chair.

" 'Tis a cruel world for the women," she mourned.

"Yeah?" he said warily. "How come?"

"There's Bernice, now," she said. "And such a fine girl, too. I feel very dispirited about her."

"What's wrong now?" he demanded.

"First, 'tis her father. She feels the disgrace of him, what with the young folks she went to school with lookin' down their impudent noses at her, and none to be her friend."

"Tough," he said with his mouth full. "But I can't moan. You ought to tell her to brighten up. She ought to bust loose and step out, and to hell with'em."

"She did that this night," Mrs. McGurk lamented, "and much to her sorrow. She came to me a bit ago, very dejected. She is in her room upstairs this minute, having herself a good cry."

"And what the heck for?" he snorted.

" 'Tis this Roger Preston, so bold. May the devil scorch him!" She patted the floor with her foot and glowered. "He took her out, all sociable, and I do not know for sure what happened. But he is not a gentleman, and Bernice is terribly sorry for herself this moment."

"Yeah," he jeered. It was after all pleasant to brawl with Mrs. McGurk. He forgot to be cautious. "And you encourage her to grieve," he charged. "She ought to know enough to stay away from that clown till she's had more experience."

He was feeling fine and expansive. He had one faint

premonition that he was being patriarchal again, but lost the symptom in his relish of the food.

Mrs. McGurk regarded him shrewdly. "Eddie," she said, "you have been all about." She beamed. "You have a very discerning eye." She nodded ponderously. "And a kind and gentle heart," she added.

That checked him. The still, small voice began to sound an alarm. Mrs. McGurk could be overpowering with her blandishments.

"It would be like you," she cooed sweetly, "to stop by her room as you go up, and say a kind word to her."

He chewed rapidly and swallowed. "What," he demanded in a panic, "are you talking about?"

"She respects you terribly, Eddie," she crooned. "She says you are awful smart. And the men, they don't pay her any attention at all; but she says you are always so polite and sociable. Now, a kind word from you, when she is depressed, would so brighten her. It would take you but a minute." Mrs. McGurk oozed guile.

He was fighting now. "At one o'clock in the morning? I'd look fine asking myself into a nice girl's room, and her crying. I can find twice too much trouble without walking right into it."

"You can leave the door open," she wheedled, "and I'll be standing by to protect you."

"A man once made millions and millions," he said desperately, "just minding his own business. His name," he informed her, "was John D. Rockerfeller."

"And a very charitable gentleman he turned out to be," she nodded.

"Why can't you let human events take their own appointed course?" he begged. "I'm trying to live to be a very kindly old gentleman, but I'll never make it by prowling of midnights."

"You were never one to think of yourself when another is in trouble," she said heartily. "And mind, I've been kind to the little boy you fetched here all wet and weary, though I mention it as shouldn't. I'll bake you one of those nice raisin pies you like so well the first thing in the mornin'."

"I warned myself," he said helplessly, "the instant I set foot in your house. Your pies are grand, but the price is too high."

Boardinghouse life could be as complicated as any, he decided bitterly.

"You have such a way with the women," she wheedled.

"Yeah!" he said scornfully, "there's only one way with a woman, and that is her way. All right," he surrendered sullenly, "lead on. And you stay by in case of need, because this is likely to develop into something outrageous."

"Now, be easy, Eddie," she begged. "Just gentle like."

He caught some subdued sniffling from the room as he rapped on Bernice's door.

"Who is it?" a choked voice drifted through the panels.

"It's Eddie Sand. Mrs. McGurk sent me, but I'll run along if you don't want to talk to me tonight," he added hopefully.

Mrs. McGurk hissed at him from the dark hallway.

There was silence from the room, then a step, and the door came open.

"What is it, Eddie?" she asked pathetically.

The evidence of grief was plain on her face. She stood straight enough, but she seemed to be drooping and broken. She was stricken—or maybe just a little baffled. It was hard to name exactly a woman's emotions.

"Mrs. Simon Legree McGurk thought I ought to do something about God knows what, but this isn't the time of night to be—"

"Come in," she invited. "Or are you afraid to?" she asked.

That wasn't the right answer. "Well, yes and no," he grinned. "She said that you went out with Roger, and that he wasn't nice to you. I'd be glad to break him in two, but that wouldn't get either of us anything but fired. He's just a guy to stay away from, that's all."

"But it isn't his fault, really, the way he treats me," she sniffed. "I am just a working girl, the daughter of an old section man, and he is the son of the president of the line. It isn't reasonable for me to think he should show me respect."

He subdued his irritation. Agree with a gal that the man who mistreated her was a miscreant, and right away she came back with an extenuation. He'd have gleefully choked Mrs. McGurk then, if he thought he wouldn't be unjustly prosecuted for it.

"That's up to you," he said shortly. "Maybe they've belittled you till you believe it yourself. Which is bad. Me, I don't think they make'em any better than I am, and I'll put up an argument any time they try to show me otherwise. By the same token, I'll root for the old home team, no matter how far in the hole they are. Haven't you got any of that famous fighting Irish spirit?"

"But Roger isn't supposed to be like—like the rest of us," she insisted.

"I don't give a hoot what he's supposed to be. He is just a guy, and not a good one at that. He got off on the wrong line, and he has never been able to get back."

He checked himself. He was getting all steamed up and arguing with a woman. That never did get you anywhere. What a fine old granny he'd eventually make out of himself.

"If he could be nice," she reflected. "He is—he is fascinating when he wants to be. I think I could like him, if he knew how to treat a girl."

"Oh," he said. "It's like that." He studied her critically. "So you'd like to play on his side," he considered.

A slow flush crawled into her cheeks.

But at that you couldn't blame her. To a mountain girl that boy would be captivating. She'd likely had a pretty dreary time, motherless most of her life, trying to have a little of the good times youngsters had a right to. She hadn't been asked to join. Her father was a section man on the railroad, and he got drunk. The other girls avoided her, and the men ignored her. She'd been pretty lonely.

"All right," he snapped. "You want it, so I'll give it to you right off the top of the deck. Get some clothes, nice ones, and learn to wear 'em—even if you have to put another mortgage on the old homestead. And do something with your hair besides wrapping it around your head. Likewise, put a little of that Irish spirit into your walk. Use your smile like you weren't afraid it would break and drop off."

"But what do I do after that?" she asked.

"I'll put you in circulation," he stated. "My working hours don't allow for much of that, but we'll arrange it. I'll step you out and show these mountaineers what they've overlooked. O. K.?"

"I think so," she said doubtfully.

"Fine! Now, get some sleep. Then blossom out. I know what you can look like if you get yourself organized."

She flushed again. "Thank you, Eddie."

He swung down the dark hall and caromed off the

solid form of his landlady. He circled quickly and made for his room.

"Good night, Eddie," Mrs. McGurk whispered sweetly in the gloom.

Eddie slammed his door.

XXXI

THE INTERMITTENT clatter of construction came up sharply through the sound of switching in the yard as Eddie came down the street, his pace moderated to Jasper's limited stride. The kid'e sober eyes circled the yard and ran along the ramp to the spans of the new bridge reaching out and nearly touching.

Jasper said, "That bridge is nearly completed," and studied it thoughtfully.

They came to the station as a road engine pushed up through the yard and grunted to a stop at the end of the passing track.

"That," Jasper pointed, "is a 4-6-2, Pacific type locomotive, built by Baldwin."

"What?" said Eddie.

"They had trouble with them derailing on the curves when they first came out," Jasper remembered. "They were too stiff."

"How did you know that?" he asked the boy.

"Everybody knows it," Jasper said.

"I didn't," Eddie objected. "Who told you about them?"

Jasper didn't reply. He held tightly to Eddie's hand as they crossed the busy waiting room to the office. He let go when they were safely inside. He prowled the office, studying the equipment.

"They are going to discontinue those ticket machines," he said, pointing, "as soon as the new ticket stock is printed. Some clerks found a way to be dishonest with them."

"I've heard that," Eddie agreed quickly, "but I've forgotten where. Who told you, Jasper?" he asked.

Jasper considered. "Everybody knows that," he said at last.

Eddie and his crew took over the station.

Bernice McFee came down the stairs. She was on her way home, and she detoured into the ticket office to post two of Superintendent Monahan's bulletins in the book. Roger Preston trailed her into the ticket office.

Roger was in a slight daze. Bernice had suddenly blossomed into something entirely feminine and very, very attractive. That had hit him with bewildering abruptness and set him adrift. The girl had discarded her mouse-like manners. You noticed her coppery hair and her quick, warm smile. She had exchanged her indifferent shirt waist and drab skirt for an array of garments that made her entirely lovely. Roger was charmed and confounded.

She greeted the third trick and gossiped with Jasper while she took the Wells-Fargo paste pot and began sticking the bulletins to a blank sheet in the book. Eddie watched her with the dubious feeling that he'd played a joke upon himself. He'd had a notion that she would emerge from her old cocoon as something bright and pleasant to look at. But the actual shift had been startling.

Now, Roger was making a pest of himself about it. He pursued her with his usual blunt impatience. The affair was creating a mild sensation at headquarters. The staff saw a hot race between Eddie and Roger, and was even making a pool on it.

Roger didn't bother to speak to anyone else in the office. "Listen, Bernice," he said. "There's a dance at Highgrove tonight. What say I hire a livery rig and we'll drive out. There's always a good crowd there on Wednesdays."

"Thank you, no," Bernice said as she pasted the sheet. "I have some work to do at home; and besides Mr. Monahan asked you to ride the manifest east tonight as far as Euston and find out about those delays at the packing house."

She'd learned fast. She might even make a Christian out of that self-centered boy.

"Aw, that," Roger grumbled. "It's not important. I could skip it and ride the hotshot tomorrow night."

"Which wouldn't be what Mr. Monahan asked you to do," she replied firmly.

His florid face shaded a darker red. He curbed his impatience but not much of it. Eddie grinned.

"I'll walk home with you anyhow" Roger insisted.

"No," she said. "You have only enough time to get your dinner before the manifest leaves. I must be going. Good night, everybody."

Very neat. Eddie considered a shot, and as she reached the door he let it fly. "Don't forget, Bernice," he said, "that you and I are stepping out tomorrow night."

"Of course," she nodded. "I'll be ready at eight o'clock." She closed the door quietly behind her.

"To hell with that manifest!" Roger snarled. He glowered at Eddie. "So she turns me down, and then makes a date with you."

"And very good taste it shows," he said agreeably.

"Just a tramp brass pounder," Roger sneered. He could let himself go now. "You'd better not get in my way, old-timer. She's my girl."

"I'll not believe that till she tells me so," he said.

Roger glared. "That gal—" He stopped. He wasn't sure why. Eddie was merely examining him with a cool, distant eye. It didn't even seem hostile. Roger smoldered.

"You'll crowd in just an inch too far some time," he said, "and be sorry for a long while after. I could give you twenty pounds and still take you apart."

"No," Eddie stated, "you couldn't. Not even at present weights. Just remember I told you that if you're ever tempted to try out your theory."

"I sure will," Roger muttered, and turned to teasing Jasper. "I'll bet your dad is a section hand," he scoffed at the kid, "and that he gets drunk every Saturday night."

"I know who you are," Jasper answered scornfully. "You are Roger Brownlow Preston, and a very big bully. They expelled you from college for ungentlemanly conduct, and nobody likes you."

The angry red flamed in Roger's cheeks. He took a light step at the boy. And then stopped. Eddie had slid off the telegraph table. He was set and waiting like a cat at a gopher hole. The telegraph instruments chattered in sudden excitement. The murmur of voices flowed in from the waiting room. Roger stood braced, holding back his storming resentment. His ice-blue eyes blazed at the kid; and then they suddenly moderated. They seemed baffled.

"Who told you that?" he demanded.

"Everybody knows it," Jasper said scornfully.

"Let the kid alone," Eddie said. "He's only repeating what he's heard around here."

"Who's been talking like that about me?" Roger flared. "I'll get his job."

"If you start that," Eddie remarked, "you might not have enough men left to run the division."

"Bullies never amount to much," Jasper stated. "Everybody knows that."

Roger seemed to catch an odd note in the boy's voice. Slowly he subsided. He shook his head and frowned. "That sounds like something I've heard before." His face puckered in thought. Then he gave it up. "Just for that," he said abruptly, "I'll take you up town and buy you an ice cream. Come along."

"If you will make it a chocolate nut sundae," Jasper suggested, "I would be glad to go."

For a pacifist, Eddie considered bleakly, he sure could get into more wrangles. Human relationships should be pleasant and so managed that you could move on to some place else on short notice without prejudice. That, however, seemed blamed hard to arrange.

The sounder babbled his call in a subdued clatter as if the impulse came from a great distance. His slim hand slipped automatically to the key.

"Hi, Eddie," the brass tongue chanted. "This is Russ Kruger down here on your old division of the Southwestern. Remember?"

His mind slipped back to that night the storm had blasted the desert, and he'd fought Russ Kruger in the little, lonely station, with the live coals from the wrecked stove under his bare feet, and Seventy-nine plowing steadily toward the washout.

"Russ," he sent, "I'm blamed glad to hear your voice again. How's the sun and silence?"

"They wouldn't let me go back there," Russ sent. "I'm over in the hills on the east end, in a big station. We've got a boom on here." He made the instrument stutter. "Bob Franklin's just gone to work here, and he said he'd seen you in Kansas City a couple months ago, and you were headed west. Then he'd heard you were with the Empire. Walley Sterling's around here some place. I heard him working the other night."

He took a long, deep breath. "See if you can't locate Walley, and have him call me." Walley wouldn't ever get himself involved with a lot of miscellaneous and conflicting projects. He took life exactly as it came to him, and rode right along. He reflected, and then inevitably put out another entangling tentacle. "Hi Wheeler is here on the Empire with me," he sent. "I wonder, do you remember that girl Gladys that he used to run around with?"

Russ clicked the sounder and pondered. "What was her other name?" he asked at last.

Eddie dug into his memory. He didn't know it. "I've forgotten, but she used to clerk at Skowinski's," he explained.

"I guess I didn't know her," said Russ. "Say," he sent, "when are you coming this way again? You kept me out of a bad one, and I'd like to say how I feel about it now."

"Some of these times, sure enough," he promised.

The circuit spluttered and broke. A blank wall slid down and shut him off from those far gray somber reaches of blasting sunlight.

XXXII

ROGER LISTENED sullenly while Bernice and Eddie planned a Sunday picnic. He was a good deal like an overgrown school boy in his first love affair, groggy and forlorn and resentful. It was ludicrous and slightly pathetic. He had found something he wanted that kicking and gouging wouldn't get him. He was rent by emotions. He was a mess.

He broke into their project morosely.

"That guy," he said to her, "is just a boomer lightning slinger, always going places. He'll move out on you some of these days—just drift along. You'd better ride with a man like me, who is permanent and respectable and responsible."

"You never can tell about boomers," Eddie said cheerfully. "Usually there comes a time when they settle down. Specially when the conditions are right."

"And I wouldn't say you were highly responsible, either," Bernice told him a little too sweetly. "When Mr. Monahan asked you to check the service on the Echo Branch today, you got interested in operating the crane out there on the bridge, and missed your train."

"Sure," Roger agreed. "It's more fun running the big hook, and I can do it better."

He liked to operate the heavy equipment, and you had to give him the credit of doing it well. He liked to run the road engines, and the enginemen said he had a feel for the big jacks. Without preliminary instructions, merely by watching the operator, he had learned to handle the huge crane with a fine, accurate skill.

"Of course, it is always easier to do the other fellow's job," Bernice reminded him.

"Aw, Monahan just ordered me to Echo to get me out of his sight," Roger said, his face puckered in a sly smile. "He's tired of my hanging around your desk, keeping you from your work."

Eddie had borrowed the track walker's velocipede for his Sunday excursion with Bernice, and in mid-morning he pumped the little vehicle slowly up the grade along the Mad River, brawling in cascades through its granite channel. Bernice sat sidewise on the flat seat beside him, and hummed and chattered. She was like a bright, alert squirrel, he thought, and apparently just as carefree. A very cheerful companion.

Lean sunlight glinted on ridges and knobs. The clumps of trees in the hollows looked like stray dark clouds. The sound of the flanged wheels on the flashing rails ran thinly over the slopes above the chuckle of the bustling stream. A jay scoffed at them from a clump of aspens. Far back, where the peaks leaned against the sky, a black dot drifted easily against the brittle blue. That old eagle up there could see things. The air made your blood bubble.

Where the stream came up almost level with the main line, by dark pines that pointed into the sky, he wheeled the car from the rails and parked it in the clear. They left their basket lunch in the shade and explored. They came back and sat on the river bank and debated, too lazy in the sun to unpack the lunch.

The sputtering sound of a laboring gas engine interrupted the chuckle of the stream and the murmur of the big trees. The roadmaster's gas car nosed into sight around the bend, chugging valiantly. You knew who was aboard that coughing machine before it came into sight. Roger had a dumb, persistent determination in his pursuit of the things he desired, and a boiler-plate resistance to ridicule. He sat forward and engineered the cranky craft, and Jasper sat behind him, his solemn eyes observing all the bright world. The motor sighed and stopped beside them. Roger lifted the heavy car easily from the rails. He beamed at them.

"Fancy meeting you here," he said. "Jasper and I had planned to picnic at this very spot. I hope we don't intrude."

"Not," said Bernice, "if you brought your own lunch."

"Oh, enough really for dozens of people," he assured her, unabashed. "And you both must share it with us." He lugged a big hamper into the shade.

They spread their lunches by the stream, and Bernice encouraged them to stuff themselves. A freight slid clanking down the grade, and then a passenger toiled up and blasted by.

Jasper wandered away. Eddie relaxed in the sun and his thoughts drifted, vague and woolly. Bernice sure had her feet on the ground now, and she was rapidly breaking Roger to harness. Eddie considered himself as a good missionary, and wasn't pleased with the thought. As a fact, he wasn't able to cheer for himself at all.

Roger was dissatisfied with the performance of the embryo gas engine. He glowered at it.

"It just could kick us up the grade," he complained.

He began to tinker with it. Soon he had the little engine off and apart. His stubby fingers handled the greasy parts deftly, almost gently. His round face had the absorbed look of a boy tinkering with an old alarm clock. He studied each part. Then he began to put it together again.

"What are you eventually going to do with Jasper, Eddie?" he inquired as he worked.

"You can't put it like that," Eddie sighed. "He'll get discovered. He belongs to somebody."

"Yes, but suppose he remains uncalled for?" Roger persisted. "What will you do about that?"

"I'll bite," Eddie said lazily. "What am I supposed to do?"

"Well," said Roger, "suppose you don't do anything about it till you let me know."

Eddie stared at him. "Sure," he agreed, "I'll let you know."

Roger worked carefully. "That roadmaster," he grumbled, "ought to take better care of his equipment." He stood up and inspected the machine all around, and then went to wash his hands in the stream.

Jasper came back and sat by Bernice. The sun slanted, and Eddie rolled over and got up reluctantly.

"I've got to slide on back in time to pick up my trick," he said. "I can make it down to the first blind siding for Forty. You three can linger, and come down behind Thirty-one."

"That's fine," Roger agreed quickly. "No use for us to hurry back, Bernice," he urged.

She vetoed that promptly. "I'll go home with the fellow that brought me," she decided.

She wasn't playing this game to his lead as she was supposed to do. He didn't feel displeased about it, though. He wondered about that.

Roger began a heavy protest, but he got no place with her. He sulked and wheedled, and then sullenly put the gas car back on the rails to proceed them down the grade. Jasper climbed aboard. The abused motor grunted and sighed under his urgings. He tinkered again, bent over the listless engine patiently, his short fingers feeling and testing.

The motor exploded with strangled fury. The car lunged. The squat wheels churned. Jasper clung and stared profoundly. The swooping twist of the grade lay blank and placid, the rails glinting in the quiet light. Forty was down there somewhere, coming up the hill. The gas car with Jasper aboard roared and ground its squat wheels into the shining steel.

The picture flickered like a mirage and dissolved. Roger stooped and snatched the broken half of a tie at his feet. He shoved it across the nearest rail in front of a grinding wheel and braced his knee against it. That motor had power on the down grade. The muscles came out in hard welts in Roger's neck. The right rear wheel chewed into the broken tie, rode it, and he shoved down and wrenched. The short wheels howled, then tipped and bucked. They slid off the rails and dug into the roadbed and kicked up ballast. Roger shut off the motor. He glowered at the machine reproachfully.

"You'd not be so cranky if I had you to take care of," he said.

XXXIII

TOURING DOWN the hall, after a session with the trick dispatcher, Eddie paused in the open doorway of the division superintendent's outer office. Bernice sat at her typewriter between stacks of papers. Her busy fingers paused and she smiled at him. Roger was slouched in a chair close by, studying with scowling intentness the carbon copy of a long telegram. He peered over the yellow sheet glumly.

"Come in," he invited, "because I know you will anyhow. But Miss McFee is busy and must not be disturbed on company time. However," he said, "I am at the moment free of pressing duties, and in the interest of the spirit of one big family, which we try to foster on the Empire Line, I am prepared to entertain you with the contents of this very interesting telegram, which is from my illustrious father, and is directed to Mr. Monahan."

"Well," said Eddie, "I might stand still for it if it doesn't keep me from taking my trick at four o'clock, and you're sure it should be imparted to a lowly employee?"

"On the contrary, my friend," Roger assured him, "this is to be given the widest possible publicity. We will, in fact, spend sums of money to spread the information far and wide. Be seated, my friend."

Roger cleared his throat peremptorily and glowered at the telegram.

"My father," he lectured, "can usually make an occasion serve many purposes. The Empire Line is building a bridge structure that is unique enough to gain notice in trade publications. But that is not enough. Therefore, bright young men are employed to call the world's attention to it in the public prints; and we will formally open the bridge to rail traffic with great acclaim."

He shook the yellow sheet at Eddie fiercely.

"Fine!" he applauded himself. "Very fine. But to go a step farther." He got up and began to take steps. "For a very long while the Western Empire Hotel has been deep in the red." He thrust his thumbs at the floor. "Not so fine. Nevertheless, can we not make the bridge—that exceptional fabrication of steel—in some way bring patronage to the caravansary?" He spread his hands, palms up. "To be sure. We will hold a banquet there in celebration of the opening, and we will invite the people who will do us the most good—the press and the politicians, and the—the—"

"I think," said Eddie, "that you are interrupting Miss McFee at her work."

"Such is not the case," Roger declared hotly. "She is merely reflecting." He refreshed his memory from the telegram.

"And that is not all," he resumed. "My father is mindful of the fact that he began his climb to success in this—in this salubrious city. Therefore, the townsman and his wife, and all others so minded, are invited to a dance in the grand ball room. Magnificent!"

He bowed. He held up his stubby hand to ward off another interruption.

"And further more," he said, "in that spirit of one big family which I have hereinbefore mentioned, all employees of the Empire Line, who can be spared from duty, will be furnished transportation and brought in for the dance and the ensuing ceremonies. Need I add more?" he declaimed.

"No," said Eddie.

Roger frowned. He brooded. "I wonder," he said darkly, "what the brothers Kincaid think of this, wherever they are?" He shook his head. "They are very tough hombres, and not at all likely to take this lying down, even tho' they are broke and busted."

"Well," said Eddie, "thank you kindly. We should have a distinguished crowd of citizens in this town on those dates."

"It," said Roger, "will indeed be something. And that being the case, Bernice, I'll date you up right now as my partner at the dance *and* the banquet." He leered at Eddie. He'd of course be expected at the banquet, together with any guests he'd care to bring along. Eddie wouldn't even be invited. Roger was gouging again.

But it meant that Bernice would be there, among the rich and haughty, at the speakers' table, right up front. The old croakers would buzz about that. Yet he still wasn't able to cheer. He felt like he was getting another one of those head colds. Maybe that was what made his head feel stuffy and his temper surly.

"But it isn't settled," he heard Bernice say blithely, and he stared at her. "Eddie, don't you remember? Roger took me to the Pioneers' ball, and you were to take me to the next thing of that kind. Now, don't try to run out on me," she chided.

He thought that wasn't quite good strategy. You could goad Roger too much. He'd sure blow up at some point.

"Sure," he said, "that's right. But," he added to give her an opening, "I'll not be expected at the banquet, so maybe you had better accept Roger's double-barreled bid, and we'll square it up later."

"Of course that's the way to do it," Roger argued.

"Not at all," he heard her say, lightly. She was using

the right tone to make it an amusing game. "I wouldn't care to sit quietly and listen to the governor and all the rest, proclaiming the glories of whatever it is they want to glorify. I would rather dance."

Roger said sullenly, "Bernice, you have been trailing along in the lower strata long enough. You ought to associate more with the higher ups."

Eddie said softly, "How high up do you mean, Roger?" and then knew he'd said the wrong thing.

"You boys quick bickering," she broke in quickly, "and get out of here. I have work to do."

"Have it your way," Roger glowered. He sulked. "But count me out of this from now on, if you feel like that. I don't stand in line any longer." He stamped out and slammed the door.

"Look," Eddie said. "Maybe you're putting too much pressure on that boy. Suppose I bring him back, and we'll compromise by letting him take you to the festival."

"Eddie Sand!" she cried. "If it's the last thing you ever do for me, you must take me to that dance."

He glanced at her quickly. He reached for the door. "Sure enough," he said.

XXXIV

HE CAME down early in the afternoon to help the agent with the rush of traffic. The mighty and the meek were converging on Crestline that day. Officers of the Empire Line, and affiliates, came in their private cars, which were switched out of the passenger trains that brought them, and set on the parking spur below the hotel. Excursion trains fetched employes and the public.

President Preston arrived on his special train, with noted guests. The special stormed in at two o'clock in the afternoon, and it was immediately switched over to the new main line, where it crossed the ramp and out onto the new bridge for a preview of the unique structure.

There was a flood of telegrams and orders, and Eddie sat at the telegraph table in the bow window, alongside the first trick operator, and copied steadily. Another exursion train came in, and the crowd around the station increased. The little tram cars shuttled up and down the incline to the hotel. There was a lull in the storm of telegrams, and he leaned back in his chair and eased out of his concentration.

Suddenly he didn't like crowds. Thoughts of those first telegraph jobs edged into his mind. A green kid he was, thin as a ladder and wide-eyed at all the world. They'd called him "a pound of rump and a pair of legs," he was that slim. The tricks were twelve hours straight through those days, but they slipped by unheeded while he kept an eye on the high iron traffic, and dreamed of the boomer trail out ahead across the world. He'd been mighty proud then, proud of his craft and the growing skill that would assure him a job wherever the railroads ran. He'd never again be able to feel that superb arrogance. It had felt good then.

Folks who worked daytimes didn't know what the **quiet night was like;** the soft, delicate scent of the dark, and the calm quiet that soaked deep and made you contented and hopeful. You felt the world turn over in dead sleep at 2 A. M., and you sensed the beginning of another day—another clean blank space to write your little piece upon. And then the dawn creeping along the rim of the world and running up the sky in vivid spokes, and the feel of the freshness of creation upon your face.

Most people dreaded loneliness. They wrote plaintive songs about it, how it was breaking their hearts. They went insane of it. Likely they were the kind that didn't get along well with themselves. They liked to get into a crowd and push, so they could avoid troublesome thoughts. He didn't remember that he'd ever been lonely. If he had it hadn't been unpleasant. He'd always been able to create things in his mind, to keep his hands busy, and be happy about the whole thing. And in the quiet sometimes you got a strange lift, a kind of hint of some better existence, a gracious and tolerant way of life, and whimsical, too. There wasn't any hint of strife. In human contacts there was always resistance that eventually wore thin spots in your charity and amiability.

The sounder in its resonator by his ear clucked metallically. The first trick operator was nodding at him.

"It's for you," he said.

His hand slid to the key as the vague thoughts drifted away.

"S—TT—U—DY" (Is that you, Eddie?) the sounder exploded, and he knew with a surge of his pulse that Walley Sterling was on the wire.

"Hi, Sorrel Top! I'm down here on the old Southwestern, and guess where. That's right—at the Cinder Patch, nights. I don't wear any clothes, and I gladly sit and watch the world go by. Listen, fella, you shouldn't delay in those altitudes. They're hard on the heart."

A dun-colored station with a pencil-like semaphore came out of a hot shimmer. A long, gray ridge sloped down and circled and climbed into smoky mountains. A glowing flat, palpitating like hot clinkers in a vast firebox, swept south and edged into the horizon. Nothing moved under the steel-blue arch of sky except the flicker of a restless mirage.

"There's things of nights—kind of friendly spirits. The stars come close and whisper. It's companionable then."

Who'd said that? Why, that operator waiting outside Chief McKeon's office down there—the long-haired man who'd let the sun and silence get inside his head.

"Walley," he sent, "you be careful of that sun. It will melt you to a grease spot."

"It don't come that bright. I had a talk with Buck Barabe, and he said he'd be tickled to have you back. And if you want that fifty bucks I still owe you, come and get it." He made a derisive clatter. "Now, here's another guy wants to talk to you. Hang on. I'll be seeing you."

The circuit closed and opened again and went into smooth signals.

"This is Russ Kruger, Eddie. About that gal of Hi

Wheeler's you were asking me about. You know who she is? She's Gladys Straightland."

"What of it?" said Eddie.

"You don't know who she is? She's been in the papers. She promoted an oil company herself, drilled on that land of hers and Hi's, and's made a hatful of money. Calls it the Hi Wheeler Petroleum Company."

"Repeat that last sentence," Eddie sent dumbly.

"It's a fact, Eddie. I told her about Hi, and she's standing right here beside me, and she wants to know in a hurry exactly where he is."

"What does she want to know that for?" he slipped in cautiously.

"Well, doggone, Eddie, I don't know. But she's standing over me in a very threatening position, and saying if I don't find out where he is, I won't be able to work again this year. She says she was to meet him in some town in Utah, and then she got entangled promoting this oil property, and wired him to come back. Altho' she practically called out the Utah militia, nobody'd ever heard of Hi in that state."

"It was Colorado," Eddie sent faintly. "How'd she ever get the idea it was Utah?"

"Don't ask me, and you can tell Hi if he wants to see her, she's here, but he'd better bring a blamed good alibi, or else a competent personal guard."

XXXV

THE CROWD milled around the president's special when it backed in to the station at five. Preston got off his private car to greet old employes and the townsfolk who had known him when he had worked here.

Roger came down the stairs and stood on the threshold, looking over the heads of the crowd. His father saw him and beckoned. They met just outside the bay window where Eddie sat at the telegraph table. The crowd stood back from the two.

Samuel T. Preston still showed evidence that he had been a brawny man. Even in these later years his shoulders bulged more than his waist. He was pink-cheeked, dynamic and masterful in a florid, magnetic way.

You could feel the sparks of dissension hop when the two met. The old man's overpowering personality irritated Roger. He sullenly resented his father's brisk dominance. Preston fretted at his son's dull rebellion without trying to fathom it.

"You will sit with me tonight at dinner," Preston said without greeting. He was absorbed in his duties as host to all this gathering. "I have asked the toastmaster to call on you for a few remarks. I should like these men I have with me to know you better."

"How are you, dad?" Roger asked ironically, and looked at his father with ice-blue eyes. "I'll come to dinner, but I won't talk."

Preston was momentarily impatient. "Anyhow, come to my car after you have dressed," he said shortly. "I want to hear how you have been doing."

Roger took his eyes away. "All right," he said.

An old timer from the dispatchers' office relieved Eddie at 7:30 and he went home to dress. Bernice was waiting for him in Mrs. McGurk's parlor when he came down. Her white dress seemed a floating mist about her, and her small face was radiant under a cloud of burnished hair. She was sweet and a little breathtaking, and he told her so with a dryness in his throat.

"Thank you, Eddie," she said. "I know you mean it."

She turned her face up to his, and he kissed her slowly on the lips.

"I'll say it again, if I get paid like that," he said with a lame grin.

She was looking at him through a bright haze across a gray distance, like a mirage. He could feel the tight vacuum silence close in, and then her voice came through like a faint echo.

"When are you leaving, Eddie?"

He listened attentively till that sound died away in the distance.

"Leaving?" he fumbled. "Why—what made you say that?"

"It's in your eyes, Eddie. You are looking at something—very far away."

"Looking at you," he said. There was a hammering on his ribs. "Anyhow, we'll have fun tonight." The drumming eased off. "And listen. You be careful how you let any one tinker with that golden heart of yours."

Mrs. McGurk bustled in, bedecked and beribboned.

"Ah, and a fine couple you make," she beamed. "Eddie, she is a lovely girl."

"I've just told her that," he said. "And you look pretty well yourself. But if you're going with us you'll have to be a good girl."

"With you, indeed!" Mrs. McGurk bridled. "I have a man of my own."

Jasper came in to say good night. He made his manners with grave politeness. He kept his solemn eyes on Bernice.

"Eddie," he murmured, "I am going to have a girl like that some day."

"You'll likely have to look far and wide," he told the kid.

The lights of Crestline came out hard and clear in the high, crisp air. The rigid beam of the searchlight on top of the hotel reached out across the peaks and spotted a distant scenic spectacle for the delight of some audience up there on the high battlement. That searchlight, brought out here from some world's fair, was still worth a paragraph in the hotel's advertising folders. Arc lights glowed and sputtered far out on the new bridge, and the big crane coughed jets of steam. They were pushing through the last odd bits of construction so that the span would be ready for the opening in the morning.

Preston's special was parked on the ramp beyond the station. The tram cars were busy picking up passengers from the platform below and swinging them aloft to the hotel. There was a great crowd in the ballroom, and on the wide terrace outside, but space here was vast and there was no crush. Chandeliers glowed dimly from the high dome of the ceiling above the dance floor. The folding doors leading to the banquet room were closed, but already, if you got close to them, you could hear an orator on the other side taking flight.

It was all on the grand scale. The orchestra on the platform loomed like a mass meeting. The music eddied and clung in the great room. They slipped into a waltz. They both had the light, easy grace that made their movements effortless. The heady feeling that had come with the contact of her lips hadn't left him. They drifted together in a grave enchantment.

The music died and picked up again to the patter of hands. His mind came slowly out of a drift of warm fancies. Mrs. McGurk and little old Johnnie McFee danced by exuberantly. Johnnie was following his daughter into the higher reaches of society, aided by Mrs. McGurk, and he was doing very well with the dance. He could still step with the best of them. He nudged Eddie impishly as he swung by.

"Everybody is having such fun," Bernice murmured. "Dad will certainly burst a blood vessel if he doesn't calm down."

"That's his inalienable right," he said. "Let him bust it."

The music faded. A lean figure loomed up beside them in the dim light, and Superintendent Monahan issued a jovial decree.

"You're outranked for the moment, young man," he declared. "It's not often an old fellow like me has a chance with the girls, and I'm not overlooking this one. I'll trouble you to relinquish the lady to your superior officer," he ordered.

"It's the only time I ever wanted to be a brass hat," Eddie mourned. "How come you're not in there listening to the gems of thought and eating rare food?" he complained.

"Not with this going on out here," Monahan said as they danced away.

He sought the punch bowl, but the mildness of the

brew discouraged him at the first swallow. The bar was supposed to be closed for that evening, which was all right, considering such a large and mixed gathering, but you couldn't be shot for trying to circumvent that. Collusion with subordinates was the answer. A high sign to the hotel clerk on duty got him piloted to an obscure entrance to the bar, which was already inhabited by a New York banker, two ex-congressmen and several members of the press. He was provided with a tall, tinkling glass.

He was in a calm mood of self-determination when he heard the music falter and die in the ballroom, and he went out quickly to find if Bernice was occupied. The division engineer had taken over from Monahan, and the chief traveling auditor was bidding for the next. The girl was knocking the brass hats over in rows. He sought Mrs. McGurk, and went through the cyclone of the next dance with her.

He detoured through the bar again and came out onto the wide terrace where the brisk air did him good. He leaned on the stone wall that guarded the abrupt fall of some hundreds of feet to the station and the yard below. A circle of grim peaks rolled away and reached for the stars. They were still tinkering with the last small jobs out there on the bridge under the arcs. Tomorrow the president's special would cross the completed structure with much rejoicing. Progress and prosperity rolled on. But somebody always got mangled in the rush. Like those what's-their-name—those Kincaid brothers that Roger bothered about.

Dim lights glowed through the length of Preston's train on the ramp. A faint wedge of light shot up from the engine's firebox. A shadow swayed in the cab as an engine watchman stoked the fire to keep the locomotive alive. The ring of the shovel came up in a clear cadence above the hum of the throng. The radiance died as the watchman closed the firebox door. He descended and scurried across the platform.

Back in the ballroom he found Bernice surrounded by the first and third trick dispatchers, Burton, the baggage smasher, the general manager's chief clerk and Big Bud Salverson, the chief special agent. The men wrangled gallantly, and the girl handled the occasion in the right spirit to make it fun. She saw him and beckoned, and he wedged in among the rest.

"Ain't a feller got any rights here with the girl he brought?" he complained. "I demand the protection of the law," he declared to Big Bud, and took Bernice's arm and they moved out onto the terrace.

He could see the folding doors to the banquet room. One was suddenly edged back and a figure with considerable expanse of white shirt front strode through. It was Roger, bored and impatient and lit with champagne. Eddie had an instant glimpse of the banquet tables lined with politely attentive faces. At the speakers' table by the farther wall, Preston had come to his feet. He was staring angrily after his son.

Roger prowled through the dim ballroom, and came out on the terrace, wedging through the crowd. He strode up to them and exploded.

"I couldn't stand that boiler shop another minute," he rumbled. "Come on, Bernice. We'll have a drink at the bar, and then we'll dance."

He was in a typhoon mood, bent on blasting everything in his way. Eddie felt himself tighten up inside, but his mind was clear and sharp-edged.

"I wouldn't care for a drink," she said quietly, "and the next dance is Eddie's."

Roger's teeth glinted in a stubborn, stormy smile.

"Always the next one is Eddie's," he said. "But he will excuse you, I know. I haven't had any fun all evening."

"But I don't want to be excused, Roger."

"Aw, come on!" He took her by the arm.

"Roger," she protested.

The tension inside Eddie slacked away in a smooth ripple of muscles. The keen edges of his thoughts cut through the shifting designs.

Roger chuckled the moist laugh that always came when he tormented someone. Then the sound was shut off as a voice spoke in his ear.

"Pipe down, Roger. Gentlemen from the higher brackets don't do that."

Roger turned. You could tell he'd been an athlete by the way he spun lightly on his feet, all set to kick and gouge. His ice-blue eyes tangled with Eddie's cold, gray glance. Their faces were close together.

The music wandered out onto the terrace. The sound of the crowd moved across the quiet slopes. Eddie stopped a passing figure without turning.

"Johnson," he said to the first trick dispatcher, "please dance this one with Miss McFee in my place."

The girl came toward him.

"Please, Bernice," he said.

She stopped and turned in quick obedience and took the trick man's arm. They moved away into the shadows.

That was quietly done within breathless seconds. The chattering groups hadn't observed the quick threat of a disturbance.

Eddie said easily, "Why don't you buy me that drink, Roger? I'd really appreciate it."

The dark red kept surging into Roger's cheeks. He quit trying to restrain himself.

"That thin skirt!" he said harshly. "That shanty Irish—"

Eddie hit Roger Preston, the president's son, on the mouth with a quick, hard blow swung from all the way back. There was second degree murder in his heart for that blinding second, and he knew how to hit. It exploded as spontaneously as the red flame in his eyes. It was like flipping a switch and turning high voltage current into a wire. It blazed that quick.

It rocked the bulk of muscle and accumulated fat, and Roger shook his head and sputtered blood from his cut lips. Then he crouched and lunged with his arms extended to grapple.

His red fury cooled to the calculated, destructive instinct that Walley Sterling had brutally drilled into him. It was easy and automatic to catch one of those big forearms in both hands, to twist and pivot and bring it over his shoulder and heave. It increased the momentum of Roger's rush, and Eddie's skill went into the wrench he gave as he pitched Roger into a flying mare. He checked the flight of the big body with a yank that slammed it down on the flagstones. Roger lit with an amazed grunt. He squirmed and clutched at the air with his stubby hands.

Eddie stood back and watched him coolly. Blurred faces drifted close, and the distant murmur of voices bumbled about his ears. A clear voice detached itself, passionless with authority.

"Stand up, Roger!"

The babble flitted away into the silence out there among the undisturbed dark peaks.

Roger's head rolled on the rock floor, and he stared up at the ring of faces. Two men stepped forward to help him to his feet.

"Stand away," the voice cut in. "Please," it added.

The faces swam into focus. Samuel L. Preston, president of the Empire Line, stood beside Eddie and stared down at his son. He wasn't paternal. He was fighting Sam Preston who had battled his way to a top place.

"On your feet!"

Roger stood up as if jerked by a violent force. He put a handkerchief to his lips and looked at his father sullenly.

You could follow a little the old man's quick calculations as the two faced each other. His impatient resentment subsided. It was probably the first time he had ever seen his son hurt. He started to speak, then checked himself.

Eddie's mind slipped into the current of immediate concerns. He reached for an easy tone of voice.

"Look, Mr. Preston," he said. "I'll take care of Roger. You go on back to your orators."

Preston turned his massive head and stared. It was like withstanding a cold needle shower to face those other ice-blue eyes. The stare moderated reflectively.

"It may be," Preston said at last, "that you can do a better job of that than ever I have."

Eddie hooked his arm through Roger's. "Come on," he said, "and buy me that drink."

Roger pulled his eyes from his father, and looked at the boomer. A slow, puzzled expression puckered on his round face.

"You're certainly quite a package of dynamite," he pondered. "Where in hell do you carry it?"

Eddie pulled at his arm. "I'll show you that trick some time," he said.

They walked slowly through the crowd. Preston followed, and then turned into the banquet room.

Eddie halted outside the bar. "I don't know what you were going to say about Bernice," he said, "but whatever

was in your mind I want you to take back right now—or
I'll bust every bone in your head."

Roger turned that over slowly. "I was wrong about
that," he decided, "but I'll make my apology to the proper
person, which isn't you." He studied the boomer again.
"It's good I know how to fall, or you'd have about killed
me. And for that I am going to take you apart one of these
days. Now, what'll you have?"

"Any time," Eddie said, "you want to pick this up and
carry it along, just help yourself. I'll take Bourbon."

XXXVI

THE DOORS to the banquet room had been thrown open when they came through the lobby. White shirt fronts showed on the dance floor and among the crowd on the terrace. Roger drew Eddie away into the shadows and hoisted himself up onto the parapet and stared moodily out over the peaks.

"My old man," he said, "doesn't think a lot of me. Never did. I suppose I wasn't worth much thought. But he might have taken some time out to see for sure, especially when I was a kid."

"It takes up a lot of a man's time, running a railroad," Eddie pointed out. "But maybe now, if you'd go to him in the right tone of voice, you two might get together."

"You're an odd fellow," Roger considered seriously.

"So are you," Eddie said.

Preston, the governor, and their party came out onto the terrace. They passed close by, and Preston turned aside and spoke to his son.

"You weren't badly hurt, were you?" he inquired.

"No," said Roger, "but it sobered me up more than I like right at this moment."

Preston's smile flickered an insant.

It was midnight and the clatter on the bridge died away. The steam crane's whistle piped and her long boom swung in. Workmen came hurrying across the ramp. The

arc lights fluttered out, leaving one glowing at the material pile out in the center where the small section remained to be filled at the ceremonies tomorrow.

Some early homebound guests boarded the tram from
the platform just above them. The car dropped slowly past
the parapet, and dodged the car coming up at a strip of
double track in the middle of the incline. The power unit
was just above the platform. The operator leaned out of
the window, watching the crowd. The searchlight on the
tower played on the eternal snow of a distant peak. A
figure in white came through the shadows.

"Eddie," Bernice said, "you have danced with me only
once."

"And I get blamed for it," he lamented. "My life's
worth practically nothing among these savages when I try
to approach you."

She took his arm, and Eddie said, "Excuse me, Roger."

"Wait a minute," Roger said.

Eddie looked at him steadily.

"Bernice," said Roger. He thought out his words doggedly. "I don't think I've ever said I was sorry to anybody
before. But I'll say it to you now."

"That was nicely spoken," she nodded brightly.

She held out her hand, and he took it gently in the
stubby fingers that could handle greasy machine parts so
deftly.

The crisp stars flickered in the velvet black of the sky,
and the music and the murmur of voices barely ruffled the
crisp silence of the heights. Then a locomotive's whistle
shouted on the ramp below. The harsh blast tossed shrill
echoes along the dark walls, and they tumbled away into
the quiet of the brooding peaks. The abrupt howl ceased,
but the silence seemed barely able to struggle back.

The headlight on the special's engine lit and slashed a

lean bar of light across the high ramp and the bridge. A cloud of lazy black smoke pushed up into the still air. Compressed air sizzled and sighed, and brakeshoes clanked as they released their hold. The engine's stack exploded and chased the cloud of smoke into a smudge across the stars. The line of coaches rolled into slow motion as the engine's exhaust snarled. The special headed out across the high approach toward the bridge with a gap in its center.

Your senses couldn't quite appreciate that it was anything but a bit of rehearsed melodrama, the way that train moved out all by itself. It hit you as weird and ominous, like a performance on the stage against a painted backdrop of mountains and stars. You felt the thrill of impending catastrophe; it was a good show, and pretty quick it would be over and no harm done.

And then Sam Preston's voice boomed out above the chug of the locomotive. "What's happening down there, Monahan? What are they doing to my train?"

"I can't think why anybody would be moving it," the division superintendent said in a tight voice.

If it wasn't a stage play, then you were watching a grim nightmare. The special moved slowly out over the ramp, the engine chugging on an easy throttle. And that seemed blasphemous. You treated the president's special with the marked respect of something sacred. Some almost took off their hats to it. Seeing it wander aimlessly away toward that gap in the bridge and destruction, made you certain that some whimsical demon spirit was playing a profane prank on the Old Man. It cut the air from your lungs.

"Monahan!" Preston cried. "Can't you have that train stopped before it gets into the river?"

Monahan was leaning over the parapet, desperately trying to figure a quick way of descent to the station platform.

There wasn't any, unless you tobogganed down the rock dome; then you wouldn't be able to do anything about it after you landed. The tramcars had no speed.

Monahan lifted up his voice and bellowed. And as that tortured sound sank into the gorge and slid away into the murmur of the rivers, compressed air sighed again, and brakeshoes mumbled. The special drew to a gentle stop as if obedient to the division superintendent's harsh command.

A figure moved vaguely on the ramp behind the special. It stooped and fumbled. It knelt and was still.

"Who are you down there?" Preston called.

The figure stood up and skipped over the open ties to the station platform.

A tight little explosion barked from the ramp. It was no louder than the report of a shotgun till the echoes took it up and multiplied it along the ridges. Two vicious balls of flame bounced on the ramp, and winked out in smoke. In the instant glow, two parallel steel beams twisted outward from the truss. A section of track lurched and sagged and fell onto the slanting rock face of the dome and slid into the river.

A voice broke through the pounding echoes. It came up resounding through the megaphone of rock walls.

"Up there on top of the hotel," the voice rang. "Turn that searchlight down here on the engine."

The hard white beam above hesitated on the skyline. Then it wandered down across the ridges and the churning water and picked out the special's locomotive. A man stood on the roof of the cab, and a figure that didn't come up to his waist line was huddled beside him. The man cupped his hands to his mouth.

"Sam Preston, up there on the terrace," his voice came singing along the gorge. "Do you recognize me?"

The beam of the searchlight cut just above Preston's head, and the white in his hair gleamed in the reflected light.

"Yes, Olin Kincaid, I'd recognize you in hell," Preston called back angrily. "What do you want?"

"Nothing!" The single word made another light explosion.

Figures crowded the terrace and faces leaned out over the parapet, staring at the two on the roof of the cab. The beam of the searchlight flowed down and distorted them in a pool of shimmering light.

Eddie said quietly, "That's the woman who was with the man who brought Jasper to the station that night, and left him there." His mind was working like a watch. "And that's Jasper he has with him now."

"What are you talking about?" Roger muttered. "That's not a woman. It's a man."

"He was dressed in women's clothes that night," Eddie said. "You'd not think I could be sure at this distance, but that woman has bothered my mind ever since. I knew it wasn't a woman then. But I didn't realize it. Now, he's got Jasper again."

"That is Jasper!" Bernice cried.

The voice funneled up from the gorge. "Listen, Sam Preston. You made your big mistake when you broke me and my brother, and then thought you wouldn't have to pay plenty for it. Now, you can watch while we give you back some of your own bad medicine."

Preston's voice rumbled. "Olin, you can destroy that bridge, and my train with it, and then they will be immediately replaced. But you will go to prison for a long time."

The laugh that skipped up along the granite walls had a good deal of vicious satisfaction in it. "Not to prison," Kincaid scoffed. "I was raised in this country, and there's a

lot of it that's never been infringed on by the law. And it
ain't your bridge I'm after," he hooted. "I'm going to work
it out on your little son Jerry. I've got him here beside
me."

"You haven't got my son there," Preston boomed at
him. "He is at our home in California."

"You mean that's where you left him," Kincaid jeered.
"Left him with servants while your wife goes to Europe,
and you mind your railroad. Servants are easy bribed,
Sam." He held up the short figure at arms' length above
him. "There's your dad up there, Jerry. Speak to him,"
he ordered.

"Hello, father," a small voice came up through the
stillness. "I wish you would come and get me."

"Jerry!" There was a trace of horror now in Sam
Preston's voice as he hung over the parapet and stared.

"We kidnapped him more than a month ago," Kincaid
called, "for ramson. But you don't keep in touch with your
family, so you never found out that he'd been stolen. That
was a joke, and it sure made us change our plans." He
rasped a laugh that wasn't funny. "Now, I'm going to
secure him in the cab of this engine, and start her up, and
let the works roll into the river." His harsh cackle fluttered like bats in the gorge. "You just saw my brother
blow a section out of this ramp so you can't get to your
train in time to stop it. And nobody can swim the river.
So you just stay up there, Sam, and watch it happen."

And he's not fooling, either, Eddie decided. The man
was wild enough to do fantastic things for vengeance.
He'd figured this one out at the last minute, after his other
schemes had been spoiled, and he was going all the way
out now. There didn't seem any way of stopping him if he
quit talking and got to moving; and it looked as if he had,

for he stooped and swung the kid in through the cab window, and then sprawled down after him.

A man leaned out beside Preston, his arm extended and at rest on the parapet. Big Bud Salverson was about to try a shot with his own .45. That was chancy, and Preston shoved his arm down.

"Don't do that," he ordered.

Roger's voice came through fitfully, as if he was talking in a gusty wind. "I could reach that engine with the crane." It sounded like that.

The engine coughed lazily. Time froze into hard, cold seconds beat out by the stamp of the stack. The picture of the still, stiff figures on the terrace, and the slowly rolling train, switched out of his mind as Eddie swung to the top of the wall and twisted to the outer edge.

"Come on, Roger," he hissed. "Snap into this."

He dropped to the tramway and scrambled up the imbedded ties to the empty car by the loading platform above. He boosted himself over the lower end and sprang up the step-like seats and spoke to the operator hanging in the engine room window.

"Lower away, George," he ordered. "Get this car down just as fast as she'll slide."

"She's got only one speed, Eddie," George said, "and here it is."

The car dropped away quietly. It shuddered as Roger came up over the lower end. Bernice leaned on the parapet as they glided past.

"Eddie," she called, "be careful."

It would have been more pious if she'd said that to Roger. You couldn't, however, debate effects when the seconds were scarce. The car slid down the incline at a reluctant crawl. Roger leaned over the side, peering down.

"Eddie," he said, "Jasper is really my half-brother, and his name is Jerry."

"Yeah," said Eddie. "I got that."

"I saw him once, when he was about three." Roger pondered. "Do you know, he isn't a bad kid."

"He's likely worth saving for the next time," Eddie said.

There were low crowd sounds on the terrace and rows of white faces peering down. You couldn't see into the engine's cab. Her bell began to toll above the lazy chuff and the mutter of coach wheels.

Roger asked, "Are you going to let me swing you over on the big hook?"

"What else?" Eddie said.

"I might bat you against the engine, or the head coach, or drop you in the water," Roger considered. "I don't know if I'm good enough to spot you at the right point, without knocking your brains out."

"You're good enough," he said. "Or'd better be. Now take it easy."

Roger slid out of his dress coat and vest. He ripped off his high collar and tore the stiff shirt from him with a quick tug. His big body bulged through his thin undershirt.

"I don't know how good my nerve is in a situation like this." Roger deliberated hard. "Or how fast I can think. But we'll soon find out. I'll try not to hurt you."

"That's not the idea," Eddie said impatiently. "You just get me across at approximately the right spot at the second I should be there. Concentrate on that."

They jumped clear of the car as it nestled into its berth at the bottom. They plunged across the platform and headed into the yard.

"I hope there's steam up in the crane's engine," Roger muttered as he ran.

Switch lights jogged past them as they ducked through the lines of rolling stock. They lunged at the embankment of the old main line. There was a feather of steam showing at the crane's safety as they pounded out onto the bench blasted into the wall of the Pinnacle. The dismal bang of the engine bell beat out unhurried notes, a kind of doleful aftertime to the deliberate chuff of the exhaust and the dragging clank of brasses. The beam of the headlight moved calmly over the bridge and flattened against the farther wall of the gorge.

Against the glint of starlight on churning water, a shadow moved down the steel leg of one of the approach trusses. A man in a boat waited just below in the quiet current close to the bank. The Kincaids would now head down the river for the wild country to the south that had spawned them.

The lone arc light glowed above the gap in the bridge. The special's engine wasn't far from that blank space in the steel structure. From the rails to the water it was a hundred and eighty feet at that point. You could make a pretty close estimate from the slow turn of the drivers how many seconds the train was from the opening. But fore-knowledge wasn't going to help much now. You still had to make the try.

The hard beam of the searchlight on top of the hotel followed the train like a bright indicator. There wasn't much reflected light on the bench. A soft glow showed at the firebox of the crane. The river snarled and raced along the granite wall below. The iron tongue of the engine bell kept up its dismal beat.

Roger stumbled over rubble beside the crane and snatched at a grab iron and swung himself up among levers. Eddie ran forward under the long steel boom. When he stopped beside the big hook, the thin air he gulped felt like a chill shower on his sweating body.

Then steam stuttered from the crane's engine and the cable drum mumbled. The boom jerked up and down above him. He set his feet in the hook and held the cable with both hands. The bench dropped from under him in a sudden swoop. The high wall of the Pinnacle backed into the gloom as he swung into cold space above the river. The boom checked so abruptly that the hook swept out over the bridge in a dizzy, pendulum stroke. The dark knob and the glowing hotel dipped in a giddy bow. The crisp air hissed in his ears and cut through his shirt in cold needles. The clang of the engine bell came from close under his ear, and the gleam of the searchlight flickered across his eyes. Smoke from the stack scratched his throat. The dim world spun as the big hook swung back through the cold darkness.

Arc lights on the bridge and along the bench sputtered into ghastly light. The black wall of the Pinnacle rushed at him. He'd sure make an unseemly splatter if he hit that solid surface. The special plodded calmly toward the blank space in the bridge. Roger had been having trouble with the levers, but suddenly you felt those stubby hands master them. A quick flip of the boom checked Eddie's wide swing, and he dangled above the water.

Roger played him like a trout fly for short seconds. The end of the boom moved smoothly out toward the engine. He kicked it to give the hook a little sway, and lowered gently and dropped Eddie to the cab window at the exact split second the engine moved by and the boom had swung out to its full length from the bench.

The searchlight was in Eddie's eyes, and he had to make a blind guess as the big hook swung in close. He let go and grabbed for the window frame. His knees came down on the arm rest. He slid into the engineer's seat and slammed the throttle shut. He fumbled for the brake valve handle and shoved it all the way over. Compressed air broke out in a soft explosion and brakeshoes grabbed and grunted. The slow motion of the special died. The air pump throbbed dully.

Jasper stared at him solemnly from the fireman's seat.

XXXVII

IT SEEMED intolerably stuffy in the luxurious office of the manager of the hotel, with all these people crowded into a space already jammed with massive furniture. Roger and his father took up most of the room, and Eddie was crowded into a corner as they tried to keep out of the way of Bernice, who was helping the doctor while he examined the boy on the couch.

Eddie got out his kerchief and ran it around the edge of his stiff collar. His hands were dirty and his blue suit mussed up from that flying trapeze stunt on the big hook. What a mess.

The doctor stood up. "There's nothing wrong with him," he said. "He isn't even badly frightened. A very sturdy lad."

The boy sat up. "Eddie," he said solemnly, "you nearly missed your holds when you swung into the cab window. I thought for a second you weren't going to make it."

"Don't I know it," he said. "I just wished myself into the cab. That searchlight was in my eyes."

The kid had a tenacious mind, too. His name was Jerry, but he'd always remember him as Jasper. It fitted him better—serious and quiet.

Roger opened the door to let in some air, and Preston

sat on the manager's desk. The old man was thinking. You could feel the thoughts plunging through his big head.

"Do you think," he asked the doctor, "that Jerry could stand a trip up into the mountains with me?"

"I think it would do him good," the doctor said.

The old man looked at Roger. "I'd planned a hunting trip, starting right after we opened the bridge, with one of our vice-presidents," he said. "I can find an excuse to send him back to headquarters, if you will go along instead, Roger. Just Jerry and you and I, with a guide and a cook. Want to try, and see what comes of it?"

Roger stared back at his father somberly. You could feel the labored thoughts working through his mind.

"Well," he said, "we might."

Preston turned a brisk eye on Eddie. "That was an extraordinary performance of yours out there," he nodded.

"It was Roger's idea," Eddie said. "All I did was grab hold, hang on and then let go at the right moment."

"Remarkable, nevertheless," Preston said, and he nodded again at some resolve. "Roger has just been telling me a little about you. We'll have a talk when I return from the mountains. I think we can make it worth while for you to stay with us."

In a flare of gratitude, the mighty would try to arrange your future for you in one quick decision. They crowded you with it in the first warm flush of thanksgiving. They were, however, pretty busy with their own affairs, and gratitude cooled quickly. You couldn't hang around and live on it. Obligations like that were incidental items. What they tried to do for you wasn't what you wanted.

They'd give you a place of authority behind a desk, and that kept you tied. The circle of your leash held you to a pin point that would quickly grow monotonous. You had to live with a steady job, and a homestead, all the days of your life. The more you acquired, the more worries you had. Position and property—and babies. They all added up fast and kept your restless feet from the careless road.

A disorderly figure shuffled to the doorway and peered into the brightly lighted room.

"Well?" said Preston shortly.

"Is Eddie Sand here?" a plaintive voice inquired. It was Hi Wheeler, just off a run, in his working clothes.

"Coming, Hi," Eddie said. He shook hands with Preston briefly. "They're calling me," he said vaguely. "Will you excuse me, Bernice? Roger," he said, "please see that Miss McFee gets home safely."

Roger's round face lighted. "Of course, Eddie," he agreed. He reflected. "I nearly snapped your head off, that first move I made with the crane," he said. "I was a little flustered at the start."

"Mister," Eddie said, "if I could handle machinery like you can, I'd get me a job in the back shop tomorrow."

"Well," Roger considered, "I might do that."

"You certainly might," said Preston and nodded again.

"I'll see you when I get back," Roger promised.

Eddie turned. He'd make it quick and careless.

Bernice fumbled with her gloves. "Good-by," she said. She glanced at him with the flicker of a smile, and then looked away. "I'll always remember," she said.

"Yeah," he nodded. "I guess I will, too." Her hand was warm with a quick pressure, and then was gone. "Good night," he said.

He edged Hi out of the doorway, and they cross the lobby.

"Listen, Eddie," Hi pleaded. "I didn't want to horn in on your social affairs, but there was a note from the trainmaster for me at the yard office when I just now got in, that said I was to turn in the company equipment I have, and where did I want my time check sent. It looked like I was fired, but they said you'd arranged it, and I was to see you right away."

"That's right," he said.

Hi looked relieved. "It didn't sound pious, but as long as you say so it's O. K. with me," he said cheerfully.

There weren't many people on the chill terrace, and the crowd had thinned out on the dance floor. The music died, then grew softly into the strains of "Home, Sweet Home."

They paused a moment outside to watch the quick shift of partners, and then the couples wove in and out to the slow melody. Bernice and Roger came across the lobby and moved quietly out upon the floor in step. They blurred and faded out among the gliding figures under the dim chandeliers.

"So that's the way you wanted it," Hi said.

"Yeah," Eddie said. "I guess it is." He grinned. "But maybe I'll have some doubts later."

The sharp stars hopped along the far line of peaks. The mountains crowded close overhead, shouldered in, held back the sky.

"Most usually," said Hi as they cross the yard, "your doubts don't last that long." He kicked headend cinders with his heavy shoes. "Right now," he asked, "have you got any idea which way we're headin'?"

"I have the sniffles again," Eddie said. "I ought to go where they'd get dried out."

"Seemed more like horse distemper to me," Hi jeered.

They turned into the yard office, and Eddie glanced at the runboard.

"We'll take the hotshot that's about due out now," he decided. "I strangled your clothes and put them in your grip, and mine too, and sent them down here."

He reached behind the counter and dragged out two

suitcases. They went down a makeup track along a line of cars, and climbed into the attached caboose. The train sounded off, and they pulled out of the yard. The conductor and rear brakeman swung aboard at the main line switch, and the two Mallets took up the burden of the train with savage grunts as the grade began.

The conductor eyed them whimsically. "You fellers have to leave town between suns?" he inquired. "If so, and do they ask me, am I to tell them which way you went?" He stacked his waybills on his desk and began his pencil work.

Hi brooded long, and then spoke. "About how far south will them sniffles take us?" he asked cautiously.

"How about down to the Southwestern?" Eddie suggested.

"Hey, back with old Buck Barabe? Do you think he'd hire us again?"

"He'd be passing up two blamed good hands, if he didn't."

"Yeah, but it might be pretty hard to make him realize that." Hi reflected suspiciously. "Is Walley Sterling down there?"

"Yeah, he's there."

"Mister," Hi said plaintively, "I hope he's in a more sober state of mind than he was in Chicago. You sure remain rapidly with that boy when he gets turbulent."

Hi began to whistle softly. Some inner contentment seemed to flood through him quietly. You couldn't find that hurt-dog look behind the oafish twinkle of his eyes. Eddie studied him sharply.

"How did you know that Gladys would be down there waiting for you?" he demanded.

Hi turned that over and over in his mind. He shook his head and puckered his brow. "Well," he said, "I can't just exactly say how I know it. I guess it's been kicking around in my head all this time that I ought to have found out about why she didn't show up when she said she would, back there on the A. S. L." His face screwed up into a tight, dubious knot. "I know she's going to be glad to see me, but at the same time she'll give me hell."

Eddie got a book out of his suitcase, and climbed into the cupola. The morning sunlight was running fast along the peaks and saddles and the bald knobs. The train snaked out ahead on the savage grades. The heights throbbed to the crack of the Mallets' exhaust. He opened the book, and the black type grated harshly across his eyeballs. He slapped it shut.

The books didn't deal with the drab stretches of head colds and mornings after and bad temper and going broke; with senseless bickerings and the long intervals when nothing happened but the bare routine of living. Maybe he was trying to live life like the books designed it, a strong-flowing river headed relentlessly for some particular sea of its own, where it would be forever content. A gross exaggeration, and his reason fiercely rejected that last concept. The theory of final, blissful, static existence was a very terrible solution. It was practically as bad as being dead.

And another thing, he lectured himself, was the restricted number of people in the books. The proposition that long friendships and permanent associations was very, very delightful—as a supposition. But the spice of life was the people you met for brief periods, and then dropped them behind. You got their best aspects that way, and if they were exceptional they remained in bright memories that you could bring forward in an association of the mind at your own convenience.

The faces of all the nice people he'd encountered back

along the high iron highway flickered across his memory, and faded out. He slid the cupola window open and cheerfully tossed the book into space. It flapped disconsolately and drifted into the sheer blue depths of the canyon toward the silver thread of the river far below.

The cluck and clatter of busy wheels under him made better music than any orchestra. The thunder of the two big locomotives as they blasted at the grade stepped up your pulse and made it sing. The yell of the whistle ripped through the dark walls and the echoes leaped to the bright sky. The flow of swift rail traffic was in his blood. He liked the exultant, screaming hotshots and the roar of storming wheels going some place else. The air from the open window leaned against his face. He felt good.

POSTSCRIPT

ABOUT THE WAR

That afternoon of Pearl Harbor, some Old-Timers, off the Rio Grande Railroad, sat together listening to the radio's staccato reports of the growing disaster. You could catch in the calm, weathered faces and quiet, thoughtful eyes the pictures that ran through those seasoned minds.

Up there on the high iron, where it climbs ten thousand feet and more over the Continental Divide, they had many times waited in lone telegraph stations, their trains snow-bound, while the little telegraph sounders chanted tidings of the blizzard's havoc. The storm had struck without warning. There wasn't a thing they could do about it at the moment, and they didn't waste energy fretting about it. At headquarters, the Old Man directed the campaign against the storm. Swiftly he moved each item of men and equipment into the conflict, with just one object in his strategy—to clear the line, to keep the traffic moving. They knew the Old Man would eventually outmaneuver the elements. Presently your turn would come and you would be shoved into the fight. Till then, keep your feet on the ground and be sure you would be ready when you got the nod.

Those Old Timers guessed the worst that had happened out there in Hawaii that Sunday, long before the official figures were posted. We faced a desperate situation. We skirted the thin edge of disaster. Still, they weren't dis-turbed. They reckoned the long fight ahead that would

317

cost much of what they had. A good many of the benefits
they had faced the daily hazards of mountain railroading
to create, would be destroyed. The price of freedom was
high. But they had the calm certainty, the absolute faith,
that whatever the price we would pay it. The country was
sound and alert. We had the men, the brains, and we had
the capacity and the resources to make the equipment.
They awaited their turn to be shoved into the fight. They
looked to headquarters to give the order. That was their
training.

HARRY BEDWELL

May 19, 1942

GLOSSARY OF RAILROAD TERMS AND SLANG

bad order
> to designate a railroad car to be in need of required maintenance or repair

blew out the flagman
> guarding a train that has made an unscheduled stop: the engineer sounds a unique whistle signal to notify the rear brakeman to depart the train a distance of approximately 300 yards and mount torpedoes (small cans of an explosive that wrap over the rail) and display a red flag to wave any approaching train to a stop; another whistle signal recalls the flagman when the train is notified to proceed

blind siding
> a siding that has a switch at one end only, requiring a train ordered to take the siding to either back in or back out

board
> a fixed signal that regulates the movement of trains

brass hat
> a railroad official or executive

brass pounder
> a telegraph operator

brownies
> demerit points for rule infractions: a specified number of demerits within a specified period of time results in the offend-

ing employee being dismissed; named for the discipline system's creator, George R. Brown

bulled a train order

to ignore or erroneously relay a train movement ordered by the dispatcher

call

the initials or abbreviation of a telegraph operator that identifies the operator or the operator's location

car-tink

an employee of the railroad's mechanical department responsible for making repairs to equipment

chief dispatcher

the person with overall responsibility for planning and ordering the movement of trains within a division of a railroad

conductor

the person designated to be in charge of a train's crew

cutting itself in two

intentionally breaking an assembled train into two sections; usually to enable a heavy train to be pulled up a grade without the assistance of a helper engine or to enable a train to fit into track space assigned to it by orders, but occasionally by an accident that will earn the engineer brownies

dicks

railroad police

dispatcher

the person who plans for and executes the movement of trains

double track

two lengths of main line track laid parallel to expedite the rapid movement of trains in two directions simultaneously and if necessary to enable a faster train to pass another traveling in the same direction

drawbar
> commonly refers to the device—couplers—that connects locomotives and cars assembled into a train

emigrant car
> a cheaply finished car used by emigrants to transport themselves and their possessions to a new settlement

extra crew
> a team of workers who lack sufficient seniority to bid on a regular job and who are called to work only when needed

given the board
> when a train has received a signal that allows it to proceed

hand car
> a small, light rail car equipped with cranks or levers and gearing so that it can be propelled along the track by hand by persons riding on the car

helper engine
> a locomotive placed at the rear of a train to help the head-end locomotive move the train up a heavy grade, after which it usually cuts off and returns to its base

Hog law
> maximum hours-of-service law that applies to a train's crew (at the time described in The Boomer, the maximum was sixteen hours)

hogger
> a locomotive engineer

home guard
> one who continues to work for a single railroad, the opposite of a boomer

house track
> track that runs alongside of or enters into a freight house

ladder track
> track from which a train enters or leaves the succession of parallel tracks that make up a railroad yard

lay out the hotshots
> issue orders to one or more fast freight trains to set up running uninterrupted over a division's right-of-way

lightning slinger
> a telegraph operator

Mallet
> a freight locomotive consisting of two engines (cylinders and driving wheels) beneath a single boiler

Malley
> railroad slang for Mallet

manifest
> a fast freight train carrying merchandise or perishables, also known as a hotshot

merchandise
> a type of freight train usually carrying time-sensitive goods

Mikado (or Mike)
> a common freight locomotive with a 2-8-2 wheel arrangement (2-wheel pilot truck, 4 driving wheels, and 2-wheel trailing truck), so named because an early order for this type of locomotive came from Nippon Railway of Japan

mixed freight
> a train made up of cars holding various cargoes

night operator
> the telegraph operator working the night shift

order board
> a fixed signal that regulates the movement of trains by instructing approaching train crews to slow or stop for train orders or on what actions to take

OS
> "on sheet," the telegraphic signal sent by an operator to report to the dispatcher that a train has passed by

parlor job
> when the rear brakeman is assigned to ride in the caboose

passing track
> a track running alongside the main line, usually with a switch at each end, that can enable two trains to pass in single-track territory

pinman (or pinner)
> the person who uncouples railroad cars during switching operations; derived from an early coupling mechanism known as the link and pin

rattler
> a slow-moving local freight train

red ball merchandise extras
> fast freight trains carrying time-sensitive merchandise or perishables that are not found on the published timetable, making them special, or "extra"

rode the cushions "on his face"
> provided a free ride on a passenger train because he was recognized as a railroad man

Rule G
> a general rule that applies to all trainmen; it reads, "The use of intoxicants or narcotics is forbidden"

saw(ed)
> a slow and complicated maneuver that enables one train to pass another on a single track line when the passing siding is too short to accommodate either of the trains passing at that point

schedule rights
> refers to the fact that a train is superior to other trains in priority if it is operating under train orders instead of by class (first, second, third, and so on) or direction

section crew
> a workforce responsible for maintaining a specified stretch of track, usually measured in miles

sections
> multiple individual trains, usually passenger trains, running in succession under the same designation, such as Sections 1, 2, and 3 of train 26, but occasionally fast freights carrying perishables; such freights could also be run as sections of passenger trains, so that in the example above, Section 1 may be a passenger train and Sections 2 and 3 freights

semaphore arms
> the semaphore is a train signal that uses protruding paddles, or arms, atop a pole to indicate instructions to approaching train crews; the position of the arms, occasionally in combination with lights, is the signal

shoo-fly
> temporary track installed to bypass an obstruction, such as a washout or derailment, or to rerail a derailed train

slack
> the unrestricted free movement between cars in a train that must be taken into account when starting and stopping a train, as the cars will run in the slack when stopping a train and run out when starting a train

sounder
> that component of telegraph equipment that converts telegraphic impulses into a sound, enabling the operator to "read" the signal

spotter
> a spy sent by the company to observe and report to management on the behavior of employees

stab the schedule
> to take an action that drastically alters or halts the scheduled movement of trains over a division

superintendent
> the executive in charge of an operating railroad division

take the hole
> occupy a siding

team track
> a railroad siding placed in a location accessible to the public for the purpose of loading or unloading goods to or from a freight car

thousand-miler
> a shirt worn by railroaders of which it was said it could travel one thousand miles between washings.

train order
> an order issued by the authorized railroad official that controls the movement of trains; a hold order, for example, would instruct a train to stop

train order hoop
> a device used to hand train orders up to crew members on a moving train. When orders were to be "hooped up" to a train's crew in this manner, two hoops were used, one for the engineer and one for the conductor. Each recipient would know, by virtue of a train order signal from the telegraph operator, to receive the order by sticking his arm through the hoop as he passed the employee holding the hoop, retrieve the attached order, and toss the hoop back to the ground.

way freight
> a freight train made up of cars being delivered locally

waybill
> a written document used to schedule and account for freight shipments

white flags
> the locomotive of an extra train, one not on the timetable, was required to display two white flags by day or two white marker lights by night, one on each side of the smokebox front, to let others know it is an extra

white man
> a common racial slur meant to imply doing things the right way

yard goat
> a locomotive intended for switching duties in a railroad yard

yelled twice
> two blasts from a locomotive's whistle

For additional information on railroad jargon and terminology, see Freeman H. Hubbard, *Railroad Avenue: Great Stories and Legends of American Railroading* (New York: McGraw-Hill, 1945); and Robert G. Lewis et al., *Railway Age's Comprehensive Railroad Dictionary* (Omaha: Simmons-Boardman Books, 1984).

PUBLICATIONS BY OR ABOUT HARRY BEDWELL

The abbreviated page counts for the stories reprinted in *Railroad Magazine* after Bedwell's death indicate the possibility the reprints may be edited versions. They are included for those interested in or with access to the later reprints.

NOVELS

Bedwell, Harry. *The Boomer: A Story of the Rails*. New York: Farrar & Rinehart, 1942. Reprint, Minneapolis: University of Minnesota Press, 2006.

———. *Priority Special*. San Francisco: Southern Pacific Company, 1945. Originally a radio broadcast on June 6, 1945. Reprinted in *Headlights and Markers: An Anthology of Railroad Stories,* ed. Frank P. Donovan and Robert Selphy Henry. (New York: Creative Age Press, 1946). (novelette)

SHORT STORIES

Bedwell, Harry. "Against Orders." *Railroad Magazine* 65 (September 1954): 16–18+.

———. "Anything's Liable to Happen." *Railroad Magazine* 27 (February 1940): 34–59. (novelette)

———. "Arizona Wires." *Action Stories* 4 (June 1925): 44–68. (novelette)

———. "Avalanche Warning." *Saturday Evening Post* 229 (May 11, 1957): 30+. (novelette)

———. "Back in Circulation." *Railroad Magazine* 28 (September 1940): 88–109. (novelette)

―――. "Campbell's Wedding Race." *Railroad Man's Magazine* 10 (October 1909): 10–19. Reprint, *Railroad Magazine* 70 (June 1959): 54–60.

―――. "The Careless Road." *Railroad Magazine* 25 (February 1939): 32–61. Reprint, *Railroad Magazine* 69 (June 1958): 48–61. (novelette)

―――. "Christmas Comes to the Prairie Central." *Railroad Magazine* 33 (January 1943): 48–72. Reprinted as "Railroaders Don't Celebrate," *Railroad Magazine* 70 (December 1958): 50+.

―――. "Code of the Boomer." *Railroad Magazine* 27 (May 1940): 40–65. Reprint, *Railroad Magazine* 68 (October 1957): 48–55. (novelette)

―――. "Desert Job." Part I, *Railroad Magazine* 37 (May 1945): 90–118; Part II, *Railroad Magazine* 37 (June 1945): 86–115. (novelette)

―――. "The Ham." *Railroad Magazine* 25 (May 1939): 17–24. Reprinted as "The Night Operator," *Railroad Magazine* 68 (August 1957): 66–70.

―――. "Imperial Pass." *Saturday Evening Post* 206 (January 13, 1934): 16–17+.

―――. "In Search of the Sun." *Railroad Magazine* 25 (January 1939): 33–47. Reprint, *Railroad Magazine* 69 (April 1958): 52+.

―――. "Indian Transfer." *Adventure* 197 (June 1942): 96–106.

―――. "Jawbone." *Railroad Magazine* 44 (November 1947): 40–65. Reprinted as "Delay at Mesquite," *Railroad Magazine* 70 (February 1959): 50–59.

―――. "Kang." *San Francisco Newsletter and Wasp* 80 (November 14, 1936): 10–11+.

―――. "Lantern in His Hand." *Saturday Evening Post* 215 (January 23, 1943): 22–23+.

―――. "Lassitude and Longitude." *Railroad Magazine* 26 (July 1939): 94–108. Reprinted as "Gods of High Iron," *Railroad Magazine* 69 (February 1958): 52–61.

―――. "The Lightning That Was Struck." *Short Stories* 119 (May 10, 1927): 134–73. (novelette)

———. "Lure of the Desert." *Los Angeles Times Illustrated Weekly Magazine* (March 1, 1908): 15.

———. "A Man Who Could Handle Trains." *Railroad Stories* 20 (November 1936): 30–44. Reprint, *Railroad Magazine* 67 (August 1956): 48–56+.

———. "Mountain Standard Time." Part I, *Railroad Magazine* 47 (January 1949): 122–40; Part II, *Railroad Magazine* 48 (February 1949): 112–29. (novelette)

———. "Mutiny on the Monte." *Adventure* 116 (November 1946): 30–37.

———. "Night of Plunder." Part I, *Saturday Evening Post* 224 (December 22, 1951): 14–15+; Part II, *Saturday Evening Post* 224 (December 29, 1951): 30–31+. (novelette)

———. "Not in the Contract." Part I, *Railroad Magazine* 40 (June 1946): 42–65; Part II, *Railroad Magazine* 40 (July 1946): 110–31. (novelette)

———. "Official Appreciation." *Railroad Magazine* 26 (October 1939): 52–68. Reprinted as "Wanderlust," *Railroad Magazine* 68 (April 1957): 56–65.

———. "Old Flighty's Deal." *Los Angeles Times Illustrated Weekly Magazine* 13 (January 10, 1909): 46.

———. "Old Mogul Mountain." *Railroad Magazine* 24 (July 1938): 32–43. Reprint, *Railroad Magazine* 67 (October 1956): 30–36.

———. "On the Night Wire." *Railroad Stories* 21 (January 1937): 91–104. Reprint, *Railroad Magazine* 67 (June 1956): 52–59.

———. "Pacific Electric." *Railroad Magazine* 29 (January 1941): 88–113. Reprint, *Railroad Magazine* 70 (August 1959): 56–64. (novelette)

———. "Pass to Seattle." *Saturday Evening Post* 214 (October 4, 1941): 18–19+.

———. "Restless Feet." *Railroad Magazine* 32 (August 1942): 52–83. Reprint, *Railroad Magazine* 69 (October 1958): 50–54+.

———. "The Return of Eddie Sand." *Railroad Magazine* 35 (February 1944): 22–42. (novelette)

———. "The Screaming Wheels." *Saturday Evening Post* 221

(February 19, 1949): 28–29+. Reprint, *Vintage Rails* 4 (Summer 1996): 70–77.

———. "The Secret Red Lights." Part I, *Railroad Man's Magazine* 14 (May 1911): 631–40; Part II, *Railroad Man's Magazine* 15 (June 1911): 151–60.

———. "Smart Boomer." *Saturday Evening Post* 213 (March 8, 1941): 20–21+. Reprinted in *Headlights and Markers: An Anthology of Railroad Stories,* ed. Frank P. Donovan and Robert Selphy Henry (New York: Creative Age Press, 1946); and *Short Lines: A Collection of Classic American Railroad Stories,* ed. Rob Johnson (New York: St. Martin's Press, 1995).

———. "The 'Snake.'" *Harper's Weekly* 55 (January 28, 1911): 14–15.

———. "Snow on the High Iron." *Saturday Evening Post* 213 (December 14, 1940): 18–19+.

———. "The Student Brakeman." *Railroad Magazine* 28 (June 1940): 34–59. (novelette)

———. "Sun and Silence." *Railroad Magazine* 23 (April 1938): 34–48. Reprint, *Railroad Magazine* 67 (April 1956): 58–67.

———. "The Switchman." *Railroad Magazine* 25 (April 1939): 52–64. Reprinted as "The Kid Switchman," *Railroad Magazine* 68 (February 1957): 58–64.

———. "Take 'Em Away, McCoy." *Argosy* 393 (September 30, 1939): 119–26.

———. "They Called Him 'Moonbeam.'" *Railroad Magazine* 27 (December 1939): 98–110. Reprinted as "Moonshine," *Railroad Magazine* 69 (August 1958): 54–61.

———. "Third Trick." *Railroad Magazine* 66 (June 1955): 30–31+.

———. "Those Merry Widow Hats." *Los Angeles Times Illustrated Weekly Magazine* 12 (November 29, 1908): 686.

———. "Thundering Rails." *Saturday Evening Post* 220 (March 27, 1948): 30–31+.

———. "The Touch of Genius." *Los Angeles Times Illustrated Weekly Magazine* 4 (August 9, 1913): 11.

———. "Tower Man." *Railroad Magazine* 29 (May 1941): 92–120. (novelette)

———. "When There's Traffic to Move." *Railroad Magazine* 23 (May 1938): 44–62. Reprint, *Railroad Magazine* 68 (December 1956): 60–71. (novelette)

———. "Where Friendship Ceases." *Los Angeles Times Illustrated Weekly Magazine* 12 (September 6, 1908): 302+.

———. "With His Fingers Crossed." *Railroad Man's Magazine* 11 (March 1910): 237–46. Reprinted as "Night Trick at Armadillo," *Railroad Magazine* 70 (April 1959): 60–64+.

———. "With the Wires Down." *Railroad Magazine* 24 (October 1938): 40–50. Reprint, *Railroad Magazine* 69 (December 1957): 48–54.

———. "Yardmaster." *Argosy* 289 (March 19, 1939): 4–31. (novelette)

———. "The Yardmaster's Story." *Railroad Magazine* 26 (August 1939): 82–107. (novelette)

AUTOBIOGRAPHICAL AND BIOGRAPHICAL

Anonymous. "Ex–Boomer." *Saturday Evening Post* 214 (October 4, 1941): 4.

———. "Rail Fiction's Most Popular Character." *Railroad* 29 (October 1942): 53.

———. "Round Trip." *Saturday Evening Post* 220 (March 27, 1948): 10.

Bedwell, Harry. "Mistakes of a Young Telegraph Operator." Part I, *American Magazine* 69 (November 1909): 71–78; Part II, *American Magazine* 69 (December 1909): 221–28.

———. "When I Was a Boomer Op." *Railroad Stories* 21 (April 1937): 112–15.

Donovan, Frank P., Jr. *Harry Bedwell: Last of the Great Railroad Storytellers*. Minneapolis: Ross & Haines, 1959.

NONFICTION

Bedwell, Harry. "Christmas Luck." As told by Gordon Montgomery. *Foreign Service* 26 (December 1938): 6–7+. (true story)

———. "CTC." *Railroad Magazine* 36 (November 1944): 100–105. (article)

———. "The Lake of Fire." As told by Gordon Montgomery. *Bluebook Magazine* 59 (July 1934): 130–32. (true story)

———. "The Superintendent's Story." *Railroad Magazine* 67 (December 1955): 52–54. (about Denver & Rio Grande Western Railroad superintendent J. R. Loftis)

REVIEWS

Burdett, Helen Ripley. "Bedwell, Harry." *Library Journal* 67 (July 1942): 629.

Conrad, George. "The Boomer." *New York Herald Tribune,* July 26, 1942, VII10.

Cournos, John. "A Saga of the Rails." *New York Times,* July 19, 1942, BR4.

HARRY BEDWELL (1888–1955) was a boomer telegraph operator until he retired in the 1930s. He wrote more than sixty short stories and is considered one of the greats of the "railroad fiction" genre. His stories were regularly published in popular magazines, such as the *Saturday Evening Post.* His life was the subject of a biography by Frank P. Donovan Jr., *Harry Bedwell: Last of the Great Railroad Storytellers.*

JAMES D. PORTERFIELD is author of *From the Dining Car: The Recipes and Stories behind Today's Greatest Rail Dining Experiences* and *Dining by Rail: The History and the Recipes of America's Golden Age of Railroad Cuisine.* His "On the Menu" column about trains and food, as well as features on railroad art and history, appears each month in *Railfan & Railroad,* a magazine for North American railroad enthusiasts.